LADY CORNELIA
THE DECEITFUL MARRIAGE
THE DIALOGUE OF THE DOGS

For Mary and Pauline

General editor: B. W. Ife
Cervantes Professor of Spanish, King's College, London

Miguel de Cervantes Saavedra

EXEMPLARY NOVELS IV
Novelas ejemplares

Lady Cornelia
La señora Cornelia

The Deceitful Marriage
El casamiento engañoso

The Dialogue of the Dogs
El coloquio de los perros

with introductions, notes and translations
by
John Jones and John Macklin

Aris & Phillips Ltd — Warminster — England

ISBN 0 85668 497 X   Volume IV cloth
ISBN 0 85668 498 8   Volume IV paper
ISBN 0 85668 557 7   Volumes I-IV complete library edition (cloth)

British Library Cataloguing-in-Publication Data
A catalogue record for this book is available from the British Library.

The Publishers gratefully acknowledge the financial assistance of the Dirección General del Libro y Bibliotecas of the Ministerio de Cultura de España with this translation.

Printed and published in England by Aris & Phillips Ltd., Teddington House, Warminster, Wiltshire BA12 8PQ

Contents

General Introduction by B. W. Ife

Life and Work   vii

The Composition of the Exemplary Novels   x

Harmless Entertainment   xi

Exemplarity   xii

Hidden Mystery   xiv

This Edition   xvi

Select Bibliography   xvii

Lady Cornelia (*La señora Cornelia*)

Introduction   1

Text and Translation   6

The Deceitful Marriage (*El casamiento engañoso*) and
The Dialogue of the Dogs (*El coloquio de los perros*)

Introduction   57

Text and Translation   66

Notes to the Stories   159

Lady Cornelia   160

The Deceitful Marriage   162

The Dialogue of the Dogs   164

Map of Spain in the sixteenth century   163

General Introduction
by B. W. Ife

Hidden among the many pages of preliminary matter which prefaced the first edition of Cervantes's *Exemplary Novels*[1] is a short, enigmatic prologue addressed to the reader. It is the most eloquent of all the introductions with which Cervantes customarily prefaced his works, and its witty and self-confident tone make it a fitting introduction to one of the most original, entertaining, and provocative collections of short novels in any language.

Cervantes begins his prologue with a characteristic joke at the expense of his publisher: since there is to be no engraved frontispiece featuring a portrait of the author, he will have to make up for it with a self-portrait in words. He paints a picture of a mature man, much-travelled and worldly-wise, an old soldier, proud of his record of military service and now, in later life, beginning to emerge as a literary figure with a growing awareness of his ability, and of his status in the public eye.

Having presented his credentials, Cervantes goes on to talk about his collection of twelve short, exemplary novels. He gives four main reasons why his readers should take them seriously, though not *too* seriously: they are harmless entertainment, contain profitable examples, each of them is Cervantes's own work, and they all contain a hidden mystery. These four claims have formed the basis of most subsequent criticism of the collection, and they continue to fascinate readers and critics to this day.

Though each of the claims is justified, none of them can be taken entirely at face value: the assertion that the stories are harmless, for example, is an interesting gloss on the amount of sex and violence they contain; and their claim to exemplarity may seem curiously at odds with the almost complete absence from them of explicit moral commentary. The purpose of this Introduction is to bring to the attention of the general reader the issues which lie behind the author's sometimes ambivalent and cryptic comments on the novels. As in Cervantes's prologue, a short biographical section is followed by a discussion of the four main points made by Cervantes about the meaning and purpose of the *Exemplary Novels*.

---

1   Preliminary matter in early Spanish printed books is copious by modern standards (c.f. José Simón Díaz, *El libro antiguo español. Análisis de su estructura*, Kassel: Edition Reichenberger, 1983), but rarely as much as in the first edition of the *Novelas ejemplares*, where tax certificates and censors' reports, royal assents, a letter of dedication and several endorsements from Cervantes's well-placed friends and supporters occupy some 22 pages. For reasons of economy, the preliminaries are omitted from this edition, with the exception of the Prologue, which is given in full in Volume I.

Life and Work

... he learned patience in adversity...

On the evidence of his books, Cervantes's life had all the ingredients of a classic literary biography: poverty, hardship and rejection. In fact, and in spite of Astrana Marín's monumental 7-volume biography, very little is known for certain about the life of Spain's greatest writer. It is clear from the works themselves that Cervantes drew frequently on his own lived experience when writing; rarely does one get a stronger sense of life being transformed into art. But the dangers inherent in extrapolating a biography from a wide range of works of fiction cannot be over-estimated. We simply do not know how much of his life Cervantes put into his work, and how much he transformed it in the process.

Cervantes alludes frequently to the formative role of poverty and adversity on his character. Born in 1547 in Alcalá de Henares to a poor professional family with pretentions to nobility, Cervantes underwent a relatively haphazard education and was largely self-taught; he studied for a while in Madrid with the Erasmian humanist Juan López de Hoyos, and read widely and – by his own admission – indiscriminately. Cervantes's originality as a writer is often attributed to the relatively unstructured education he enjoyed as a youth.

In 1569 Cervantes left Madrid for Italy, and entered the service of Giulio Acquaviva before enlisting in the Spanish army. He fought under Don John of Austria in the great victory over the Turks at Lepanto in 1571, and lost his left hand, an injury of which he was inordinately proud 'since it was collected in the greatest and most memorable event that past centuries have ever seen'. Other military operations followed, in Corfu, Navarino and Tunis, and during his return journey to Spain in 1575, he was captured at sea by Turkish corsairs and taken to Algiers. There he spent five years in captivity before being redeemed by the payment of a ransom in 1580. Cervantes's experiences of military life in Italy, and more especially of prison life in north Africa, colour a great deal of his writing, and, in particular, several of the *Exemplary Novels*.

Back in Spain, Cervantes found the life of a 'returnee' frustrating and disappointing, and his attempts to build a literary career for himself met with little success in the early years. His first attempts at writing were in the popular genres of pastoral romance and the theatre. *La Galatea* appeared in 1585, but he proved to be an untalented practitioner of the one thing on which pastoral depends heavily for its success – lyric verse. His first attempts at writing plays were only slightly more successful. An unhappy marriage to a much younger girl and continued financial difficulties forced him to take a post as tax-collector in Andalusia. He travelled widely and gained considerable knowledge of rural Spain - knowledge displayed most obviously in *Don Quixote* – but he was accused of fraudulent accounting and spent at least two periods of time in prison in Seville. There he learned a great deal about organised crime and the Seville underworld, including *germanía*, the language of criminals featured in the novel *Rinconete and Cortadillo*.

In 1605 Cervantes, now settled in Valladolid, published Part I of *Don Quixote*. Although the work brought few financial rewards, it was well received in some circles and earned him a place on the fringes of the literary establishment there, and later in Madrid. The last four years of his life saw the culmination of his literary career: the

Exemplary Novels were followed in 1614 by a long allegorical poem, the *Viaje del Parnaso*; 1615 brought Part II of *Don Quixote* and the *Eight Plays and Eight Entr'actes*. His great epic novel *The Travails of Persiles and Sigismunda* was published posthumously in 1617. The prologue to this work, full of inconsequential jesting and self-deprecation, contains an uncanny prediction of the author's death, on 23 April 1616, four days after it was written.

Cervantes was the most notable of a group of writers emerging in Spain around the end of the sixteenth century who can be said to be the first practitioners of literature as a profession. Unlike virtually every Spanish writer before him, Cervantes wrote to make money. That fact alone is an important clue to the kind of writer he was, and to the nature of his success. In order to make ends meet, Cervantes *had* to be popular, and, although he was not always successful at what he attempted, he nevertheless turned his hand to virtually every major literary genre of his day. He did not attempt the verse epic, though he produced an epic in prose, and although he did not write a picaresque novel in the standard format of the genre, he made much use of picaresque conventions and low-life settings in other ways. He knew what the public liked and he tried to make sure they got it.

Cervantes's professionalism has a double significance for the *Exemplary Novels*. As a collection, the novels illustrate the enormous variety which is characteristic of his work as a whole, and, in particular, the mixing of features from established and popular genres to create something new and specifically Cervantine. Of equal significance is the way in which he consistently moves back and forth between two types of genre which at first sight might seem mutually exclusive: the high romance of the chivalresque, pastoral and Byzantine novels, and his own literary version of everyday life in contemporary Spain.[2]

Cervantes's interest in the full spectrum of genres available to him is important in view of the fact that he is widely perceived as a writer who made his name from debunking romance. The origin of this view undoubtedly lies in the success of *Don Quixote*. This starts out, admittedly, as a fairly conventional piece of satire. Quixote's hare-brained determination to re-enact the fantasies of chivalresque literature is shown to be an inadequate and ultimately ridiculous response to the nature of the 'real' world. But, as the novel develops, literary issues begin to predominate, and Quixote is increasingly able to make the world, not himself, look out of step.

Towards the end of Part I, he engages another character, the Canon of Toledo, in a long debate about the merits of novels of chivalry. The Canon offers some routine criticism of their implausibility, their poor construction and the adverse effects they can have on impressionable readers, like Quixote himself. But in his reply Quixote makes a strangely compelling case for the power of fiction over the rational mind, and in the story of the Knight of the Boiling Lake he evokes brilliantly the ecstasy of reading and of being transported to another world with a reality of its own.

---

2   For a discussion of this key aspect of Cervantes's style see E.C. Riley, 'Cervantes: a Question of Genre' in *Medieval and Renaissance Studies on Spain and Portugal in Honour of P.E. Russell*, ed. F.W. Hodcroft *et al.*, Oxford, 1981, pp. 69–85.

These issues – the persuasiveness of fiction, its pleasurable therapy, and the craft of persuasion required of the author – lie at the heart of all Cervantes's work, and the *Exemplary Novels* most of all.

The Composition of the Exemplary Novels

... I am the first to write novels in Castilian...

Although Cervantes did not apply for a licence to publish the *Exemplary Novels* as a collection until 1612, there is considerable evidence to suggest that some of them, at least, had been in preparation since the early 1590s. Two of them, *Rinconete and Cortadillo* and *The Jealous Old Man from Extremadura*, had already been collected in a manuscript anthology, the so-called Porras manuscript, now lost, compiled for the Archbishop of Seville, Fernando Niño de Guevara, around 1604, and both stories underwent considerable subsequent revision by Cervantes before finally being published in 1613.

Cervantes's interest in the short novel as a separate entity in its own right therefore predates his own use of the form as an interpolated narrative in a longer work. Part I of *Don Quixote* contains six such interludes, one of which, *Misguided Curiosity*, is often considered one of the best examples of the genre, while another, *The Captive's Tale*, appears to be a heavily autobiographical account of being held hostage in Algiers.

In using substantial narrative interludes in this way, to add variety to the extended romance format, Cervantes was not himself breaking new ground. Frame-stories like *The Canterbury Tales* and the *Arabian Nights* were a commonplace of medieval literature, and were undoubtedly the precedent used by writers of chivalresque and pastoral romances to build up large-scale narratives. Each time a new character is introduced, questions are asked about their past history and exploits which give rise to prolonged bouts of autobiography which can be substantial enough to constitute short, self-contained novels. The writers of picaresque novels also picked up and developed this episodic structure; *Lazarillo de Tormes* (1554) contains a number of semi-autonomous anecdotes, some of popular origin, and *Guzmán de Alfarache* (1599) is frequently interrupted by substantial interpolated narratives running to many thousands of words in length.

The essence of Cervantes's claim to originality, however, lies in the way in which he took the form and gave it a life of its own, liberating it from dependence on a larger structure. In this, his antecedents are Italian rather than Spanish: the *Decameron* (c. 1348) of Giovanni Boccaccio, and two collections of stories by sixteenth-century writers, the *Novelliere* (1554, 1573) of Matteo Bandello and the *Hecatommithi* (1565) of Giambattista Giraldi Cinthio. Such collections were popular throughout Europe and provided playwrights in several countries, Shakespeare among them, with handy ideas for plots. Similar collections of anecdotes were published in Spain, but as Cervantes says in his prologue, they were usually translated or loosely adapted from foreign models; and as he does not say, but clearly implies, they were artistically vastly inferior to his own work, with thin, single-strand plots and minimal characterisation.

Cervantes claims that all his stories are his own work: 'conceived in my imagination, given birth by my pen'. This claim appears to be largely justified. Much effort has gone into tracking down sources for the novels,[3] but little definitive evidence has come to light to suggest that he drew on the work of other writers; indeed, two of the censors of the first edition comment with approval on the fertility of his imagination and outstanding invention. Nevertheless, as a professional writer, Cervantes needed to be closely attuned to the tastes of his readership, and his novels have an unmistakably fashionable feel to them. No one novel may be derived from a particular source in Spanish or Italian, but the novels undoubtedly share features of plot and ethos with a wide range of popular fiction and drama throughout late sixteenth- and early seventeenth-century Europe.

Harmless Entertainment

... they could not provoke anyone into evil thoughts...

The Italianate origins of the short novel become apparent when we come to consider the title Cervantes chose for the collection as a whole. When he originally applied for permission to publish them, he appears to have done so under the title *Novelas ejemplares de honestísimo entretenimiento* (*Exemplary Novels of the Most Harmless Entertainment*).[4] We do not know why Cervantes eventually preferred the shorter form, or if, indeed, the choice was his. The change may have been for reasons of euphony, or perhaps, more likely, in order to project more effectively the antithesis implicit in the collocation of *exemplary* and *novel* – for most contemporary readers, the title *Exemplary Novels* would have been a striking contradiction in terms.

In Cervantes's day, the term *novela* (Italian *novella*) was a recent coining which had not yet acquired any of the respectability which the term 'novel' now enjoys. Works of prose fiction were either called simply *libro* ('book') or *historia* ('history'), and a short, self-contained anecdote was called a *cuento* ('story'). *Novela* was rarely used in Spain to refer to a work of fiction before Cervantes's time; when it was, it suggested a low, disreputable and bawdy narrative in the style of the medieval *fabliaux*. The anecdotal origins of the *novela* can clearly be seen in such stories as *The Deceitful Marriage*.

By calling the novels 'novels' and then by qualifying them as 'exemplary' Cervantes was being deliberately provocative; he uses oxymoron in a similar way in the titles of *The Illustrious Kitchen Maid* and *The English Spanish Girl*. He was in effect challenging received opinions about the *novella* by suggesting that it was capable of greater seriousness and sophistication than had previously been thought. It is clear that Cervantes was consciously trying to extend the range of forms available to him, and to break the dominance of the long, episodic chivalresque and pastoral romances and their close cousin, the picaresque.

---

3   A. González de Amezúa y Mayo, *Cervantes creador de la novela corta española*. 2 vols. Madrid, 1956–8.
4   This is the form of words in which the collection is referred to by one of the censors, Salas Barbadillo, and in the royal warrant signed by the King in November 1612.

Cervantes's abiding interest in the power of fiction, and his talent for exploiting it for his readers' amusement, also made him more sensitive than most to its inherent dangers. *Don Quixote*, after all, illustrates how the mind of a gullible reader can be invaded by a potentially destructive set of moral values embodied in a fictional form. The dangers of imaginative identification with the fictional world, and the vicarious experience to which this can lead, were much commented on in Cervantes's day.[5] In view of these concerns, it is hardly surprising that Cervantes should stress the harmlessness of the novels he is putting before his public.

In the *Exemplary Novels*, then, Cervantes was offering his readership a new, more respectable and worthwhile form of narrative which, contrary to their expectations, would not shock or offend them. And he backed up this assertion by saying that he would rather cut off the hand with which he wrote them than have anyone come to harm from reading them; no idle promise, in view of what he has just told us about having lost his other hand in battle.

The importance of entertainment – signalled in that part of the title which was eventually dropped – must also not be overlooked. Cervantes goes to some length in his prologue to stress the recreational role of literature, specifically likening his work to a popular pastime, billiards, and going on to suggest that excessive attention to work, and even to serious matters like religion, is not healthy. This stress on the value of entertainment for its own sake is further underlined by one of the censors of the first edition, Fr. Juan Bautista, who points out that both Aristotle and St. Thomas Aquinas considered harmless fun to be a virtue.

In the interests of entertainment, Cervantes consciously cultivated in the novels those popular themes which he knew were fashionable and which would appeal to his readers. The standard features of high romance are never far away: star-crossed lovers, journeys, ordeals, reconciliations between long-lost relatives, murder, rape, piracy and transvestite disguise. These were the stuff of popular fiction and, in particular, of the theatre, with which many of the *Exemplary Novels* bear a close relationship. Cervantes is also alert to the popularity of the picaresque, and several of the novels exploit and develop the conventions of this genre, giving him the opportunity to display his wide knowledge and experience of contemporary Spain and Italy, and the low-life settings which obviously fascinated the mainly professional and upper-class readership for which he was writing.

Exemplarity

... if you look closely, you will see that there is not one from which you cannot extract some profitable example...

Mere harmlessness, however, was not enough, particularly when the plots of most of these novels turn on such unsavoury topics as murder, rape and abduction. In these circumstances, the appeal to a 'profitable example' was not just a piece of conventional appeasement aimed at disapproving readers, but was an essential feature of Cervantes's

5   See the first two chapters of B.W. Ife, *Reading and Fiction in Golden-Age Spain*, Cambridge, 1985.

determination to raise the level of complexity and sophistication of the *novella* form. Hence the claim that the novels are called 'exemplary' because each one contains a moral, as does the collection as a whole.

But, here again, Cervantes appears open to the charge that he is being disingenuous. As far as explicit moral lessons are concerned, the stories appear to contain none – at least, nothing more than an occasional, very banal gesture towards the conventional morality of fables. The *fabliau*-type origin of *The Deceitful Marriage*, for example, is obvious enough, and in case there should be any doubt, two lines of Petrarch are quoted as a summary of the story's findings: he who succeeds by deceit will surely fail by it. *The English Spanish Girl* also has a short codetta to remind us what beauty and virtue can achieve in the face of adverse fortune, though it must be doubted if Cervantes seriously expects an intelligent reader to accept such a conclusion.

The exemplarity of the *Exemplary Novels* is, therefore, a good deal more problematic than Cervantes seems to allow at first glance. By inviting his reader to look for profitable examples which are not explicit, or explicit lessons which are banal or which offend against common sense and experience, Cervantes is underlining the way in which the 'delicious and wholesome fruit' has to be extracted by dint of careful consideration and close reading. This is not always as difficult as it may seem, for the educated reader then, as now, was perfectly capable of reading between the lines. The censor, Fr. Juan Bautista, had no trouble in finding profitable examples in both the positive and the negative senses: '[the novels] teach us by their examples to flee vice and follow virtue'. The examples may be there for us either to imitate or to shun, and we do not necessarily have to be told explicitly which is which.

The fascination of the *Exemplary Novels*, however, lies in the way they show that life is hardly ever a simple matter of black and white. So often, characters are forced to respond to events and situations which are not of their own making, in ways which at the time may seem perfectly understandable but which may lead to untold misery or undreamed-of happiness. Human nature – and divine providence – are complex matters which do not lend themselves readily to clear-cut judgments. Why are Juana Carducha's desperate measures in the face of overwhelming desire any more reprehensible than Andrés Caballero's (*The Little Gypsy Girl*)? Why are Carrizales's attempts to preserve his wife's virtue any worse than Loaysa's attempts to destroy it (*The Jealous Old Man from Extremadura*)? Why are so many wrong-doers rewarded with happy outcomes they do not appear to deserve?

What Cervantes shows is that it is both impossible and undesirable to stick the 'profitable example' onto the end of the story as an afterthought; the moral is woven into the fabric of the novel[6] and is inextricably bound up not just with the way the tale is told, but also with the way it is read. That is why Cervantes's most typical stance is non-committal. He illustrates and leaves the reader to conclude; the quest for profit is part of the pleasure. In this way, it is perhaps better to think of the *Exemplary Novels* as providing not *examples* but *samples*, illustrations of the complexities of life and human nature, showing the kinds of ways in which people are apt to behave in a given set of

---

6   See B.W. Ife, 'From Salamanca to Brighton Rock', in *Essays in Honour of R.B. Tate*, ed. R.A. Cardwell, Nottingham, 1984, pp. 46–52.

circumstances. As a noun, the word *ejemplar* in Spanish can mean precisely that: a copy of a book, one instance of many, a part which stands for the whole.

But what of Cervantes's many 'samples' of circumstances and events which manifestly do not happen in real life, when the example contradicts common experience? What lessons are to be drawn from these? There are three novels in particular which appear to fly in the face of common sense, and they all concern the redemption of a heroine from circumstances into which she was placed by a criminal or immoral act. The heroines of *The Little Gypsy Girl, The English Spanish Girl* and *The Illustrious Kitchen Maid* are all young, beautiful, virtuous and noble, and they all help to bring about their own rescue by displaying outstanding personal qualities in the face of overwhelmingly hostile surroundings. They are all exceptional women, and their beauty and their virtue draw to them the three men who will redeem them from their alien environment and restore them to the noble, Christian world from which they were wrongfully abducted.

Such stories – and there are others which, although they do not fit this paradigm exactly, presuppose an equivalent set of values – pose a number of difficult questions to the reader in search of a profitable example. It is unlikely that anyone would reasonably conclude that Cervantes is making virtue contingent upon noble birth, or on youth and physical beauty, or that he is suggesting that integrity and truth to self will inevitably be rewarded. The reader's own experience will always reply that, in these unlikely circumstances, social conditioning would prove more powerful than innate virtue, and that, even if a gallant knight did come to the rescue, he would most likely turn out to be a blackguard in disguise.

To these objections, Cervantes would no doubt reply that his heroes and heroines are by definition exceptional – Preciosa (*The Little Gypsy Girl*) is the most strikingly beautiful, outstandingly gifted, witty, intelligent, fair-skinned, blonde-haired gypsy Andrés or anyone else has ever seen – and as such, they are the exceptions that prove the rule. And if we find it so difficult to believe that a man like Ricaredo (*The English Spanish Girl*) could make such fervent declarations of love, and mean them, and act on them to the exclusion of all other considerations, then what conclusions must we draw about the lives we lead and the cynicism with which they are shot through?

The striking, provocative and often far-fetched examples which Cervantes gives us in the more heroic of his novels provide the reader with a fascinating insight into his own response to the various forms of idealism to which the world pays lip-service every day. He gives us outstanding examples of heroism and virtue and invites us to consider why we find these examples so difficult to attain in our own lives and so difficult to accept in those of his characters. The exemplarity of each novel, then, is that of the collection as a whole, and it lies in the ability of these fictions to provoke thought and invite judgment about serious issues of moral conduct which are not nearly so distant from our own experience as their escapism might suggest.

Hidden Mystery

... since I have been bold enough to dedicate these novels to the Count of Lemos, they must contain some hidden mystery which elevates them to that level...

There is another sense in which the novels are exemplary, one which is tied up with Cervantes's claim that they contain a hidden mystery: the sense in which the novels are examples of the writer's art. At first glance, Cervantes's rather feeble joke about the elevation of the sacrament during the mass may strike the reader as in dubious taste. But the mysterious ingredient which helps to make the novels worthy of dedication to such an eminent patron is a mystery of almost comparable significance to Cervantes, the mystery of skill, of craft.[7]

Taken as a whole, the *Exemplary Novels* constitute an anthology of the many skills which the writer must exemplify, and underlying them all is an implied challenge, to Cervantes himself as well as to the reader. The task is to extend the boundaries of what is possible in fiction without losing the reader's goodwill in the process. At a key moment in *The Little Gypsy Girl*, Andrés, dissatisfied with the poet's explanation of his sudden appearance in the gypsy encampment – he claims to have lost his way –, tells him that if he must lie, he should do so with a greater semblance of truth. The poet then goes on to give an alternative, apparently more acceptable, explanation, which is much more fantastic than the first. This exchange illustrates Cervantes's fascination with making improbable things seem possible, rejecting as too facile events and situations which have the all too plausible quality of day-to-day reality.

To do this successfully involves stretching the reader's credulity while at the same time maintaining the overall credibility of the fiction. Cervantes achieves this balance by a skilful mix of two characteristic ingredients: wonder and verisimilitude. He excites the reader's amazement by offering a string of extremely unlikely occurrences, while simultaneously ensuring that, improbable though they may be, they are never quite beyond the bounds of possibility. In order to achieve this sleight of hand, he prepares each improbable turn of events with such skill that the reader is first intrigued and then captivated; and, having led the reader often further than he might otherwise have been prepared to go, he never leaves him exposed and stranded but always brings him back to safety. It is often only when we look back that we see how far we have been led by the power of fiction.

This process is most clearly illustrated in the final two stories of the collection, *The Deceitful Marriage* and *The Dialogue of the Dogs*. They are linked thematically and formally by the device of presenting the second story as having been written by the protagonist of the first. Campuzano prepares the ground with a conventional tale of confidence trickery and then persuades his interlocutor, Peralta, to read an account of a conversation between two dogs he claims to have overheard while recovering in hospital

---

7   The etymology of 'mystery' is in itself mysterious. Latin 'mysterium' meaning 'sacrament' is contaminated by association with 'ministerium' and acquires a secular meaning akin to 'guild', to which members or initiates are admitted by virtue of a trade or skill. Cervantes appears to combine the religious and secular implications of the word in what he says about the mystery of his own work.

from a dose of the pox. Campuzano admits many times that the story is incredible, but Peralta's understandable reluctance to believe it is gradually overcome as he is engulfed in a deepening spiral of implausibility involving magic, witchcraft and reincarnation. At the end of the story, which marks the end of the volume, Peralta emerges from the reading experience by having to concede that, even though it was incredible, it was very entertaining and very well done.

Any reader might conclude the same of the collection as a whole, and, indeed, is frequently invited to do so. It is common for characters as well as narrator to comment on the inherent unlikeliness of the very events in which they are taking part. The most improbable plots and coincidences are carefully prepared and lovingly presented in the most convincing settings, usually real places in contemporary Spain; outrageous outcomes are shown to develop with inexorable logic; and all this is done with the imperceptible craftsmanship of the pickpocket.

A key factor in his success is Cervantes's mixing of genre. Critics have often tried to categorise each of the stories, and the predominance of one or other genre has been used unsuccessfully as a guide to the date of composition of individual novels.[8] In fact, none of the stories is entirely untouched by the imaginative freedom which is characteristic of romance, and none – even those with plots which are most obviously reminiscent of romance – is entirely divorced from the contemporary world in which they were written. *The Power of Blood* opens with a casual stroll on a warm evening in Toledo, *The English Spanish Girl* is steeped in the religious and political struggles of contemporary Europe, *The Illustrious Kitchen Maid* is largely set in a well-known inn in Toledo.

This mixture of the palpably real and the improbably fantastic is the essence of the Cervantine trade mark, and it serves two main purposes. In purely functional terms, the creation of a strong sense of place, not common in European fiction at the time, provides a kind of anchor for the flights of fancy: a solid foundation on which tall stories can be built with greater confidence. But descriptions of interiors, dress, the rigging of ships, squares and fountains do not in themselves guarantee a convincing fiction, and Cervantes would be the first to admit that the greater conviction comes from the inherent truth, the psychological and moral plausibility of the story.

In broader terms, the purpose of mixing genres lies in the potential to show the spiritual truth which underlies the commonplace exterior, and in this way the exemplarity and the wonderment are made to work together. What Cervantes is doing in creating a character like Costanza, for example, a beacon of moral and spiritual probity in a world of decadence and corruption, is akin to what Velázquez does in pictures like *The Drunkards* and *Vulcan's Forge*: both artists bring the mythical world into contact with the real. Like Velázquez, Cervantes imbues the tawdry and the down-at-heel with beauty and nobility, and shows the human spirit triumphantly at odds with its surroundings. The truthfulness of this story comes not from its low-life setting, its thieves and prostitutes, but from Cervantes's demonstration that integrity and steadfastness can not only redeem Costanza, but illuminate the lives of all those with whom she comes into contact.

---

8 A. González de Amezúa y Mayo, *Cervantes creador*, argues that the trajectory of Cervantes's work is from idealistic fiction towards realism, while Ruth El Saffar, *Novel to Romance*, Baltimore, 1974, argues the contrary.

All the novels in the collection, in their different ways, operate on the reader in a similar fashion. They are intriguing, compelling and ultimately persuasive if, like Peralta, we are prepared to go with the flow; and if we care to examine the basis of our own response to them, they are full of profitable examples. Like Costanza, they all have that quality of entertaining and elevating mystery which makes them shining examples of their kind.

This Edition

The Spanish text of this, the first complete parallel edition of the *Exemplary Novels,* has been established with reference to the 1613 edition, and to those of Schevill and Bonilla, Avalle-Arce and Sieber. The translations have been newly commissioned for this series.

General Bibliography

Biographies of Cervantes

Jean Canavaggio, *Cervantes*, London 1990

Luis Astrana Marín, *Vida ejemplar y heroica de Miguel de Cervantes Saavedra*, 7 vols Madrid 1948–58.

William Byron, *Cervantes: A Biography*, London, 1979.

Melveena McKendrick, *Cervantes*, Boston, 1980.

P.E. Russell, *Cervantes*, London, 1986.

General

J.B. Avalle-Arce and E.C. Riley (eds.), *Suma cervantina*, London, 1973.

Marcel Bataillon, 'El erasmismo de Cervantes' in *Erasmo y España*, Mexico City, 1950, Vol. 2, pp. 400–27.

Américo Castro, *Hacia Cervantes*, Madrid, 1967.

Américo Castro, *El pensamiento de Cervantes*, Barcelona/Madrid, 1972.

A. J. Close, *Cervantes: Don Quixote*, Cambridge University Press, 1990.

Alban K. Forcione, *Cervantes, Aristotle and the 'Persiles'*, Princeton, 1970.

B.W. Ife, 'Cervantes and the Credibility Crisis in Spanish Golden Age Fiction', *Renaissance and Modern Studies*, XXVI (1982), 52-74.

E.C. Riley, *Cervantes's Theory of the Novel*, Oxford, 1962.

E.C. Riley, 'Cervantes: a question of genre', in F.W. Hodcroft *et al.* (eds.), *Medieval and Renaissance Studies on Spain and Portugal in Honour of P.E. Russell*, Oxford, 1981, 69–85.

E.C. Riley, *Don Quixote*, London, 1986.

Exemplary Novels

Joaquín Casalduero, *Sentido y forma de las Novelas ejemplares*, Madrid, 1967.

Américo Castro, 'La ejemplaridad de las novelas cervantinas', in *Hacia Cervantes*, Madrid, 1967, pp. 451–74.

Alban K. Forcione, *Cervantes and the Humanist Vision: A Study of Four 'Exemplary Novels'*, Princeton, 1982.

Northrop Frye, *The Secular Scripture*, Cambridge, Mass., 1976.

A. González de Amezúa y Mayo, *Cervantes, creador de la novela corta española*, 2 vols, Madrid, 1958.

Ruth El Saffar, *Novel to Romance: A Study of Four Novelas ejemplares*, Princeton, 1982.

Frank Pierce, 'Reality and Realism in the Exemplary Novels', *BHS* 30 (1953), 134–42.

José Jesús de Bustos Tovar, *Lenguaje, ideología y organización textual en las 'Novelas ejemplares'*, Madrid, 1983.

Texts and translations

Juan Bautista Avalle-Arce, *Novelas ejemplares,* 3 vols., Madrid, 1987.
Rodolfo Schevill and Adolfo Bonilla, *Novelas exemplares,* 3 vols., Madrid, 1922-5.
Harry Sieber, *Novelas ejemplares,* 2 vols , Madrid, 1980.

C. A. Jones *Exemplary Stories,* Harmondsworth, 1972.
Harriet de Onis, *Six Exemplary Novels,* New York, 1961.

LADY CORNELIA

Introduction

Lady Cornelia is the story of two young Spanish noblemen, Don Juan de Gamboa and Don Antonio de Isunza, and their role in bringing about, after many mishaps, the eventual marriage of Cornelia Bentibolli and the Duke of Ferrara, by whom she has had a child. Considered to be one of the Italianate, idealistic exemplary novels, the action of *Lady Cornelia* takes place mainly in Italy and is infused with aristocratic values (nobility, honour, generosity, dignity, religion) which serve to produce a happy outcome after a series of adventures and misunderstandings which add excitement and suspense to the tale. Cornelia, an orphan renowned for her beauty, is kept secluded from society by her brother Lorenzo, but is seen at a wedding by the Duke of Ferrara. They fall in love and by a series of stratagems manage to see each other, and eventually Cornelia becomes pregnant. Apparently out of consideration for his dying mother, the Duke is unable to marry her, but on the night he intends to take her under his protection she gives birth and the child is handed over by mistake to Don Juan, who takes it home. Later, he rescues the Duke who is being attacked by a group of men, while his friend, Don Antonio, encounters the distressed Cornelia and takes her home. By telling each other the night's events the truth emerges and the full story is eventually told by Cornelia, who is reunited with her child and now fears for the lives of both her brother and the Duke. Lorenzo inexplicably arrives at the house and asks Don Juan to help him find the Duke and restore his family honour. In the end, the two friends effect a reconciliation between the Duke and Lorenzo and undertake to restore to them Cornelia and the child. Meanwhile, however, Cornelia, encouraged by the housekeeper, escapes to an unknown destination, so that on their return the friends and the Duke find only a prostitute named Cornelia who is sleeping with a page. Disconcerted the Duke makes for Ferrara but on the way stops at the house of a friend, a priest, where he finds the real Cornelia and his son. He sends for Juan, Antonio and Lorenzo, who have remained in Bologna and, on their arrival, he at first tricks them by saying that he intends to marry a peasant girl since Cornelia has disappeared, and just as the three are about to set upon him, he presents Cornelia and the child, the priest blesses their union, and the story ends happily.

It will be clear from the above summary that *Lady Cornelia*, with its duels, mistaken identities and misadventures, is in the tradition of the Byzantine or adventure novel in which the action, after a series of complications, is brought to a satisfactory resolution. The plot pattern is fundamentally that of separation and return. In the first instance, it is the separation of Don Juan and Don Antonio which sets the whole process in motion, as normally they went out together. The other separation is, of course, that of Cornelia and the Duke, firstly through family circumstances (the protection of the brother, the existence of the Duke's mother) and then through the events of the night in question.

The events of the night also separate Cornelia and Lorenzo and, more importantly, the mother and the child. The coming together again of the two friends is the first step in the reuniting of the couple, and the first phase of that process is the reuniting, after some postponement caused by the changing of his rich clothes for poor ones, of Cornelia with her son. This pattern of deferral is repeated throughout the text. Just as Don Juan and Don Antonio succeed in bringing Lorenzo and the Duke together, thereby ending the narrative, Cervantes adds a new twist. Not only does Cornelia disappear, but in her place is another Cornelia, a prostitute, and this picaresque episode serves to delay the resolution of the plot, as well as providing a thematic contrast between pure and impure love. Similarly, the Duke's trick at the end is a mere device which arguably fools the protagonists but not the reader who is kept in the know by the narrator.

Deferral is not the only structuring device in the novel, however, for it is built upon a number of dualities and polarities which are very characteristic of Cervantes. The most obvious duality is the existence of a pair of friends who complement each other. Similar in age and appearance, they both become the protectors of Cornelia. Don Juan is, in fact, the more prominent in that he is more active in the resolution of the plot, whereas Don Antonio merely follows his friend. In the opening scenes, however, their actions complement each other in that Don Juan rescues the child and the Duke while Don Antonio saves the mother. There are two Cornelias, from different social classes and with different moral standards. There are two contrasting encounters between Lorenzo and the Duke, in one they are fighting, in the other they meet as equals and brothers. Cornelia flees twice from the house in which she is protected. Two picaresque scenes (the housekeeper and the false Cornelia) are introduced into an otherwise idealistic narrative.

Although it is set in the social world of sixteenth-century Italy, *Lady Cornelia* is essentially idealistic in the values it espouses and the characters it portrays. Despite appearances, all the characters are high-minded and principled, and particular emphasis is laid on the fact that the two protagonists are Spaniards. Their Spanishness underlies all their conduct and is the principal basis of the trust that is placed in them by others. Here Cervantes is offering a view of the Spanish nobility of the sixteenth and seventeenth centuries in which the emphasis is on dignity and the higher reaches of the human soul, and which contrasts very sharply with the picaresque and the literature of *desengaño* (disillusionment). From the very first paragraph, the narrator insists on the qualities of the two men and their academic and artistic leanings. Their decision to go to Flanders is a desire to serve their country and, being unable to do so, they decide to return to their studies. Their resolve to visit Italy is an affirmation of their commitment to humanist values, and the esteem in which they are held there is further testimony to their worth which the narrator contrasts with the famed Spanish defect of arrogance. Their conventional piety is evidenced by Don Antonio's wish to remain indoors and pray. Interestingly, however, the whole chain of events is set in motion by Don Juan's untruth, his acceptance of another identity. It is, of course, a minor transgression, committed in the heat of the moment and redeemed immediately by the good actions which follow, and is above all fictionally necessary if the novel is to be written at all.

Cervantes uses other novelistic devices in *Lady Cornelia*. One of these is the use of clothing and jewellery which is, of course, perfectly compatible with the status of the principal protagonists. Don Juan has the child's clothes and wrappings changed on his

return to the house in order to hide from the wet-nurse his noble lineage. This initially misleads Cornelia, but when the child is dressed in its original clothes his identity is eventually made known. The question of identity is essential to the novel. When the child is handed over it loses its identity for a time and only fully acquires it again when recognised by its father, in other words, when it is made legitimate. On a more simple narrative level, attire is used for the purposes of establishing identity. Cornelia's jewels, her cross and the *agnus*, gifts from the Duke, play a part in her final presentation to him. The hat which Don Juan acquires as a result of the street fight and which belongs to the Duke enables him to be recognised as his saviour by the Duke on the road to Ferrara. Earlier, it causes him to be mistaken for the Duke by Cornelia, gains him entrance to her room and provokes the telling of her story. Dress then metonymically designates class (as do food and language), but it also provides narrative motivation. The various movements and journeys of the characters likewise play an important role in the action. The decision of Don Juan and Don Antonio to go first to Flanders and then to Italy sets the whole chain of events in train. Don Juan's desire to go for a walk, and thus be separated from Don Antonio, initiates the major phase of the action, which Cornelia's exit from her house continues. Don Juan and Don Antonio's departure, followed by Cornelia's flight, move the action forward. It is then complicated by the return of the male protagonists to Bologna and resolved by the Duke's subsequent departure for Ferrara. The novel is only static at those points where a character is narrating his or her part in the story, for all of them are narrators at some point. Juan and Antonio tell of their night's adventures, Cornelia tells her story (to Don Juan and Don Antonio, to the housekeeper, and to the priest), which is told from a different perspective by Lorenzo and by the Duke himself. It is only when all the narratives are put together that the full story of Cornelia and the Duke emerges, for doubts and uncertainties grow in the lacunae between them.

The fundamental motif of the story is honour, the aristocratic code on which public reputation was based. As often as not, questions of honour arose in the area of sexual relations. Cornelia is kept secluded by her brother to protect her honour and consequently that of her family, in this case essentially his own. Her unique beauty is an attraction to men and therefore her honour is constantly in jeopardy. Her seduction by the Duke is an affront to the honour of the Bentibolli family and must be avenged, hence the attack on the Duke by Lorenzo and his companions. The only way in which the stain of honour could be cleansed in this case is by marriage which would signify compliance with the established social code. This is important to Cornelia on one level. On another level, however, she is genuinely in love with the Duke and so marriage will fulfil her emotional needs. Indeed, it transpires that the Duke's promise to marry her is a genuine one, delayed only by certain circumstances, so that he can be seen to be acting honourably. The Spaniards' action in helping them is also motivated by codes of conduct which are inherent in the nobility, and therefore the whole novel is an exemplification of certain perfect values and standards of behaviour. The novel is enacted in the public and social sphere. Interestingly, the characters who do not conform to these standards are not of the same aristocratic class. The false Cornelia is motivated only by self-interest and the quest for pleasure, as is the page, and the housekeeper's slander of the Spaniards is shown to be wholly without foundation, for their behaviour with Cornelia is beyond reproach. It is suggested early in the novel that

they were, as would be appropriate to their age, interested in the young ladies, both single and married. The whole emphasis of the novel is on the impeccable standards and high ideals of the nobility.

The highly idealistic portrait of upper class society is inseparable from certain religious ideas, though not necessarily conventional ones. The emphasis in the story is less on the external worth of individuals than on certain inner values. Arguably, the insistence on externals conceals a greater truth within. The relationship of the Duke and Cornelia represents an inversion of the conventional situation. Their relationship is consummated and their child is born outside of wedlock, before their marriage is blessed by the Church. By insisting, however, on their purity of intention rather than on their observance of a social ritual, Cervantes makes it clear that the final outcome is appropriate and deserved. That heaven will not permit anything other than a happy resolution of Cornelia's tribulations is asserted by Don Juan on hearing her story. This is a premonition of the outcome and of the Spaniards' role in bringing it about. They ensure that honour and virtue are rewarded, so that sincere feeling and pure motives are publicly acknowledged. Only in this spiritual context does the social have any ultimate validity. In fact, in retrospect we can see that by having Cornelia and the Duke meet at a wedding, their relationship had been set in the context of marriage from the outset, and their whole story, as we know it, is framed between the two ceremonies.

Bibliography, *Lady Cornelia*

Dunn, Peter N., 'La señora Cornelia', in J.B. Avalle-Arce & E.C. Riley, eds., *Suma cervantina* (London, 1973), 106-12.
El Saffar, Ruth, 'La señora Cornelia', in *Novel to Romance* (Baltimore, 1974), 118-28.
Lacadena y Calero, Esther, 'La señora Cornelia y su técnica narrativa', *Anales cervantinos*, 15 (1976), 199-210.
Pabón, T., 'Secular Resurrection through Marriage in Cervantes's *La señora Cornelia, Las dos doncellas* and *La fuerza de la sangre*', *Anales cervantinos*, 16 (1977), 109-24.

Novela de la señora Cornelia

Don Antonio de Isunza y don Juan de Gamboa, caballeros principales, de una edad, muy discretos y grandes amigos, siendo estudiantes en Salamanca determinaron de dejar sus estudios por irse a Flandes, llevados del hervor de la sangre moza y del deseo, como decirse suele, de ver mundo, y por parecerles que el ejercicio de las armas, aunque arma y dice bien a todos, principalmente asienta y dice mejor en los bien nacidos y de ilustre sangre.

Llegaron, pues, a Flandes a tiempo que estaban las cosas en paz, o en conciertos y tratos de tenerla presto. Recibieron en Amberes cartas de sus padres, donde les escribieron el grande enojo que habían recibido por haber dejado sus estudios sin avisárselo, para que hubieran venido con la comodidad que pedía el ser quién eran. Finalmente, conociendo la pesadumbre de sus padres, acordaron de volverse a España, pues no había que hacer en Flandes; pero antes de volverse quisieron ver todas las más famosas ciudades de Italia; y habiéndolas visto todas pararon en Bolonia, y admirados de los estudios de aquella insigne universidad, quisieron en ella proseguir los suyos. Dieron noticia de su intento a sus padres, de que se holgaron infinito, y lo mostraron con proveerles magníficamente y de modo que mostrasen en su tratamiento quién eran y qué padres tenían; y desde el primero día que salieron a las escuelas fueron conocidos de todos por caballeros, galanes, discretos y bien criados.

Tendría don Antonio hasta veinticuatro años y don Juan no pasaba de veintiséis. Y adornaban esta buena edad con ser muy gentiles hombres, músicos, poetas, diestros y valientes, partes que los hacían amables y bien queridos de cuantos los comunicaban.

Tuvieron luego muchos amigos, así estudiantes españoles, de los muchos que en aquella universidad cursaban, como de los mismos de la ciudad y de los extranjeros. Mostrábanse con todos liberales y comedidos, y muy ajenos de la arrogancia que dicen que suelen tener los españoles. Y como eran mozos y alegres, no se disgustaban de tener noticia de las hermosas de la ciudad; y aunque había muchas señoras doncellas y casadas con gran fama de ser honestas y hermosas, a todas se aventajaba la señora Cornelia Bentibolli, de la antigua y generosa familia de los Bentibollis, que un tiempo fueron señores de Bolonia.

Era Cornelia hermosísima en extremo, y estaba debajo de la guarda y amparo de Lorenzo Bentibolli, su hermano, honradísimo y valiente caballero, huérfanos de padre y madre; que aunque los dejaron solos, los dejaron ricos, y la riqueza es grande alivio de la orfandad.

Era el recato de Cornelia tanto y la solicitud de su hermano tanta en guardarla, que ni ella se dejaba ver ni su hermano consentía que la viesen. Esta fama traía deseosos a don Juan y a don Antonio de verla, aunque fuera en la iglesia; pero el trabajo que en ello pusieron fue en balde, y el deseo, por la imposibilidad, cuchillo de la esperanza, fue

Lady Cornelia

Don Antonio de Isunza and Don Juan de Gamboa, two noblemen of great discretion, who were about the same age and very close friends, decided, while studying at Salamanca, to abandon their studies and go to Flanders,[1] fired by the impetuousness of youth and by the desire, as people often say, to see the world. It also seemed to them that the profession of arms, although befitting and suiting everyone, is especially befitting to those of high birth and noble blood.

They arrived in Flanders at a time of peace or, at any rate, when negotiations and agreements would shortly lead to it. In Antwerp, they received letters from their fathers expressing great annoyance at the way their sons had abandoned their studies without letting them know first so as to ensure that they travelled back home in the comfort that befitted men such as they were. So it was that, conscious of their fathers' anxiety, they decided to return to Spain since there was nothing to do in Flanders but, before returning, they decided to see all the most famous cities of Italy; and having seen them all, they stopped at Bologna where, amazed at the subjects studied in that distinguished university, they wished to continue their own studies.[2] They sent news of their intentions to their fathers who were extremely pleased and showed it by providing for them magnificently so that their sons might show in their dealings with others who they were and the kind of fathers they had; and from the very first day in the lecture rooms they were acknowledged by all as gentlemen of discretion, fine manners and good breeding.

Don Antonio must have been twenty-four years old and Don Juan was no more than twenty-six. Their fine ages were enhanced by the fact that they were gentlemen, musicians, poets, as well as being skilled and brave, qualities which made them popular and well loved by everyone who came into contact with them.

They therefore soon made many friends both among the many Spanish students studying in that university and among the local students of the city and those from abroad. They showed generosity and courtesy to everyone and none of the arrogance which Spaniards are said to possess. As they were young and high-spirited, they were not averse to finding out who were the beautiful women of the city; and although there were many married and unmarried ladies whose chastity and beauty were renowned, they were all surpassed by Lady Cornelia Bentibolli, of the old and noble family of the Bentibollis, one-time lords of Bologna.[3]

Cornelia, who was extremely beautiful, was under the care and protection of her brother, Lorenzo Bentibolli, a brave and very honourable nobleman; they were orphans, having lost both father and mother who, although leaving them alone, left them wealthy, and wealth can be a great comfort to orphans.

Cornelia's modesty and her brother's solicitude in protecting her were such that she did not allow herself to be seen nor did her brother allow anyone to see her. This reputation had made Don Juan and Don Antonio keen to set eyes on her if only in church, but all their efforts were in vain and their desire gradually diminished because of

menguado. Y así, con sólo el amor de sus estudios y entretenimiento de algunas honestas mocedades, pasaban una vida tan alegre como honrada. Pocas veces salían de noche, y si salían iban juntos y bien armados.

Sucedió, pues, que habiendo de salir una noche, dijo don Antonio a don Juan que él se quería quedar a rezar ciertas devociones, que se fuese, que luego le seguiría.

–No hay para qué –dijo don Juan–, que yo os aguardaré, y si no saliéremos esta noche, importa poco.

–No, por vida vuestra –replicó don Antonio–, salid a coger el aire, que yo seré luego con vos, si es que vais por donde solemos ir.

–Haced vuestro gusto –dijo don Juan–; quedaos en buena hora, y si saliéredes, las mismas estaciones andaré esta noche que las pasadas.

Fuese don Juan, y quedóse don Antonio. Era la noche entre oscura, y la hora, las once; y habiendo andado dos o tres calles y viéndose solo y que no tenía con quién hablar, determinó volverse a casa, y poniéndolo en efecto, al pasar por una calle que tenía portales sustentados en mármoles oyó que de una puerta le ceceaban. La oscuridad de la noche y la que causaban los portales no le dejaban atinar al ceceo. Detúvose un poco, estuvo atento, y vio entreabrir una puerta; llegóse a ella, y oyó una voz baja que dijo:

–¿Sois por ventura Fabio?

Don Juan, por sí o por no, respondió sí.

–Pues tomad –respondieron de dentro–, y ponedlo en cobro, y volved luego, que importa.

Alargó la mano don Juan, y topó un bulto, y queriéndolo tomar, vio que eran menester las dos manos, y así le hubo de asir con entrambas; y apenas se le dejaron en ellas, cuando le cerraron la puerta, y él se halló cargado en la calle y sin saber de qué. Pero casi luego empezó a llorar una criatura, al parecer recién nacida, a cuyo lloro quedó don Juan confuso y suspenso, sin saber qué hacerse ni qué corte dar en aquel caso; porque en volver a llamar a la puerta le pareció que podía correr algún peligro cuya era la criatura, y en dejarla allí, la criatura misma; pues el llevarla a su casa, no tenía en ella quien la remediase, ni él conocía en toda la ciudad persona adonde poder llevarla. Pero viendo que le habían dicho que la pusiese en cobro y que volviese luego, determinó de traerla a su casa y dejarla en poder de una ama que los servía, y volver luego a ver si era menester su favor en alguna cosa, puesto que bien había visto que le habían tenido por otro y que había sido error darle a él la criatura.

Finalmente, sin hacer más discursos, se vino a casa con ella, a tiempo que ya don Antonio no estaba en ella. Entróse en un aposento, y llamó al ama, descubrió la criatura y vio que era la más hermosa que jamás hubiese visto. Los paños en que venía envuelta mostraban ser de ricos padres nacida. Desenvolvióla el ama, y hallaron que era varón.

–Menester es –dijo don Juan– dar de mamar a este niño, y ha de ser de esta manera: que vos, ama, le habéis de quitar estas ricas mantillas y ponerle otras más humildes, y sin decir que yo le he traído la habéis de llevar en casa de una partera, que las tales siempre suelen dar recado y remedio a semejantes necesidades. Llevaréis dineros con

its impossibility which is the killer of hope. And so, with only the love of their studies and the innocent pastimes of youth, they led a life which was as happy as it was honourable. They rarely went out at night, and when they did so they went together and well armed against possible attackers.

It happened one night when they were about to go out that Don Antonio told Don Juan to go on ahead because he wished to stay behind to say some prayers and he would catch up with him later:

"There's no need for that," replied Don Juan. "I shall wait for you, and if in the end we do not go out tonight, it does not matter."

"No, upon my soul," Don Antonio replied, "go out and take some fresh air. I shall catch up with you later, that is, assuming you take the usual route."

"As you wish," replied Don Juan. "I leave you in peace, and if you do come out tonight, I shall be walking along the same streets as usual."

Don Juan went out, and Don Antonio stayed behind. The night was rather dark, the time eleven o'clock. After walking through one or two streets and still finding himself alone, with no one to talk to, Don Juan decided to return home, and as he was walking along a street which had doorways with marble pillars he heard someone whispering to him from one of the doors. The darkness of the night and of the doorways made it difficult to locate the whispering. He stopped a while, listened carefully, and saw a door open a little; he went towards it and heard a voice whisper:

"Are you Fabio by any chance?"

Don Juan, to play safe, replied that he was.

"Take this then," the reply came from inside, "put it in a safe place, and then come back. It's important."

Don Juan reached out and felt a bundle and when he tried to take it he realized he needed to use both hands. He had hardly taken hold of it when the door was shut, and he was left in the street with this burden, not knowing what it was. But almost immediately, crying like that of a new-born baby was heard, and Don Juan was confused and amazed, not knowing what to do or where to turn in order to resolve the situation; for, if he knocked on the door again, he felt there would be some risk to the person whose child it was, and if he left the child there, the child itself would be at risk; if he took the child home, there was no one there to look after it, nor did he know anyone else in the whole of the city with whom he could leave it. But seeing that he had been told to put it in a safe place and to come back later, he decided to take it to his own home and leave it in the care of their housekeeper and to go back to see if his help were needed, since it was clear to him that he had been mistaken for someone else and had been given the child in error.

In the end, without debating the matter further, he went home with the child, by which time Don Antonio was no longer there. He went into one of the rooms and called the housekeeper; he uncovered the child and saw that it was the most beautiful he had ever seen. The garments in which it was wrapped showed that it was born of wealthy parents, and when the housekeeper undressed the child they saw that it was a boy.

"We must find someone to suckle this child," Don Juan said to the housekeeper, "and we shall do it as follows: you must take him out of these expensive shawls and put him in humbler ones and, without mentioning that I brought him here, take him to the house of a midwife, who can provide the advice and help that we need in a moment such as

que la dejéis satisfecha y daréisle los padres que quisiéredes, para encubrir la verdad de haberlo yo traído.

Respondió el ama que así lo haría, y don Juan, con la prisa que pudo, volvió a ver si le ceceaban otra vez; pero un poco antes que llegase a la casa adonde le habían llamado oyó gran ruido de espadas, como de mucha gente que se acuchillaba. Estuvo atento, y no sintió palabra alguna. La herrería era a la sorda; y a la luz de las centellas que las piedras heridas de las espadas levantaban, casi pudo ver que eran muchos los que a uno solo acometían, y confirmóse en esta verdad oyendo decir:

–¡Ah traidores, que sois muchos, y yo solo! Pero con todo eso no os ha de valer vuestra superchería!

Oyendo y viendo lo cual don Juan, llevado de su valeroso corazón, en dos brincos se puso al lado, y metiendo mano a la espada y a un broquel que llevaba, dijo al que defendía, en lengua italiana, por no ser conocido por español:

–No temáis, que socorro os ha venido que no os faltará hasta perder la vida; menead los puños, que traidores pueden poco, aunque sean muchos.

A estas razones respondió uno de los contrarios:

–Mientes, que aquí no hay ningún traidor; que el querer cobrar la honra perdida, a toda demasía da licencia.

No le habló más palabras, porque no les daba lugar a ello la prisa que se daban a herirse los enemigos, que al parecer de don Juan debían de ser seis. Apretaron tanto a su compañero que de dos estocadas que le dieron a tiempo en los pechos dieron con él en tierra. Don Juan creyó que le habían muerto, y con ligereza y valor extraño se puso delante de todos y los hizo arredrar a fuerza de una lluvia de cuchilladas y estocadas. Pero no fuera bastante su diligencia para ofender y defenderse, si no le ayudara la buena suerte con hacer que los vecinos de la casa sacasen lumbres a las ventanas y a grandes voces llamasen a la justicia: lo cual, visto por los contrarios, dejaron la calle y a espadas vueltas se ausentaron.

Ya en esto se había levantado el caído, porque las estocadas hallaron un peto como de diamante, en que toparon. Habíasele caído a don Juan el sombrero en la refriega, y buscándole, halló otro, que se puso acaso, sin mirar si era suyo o no. El caído se llegó a él y le dijo:

–Señor caballero, quienquiera que seáis, yo confieso que os debo la vida que tengo, la cual con lo que valgo y puedo, gastaré a vuestro servicio. Hacedme merced de decirme quién sois y vuestro nombre, para que yo sepa a quién tengo que mostrarme agradecido.

A lo cual respondió don Juan:

–No quiero ser descortés, ya que soy desinteresado. Por hacer, señor, lo que me pedís, y por daros gusto, solamente os diré que soy un caballero español y estudiante en esta ciudad; si el nombre os importara saberlo, os lo dijera; mas por si acaso quisiéredes servir de mí en otra cosa, sabed que me llamo don Juan de Gamboa.

–Mucha merced me habéis hecho – respondió el caído–; pero, señor don Juan de Gamboa, no quiero deciros quién soy ni mi nombre, porque he de gustar mucho de que lo sepáis de otro que de mí, y yo tendré cuidado de que os hagan sabidor de ello.

this. Take sufficient money to pay what she asks and give the child whatever parents you choose so as to cover up the fact that I brought him here."

The housekeeper replied that she would do as he asked, and Don Juan went back as quickly as he could to see if anyone would whisper to him again; but a little before reaching the house from which the voice had called to him he heard the clash of swords, as though many men were fighting. He listened carefully but he could not hear a single word. The sword fight was being carried out in silence, and by the light of the sparks which flew off the stones struck by the swords, he was just able to make out that a group of men were attacking a single individual, and this was confirmed when he heard a man shout:

"Ah, traitors, you are many and I am one! But, despite that, your knavery will be of no avail to you."

Hearing and seeing this, Don Juan, spurred on by his courageous spirit, immediately leapt to the man's aid and, taking hold of his sword and shield, addressed the person he was defending in Italian so that he would not be recognised as a Spaniard:

"Do not fear, I shall help you even if I have to lose my life; fight skilfully for traitors cannot do very much even if they are many in number."

To these arguments one of the adversaries responded:

"You lie, for there is no traitor here; all is justified when honour is at stake."

Don Juan did not have time to say anything else because of the speed with which the enemies, of whom it seemed to Don Juan there were six, sought to wound or be wounded. They pressed Don Juan's companion very hard and brought him down with two simultaneous sword thrusts to the chest. Don Juan thought they had killed him and with great speed and a rare courage he stood in front of them all and made them retreat through the thrusts and blows of the sword that he showered on them. But his efforts in attacking and defending himself would not have been sufficient if good fortune had not aided him through the residents of the street who appeared at their windows with lights, and shouted for the law. Seeing this, the adversaries put away their swords and left the street.

By now, the man who had been struck to the ground had got up, for the blows of the swords had struck a breastplate which was hard as diamond. During the fight, Don Juan's hat had fallen off, and looking for it now he picked up another which he put on without looking to see whether it was his or not. The man approached him and said:

"Sir, whoever you are, I must confess that I owe my life to you, and that life together with all the wealth and power I have, I put at your service. Please tell me who you are and what your name is so that I may know to whom I am indebted."

To which Don Juan replied:

"Although I have no interest at stake in this, I do not wish to be discourteous. Sir, it is only to do as you ask and to please you that I tell you that I am a Spanish gentleman and a student in this city; if it matters to you to know my name, I shall tell you it; in case you wish to avail yourself of my services in the future, I inform you that my name is Don Juan de Gamboa."

"You have done me a great favour," replied the other, "but, Don Juan de Gamboa, I do not wish to tell you who I am or what my name is because I would much rather you learned this from someone other than myself, and I will see to it that you are so informed."

Habíale preguntado primero don Juan si estaba herido, porque le había visto dar dos grandes estocadas, y habíale respondido que un famoso peto que traía puesto, después de Dios, le había defendido; pero que con todo eso, sus enemigos le acabaran si él no se hallara a su lado. En esto vieron venir hacia ellos un bulto de gente, y don Juan dijo:

−Si éstos son los enemigos que vuelven, apercibíos, señor, y haced como quien sois. A lo que yo creo, no son enemigos, sino amigos los que aquí vienen.

Y así fue la verdad, porque los que llegaron, que fueron ocho hombres, rodearon al caído y hablaron con él pocas palabras, pero tan calladas y secretas que don Juan no las pudo oír. Volvió luego el defendido a don Juan y díjole:

−A no haber venido estos amigos, en ninguna manera, señor don Juan, os dejara hasta que acabárades de ponerme en salvo; pero ahora os suplico con todo encarecimiento que os vais y me dejéis, que me importa.

Hablando esto se tentó la cabeza, y vio que estaba sin sombrero, y volviéndose a los que habían venido pidió que le diesen un sombrero, que se le había caído el suyo. Apenas lo hubo dicho, cuando don Juan le puso el que había hallado en la calle. Tentóle el caído, y volviéndose a don Juan, le dijo:

−Este sombrero no es mío; por vida del señor don Juan, que se le lleve por trofeo de esta refriega, y guárdele, que creo que es conocido.

Diéronle otro sombrero al defendido, y don Juan, por cumplir lo que le había pedido, pasando otros algunos, aunque breves comedimientos, le dejó sin saber quién era, y se vino a su casa, sin querer llegar a la puerta donde le habían dado la criatura, por parecerle que todo el barrio estaba despierto y alborotado con la pendencia.

Sucedió, pues, que volviéndose a su posada, en la mitad del camino encontró con don Antonio de Isunza, su camarada, y conociéndose, dijo don Antonio:

−Volved conmigo, don Juan, hasta aquí arriba, y en el camino os contaré un extraño cuento que me ha sucedido, que no le habréis oído tal vez en toda vuestra vida.

−Como esos cuentos os podré contar yo −respondió don Juan−; pero vamos donde queréis, y contadme el vuestro.

Guió don Antonio, y dijo:

−Habéis de saber que poco más de una hora después que salisteis de casa salí a buscaros, y no treinta pasos de aquí vi venir casi a encontrarme un bulto negro de persona, que venía muy aguijando, y llegándose cerca conocí ser mujer en el hábito largo, la cual, con voz interrumpida de sollozos y de suspiros, me dijo: "¿Por ventura, señor, sois extranjero o de la ciudad?". "Extranjero soy y español", respondí yo. Y ella. "Gracias al cielo, que no quiere que muera sin sacramentos". "¿Venís herida, señora − repliqué yo−, o traéis algún mal de muerte?" "Podría ser que el que traigo lo fuese, si presto no se me da remedio; por la cortesía que siempre suele reinar en los de vuestra nación, os suplico, señor español, que me saquéis de estas calles y me llevéis a vuestra posada con la mayor prisa que pudiéredes, que allá, si gustáredes de ello, sabréis el mal que llevo y quién soy, aunque sea a costa de mi crédito." Oyendo lo cual, pareciéndome

Don Juan had first asked him if he was wounded because he had seen him struck twice, and he had replied that a famous breastplate he was wearing had, next to God, been his protection, but that even so, his enemies would have killed him if Don Juan had not stood at his side. At that point, they saw a group of people heading towards them, and Don Juan said:

"If these are your enemies coming back, get ready, sir, and behave as befits who you are. But I think that those people who are coming are not enemies but friends."

And he was right, for those who arrived, eight men in all, surrounded the man who had been attacked and exchanged a few words with him, but so quietly and secretively that Don Juan was unable to hear them. Then the man he had defended turned to Don Juan and said to him:

"If these friends had not come, there would have been no chance of my letting you go until you had placed me in complete safety; but I now ask you most earnestly to go away[4] and leave me, for it is important to me that you should do so."

As he was saying this, he felt his head and realized he had lost his hat and, turning to those who had arrived, he asked them to give him a hat, for his own had fallen off. Hardly had he said this than Don Juan put on him the one he had found in the street, and as he felt it he turned to Don Juan and said:

"This is not my hat. Don Juan, you are free to take it as a trophy from the fight. Please take good care of it for I think it is a famous hat."

The man was given another hat, and Don Juan, in order to do as he had been asked, exchanged some other brief words of politeness and left without knowing who the man was, and he went home without going near the door from which the child had been handed over to him, since it seemed to him that the whole district was awake and disturbed by the fight.

It so happened that when he was half-way back to his lodgings he met Don Antonio de Isunza, his comrade, who was also returning, and as they saw each other, Don Antonio said:

"Come with me a little way, Don Juan, and as we go I shall relate to you a strange event which has happened to me, the likes of which you will not have heard in all your life."

"I think I could tell you a similar one," replied Don Juan, "but let's go the way you want and you tell me yours first."

Don Antonio led the way and said:

"Just over an hour after you left home, I went to look for you, and no more than thirty yards from here I saw the dark outline of a person heading straight towards me, walking very quickly, and as the person drew near I saw, by the length of the dress, that it was a woman who, through her sobs and sighs, said to me: `Sir, are you by any chance from this city or are you a stranger to these parts?' `I am a stranger, I am a Spaniard,' I replied. And she said: `I give thanks to God who will not allow me to die without receiving the sacraments.' `Are you wounded, madam?' I asked, `or are you suffering from some deadly sickness?' `The sickness I have could well be deadly if a cure for it is not found soon; I beseech you by the gallantry which is typical of your countrymen[5] to take me away as quickly as possible from these streets to your lodgings and there, if you wish, you will find out what ails me and who I am, even though it be at the expense of my reputation.' Hearing this and believing that she really was in need of what she asked,

que tenía necesidad de lo que pedía, sin replicarla más, la así de la mano y por calles desviadas la llevé a la posada. Abrióme Santisteban el paje, hícele que se retirase, y sin que él la viese la llevé a mi estancia, y ella en entrando se arrojó encima de mi lecho, desmayada. Lleguéme a ella y descubríla el rostro, que con el manto traía cubierto, y descubrí en él la mayor belleza que humanos ojos han visto; será a mi parecer de edad de diez y ocho años, antes menos que más. Quedé suspenso de ver tal extremo de belleza; acudí a echarle un poco de agua en el rostro, con que volvió en sí, suspirando tiernamente, y lo primero que me dijo fue: "¿Conocéisme, señor?" "No –respondí yo–, ni es bien que yo haya tenido ventura de haber conocido tanta hermosura." "Desdichada de aquella –respondió ella– a quien se la da el cielo para mayor desgracia suya; pero, señor, no es tiempo éste de alabar hermosuras, sino de remediar desdichas; por quien sois, que me dejéis aquí encerrada, y no permitáis que ninguno me vea, y volved luego al mismo lugar que me topastéis y mirad si riñe alguna gente, y no favorezcáis a ninguno de los que riñeren, sino poned paz, que cualquier daño de las partes ha de resultar en acrecentar el mío." Déjola encerrada y vengo a poner en paz esta pendencia.

–¿Tenéis más que decir, don Antonio? –preguntó don Juan.

–¿Pues no os parece que he dicho harto? –respondió don Antonio–. Pues he dicho que tengo debajo de llave y en mi aposento la mayor belleza que humanos ojos han visto.

–El caso es extraño, sin duda –dijo don Juan–; pero oíd el mío.

Y luego le contó todo lo que le había sucedido, y como la criatura que le habían dado estaba en casa en poder de su ama, y la orden que le había dejado de mudarle las ricas mantillas en pobres y de llevarle adonde le criasen o a lo menos socorriesen la presente necesidad. Y dijo más: que la pendencia que él venía a buscar ya era acabada y puesta en paz, que él se había hallado en ella, y que a lo que él imaginaba todos los de la riña debían de ser gentes de prendas y de gran valor.

Quedaron entrambos admirados del suceso de cada uno y con prisa se volvieron a la posada, por ver lo que había menester la encerrada. En el camino dijo don Antonio a don Juan que él había prometido a aquella señora que no la dejaría ver de nadie ni entraría en aquel aposento sino él solo, en tanto que ella no gustase otra cosa.

–No importa nada –respondió don Juan–, que no faltará orden para verla, que ya lo deseo en extremo, según me la habéis alabado de hermosa.

Llegaron en esto, y a la luz que sacó uno de tres pajes que tenían, alzó los ojos don Antonio al sombrero que don Juan traía, y viole resplandeciente de diamantes; quitósele, y vio que las luces salían de muchos que en un cintillo riquísimo traía. Miráronle y remiráronle entrambos, y concluyeron que, si todos eran finos como parecían, valía más de doce mil ducados. Aquí acabaron de conocer ser gente principal la de la pendencia, especialmente el socorrido de don Juan, de quien se acordó haberle dicho que trajese el sombrero y le guardase, porque era conocido. Mandaron retirar los pajes y don Antonio abrió su aposento, y halló a la señora sentada en la cama, con la mano en la mejilla, derramando tiernas lágrimas. Don Juan, con el deseo que tenía de verla, se asomó a la

without saying anything else to her, I took her by the hand and led her through some back streets to my lodgings. The page Santisteban opened the door for me. I asked him to withdraw, and without his seeing her I took her to my room where, as soon as she went in, she fell on my bed and fainted. I went up to her and removed the shawl which covered her face, and I beheld the greatest beauty that human eyes have ever seen; she must have been about eighteen years old, or even younger. I was amazed at her extreme beauty. I quickly sprinkled a little water on her face, whereupon she came to, sighing gently, and the first thing she said to me was: `Do you know me, sir?' `No,' I replied, `nor does it necessarily befit me to have the fortune of knowing such great beauty.' `Unfortunate is the woman on whom heaven bestows such beauty for her own unhappiness,' she replied, `but, sir, this is no time to praise beauty but rather to remedy misfortunes; I beseech you by whom you are to leave me shut away here and not allow anyone to see me, and to return presently to the same place where you came across me to see if any people are fighting. Do not take sides but make peace, for any harm to either side may result in greater harm to me.' I have left her shut away," Don Antonio said, "and I have come to settle this fight."

"Do you have anything more to tell me, Don Antonio?" asked Don Juan.

"Don't you think I have said enough?" Don Antonio replied. "I have said that I have under lock and key in my room the greatest beauty that human eyes have ever seen."

"It is certainly a strange story," Don Juan said, "but listen to mine."

And he then narrated all that had happened to him, and how the child he had been given was in his house being looked after by the housekeeper, and the instruction he had given her to exchange the expensive shawls for simpler ones and to take the child where it could be suckled or at least where it would be looked after for the time being. And he went on to say more: that the fight Don Antonio was enquiring about was now over and that peace had been restored, that he himself had been involved in it and that as far as he could see all those who had taken part were people of standing and great worth.

They were both filled with wonder at each other's experiences and they hurried back to their lodgings to see if the lady needed anything. On the way, Don Antonio told Don Juan that he had promised her that he would not allow anyone to see her and that he himself would be the only one to enter her room until such time as she might decide otherwise.

"It doesn't matter at all," Don Juan replied, "for there will be opportunity to see her in due course, but I must confess that I already feel a great desire to do so, seeing how you have extolled her beauty."

They arrived home at that point and by the light brought out by one of their three pages, Don Antonio saw that Don Juan's hat was covered with glittering diamonds; he took it off him and saw that the reflections came from the many diamonds on the richest of hat-bands. They examined and reexamined it and concluded that if the diamonds were all as fine as they looked the hat must be worth more than twelve thousand ducats. This finally convinced them that the people involved in the fight were important people, especially the man who had been aided by Don Juan, whom he remembered saying that he should take the hat and look after it, for it was a famous one. They ordered the pages to withdraw and Don Antonio opened his room and found the lady sitting on the bed, with her hand on her cheek, shedding tender tears. Don Juan, having a great desire to

puerta tanto cuanto pudo entrar la cabeza, y al punto la lumbre de los diamantes dio en los ojos de la que lloraba, y alzándolos, dijo:

–Entrad, señor duque, entrad, ¿para qué me queréis dar con tanta escaseza el bien de vuestra vista?

A esto dijo don Antonio:

–Aquí, señora, no hay ningún duque que se excuse de veros.

–¿Cómo no? –replicó ella–. El que allí se asomó ahora es el duque de Ferrara, que mal le puede encubrir la riqueza de su sombrero.

–En verdad, señora, que el sombrero que vistes no le trae ningún duque; y si queréis desengañaros con ver quien le trae, dadle licencia que entre.

–Entre enhorabuena –dijo ella–, aunque si no fuese el duque mis desdichas serían mayores.

Todas estas razones había oído don Juan, y viendo que tenía licencia de entrar, con el sombrero en la mano entró en el aposento, y así como se le puso delante y ella conoció no ser quien decía el del rico sombrero, con voz turbada y lengua presurosa, dijo:

–¡Ay, desdichada de mí! Señor mío, decidme luego, sin tenerme más suspensa: ¿conocéis el dueño de ese sombrero? ¿Dónde le dejastes o cómo vino a vuestro poder? ¿Es vivo por ventura, o son ésas las nuevas que me envía de su muerte? ¡Ay, bien mío, qué sucesos son éstos! ¡Aquí veo tus prendas, aquí me veo sin ti encerrada y en poder que, a no saber que es de gentiles hombres españoles, el temor de perder mi honestidad me hubiera quitado la vida!

–Sosegaos, señora –dijo don Juan–, que ni el dueño de este sombrero es muerto ni estáis en parte donde se os ha de hacer agravio alguno, sino serviros con cuanto las fuerzas nuestras alcanzaren, hasta poner las vidas por defenderos y ampararos; que no es bien que os salga vana la fe que tenéis de la bondad de los españoles; y pues nosotros lo somos y principales (que aquí viene bien ésta que parece arrogancia), estad segura que se os guardará el decoro que vuestra presencia merece.

–Así lo creo yo –respondió ella–; pero con todo eso, decidme, señor, ¿cómo vino a vuestro poder ese rico sombrero, o adónde está su dueño, que, por lo menos, es Alfonso de Este, duque de Ferrara?

Entonces don Juan, por no tenerla más suspensa, le contó cómo le había hallado en una pendencia, y en ella había favorecido y ayudado a un caballero que, por lo que ella decía, sin duda debía de ser el duque de Ferrara, y que en la pendencia había perdido el sombrero y hallado aquél, y que aquel caballero le había dicho que le guardase, que era conocido, y que la refriega se había concluido sin quedar herido el caballero ni él tampoco, y que después de acabada, había llegado gente que al parecer debían de ser criados o amigos del que él pensaba ser el duque, el cual le había pedido le dejase y se viniese; "mostrándose muy agradecido al favor que yo le había dado".

–De manera, señora mía, que este rico sombrero vino a mi poder por la manera como os he dicho, y su dueño, si es el duque, como vos decís, no ha una hora que le dejé bueno, sano y salvo; sea esta verdad parte para vuestro consuelo, si es que le tendréis con saber del buen estado del duque.

see her, put his head round the door as best he could, and straightaway the glittering diamonds caught the tearful eyes of the lady who looked up and said:

"Come in, Duke, come in, why do you not let me see more of you?"

To which Don Antonio replied:

"My lady, there is no duke here who is trying to elude your eyes."

"What do you mean, no duke? The person who looked through the door a minute ago was the Duke of Ferrara, for his rich hat can conceal him but poorly."

"Truly, my lady, the hat you saw was worn by no duke; and if you wish to ascertain who, in fact, is wearing it, give him leave to enter."

"Let him enter then," she said, "although if he is not the Duke, my misfortunes will be even greater."

Don Juan had listened to all these comments and, seeing that he had permission to enter, he went into the room with the hat in his hand, and as soon as he stood in front of her and she saw that the man wearing the rich hat was not the one whom she claimed, she said hastily in an upset voice:

"Oh, wretched me! Sir, tell me then, without keeping me in suspense any longer, do you know the owner of that hat? Where did you leave him and how did it come into your possession? Is he alive by any chance, or does your possession of that hat mean he is dead? Oh, my love, what events are these? I see your clothes here, I find myself locked away without you and in the power of men who, did I not know them to be gallant Spanish gentlemen, would make me fear for my life through fear of losing my honour!"

"Calm yourself, my lady," Don Juan said, "for the owner of this hat is not dead nor are you in a place where any harm will come to you. On the contrary, we shall help you as much as we can, even to the point of laying down our lives in your defence and protection; for it is not right that the faith you put in Spanish men should turn out to be misplaced. And so, since we are Spaniards, and noble ones at that (and in this case our show of arrogance is quite justified), rest assured that you will be accorded the respect that your person deserves."

"I believe you," she replied, "but even so, tell me, sir, how did that rich hat come into your possession, or where is its owner who must be no less than Alfonso de Este, Duke of Ferrara?"[6]

Then, so as not to keep her in suspense any longer, Don Juan related to her how he had acquired it in a fight in which he had aided and helped a gentleman who, from what she said, must undoubtedly be the Duke of Ferrara, and that in the same fight he had lost his own hat and gained that one, and that the gentleman had asked him to look after it carefully for it was well known, and that the fight had ended with neither the gentleman nor himself being wounded. After it had finished, some people had arrived who appeared to be servants or friends of the man that he took to be the Duke, who had then asked him to take his leave of him and to go away, "displaying great gratitude for the support I had given him."

"And so, my lady, this hat came into my possession in the manner I have described, and its owner, if it is the Duke, as you say, I left not one hour ago safe and sound and in good health; I hope this fact will serve to console you, if indeed knowing of the Duke's safety is a consolation to you."

–Para que sepáis, señores, si tengo razón y causa para preguntar por él, estadme atentos y escuchad la no sé si diga mi desdichada historia.

Todo el tiempo en que esto pasó le entretuvo el ama en paladear al niño con miel y en mudarle las mantillas de ricas en pobres; y ya que lo tuvo aderezado, quiso llevarla en casa de una partera, como don Juan se lo dejó ordenado, y al pasar con ella junto a la estancia donde estaba la que quería comenzar su historia lloró la criatura de modo que lo sintió la señora, y levantándose en pie púsose atentamente a escuchar, y oyó más distintamente el llanto de la criatura, y dijo:

–Señores míos, ¿qué criatura es aquella que parece recién nacida?

Don Juan respondió:

–Es un niño que esta noche nos han echado a la puerta de casa, y va el ama a buscar quién le dé de mamar.

–Tráiganmele aquí, por amor de Dios –dijo la señora–, que yo haré esa caridad a los hijos ajenos, pues no quiere el cielo que la haga con los propios.

Llamó don Juan al ama y tomóle el niño, y entrósele a la que le pedía, púsosele en los brazos, diciendo:

–Veis aquí, señora, el presente que nos han hecho esta noche, y no ha sido éste el primero, que pocos meses se pasan que no hallamos a los quicios de nuestras puertas semejantes hallazgos.

Tomóle ella en los brazos y miróle atentamente así el rostro como los pobres aunque limpios paños en que venía envuelto, y luego, sin poder tener las lágrimas, se echó la toca de la cabeza encima de los pechos, para poder dar con honestidad de mamar a la criatura, y aplicándosela a ellos, juntó su rostro con el suyo, y con la leche le sustentaba y con las lágrimas le bañaba el rostro. Y de esta manera estuvo sin levantar el suyo tanto espacio cuanto el niño no quiso dejar el pecho. En este espacio guardaban todos cuatro silencio; el niño mamaba; pero no era así, porque las recién paridas no pueden dar el pecho, y así, cayendo en la cuenta la que se lo daba, se volvió a don Juan, diciendo:

–En balde me he mostrado caritativa; bien parezco nueva en estos casos. Haced, señor, que a este niño le paladeen con un poco de miel, y no consintáis que a estas horas le lleven por las calles. Dejad llegar el día, y antes que le lleven vuélvanmele a traer, que me consuelo en verle.

Volvió el niño don Juan al ama y ordenóle le entretuviese hasta el día y que le pusiese las ricas mantillas con que le había traído, y que no le llevase sin primero decírselo. Y volviendo a entrar, y estando los tres solos, la hermosa dijo:

–Si queréis que hable, dadme primero algo que coma, que me desmayo, y tengo bastante ocasión para ello.

Acudió prestamente don Antonio a un escritorio y sacó de él muchas conservas, y de algunas comió la desmayada, y bebió un vidrio de agua fría, con que volvió en sí, y algo sosegada, dijo:

–Sentaos, señores, y escuchadme.

Hiciéronlo así, y ella, recogiéndose encima del lecho y abrigándose bien con las faldas del vestido, dejó descolgar por las espaldas un velo que en la cabeza traía, dejando el rostro exento y descubierto, mostrando en él el mismo de la luna o, por mejor decir, del mismo sol, cuando más hermoso y más claro se muestra. Llovíanle

"So that you may see whether I have cause and reason to ask after him, gentlemen, be attentive and listen to this unhappy story of mine if I am right in so describing it."

While all this was going on, the housekeeper was busy giving the baby some honey to taste and changing his expensive shawls for humbler ones. When she had everything ready, she decided to take the child to the house of a midwife as Don Juan had ordered, and as she carried him past the room where the lady was about to begin her story, the child cried so that the lady heard it, got up, listened attentively, ascertained that it was the crying of a child, and asked: "Gentlemen, what child is that for it appears to be newly-born?"

Don Juan replied:

"It is a boy who this very night has been left at our doorstep and who is being taken by the housekeeper to someone who may suckle it."

"Bring him here, for the love of God,", the lady said, "for I will perform that act of love for the child of others since heaven has not willed that I should perform it for my own."

Don Juan called the housekeeper and taking the boy from her, gave him to the lady, saying as he placed him in her arms:

"Here, my lady, look at the gift we have been given this night, and it is not the first, for few months go by without our making such discoveries on our doorsteps."

She took the baby in her arms and looked carefully both at his face and at the humble but clean garments in which he was swathed, and then, not being able to hold back her tears, she pulled her headscarf over her breasts so that she might be able to suckle the child decorously, took the child to her breasts, put her face next to his and tried to feed him with her milk as she bathed his face with her tears. And she continued in this manner without raising her head for as long as the child continued at her breast. During this time, all four of them kept silent; the boy sucked but was not fed, for women who have recently given birth have no milk, and so, realizing this, the lady turned to Don Juan and said:

"In vain have I tried to be kind; I appear to be a novice in these matters. See to it that this boy is given a little honey to taste and do not allow him to be carried through the streets at this time of night. Wait until daybreak, and before he is taken away bring him to me again, for seeing him is of great comfort to me."

Don Juan gave back the boy to the housekeeper and instructed her to look after him until the morning and to put on him the rich shawls in which she had brought him and not to take him away without first letting him know. And when he went back in and the three of them were alone, the beautiful lady said:

"If you want me to talk, first give me something to eat for I am faint with hunger, and I shall have plenty of time to talk later."

Don Antonio straightaway went to a writing-table and took out from it several preserved foods from which the lady ate, and she drank a glass of cold water, and having thus regained her strength, and feeling somewhat calmer, she said:

"Sit down, gentlemen, and listen to me."

They did as she asked and she, sitting on the bed and gathering her skirt around her, let fall over her back a veil which she was wearing on her head, leaving her face uncovered and clear, like the face of the moon, or rather the sun when it appears at its most beautiful and clearest. Her eyes shed tears like pearls and she wiped them with

líquidas perlas de los ojos, y limpiábaselas con un lienzo blanquísimo y con unas manos tales, que entre ellas y el lienzo fuera de buen juicio el que supiera diferenciar la blancura. Finalmente, después de haber dado muchos suspiros y después de haber procurado sosegar algún tanto el pecho, con voz algo doliente y turbada, dijo:

–Yo, señores, soy aquella que muchas veces habréis, sin duda alguna, oído nombrar por ahí, porque la fama de mi belleza, tal cual ella es, pocas lenguas hay que no la publiquen. Soy, en efecto, Cornelia Bentibolli, hermana de Lorenzo Bentibolli, que con deciros esto quizá habré dicho dos verdades: la una, de mi nobleza; la otra, de mi hermosura. De pequeña edad quedé huérfana de padre y madre, en poder de mi hermano, el cual desde niña puso en mi guarda al recato mismo, puesto que más confiaba de mi honrada condición que de la solicitud que ponía en guardarme. Finalmente, entre paredes y entre soledades, acompañadas no más que de mis criadas, fui creciendo, y juntamente conmigo crecía la fama de mi gentileza, sacada en público de los criados y de aquellos que en secreto me trataban y de un retrato que mi hermano mandó hacer a un famoso pintor, para que, como él decía, no quedase sin mí el mundo, ya que el cielo a mejor vida me llevase. Pero todo esto fuera poca parte para apresurar mi perdición si no sucediera venir el duque de Ferrara a ser padrino de unas bodas de una prima mía, donde me llevó mi hermano con sana intención y por honra de mi parienta. Allí miré y fui vista; allí, según creo, rendí corazones, avasallé voluntades; allí sentí que daban gusto las alabanzas, aunque fuesen dadas por lisonjeras lenguas; allí, finalmente, vi al duque y él me vio a mí, de cuya vista ha resultado verme ahora como me veo. No os quiero decir, señores, porque sería proceder en infinito, los términos, las trazas, y los modos por donde el duque y yo vinimos a conseguir, al cabo de dos años, los deseos que en aquellas bodas nacieron, porque ni guardas, ni recatos, ni honrosas amonestaciones, ni otra humana diligencia fue bastante para estorbar en juntarnos, que en fin hubo de ser debajo de la palabra que él me dio de ser mi esposo, porque sin ella fuera imposible rendir la roca de la valerosa y honrada presunción mía. Mil veces le dije que públicamente me pidiese a mi hermano, pues no era posible que me negase, y que no había que dar disculpas al vulgo de la culpa que le pondrían de la desigualdad de nuestro casamiento, pues no desmentía en nada la nobleza del linaje Bentibolli a la suya Estense. A esto me respondió con excusas, que yo las tuve por bastantes y necesarias, y confiada como rendida, creí como enamorada, y entreguéme de toda mi voluntad a la suya por intercesión de una criada mía, más blanda a las dádivas y promesas del duque que lo que debía a la confianza que de su fidelidad mi hermano hacía. En resolución, a cabo de pocos días, me sentí preñada, y antes que mis vestidos manifestasen mis libertades, por no darles otro nombre, me fingí enferma y melancólica e hice con mi hermano me trajese en casa de aquella mi prima de quien había sido padrino el duque. Allí le hice saber en el término en que estaba y el peligro que me amenazaba y la poca seguridad que tenía de mi vida, por tener barruntos de que mi hermano sospechaba mi desenvoltura. Quedó de acuerdo entre los dos que en entrando en el mes mayor se lo avisase, que él vendría por mí con otros amigos suyos y me llevaría a Ferrara, donde en la sazón que esperaba se casaría públicamente conmigo. Esta noche en que estamos fue la del concierto de su venida, y esta misma noche, estándole esperando, sentí pasar a mi hermano con otros muchos hombres, al parecer armados, según les crujían las armas, de cuyo sobresalto de improviso me sobrevino el parto, y en un instante parí un hermoso

such a white handkerchief and such white hands that only a person of very fine judgement could tell the difference between the whiteness of the hands and that of the handkerchief. Finally, after having sighed many times and after trying to calm her heart a little, with a somewhat grieving and disturbed voice, she said:

"Sirs, I am that lady whom you must doubtless have heard mentioned in various places, because those who do not proclaim my beauty, such as it is, are few. I am, in fact, Cornelia Bentibolli, sister of Lorenzo Bentibolli, and by telling you this I may perhaps have told you two truths: one concerning my nobility, the other concerning my beauty. At an early age, I lost my father and mother, and was left an orphan and in the care of my brother who, from the time when I was a young girl, placed modesty itself as my guardian since he trusted more in my sense of honour than in his own care in protecting me. In the end, I grew up enclosed by walls and all alone, accompanied only by maids, and growing with me was the fame of my beauty which was made public by the servants and those who visited me in secret, and by a portrait of me that my brother had painted by a famous painter so that, as he used to say, the world should not be deprived of me should heaven lead me to a better life. But all this would not have been enough to hasten my undoing had not the Duke of Ferrara happened to come to witness the wedding of a cousin of mine to which my brother took me in all good faith to honour my relative. There I saw and was seen; there, so I understand, I won hearts and enslaved wills; there I experienced the pleasure of praise, even when given by flattering tongues; there, finally, I saw the Duke and he saw me and, as a result, I find myself in my present plight. Gentlemen, because it would mean carrying on *ad infinitum*, I do not wish to tell you the stratagems and the ways and means by which the Duke and I managed to satisfy, at the end of two years, the desires that had been born at that wedding, for neither protection nor caution nor honourable advice nor any other form of human effort were sufficient to impede our coming together, which in the end was possible only because he gave his word to become my husband for, without this promise, it would have been impossible to break the rock on which my valour, pride and honour rested. A thousand times I told him to ask my brother openly for my hand, for it would be impossible for him to refuse it, and that there was no need to offer excuses to those people who would criticize our unequal marriage, for the noble line of the Bentibollis in no way discredited his own of the Estes. To this he replied with excuses which I accepted as substantial and valid. Full of trust and won over, I believed him, in love as I was, and with the help of a servant of mine who responded more readily to the gifts and promises of the Duke than to the trust that my brother placed in her fidelity, I surrendered my entire will to his. In short, in no time at all, I realized I was pregnant, and before my dress should reveal the liberties I had taken, for this is what they were, I pretended to be ill and depressed[7] and I made my brother take me to the house of that married cousin of mine for whom the Duke had acted as witness. There I told her of my condition and of the danger that threatened me, and that I feared for my life because I felt that my brother had suspicions about my looseness. The Duke and I agreed that when I entered the last month of my pregnancy I should let him know and he would come for me with some other friends of his to take me to Ferrara where, at the appropriate time, he would marry me in public. This very night was the one agreed for his coming, and this very night, whilst I was waiting for him, I heard my brother go past with other men. The sounds they made indicated that they were armed and from the fright this gave me, I suddenly went into

niño. Aquella criada mía, sabidora y medianera de mis hechos, que estaba ya prevenida para el caso, envolvió la criatura en otros paños que no los que tiene la que a vuestra puerta echaron, y saliendo a la puerta de la calle la dio, a lo que ella dijo, a un criado del duque. Yo desde allí a un poco, acomodándome lo mejor que pude, según la presente necesidad, salí de la casa, creyendo que estaba en la calle el duque, y no lo debiera hacer hasta que él llegara a la puerta; mas el miedo que me había puesto la cuadrilla armada de mi hermano, creyendo que ya esgrimía su espada sobre mi cuello, no me dejó hacer otro mejor discurso; y así, desatentada y loca, salí donde me sucedió lo que habéis visto; y aunque me veo sin hijo y sin esposo y con temor de peores sucesos, doy gracias al cielo, que me ha traído a vuestro poder, de quien me prometo todo aquello que de la cortesía española puedo prometerme, y más de la vuestra, que la sabréis realzar por ser tan nobles como parecéis.

Diciendo esto se dejó caer del todo encima del lecho, y acudiendo los dos a ver si se desmayaba, vieron que no, sino que amargamente lloraba, y díjole don Juan:

–Si hasta aquí, hermosa señora, yo y don Antonio, mi camarada, os teníamos compasión y lástima por ser mujer, ahora, que sabemos vuestra calidad, la lástima y compasión pasa a ser obligación precisa de serviros. Cobrad ánimo y no desmayéis, y aunque no acostumbrada a semejantes casos, tanto más mostraréis quién sois cuanto más con paciencia supiéredes llevarlos. Creed, señora, que imagino que estos tan extraños sucesos han de tener un feliz fin, que no han de permitir los cielos que tanta belleza se goce mal y tan honestos pensamientos se malogren. Acostaos, señora, y curad de vuestra persona, que lo habéis menester, que aquí entrará una criada nuestra que os sirva, de quien podéis hacer la misma confianza que de nuestras personas: tan bien sabrá tener en silencio vuestras desgracias como acudir a vuestras necesidades.

–Tal es la que tengo, que a cosas más dificultosas me obliga –respondió ella–. Entre, señor, quien vos quisiéredes, que encaminada por vuestra parte no puedo dejar de tenerla muy buena en la que menester hubiere; pero, con todo, os suplico que no me vean más que vuestra criada.

–Así será –respondió don Antonio.

Y dejándola sola se salieron, y don Juan dijo al ama que entrase dentro y llevase la criatura con los ricos paños, si se los había puesto. El ama dijo que sí, y que ya estaba de la misma manera que él la había traído. Entró el ama advertida de lo que había de responder a lo que acerca de aquella criatura la señora que hallaría allí dentro le preguntase.

En viéndola Cornelia, le dijo:

–Vengáis en buena hora, amiga mía; dadme esa criatura y llegadme aquí esa vela.

Hízolo así el ama, y tomando el niño Cornelia en sus brazos se turbó toda y le miró ahincadamente, y dijo al ama:

–Decidme, señora, ¿este niño y el que me trajiste o me trajeron poco ha es todo uno?

–Sí, señora –respondió el ama.

labour, and a moment later I had given birth to a lovely boy. That servant of mine I mentioned, who knew of my affairs and was involved in them, being already forewarned in the matter, wrapped the child in garments different from those worn by the child left at your door, and going to the front door gave it, so she said, to a servant of the Duke. A little later, getting ready as best I could, given my plight, I went out of the house thinking that the Duke was in the street, and I should not have done so until he had come to the door; but the fear my brother's armed band had instilled in me, since it seemed to me that their swords were already being wielded over my neck, did not allow me to reason more clearly and so, rashly and madly, I went out and found myself in the situation you have witnessed, and although I am left without child and husband and in fear of even worse events, I give thanks to Heaven for leading me into your power, gentlemen, from whom I am guaranteed to receive all that Spanish gallantry guarantees, and even more from you, for you will give it in increased measure since you are as noble as you appear."

Having said this, she let herself fall on the bed, and both of them went to her to see if she had fainted and saw that she had not but that she was weeping bitterly, whereupon Don Juan said to her:

"My beautiful lady, if up to now my comrade, Don Antonio, and I have felt pity and compassion for you as a woman, now that we know your worth, our pity and compassion become a duty and an obligation to serve you. Take heart and do not weaken, and even though you are not accustomed to events such as these, you will the better show who you are the more patiently you cope with them. Believe me, my lady, I think these strange events will have a happy ending, for heaven will not allow so much beauty not to be properly enjoyed and such honourable thoughts to come to nothing. Go to bed, my lady, for you need to take care of yourself; a servant of ours will come and see to you, and you will be able to confide in her as you do in us; she will be able both to keep your misfortunes secret and to attend to your needs."

"So great is my need now that it is driving me into more difficult things," she replied. "Sir, whoever you wish may come in, for I cannot fail to value whomsoever you send to help me in my hour of need, but still, I beseech you not to allow anyone else to see me except your servant."

"So be it," replied Don Antonio.

And leaving her alone they went out. Don Juan told the housekeeper to go in and to take with her the child dressed in the rich garments, if she had now put them on him. The housekeeper said she had done so and that the child was now dressed as when he had first brought it in. She went in instructed as to what she should reply to anything the lady inside might ask about the child.

On seeing her, Cornelia said:

"Welcome, my friend; give me that child and pass me that candle."

The housekeeper did as she was asked and Cornelia, taking the boy from her arms, became very disturbed and looked at him intently, and said to the housekeeper:

"Tell me, is this boy and the one that was brought to me a short while ago one and the same?"

"Yes, my lady," the housekeeper replied.

–Pues, ¿cómo trae tan trocadas las mantillas? –replicó Cornelia–. En verdad, amiga, que me parece o que éstas son otras mantillas o que ésta no es la misma criatura.

–Todo podía ser –respondió el ama.

–Pecadora de mí –dijo Cornelia–, ¿cómo todo podía ser? ¿Cómo es esto, ama mía? Que el corazón me revienta en el pecho hasta saber ese trueco. Decídmelo, amiga, por todo aquello que bien queréis. Digo que me digáis de dónde habéis habido estas tan ricas mantillas, porque os hago saber que son mías, si la vista no me miente o la memoria no se acuerda. Con estas mismas u otras semejantes entregué yo a mi doncella la prenda querida de mi alma; ¿quién se las quitó? ¡Ay, desdichada! Y ¿quién las trajo aquí? ¡Ay, sin ventura!

Don Juan y don Antonio, que todas estas cosas escuchaban, no quisieron que más adelante pasase en ellas ni permitieron que el engaño de las trocadas mantillas más la tuviese en pena, y así, entraron, y don Juan le dijo:

–Esas mantillas y ese niño son cosa vuestra, señora Cornelia.

Y luego le contó punto por punto como él había sido la persona a quien su doncella había dado el niño, y de como le había traído a casa, con la orden que había dado al ama del trueco de las mantillas y la ocasión por qué lo había hecho, aunque después que le contó su parto siempre tuvo por cierto que aquél era su hijo, y que si no se lo había dicho había sido porque tras el sobresalto del estar en duda de conocerle, sobreviniese la alegría de haberle conocido.

Allí fueron infinitas las lágrimas de alegría de Cornelia, infinitos los besos que dio a su hijo, infinitas las gracias que rindió a sus favorecedores, llamándolos ángeles humanos de su guarda y otros títulos que de su agradecimiento daban notoria muestra. Dejáronla con el ama, encomendándola mirase por ella y la sirviese cuanto fuese posible, advirtiéndola en el término en que estaba, para que acudiese a su remedio, pues ella, por ser mujer, sabía más de aquel menester que no ellos.

Con esto se fueron a reposar lo que faltaba de la noche, con intención de no entrar en el aposento de Cornelia si no fuese o que ella los llamase o a necesidad precisa. Vino el día, y el ama trajo a quien secretamente y a oscuras diese de mamar al niño, y ellos preguntaron por Cornelia. Dijo el ama que reposaba un poco. Fuéronse a las escuelas y pasaron por la calle de la pendencia y por la casa de donde había salido Cornelia, por ver si era ya pública su falta o si hacían corrillos de ella; pero en ningún modo sintieron ni oyeron cosa ni de la riña ni de la ausencia de Cornelia. Con todo, oídas sus lecciones, se volvieron a su posada.

Llamólos Cornelia con el ama, a quien respondieron que tenían determinado de no poner los pies en su aposento, para que con más decoro se guardase el que a su honestidad se debía; pero ella replicó con lágrimas y con ruegos que entrasen a verla, que aquél era el decoro más conveniente, si no para su remedio, a lo menos para su consuelo. Hiciéronlo así, y ella los recibió con rostro alegre y con mucha cortesía; pidióles le hiciesen merced de salir por la ciudad y ver si oían algunas nuevas de su atrevimiento. Respondiéronle que ya estaba hecha aquella diligencia con toda curiosidad, pero no se decía nada.

"Well, in that case, how is it that the shawls are so different?" Cornelia asked. "Truly, my friend, I think that either these are different shawls or that this is not the same child."

"Both things are possible," the housekeeper replied.

"Sinner that I am," Cornelia said, "how can both things be possible? How can it be, housekeeper? My heart is going to burst if I don't find out what is afoot here. Please tell me, my friend, by all that you hold most dear. Please say where you have obtained these rich shawls, for they are mine, if my eyes and my memory do not deceive me. Having dressed him in these very shawls or similar ones, I handed over to my maidservant the child I loved so dearly. Who removed them from him? Oh, wretched creature! And who brought them here? Oh, unfortunate creature!"

Don Juan and Don Antonio, who had been listening to all this, did not want it to go any further, and did not allow the device of exchanging the shawls to keep her in misery any longer, and so they went in and Don Juan said to her:

"Those shawls and that child are yours, Lady Cornelia."

And then he related to her step by step how he had been the person to whom the maidservant had given the boy, and how he had brought him home and had instructed the housekeeper to change the shawls and why he had done so, although after Cornelia had told him about giving birth he had been certain that that was her son, and that he had not told her so that the sudden doubt as to whether she knew him or not should give way to the joy of recognition.

Endless were the tears of happiness that Cornelia then shed, endless the kisses she gave her son and endless the thanks she expressed to her helpers, calling them human guardian angels and other names which showed clearly the extent of her gratitude. They left her with the housekeeper, charging her with looking after Cornelia and serving her in whatever way possible, making clear to her the state she was in so that the housekeeper might help her since, being a woman, she understood better than they did what was required in such a situation.

They then went off to rest during what was left of the night, with the intention of not entering Cornelia's room unless she called them or there was specific need to do so. Daybreak came, and the housekeeper brought someone who would secretly suckle the boy in some hidden corner of the house, and Don Juan and Don Antonio asked after Cornelia, to which the housekeeper replied that she was resting a little. They went off to their classes and walked along the street in which the fight had taken place and past the house from where Cornelia had emerged so as to see if her absence had been noticed already or if people were standing around talking about her; but nothing that they listened to or overheard had anything to do either with the fight or the absence of Cornelia. After their classes, they returned to their lodgings.

Cornelia asked the housekeeper to call them and they replied that they had decided not to set foot in her room so that her honour, to which proper consideration was due, might be the more decorously respected, but she replied with tears and entreaties that they should go in to see her, for that was what was most fitting, if not as a remedy for her, at least as a consolation. They did so, and Cornelia received them with a smiling face and with great politeness. She asked them to do her the favour of going out into the city to see if there was any talk of her shameful behaviour. They replied that they had very carefully seen to that already but that they had not heard anything.

En esto llegó un paje, de tres que tenían, a la puerta del aposento, y desde fuera dijo:

–A la puerta está un caballero con dos criados que dice se llama Lorenzo Bentibolli, y busca a mi señor don Juan de Gamboa.

A este recado cerró Cornelia ambos puños y se los puso en la boca, y por entre ellos salió la voz baja y temerosa y dijo:

–¡Mi hermano, señores; mi hermano es ése! Sin duda debe de haber sabido que estoy aquí, y viene a quitarme la vida; ¡socorro, señores, y amparo!

–Sosegaos, señora –le dijo don Antonio–, que en parte estáis y en poder de quien no os dejará hacer el menor agravio del mundo. Acudid vos, señor don Juan, y mirad lo que quiere ese caballero, y yo me quedaré aquí a defender, si menester fuere, a Cornelia.

Don Juan, sin mudar semblante, bajó abajo, y luego don Antonio hizo traer dos pistoletes armados y mandó a los pajes que tomasen sus espadas y estuviesen apercibidos.

El ama, viendo aquellas prevenciones, temblaba; Cornelia, temerosa de algún mal suceso, tremía; solos don Antonio y don Juan estaban en sí, y muy bien puestos en lo que habían de hacer. En la puerta de la calle halló don Juan a don Lorenzo, el cual en viendo a don Juan, le dijo:

–Suplico a V. S. –que ésta es la merced de Italia– me haga merced de venirse conmigo a aquella iglesia que está allí frontero, que tengo un negocio que comunicar con V. S. en que me va la vida y la honra.

–De muy buena gana –respondió don Juan–; vamos, señor, donde quisiéredes.

Dicho esto, mano a mano se fueron a la iglesia, sentándose en un escaño y en parte donde no pudiesen ser oídos, Lorenzo habló primero y dijo:

–Yo, señor español, soy Lorenzo Bentibolli, si no de los más ricos, de los más principales de esta ciudad. Ser esta verdad tan notoria servirá de disculpa del alabarme yo propio. Quedé huérfano algunos años ha, y quedó en mi poder una mi hermana, tan hermosa, que a no tocarme tanto quizá os la alabara de manera que me faltaran encarecimientos por no poder ningunos corresponder del todo a su belleza. Ser yo honrado y ella muchacha y hermosa me hacían andar solícito en guardarla; pero todas mis prevenciones y diligencias las ha defraudado la voluntad arrojada de mi hermana Cornelia, que éste es su nombre. Finalmente, por acortar, por no cansaros este que pudiera ser cuento largo, digo que el duque de Ferrara, Alfonso de Este, con ojos de lince venció a los de Argos, derribó y triunfó de mi industria venciendo a mi hermana, y anoche me la llevó y sacó de casa de una parienta nuestra, y aun dicen que recién parida. Anoche lo supe, y anoche le salí a buscar, y creo que le hallé y acuchillé; pero fue socorrido de algún ángel, que no consintió que con su sangre sacase la mancha de mi agravio. Hame dicho mi parienta, que es la que todo esto me ha dicho, que el duque engañó a mi hermana debajo de palabra de recibirla por mujer. Esto yo no lo creo, por ser desigual el matrimonio en cuanto a los bienes de fortuna, que en los de naturaleza el mundo sabe la calidad de los Bentibollis de Bolonia. Lo que creo es que él se atuvo a lo que se atienen los poderosos que quieren atropellar [a] una doncella temerosa y recatada, poniéndole a la vista el dulce nombre de esposo, haciéndola creer que por

Then one of their three pages came up and said from the other side of the door:

"There is a gentleman at the door with two servants who says he is Lorenzo Bentibolli and that he is looking for my master, Don Juan de Gamboa."

On hearing these words, Cornelia clenched both fists and took them to her mouth and through them her low and fearful voice said:

"My brother, gentlemen, that man is my brother! Without doubt he has learned I am here and he has come to take my life; help me, gentlemen, protect me!"

"Calm yourself, my lady," Don Antonio said to her, "for you are in a safe place and in the power of people who will not allow the least injury in the world to be done to you. Go, Don Juan, and see what that gentleman wants, and I shall remain here to defend Cornelia if need be."

Don Juan, without altering his expression, went downstairs, and then Don Antonio had two loaded pocket pistols brought to him and ordered the pages to take up their swords and to be ready.

The housekeeper, seeing those preparations, was shaking; Cornelia, fearful of an unhappy outcome, was trembling; only Don Antonio and Don Juan were composed and were clear in their minds as to what they would do. At the main door, Don Juan found Don Lorenzo who, on seeing him, said:

"I entreat your Lordship - for this is how respect is shown in Italy[8] - to do me the favour of coming with me to that Church opposite for I have some business to communicate to your Lordship upon which my life and honour depend."

"Very gladly," Don Juan replied. "Let's go, sir, wherever you wish."

This said, they went together to the church, and sitting down on a pew where they could not be overheard, Lorenzo spoke first and said:

"My dear Spanish gentleman, I am Lorenzo Bentibolli, if not one of the wealthiest, certainly one of the leading men of this city. The fact that this is so well known should serve to excuse the way I praise myself. I was left an orphan some years ago, and in my care was a sister of mine, so beautiful that were it not for the fact that she is so closely related to me, I should wish to praise her so highly that no words would in my opinion adequately express her beauty. As I was a man of honour and she a beautiful young woman, I was careful in protecting her; but all the precautions and care on my part have been frustrated by the daring will of my sister Cornelia, for this is her name. Finally, in order to cut things short, so that this story which could be long may not tire you, I will merely say that the Duke of Ferrara, Alfonso de Este, with lynx-sharp eyes conquered those of Argos,[9] overthrew and triumphed over my efforts and won over my sister, and last night he took her away from the house of a relative of ours, so it is said, shortly after she had given birth to a child. I learned of this last night and at once I went in search of him, and I think I found him and wounded him with my sword; but he was aided by some angel who did not allow that his blood should wash away the stain of my dishonour. I have been told by a relative of mine, who has been my informant in all of this, that the Duke deceived my sister by promising to marry her. This I do not believe, for this marriage is an unequal one in relation to material things, although in those which relate to natural qualities everyone knows the quality of the Bentibollis of Bologna. What I believe happened is that he acted in the way powerful men act when they wish to overcome a young lady who is fearful and cautious, dangling before her eyes the sweet name of husband, then making her believe that there are certain reasons

ciertos respetos no se desposa luego; mentiras aparentes de verdades, pero falsas y malintencionadas. Pero sea lo que fuere, yo me veo sin hermana y sin honra, puesto que todo esto hasta ahora por mi parte lo tengo puesto debajo de la llave del silencio, y no he querido contar a nadie este agravio hasta ver si le puedo remediar y satisfacer en alguna manera; que las infamias mejor es que se presuman y sospechen que no que se sepan de cierto y distintamente, que entre el sí y el no de la duda cada uno puede inclinarse a la parte que más quisiere, y cada una tendrá sus valedores. Finalmente, yo tengo determinado de ir a Ferrara y pedir al mismo duque la satisfac[c]ión de mi ofensa, y si la negare, desafiarle sobre el caso; y esto no ha de ser con escuadrones de gente, pues no los puedo ni formar ni sustentar, sino de persona a persona, para lo cual quería el ayuda de la vuestra y que me acompañásedes en este camino, confiado en que lo haréis por ser español y caballero, como ya estoy informado. Y por no dar cuenta a ningún pariente ni amigo mío, de quien no espero sino consejos y disuasiones, y de vos puedo esperar los que sean buenos y honrosos, aunque rompan por cualquier peligro. Vos, señor, me habéis de hacer merced de venir conmigo, que llevando un español a mi lado, y tal como vos me parecéis, haré cuenta que llevo en mi guardia los ejércitos de Jerjes. Mucho os pido, pero a más obliga la deuda de responder a lo que la fama de vuestra nación pregona.

–No más, señor Lorenzo –dijo a esta sazón don Juan, que hasta allí, sin interrumpirle, le había estado escuchando–, no más, que desde aquí me constituyo por vuestro defensor y consejero y tomo a mi cargo la satisfac[c]ión o venganza de vuestro agravio; y esto no sólo por ser español, sino por ser caballero y serlo vos tan principal, como habéis dicho y como yo sé y todo el mundo sabe. Mirad cuándo queréis que sea vuestra partida, y sería mejor que fuese luego, porque el hierro se ha de labrar mientras estuviere encendido, y el ardor de la cólera acrecienta el ánimo y la injuria reciente despierta la venganza.

Levantóse Lorenzo y abrazó apretadamente a don Juan [y] dijo:

–A tan generoso pecho como el vuestro, señor don Juan, no es menester moverle con ponerle otro interés delante que el de la honra que ha de ganar en este hecho, la cual desde aquí os la doy si salimos felizmente de este caso, y por añadidura os ofrezco cuanto tengo, puedo y valgo. La ida quiero que sea mañana, porque hoy pueda prevenir lo necesario para ella.

–Bien me parece –dijo don Juan–, y dadme licencia, señor Lorenzo, que yo pueda dar cuenta de este hecho a un caballero, camarada mío, de cuyo valor y silencio os podéis prometer harto más que del mío.

–Pues vos, señor don Juan, según decís, habéis tomado mi honra a vuestro cargo, disponed de ella como quisiéredes y decid de ella lo que quisiéredes y a quien quisiéredes, cuanto más que camarada vuestra, ¿quién puede ser que muy bueno no sea?

Con esto se abrazaron y despidieron, quedando que otro día por la mañana le enviaría a llamar para que fuera de la ciudad se pusieran a caballo y siguiesen disfrazados su jornada.

Volvió don Juan, y dio cuenta a don Antonio y a Cornelia de lo que con Lorenzo había pasado y el concierto que quedaba hecho.

why he cannot get married; lies masquerading as truths, but false and with evil intent. Be that as it may, I find myself without my sister and my honour, although all of this up to now I have kept locked away in silence, and I have not wished to tell anyone about this injury until I see whether I can remedy it or avenge it in some way; for it is better that injuries should be presumed or suspected rather than known for certain, for where there is uncertainty each person can incline towards the side that he prefers, and each side will have its own supporters. In short, I am determined to go to Ferrara to ask the Duke himself for satisfaction of my offence, and if he should refuse it, to challenge him on the issue; and this not with squadrons of followers, for I cannot get them together nor maintain them, but rather person to person, for which I should like your help and your company along the way, and I am confident you will oblige because you are a Spaniard and a gentleman, as I have already been told. I do not want to inform any relative or friend of mine, from whom I can expect nothing but discouragement, whereas from you I can expect good and honourable counsel, even though I may not be able to follow it because of possible risks. Please, sir, do me the favour of coming with me, for having a Spaniard at my side, and furthermore one such as you seem to be, will make me feel as though the armies of Xerxes[10] are protecting me. I am asking a great deal of you, but you are obliged to do much more by having to live up to the reputation of men from your country."

Don Juan, who had been listening to him up to then without interrupting, said at that point:

"Say no more, my Lord Lorenzo, say no more, for from this moment onwards I become your champion and adviser and take upon myself the expiation or avenging of your injury; and this, not only because I am a Spaniard, but because I am a gentleman and you are such a leading man, as you yourself have said and I and the whole world know. Decide when you wish to set off, but it had better be soon, for iron has to be struck when it is hot, and the heat of anger gives courage, and a recent injury arouses vengeance."

Lorenzo got up, embraced Don Juan affectionately and said:

"My Lord Don Juan, your heart is so generous that it is not moved by any interest other than the honour deriving from this cause. From this very moment I grant you that honour provided we come out of this affair happily, and in addition I offer you all that I have, all my power and all that I am worth. As for our departure, I want it to be tomorrow so that today I may prepare what we need for it."

"That seems fine to me," Don Juan said, "and, my Lord Lorenzo, I ask your permission to communicate this matter to a certain gentleman, a companion of mine, in whose courage and silence you can trust much more than in mine."

"Don Juan, since, as you say, you have assumed responsibility for my honour, do with it as you think fit and say whatever you wish about it to whomsoever you wish, for if it is a companion of yours can it possibly be anyone who is not good?"

After this, they embraced each other and parted, having agreed that the following morning Lorenzo would send for Don Juan so that they would mount their horses outside the city and continue their journey in disguise.

Don Juan went home and related to Don Antonio and Cornelia what had happened with Lorenzo and the agreement they had made.

–¡Válame Dios! –dijo Cornelia–; grande es, señor, vuestra cortesía y grande vuestra confianza. ¿Cómo? ¿Y tan presto os habéis arrojado a emprender una hazaña llena de inconvenientes? ¿Y qué sabéis vos, señor, si os lleva mi hermano a Ferrara o a otra parte? Pero dondequiera que os llevare, bien podéis hacer cuenta que va con vos la fidelidad misma, aunque yo, como desdichada, en los átomos del sol tropiezo, de cualquier sombra temo; y ¿no queréis que tema, si está puesta en la respuesta del duque mi vida o mi muerte, y qué sé yo si responderá tan atentamente que la cólera de mi hermano se contenga en los límites de su discreción? Y cuando salga, ¿paréceos que tiene flaco enemigo? Y ¿no os parece que los días que tardáredes he de quedar colgada, temerosa y suspensa, esperando las dulces o amargas nuevas del suceso? ¿Quiero yo tan poco al duque o a mi hermano que de cualquiera de los dos no tema las desgracias y las sienta en el alma?

–Mucho discurrís y mucho teméis, señora Cornelia –dijo don Juan–; pero dad lugar entre tantos miedos a la esperanza y fiad en Dios, en mi industria y buen deseo, que habéis de ver con toda felicidad cumplido el vuestro. La ida de Ferrara no se excusa, ni el dejar de ayudar yo a vuestro hermano, tampoco. Hasta ahora no sabemos la intención del duque ni tampoco si él sabe vuestra falta, y todo esto se ha de saber de su boca, y nadie se lo podrá preguntar como yo. Y entended, señora Cornelia, que la salud y contento de vuestro hermano y el del duque llevo puestos en las niñas de mis ojos, yo miraré por ellos como por ellas.

–Si así os da el cielo, señor don Juan –respondió Cornelia–, poder para remediar como gracia para consolar, en medio de estos mis trabajos me cuento por bien afortunada. Ya querría veros ir y volver, por más que el temor me aflija en vuestra ausencia o la esperanza me suspenda.

Don Antonio aprobó la determinación de don Juan y le alabó la buena correspondencia que en él había hallado la confianza de Lorenzo Bentibolli. Díjole más: que él quería ir a acompañarlos, por lo que podía suceder.

–Eso no –dijo don Juan–; así porque no será bien que la señora Cornelia quede sola, como porque no piense el señor Lorenzo que me quiero valer de esfuerzos ajenos.

–El mío es el vuestro mismo –replicó don Antonio–; y así, aunque sea desconocido y desde lejos, os tengo que seguir, que la señora Cornelia sé que gustará de ello y no queda tan sola que le falte quien la sirva, la guarde y acompañe.

A lo cual Cornelia dijo:

–Gran consuelo será para mí, señores, si sé que vais juntos, o a lo menos de modo que os favorezcáis el uno al otro si el caso lo pidiere; y pues al que vais a mí se me semeja ser de peligro, hacedme merced, señores, de llevar estas reliquias con vosotros.

Y diciendo esto, sacó del seno una cruz de diamantes de inestimable valor y un *agnus* de oro tan rico como la cruz. Miraron los dos las ricas joyas, y apreciáronlas aún más que lo que habían apreciado el cintillo; pero volviéronselas, no queriendo tomarlas en ninguna manera, diciendo que ellos llevarían reliquias consigo, si no tan bien adornadas, a lo menos en su calidad tan buenas. Pesóle a Cornelia el no aceptarlas; pero al fin hubo de estar a lo que ellos querían.

"Good heavens!" Cornelia exclaimed. "Sir, great is your courtesy and great your trust. How is it that you have so readily dared to undertake an enterprise so full of pitfalls? And how do you know, sir, whether my brother will take you to Ferrara or to some other place? But wherever he may take you, you can rest assured that fidelity itself travels with you, although I myself, as a wretched creature, stumble on the very specks of dust in the sun's rays, and fear any shadow. How do you expect me not to be afraid if my life or death rests on the response of the Duke, and how do I know whether he will reply politely enough so that my brother's anger may be kept within the limits of discretion? And should his anger erupt, do you think he will encounter a weak enemy? And don't you think that those days you are away I will be left wondering, full of fear and suspense, awaiting the happy or bitter news of the outcome? Do you think I love either the Duke or my brother so little that I will not fear or feel in my heart the misfortunes of each one of them?"

"You say many things and you fear many things, Lady Cornelia," Don Juan said, "but in the midst of so many fears allow some room for hope, and trust in God and in my efforts and good intentions, for you will thus happily see your own fulfilled. There is no question but that the journey to Ferrara must be made or that I must help your brother. So far we do not know the Duke's intentions nor whether he knows about your absence, and all of this we must learn from his own lips, and who better to ask him than me? Understand, Lady Cornelia, that the health and happiness of your brother and the Duke are as precious to me as my own life, and I will look after them as I look after that life itself."

"Don Juan," replied Cornelia, "if God thus gives you the power and kindness to bring me remedies and consolation in the midst of these troubles of mine, I can consider myself fortunate. I wish you had gone and come back already, no matter how strongly fear may afflict me in your absence or hope keep me in suspense."

Don Antonio agreed with Don Juan's decision and praised the fitting response that Lorenzo Bentibolli's trust had found in him. He also said to him that he wished to accompany them, in case they might need his help.

"No," Don Juan replied, "for Lady Cornelia should not be left alone nor should Lorenzo think that I am relying on the help of others."

"My help is part of yours," Don Antonio said, "and so, I have to follow you, even if unnoticed and from afar, for I know that Lady Cornelia will be pleased by this, and she will not be left without someone to protect her, keep her company and see to her needs."

To which Cornelia replied:

"It will be a great comfort to me, gentlemen, to know that you are travelling together, or at least, that you will be able to help each other should the occasion demand it; and since it seems to me that you are heading towards danger, be good enough, gentlemen, to carry these relics with you."

And saying this, she took from her bosom a diamond cross of priceless value and a golden *agnus*[11] of equal value to the cross. Don Juan and Don Antonio looked at the rich jewels and saw that they were even more valuable than the hat-band, but they gave them back to her saying they could not possibly accept them and that they would be taking their own relics with them which, if not as richly adorned, were certainly at least of similar quality. Cornelia was sorry they would not take them but in the end had to respect their wishes.

El ama tenía gran cuidado de regalar a Cornelia, y, sabiendo la partida de sus amos, de que le dieron cuenta, pero no a lo que iban ni adónde iban, se encargó de mirar por la señora, cuyo nombre aun no sabía, de manera que sus mercedes no hiciesen falta. Otro día, bien de mañana, ya estaba Lorenzo a la puerta, y don Juan de camino con el sombrero del cintillo, a quien adornó de plumas negras y amarillas y cubrió el cintillo con una toquilla negra. Despidiéronse de Cornelia, la cual, imaginando que tenía a su hermano tan cerca, estaba tan temerosa, que no acertó a decir palabra a los dos que de ella se despidieron.

Salió primero don Juan, y con Lorenzo se fue fuera de la ciudad, y en una huerta algo desviada hallaron dos muy buenos caballos, con dos mozos que de diestro los tenían. Subieron en ellos y los mozos delante, por sendas y caminos desusados caminaron a Ferrara. Don Antonio sobre un cuartago suyo, y otro vestido y disimulando, los seguía; pero parecióle que se recataban de él, especialmente Lorenzo, y así acordó de seguir el camino derecho de Ferrara, con seguridad que allí los encontraría.

Apenas hubieron salido de la ciudad, cuando Cornelia dio cuenta al ama de todos sus sucesos, y de cómo aquel niño era suyo y del duque de Ferrara, con todos los puntos que hasta aquí se han contado tocantes a su historia, no encubriéndole cómo el viaje que llevaban sus señores era a Ferrara, acompañando a su hermano, que iba a desafiar al duque Alfonso. Oyendo lo cual el ama –como si el demonio se lo mandara, para intricar, estorbar o dilatar el remedio de Cornelia–, dijo:

–¡Ay señora de mi alma! ¿Y todas esas cosas han pasado por vos y estáisos aquí descuidada y a pierna tendida? O no tenéis alma, o tenéisla tan desmazalada que no siente. ¿Cómo, y pensáis vos por ventura que vuestro hermano va a Ferrara? No lo penséis, sino pensad y creed que ha querido llevar a mis amos de aquí y ausentarlos de esta casa para volver a ella y quitaros la vida, que lo podrá hacer como quien bebe un jarro de agua. Mirá debajo de qué guarda y amparo quedamos sino en la de tres pajes, que harto tienen ellos que hacer en rascarse la sarna de que están llenos que en meterse en dibujos; a lo menos, de mí sé decir que no tendré ánimo para esperar el suceso y ruina que a esta casa amenaza. ¡El señor Lorenzo, italiano, y que se fíe de españoles, y les pida favor y ayuda! Para mi ojo si tal crea –y diose ella misma una higa –; si vos, hija mía, quisiéredes tomar mi consejo, yo os le daría tal que os luciese.

Pasmada, atónita y confusa estaba Cornelia oyendo las razones del ama, que las decía con tanto ahinco y con tantas muestras de temor que le pareció ser todo verdad lo que le decía, y quizá estaban muertos don Juan y don Antonio, y que su hermano entraba por aquellas puertas y la cosía a puñaladas; y así, le dijo:

–¿Y qué consejo me daríades vos, amiga, que fuese saludable y que previniese la sobrestante desventura?

–Y como que le daré tal y tan bueno que no pueda mejorarse –dijo el ama–: yo, señora, he servido a un piovano, a un cura, digo, de una aldea que está a dos millas de Ferrara; es una persona santa y buena y que hará por mí todo lo que yo le pidiere,

The housekeeper was eager to treat Cornelia well and, knowing that her masters were going to depart, for they had informed her of this but not of where they were going nor on what business, she decided to look after the lady, whose name she still did not know, in such a manner that her masters would not be missed. The next day, very early in the morning, Lorenzo was already at the door, and Don Juan ready to set off wearing the hat with the hat-band. The hat-band was now covered with a black headscarf and the hat was adorned with black and yellow feathers. They took their leave of Cornelia who, aware that her brother was so near, did not manage to say a single word to the two men who were taking their leave of her, so fearful was she.

Don Juan set off first, and together with Lorenzo, he went outside the city to a remote orchard where two fine horses which two young men had bridled were waiting for them. They mounted the horses and with the young men leading the way they travelled to Ferrara by hidden paths and roads. Don Antonio followed them, riding on a small horse, wearing different clothes and trying not to attract attention; but he thought they were becoming suspicious of him, particularly Lorenzo, and so he decided to follow the direct route to Ferrara, knowing that he was bound to find them there.

They had all hardly left the city when Cornelia informed the housekeeper of everything that had happened to her, and of how that child was hers and the Duke of Ferrara's, with all the details that have so far been given concerning her story, not keeping from her the fact that the journey that their lordships had undertaken was to Ferrara, in the company of her brother who had gone to challenge the Duke Alfonso. On hearing this, the housekeeper said - as if the devil himself had commanded her, whether to complicate, hinder or prolong a solution for Cornelia:

"Oh, my dearest lady! All these things have happened to you and yet you are here relaxed and without a care! Either you have no soul or it is so destroyed that it has no feeling. How can you possibly think that your brother is really going to Ferrara? Don't believe that, rather believe and accept the fact that he has decided to take away my lordships from here and keep them away from this house in order to return and take your life, which he will be able to do as easily as he can drink a glass of water. Think, my lady, what guard and protection do we have except for three pages who have enough to do scratching their itchy bodies covered in scabies without getting involved in risky business; speaking for myself at least, I can say that I will not be able to await the events and ruin which threaten this house. The Lord Lorenzo, an Italian, who trusts Spaniards and seeks their help and favour! Who would believe that?" she said with a gesture of contempt.[12] "If you wish to take my advice, my child, I can give you some which will be of great value to you."

Astounded, amazed and confused, Cornelia listened to the arguments put forward by the housekeeper who expressed them so earnestly and with such a show of fear that Cornelia thought all that she was saying must be true, and that perhaps Don Juan and Don Antonio might even be dead by now, and her brother about to come in through those doors any minute and cut her to pieces, and so she said to her:

"And what advice would you give me, my friend, which might be sound and sufficient to forestall the impending misfortune?"

"Such good advice that it cannot be bettered," the housekeeper said. "I, my lady, have been in the service of a *piovano,* that is a parish priest, of a village which is two miles from Ferrara; he is a good and holy man who will do anything I ask of him

porque me tiene obligación más que de amo. Vámonos allá, que yo buscaré quien nos lleve luego, y la que viene a dar de mamar al niño es mujer pobre y se irá con nosotras al cabo del mundo. Y ya, señora, que presupongamos que has de ser hallada, mejor será que te hallen en casa de un sacerdote de misa, viejo y honrado, que en poder de dos estudiantes, mozos y españoles, que los tales, como soy buen testigo, no desechan ripio. Y ahora, señora, como estás mala, te han guardado respeto; pero si sanas y convaleces en su poder, Dios lo podrá remediar, porque en verdad que si a mí no me hubieran guardado mis repulsas, desdenes y enterezas, ya hubieran dado conmigo y con mi honra al traste; porque no es todo oro lo que en ellos reluce; uno dicen y otro piensan; pero hanlo habido conmigo, que soy taimada, y sé dónde me aprieta el zapato, y sobre todo soy bien nacida, que soy de los Cribelos de Milán, y tengo el punto de la honra diez millas más allá de las nubes; y en esto se podrá echar de ver, señora mía, las calamidades que por mí han pasado, pues con ser quien soy, he venido a ser masara de españoles, a quien ellos llaman ama, aunque a la verdad no tengo de qué quejarme de mis amos, porque son unos benditos, como no estén enojados y en esto parecen vizcaínos, como ellos dicen que lo son. Pero quizá para consigo serán gallegos, que es otra nación, según es fama, algo menos puntual y bien mirada que la vizcaína.

En efecto, tantas y tales razones le dijo, que la pobre Cornelia se dispuso a seguir su parecer; y así, en menos de cuatro horas, disponiéndolo el ama y consintiéndolo ella, se vieron dentro de una carroza las dos y el ama del niño, y sin ser sentidas de los pajes se pusieron en camino para la aldea del cura; y todo esto se hizo a persuasión del ama y con sus dineros, porque había poco que la habían pagado sus señores un año de su sueldo, y así no fue menester empeñar una joya que Cornelia le daba. Y como habían oído decir a don Juan que él y su hermano no habían de seguir el camino derecho de Ferrara, sino por sendas apartadas, quisieron ellas seguir el derecho, y poco a poco, por no encontrarse con ellos, y el dueño de la carroza se acomodó al paso de la voluntad de ellas porque le pagaron al gusto de la suya.

Dejémoslas ir, que ellas van tan atrevidas como bien encaminadas, y sepamos qué les sucedió a don Juan de Gamboa y al señor Lorenzo Bentibolli; de los cuales se dice que en el camino supieron que el duque no estaba en Ferrara, sino en Bolonia. Y así, dejando el rodeo que llevaban, se vinieron al camino real, o a la estrada maestra, como allá se dice, considerando que aquélla había de traer el duque cuando de Bolonia volviese. Y a poco espacio que en ella habían entrado, habiendo tendido la vista hacia Bolonia por ver si por él alguno venía, vieron un tropel de gente de a caballo, y entonces dijo don Juan a Lorenzo que se desviase del camino porque si acaso entre aquella gente viniese el duque, le quería hablar allí antes que se encerrase en Ferrara, que estaba poco distante. Hízolo así Lorenzo, y aprobó el parecer de don Juan.

Así como se partió Lorenzo, quitó don Juan la toquilla que encubría el rico cintillo, y esto no sin falta de discreto discurso, como él después lo dijo.

En esto llegó la tropa de los caminantes, y entre ellos venía una mujer sobre una pía, vestida de camino y el rostro cubierto con una mascarilla, o por mejor encubrirse, o por guardarse del sol y del aire. Paró el caballo don Juan en medio del camino, y estuvo con el rostro descubierto a que llegasen los caminantes, y en llegando cerca, el talle, el brío,

because he is more than a master to me. Let's go there; I'll find someone to take us later, and the woman who comes to suckle the boy is a poor woman who will follow us to the ends of the earth. My lady, if you are going to be found, it will be better to be found in the house of a parish priest who is old and honourable, than in the power of two young Spanish students who, as I can testify, do not waste opportunities. Up to now, they have respected you because you are ill; but if you get better and convalesce in their power, only God will be able to save you, for in truth, if it had not been for my rebuffs, contempt and integrity, they would have ruined me and my honour by now, because in their case all that glitters is not gold; they say one thing and mean another, but they have met their match in me for I am crafty and know what's what, and above all I am of good birth, for I am descended from the Crivelli of Milan,[13] and I have an extremely high sense of honour and, my lady, you will be able to appreciate the calamities I have undergone through the fact that, despite being who I am, I have come to be *masara* to Spaniards, or housekeeper as they call me, although truly I have no complaints against them for they are saints, except when they are annoyed and then they are true Vizcayans, as they themselves admit. But perhaps they are really Galicians which is another race with a reputation for being somewhat less reliable and less well thought of than the Vizcayans."[14]

In fact, she put forward such arguments and so many of them that poor Cornelia decided to follow her advice and so, in less than four hours, the housekeeper having arranged everything and Cornelia agreeing to it, they and the boy's nurse found themselves inside a coach and, unknown to the pages, they set off for the priest's village. All this was done at the instigation of the housekeeper and with her money since a short while before her lordships had paid her a year's wages, so it was not necessary to pawn a jewel which Cornelia offered her. As they had heard Don Juan say that he and her brother would not be taking the direct route to Ferrara but would go by out-of-the-way paths, they decided to follow the direct route, and at a slow pace so that they would not meet them, to which the owner of the coach agreed since they had paid him as much as it pleased him to ask.

But let us leave them on their way, full of daring on the road they have taken, and let us find out what happened to Don Juan de Gamboa and Lord Lorenzo Bentibolli. It is said that on the way to Ferrara they found out that the Duke was not there but in Bologna. And so, leaving the circuitous route they were following, they came to the royal road, or the main road, as they say over there, reckoning that the Duke would return by it from Bologna. After they had travelled along it for a while, they glanced towards Bologna to see if anyone was coming from that direction and saw a crowd of people on horseback, at which Don Juan told Don Lorenzo to get off that road because if by any chance the Duke was amongst that throng, he wished to speak to him there and then before he shut himself away in Ferrara, which was not far away. Lorenzo did as he asked knowing Don Juan to be right.

As soon as Lorenzo departed, Don Juan removed the headscarf which covered the rich hat-band, making some fitting comments at the same time, as he later recounted.

Then the crowd of travellers approached, and amongst them there was a lady on a steed, dressed in riding clothes and wearing a mask either to conceal herself better or to protect herself against the sun and wind. Don Juan brought his horse to a halt in the middle of the road and waited for the travellers to reach him, and when they were near,

el poderoso caballo, la bizarría del vestido y las luces de los diamantes llevaron tras sí los ojos de cuantos allí venían, especialmente los del duque de Ferrara, que era uno de ellos, el cual, como puso los ojos en el cintillo, luego se dio a entender que el que le traía era don Juan de Gamboa, el que le había librado en la pendencia; y tan de veras aprehendió esta verdad, que sin hacer otro discurso, arremetió su caballo hacia don Juan diciendo:

–No creo que me engañaré en nada, señor caballero, si os llamo don Juan de Gamboa, que vuestra gallarda disposición y el adorno de ese capelo me lo están diciendo.

–Así es la verdad –respondió don Juan–, porque jamás supe ni quise encubrir mi nombre; pero decidme, señor, quién sois, por que yo no caiga en alguna descortesía.

–Eso será imposible –respondió el duque–, que para mí tengo que no podéis ser descortés en ningún caso. Con todo eso os digo, señor don Juan, que yo soy el duque de Ferrara y el que está obligado a serviros todos los días de su vida, pues no ha cuatro noches que vos me la distes.

No acabó de decir esto el duque cuando don Juan, con extraña ligereza, saltó del caballo y acudió a besar los pies del duque; pero por presto que llegó, ya el duque estaba fuera de la silla, de modo que se acabó de apear en brazos [de] don Juan.

El señor Lorenzo, que desde algo lejos miraba estas ceremonias, no pensando que lo eran de cortesía, sino de cólera, arremetió su caballo; pero en la mitad del repelón le detuvo, porque vio abrazados muy estrechamente al duque y a don Juan, que ya había conocido al duque. El duque, por encima de los hombros de don Juan, miró a Lorenzo y conocióle, de cuyo conocimiento algún tanto se sobresaltó, y así como estaba abrazado preguntó a don Juan si Lorenzo Bentibolli, que allí estaba, venía con él o no. A lo cual don Juan respondió:

–Apartémonos algo de aquí, contaréle a Vuestra Excelencia grandes cosas.

Hízolo así el duque, y don Juan le dijo:

–Señor, Lorenzo Bentibolli, que allí véis, tiene una queja de vos, no pequeña. Dice que habrá cuatro noches que le sacastes a su hermana, la señora Cornelia, de casa de una prima suya, y que la habéis engañado y deshonrado, y quiere saber de vos qué satisfac[c]ión le pensáis hacer para que él vea lo que le conviene. Pidióme que fuese su valedor y medianero; yo se lo ofrecí, porque por los barruntos que él me dio de la pendencia conocí que vos, señor, érades el dueño de este cintillo, que por liberalidad y cortesía vuestra quisiste que fuese mío, y viendo que ninguno podía hacer vuestras partes mejor que yo, como ya he dicho, le ofrecí mi ayuda. Querría yo ahora, señor, me dijésedes lo que sabéis acerca de este caso y si es verdad lo que Lorenzo dice.

–¡Ay amigo! –respondió el duque–; es tan verdad, que no me atrevería a negarla aunque quisiese; yo no he engañado ni sacado a Cornelia, aunque sé que falta de la casa que dice; no la he engañado, porque la tengo por mi esposa; no la he sacado, porque no sé de ella; si públicamente no celebré mis desposorios fue porque aguardaba que mi madre (que está ya en lo último) pasase de ésta a mejor vida, que tiene deseo que sea mi esposa la señora Livia, hija del duque de Mantua, y por otros inconvenientes quizá más eficaces que los dichos, y no conviene que ahora se digan. Lo que pasa es que la noche que me socorristes la había de traer a Ferrara, porque estaba ya en el mes de dar a luz la

his stature, his elegance, his powerful horse, the striking clothes he was wearing and the glittering diamonds all attracted the glances of everyone in the group, especially the Duke of Ferrara who was one of them and who, as soon as he set eyes on the hat-band, realized that the person wearing it was Don Juan de Gamboa who had saved him in the fight. When he realized this he was so moved that, without any explanation to the others, he charged on his horse towards Don Juan, saying:

"I believe I am not in the least mistaken, my dear gentleman, if I call you Don Juan de Gamboa, for your bearing and presence and that well-adorned hat tell me you are so."

"That is the truth," replied Don Juan, "for I never wished to conceal my name; but tell me, sir, who you are, so that I may not show any disrespect."

"That would be impossible," the Duke replied, "for I am sure you cannot be disrespectful in anything. In any case, my lord Don Juan, I inform you that I am the Duke of Ferrara who is obliged to serve you for the rest of his life because barely four nights ago you gave that life to me."

The Duke had hardly finished saying this when Don Juan, with unusual speed, jumped off his horse and made to kiss the Duke's feet but, quick as he was, the Duke was already off his saddle so that he ended up dismounting into Don Juan's arms.

Lord Lorenzo who was watching these ceremonious actions some distance away, thinking that they were not the result of courtesy but of anger, charged at them on his horse, but in the middle of the charge, he halted because he saw the Duke and Don Juan embracing each other warmly, for he had now recognised the Duke. The Duke looked over Don Juan's shoulders at Lorenzo and recognised him, at which he was quite startled, and still embracing Don Juan, he asked whether Lorenzo Bentibolli was there in his company or not. To which Don Juan replied:

"Let us move a little away from here and I shall relate great things to your lordship."

The Duke did as asked and Don Juan said to him:

"My lord, Lorenzo Bentibolli, whom you see over there, has a complaint against you, and not a small one at that. He claims that four nights ago you took away his sister, Lady Cornelia, from the house of a cousin of his, and that you deceived and dishonoured her, and he wishes to know from you what satisfaction you are going to render so that he may see whether it is fitting. He asked me to be his champion and mediator; I offered to do so because from the indications he gave me of the fight I realised that you, sir, were the owner of the hat-band which through your generosity and politeness you deigned to give me and, seeing that no one could defend your interests better than I, as I have already said, I offered my help. I should now be grateful if you would tell me, sir, what you know about this affair and if what Lorenzo says is true."

"Oh, my friend," the Duke replied, "it is so true that I would not dare to deny it even if I wanted to; I have neither deceived nor taken Cornelia away, although I know she is missing from the house in question; I have not deceived her because I consider her as my wife; I have not taken her away because I know nothing of her whereabouts; if I did not proclaim our betrothal in public it was because I was awaiting my mother's passage from this life to a better one (since she is already on the point of death), for she wishes that my wife should be Lady Livia, daughter of the Duke of Mantua, and because of other obstacles perhaps greater than the ones I have mentioned and which are better not talked about now. The truth of the matter is that on the night you came to my help I was to bring her to Ferrara because it was then the month in which she was due to give birth

prenda que ordenó el cielo que en ella depositase; o ya fuese por la riña, o ya por mi descuido, cuando llegué a su casa hallé que salía de ella la secretaria de nuestros conciertos. Pregúntéle por Cornelia, díjome que ya había salido, y que aquella noche había parido un niño, el más bello del mundo, y que se le había dado a un Fabio, mi criado. La doncella es aquella que viene allí; el Fabio está aquí, y el niño y Cornelia no parecen. Yo he estado estos dos días en Bolonia, esperando y escudriñando oír algunas nuevas de Cornelia, pero no he sentido nada.

–De modo, señor –dijo don Juan–, cuando Cornelia y vuestro hijo pareciesen ¿no negaréis ser vuestra esposa y él vuestro hijo?

–No por cierto; porque aunque me precio de caballero, más me precio de cristiano; y más que Cornelia es tal que merece ser señora de un reino. Pareciese ella, y viva o muera mi madre, que el mundo sabrá que si supe ser amante, supe la fe que di en secreto guardarla en público.

–Luego, ¿bien diréis –dijo don Juan– lo que a mí me habéis dicho a vuestro hermano el señor Lorenzo?

–Antes me pesa –respondió el duque– de que tarde tanto en saberlo.

Al instante hizo don Juan de señas a Lorenzo que se apease y viniese donde ellos estaban, como lo hizo, bien ajeno de pensar la buena nueva que le esperaba. Adelantóse el duque a recibirle con los brazos abiertos y la primera palabra que le dijo fue llamarle hermano.

Apenas supo Lorenzo responder a salutación tan amorosa ni a tan cortés recibimiento; y estando así suspenso, antes que hablase palabra, don Juan le dijo:

–El duque, señor Lorenzo, confiesa la conversación secreta que ha tenido con vuestra hermana, la señora Cornelia. Confiesa asimismo que es su legítima esposa, y que como lo dice aquí lo dirá públicamente cuando se ofreciere. Concede asimismo que fue ha cuatro noches a sacarla de casa de su prima para traerla a Ferrara y aguardar coyuntura para celebrar sus bodas, que las ha dilatado por justísimas causas que me ha dicho. Dice asimismo la pendencia que con vos tuvo, y que cuando fue por Cornelia encontró con Sulpicia, su doncella, que es aquella mujer que allí viene, de quien supo que Cornelia no había una hora que había parido, y que ella dio la criatura a un criado del duque, y que luego Cornelia, creyendo que estaba allí el duque, había salido de casa medrosa, porque imaginaba que ya vos, señor Lorenzo, sabíades sus tratos. Sulpicia no dio el niño al criado del duque, sino a otro en su cambio. Cornelia no parece, él se culpa de todo, y dice que cada y cuando que la señora Cornelia parezca la recibirá como a su verdadera esposa. Mirad, señor Lorenzo, si hay más que decir ni más que desear si no es el hallazgo de las dos tan ricas como desgraciadas prendas.

A esto respondió el señor Lorenzo arrojándose a los pies del duque, que porfiaba por levantarlo:

–De vuestra cristiandad y grandeza, serenísimo señor y hermano mío, no podíamos mi hermana y yo esperar menor bien del que a entrambos nos hacéis: a ella, en igualarla con vos, y a mí, en ponerme en el número de vuestro.

to the precious child Heaven ordained I should give her. Whether it was because of the fight or through carelessness on my part, when I arrived at her house I found that the woman who had made our arrangements was on the point of leaving it. I asked after Cornelia and she told me that she had already left after having given birth the previous night to a boy, the most beautiful in the world, and that she had handed him over to Fabio, one of my servants. That's the woman in question over there heading this way; Fabio is here, and the boy and Cornelia are missing. I have been in Bologna the past two days, waiting and listening for any news of Cornelia, but I have heard nothing."

"Therefore, sir," Don Juan said, "do I take it that when Cornelia and your son turn up you will not deny that she is your wife and he your son?"

"Certainly not; for although I pride myself on being a gentleman, I pride myself even more on being a Christian; and what's more, Cornelia's quality is such that she deserves to be mistress of a great kingdom. Let her appear and then, whether my mother is dead or alive, the world will discover that not only was I capable of loving well but also of honouring in public the promise I made in private."

"Then," Don Juan asked, "will you also say to your brother Lorenzo what you have said to me?"

"It pains me," the Duke replied, "that he does not already know it."

Straightaway Don Juan signalled to Lorenzo to dismount and to come over to them, which he did, hardly expecting the good news that awaited him. The Duke stepped forward to welcome him with open arms and the first word he said to him was to call him brother.

Lorenzo hardly knew how to reply to such a loving greeting and such a polite welcome, and being thus in a state of suspense, before he could utter a word, Don Juan said to him:

"My Lord Lorenzo, the Duke admits to the secret conversation he had with your sister, Lady Cornelia. He likewise acknowledges that she is his legitimate wife, and just as he says so here he will say so in public whenever it is necessary. He also admits that four nights ago he went to take her away from her cousin's house to Ferrara and there await a suitable moment to celebrate their wedding, delayed by him for very valid reasons which he has communicated to me. He also admits to the fight he had with you and that when he went for Cornelia he found Sulpicia, her maidservant, who is that lady approaching us over there, from whom he learned that less than an hour previously Cornelia had given birth, and that she gave the child to a servant of the Duke, and that later Cornelia, thinking the Duke was there, had gone out of the house in fear because she thought that you, Lorenzo, knew of her affair. Sulpicia did not give the boy to the Duke's servant but to someone else instead. Cornelia is missing, he blames himself for everything and he says that whenever Cornelia appears, he will take her as his true wife. See, therefore, my Lord Lorenzo, if there is anything more to say or wish for except to find the two beloved creatures who are as precious as they are unfortunate."

Throwing himself at the feet of the Duke, who protested and tried to lift him up, Lorenzo replied:

"Most serene lord and brother of mine, my sister and I could not expect anything less from you as a great Christian gentleman than what you are doing for us: in my sister's case, by putting her on your own level, and in mine by counting me as one of your own."

Ya en esto se le arrasaban los ojos de lágrimas, y al duque lo mismo, enternecidos, el uno con la pérdida de su esposa, y el otro, con el hallazgo de tan buen cuñado; pero consideraron que parecía flaqueza dar muestras con lágrimas de tanto sentimiento, las reprimieron y volvieron a encerrar en los ojos, y los de don Juan, alegres, casi les pedían albricias de haber parecido Cornelia y su hijo, pues los dejaba en su misma casa.

En esto estaban, cuando se descubrió don Antonio de Isunza, que fue conocido de don Juan en el cuartago desde algo lejos; pero cuando llegó cerca se paró, y vio los caballos de don Juan y de Lorenzo, que los mozos tenían de diestro y acullá desviados. Conoció a don Juan y a Lorenzo, pero no al duque, y no sabía qué hacerse, si llegaría o no adonde don Juan estaba. Llegándose a los criados del duque, les preguntó si conocían aquel caballero que con los otros dos estaba, señalando al duque. Fuele respondido ser el duque de Ferrara, con que quedó más confuso y menos sin saber qué hacerse; pero sacóle de su perplejidad don Juan llamándole por su nombre. Apeóse don Antonio, viendo que todos estaban a pie, y llegóse a ellos; recibióle el duque con mucha alegría, porque don Juan le dijo que era su camarada. Finalmente, don Juan contó a don Antonio todo lo que con el duque le había sucedido hasta que él llegó. Alegróse en extremo don Antonio, y dijo a don Juan:

–¿Por qué, señor don Juan, no acabáis de poner la alegría y el contento de estos señores en su punto pidiendo las albricias del hallazgo de la señora Cornelia y de su hijo?

–Si vos no llegárades, señor don Antonio, yo las pidiera; pero pedidlas vos, que yo seguro que os las den de muy buena gana.

Como el duque y Lorenzo oyeron tratar del hallazgo de Cornelia y de albricias, preguntaron qué era aquello.

–¿Qué ha de ser –respondió don Antonio– sino que yo quiero hacer un personaje en esta trágica comedia, y ha de ser el que pide las albricias del hallazgo de la señora Cornelia y de su hijo que quedan en mi casa?

Y luego les contó punto por punto todo lo que hasta aquí se ha dicho, de lo cual el duque y el señor Lorenzo recibieron tanto placer y gusto, que don Lorenzo se abrazó con don Juan y el duque con don Antonio. El duque prometió todo su estado en albricias, y el señor Lorenzo, su hacienda, su vida y su alma. Llamaron a la doncella que entregó a don Juan la criatura, la cual, habiendo conocido a Lorenzo, estaba temblando; preguntáronle si conocería al hombre a quien ella había dado el niño. Dijo que no, sino que ella le había preguntado si era Fabio, y él había respondido que sí, y con esta buena fe se le había entregado.

–Así es la verdad –respondió don Juan–; y vos, señora, cerraste la puerta luego, y me dijiste que la pusiese en cobro y diese luego la vuelta.

–Así es, señor –respondió la doncella llorando.

Y el duque dijo:

–Ya no son menester lágrimas aquí, sino júbilos y fiestas. El caso es que yo no tengo que entrar en Ferrara, sino dar la vuelta luego a Bolonia, porque todos estos contentos son en sombra hasta que los haga verdaderos la vista de Cornelia.

Y sin más decir, de común consentimiento dieron la vuelta a Bolonia.

Adelantóse don Antonio para apercibir a Cornelia, por no sobresaltarla con la improvisa llegada del duque y de su hermano; pero como no la halló, ni los pajes le

As he said this his eyes were filling up with tears, as were the Duke's. Both of them were moved, the one by the loss of his wife, the other by the discovery of such a good brother-in-law, but they thought it might seem a weakness on their part to express this deep feeling through tears and they restrained and contained them within their eyes; and Don Juan's eyes were so full of happiness that they were almost begging for a reward at finding Cornelia and her son, whom he had left in his own house.

In the midst of this, Don Antonio de Isunza took off his disguise and was recognised by Don Juan who saw him coming on his horse from some distance away; but when Don Antonio came near he stopped and saw Don Juan and Lorenzo's horses which the young men had bridled and led to this spot. He recognised Don Juan and Lorenzo but not the Duke, and he did not know what to do, whether to go up to Don Juan or not. Approaching the Duke's servants, he asked them if they knew the gentleman who was with the other two, pointing to the Duke. He was told in reply that he was the Duke of Ferrara, at which he was left more confused and less certain as to what to do, but Don Juan took him out of his bewilderment by calling out his name. Don Antonio dismounted, seeing that everyone else was on foot, and he approached them; the Duke received him with great happiness, because Don Juan told him that Don Antonio was his companion. Finally, Don Juan related to Don Antonio all that had happened to him with the Duke before he arrived. Antonio was overjoyed and he said to Don Juan:

"Don Juan, sir, why don't you complete the happiness and joy of these gentlemen by asking them to reward you for having found Lady Cornelia and her son?"

"If you had not arrived, Don Antonio, I should have asked; but you ask for it instead for I am sure they will willingly oblige."

As the Duke and Lorenzo heard talk of the finding of Cornelia and of rewards, they asked what it all meant.

"What can it mean," replied Don Antonio, "except that I wish to play a part in this tragicomedy, and the part is that of the person who seeks the reward for finding Lady Cornelia and her son, who are both in my house?"

And then he related to them step by step all that has been said up to now, which gave the Duke and Lorenzo so much satisfaction and pleasure that Lorenzo embraced Don Juan and the Duke Don Antonio. The Duke promised all his estate in reward and Lorenzo his property, his life and his soul. They called the maidservant who had handed the child to Don Juan and who, having recognised Lorenzo, was trembling; they asked her if she would recognise the man to whom she had given the boy. She replied that she would not, but that she had asked him if he was Fabio, and he had confirmed that he was and trusting in his good faith, she had handed him the child.

"That is the truth," Don Juan replied, "and you then closed the door, my lady, and asked me to place the child in safety and to come back later."

"That is so," the maidservant replied in tears. And the Duke said:

"Tears are no longer called for here but rather rejoicing and celebrations. The fact is I do not have to go into Ferrara now but instead turn back towards Bologna, because all this happiness is unreal until the sight of Cornelia gives it substance."

And without further ado, and by general agreement, they turned back towards Bologna.

Don Antonio went on ahead to warn Cornelia so that she would not be startled by the sudden arrival of the Duke and her brother but, as he did not find her and the pages were

supieron decir nuevas de ella, quedó el más triste y confuso hombre del mundo; y como vio que faltaba el ama, imaginó que por su industria faltaba Cornelia. Los pajes le dijeron que faltó el ama el mismo día que ellos habían faltado, y que la Cornelia por quien preguntaban nunca ellos la vieron. Fuera de sí quedó don Antonio con el no pensado caso, temiendo que quizá el duque los tendría por mentirosos o embusteros, o quizá imaginaría otras peores cosas que redundasen en perjuicio de su honra y del buen crédito de Cornelia. En esta imaginación estaba, cuando entraron el duque, y don Juan y Lorenzo, que por calles desusadas y encubiertas, dejando la demás gente fuera de la ciudad, llegaron a la casa de don Juan, y hallaron a don Antonio sentado en una silla, con la mano en la mejilla y con una color de muerto.

Preguntóle don Juan qué mal tenía y dónde estaba Cornelia.

Respondió don Antonio:

–¿Qué mal queréis que no tenga? Pues Cornelia no parece, que con el ama que le dejamos para su compañía, el mismo día que de aquí faltamos, faltó ella.

Poco le faltó al duque para expirar, y a Lorenzo para desesperarse, oyendo tales nuevas. Finalmente, todos quedaron turbados, suspensos e imaginativos. En esto se llegó un paje a don Antonio y al oído le dijo:

–Señor, Santisteban, el paje del señor don Juan, desde el día que vuesas mercedes se fueron, tiene una mujer muy bonita encerrada en su aposento, y yo creo que se llama Cornelia, que así la he oído llamar.

Alborotóse de nuevo don Antonio, y más quisiera que no hubiera parecido Cornelia, que sin duda pensó que era la que el paje tenía escondida, que no que la hallaran en tal lugar. Con todo eso no dijo nada, sino callando se fue al aposento del paje, y halló cerrada la puerta y que el paje no estaba en casa: llegóse a la puerta, y dijo con voz baja:

–Abrid, señora Cornelia, y salid a recibir a vuestro hermano y al duque vuestro esposo, que vienen a buscaros.

Respondiéronle de dentro:

–¿Hacen burla de mí? Pues en verdad que no soy tan fea ni desechada que no podían buscarme duques y condes, y eso se merece la persona que trata con pajes.

Por las cuales palabras entendió don Antonio que no era Cornelia la que respondía. Estando en esto vino Santisteban el paje, y acudió luego a su aposento, y hallando allí a don Antonio, que pedía que le trajesen las llaves que había en casa, por ver si alguna hacía a la puerta. El paje, hincado de rodillas y con la llave en la mano, le dijo:

–El ausencia de vuesas mercedes y mi bellaquería, por mejor decir, me hizo traer una mujer estas tres noches a estar conmigo. Suplico a vuesa merced, señor don Antonio de Isunza, así oiga buenas nuevas de España, que si no lo saben mi señor don Juan de Gamboa que no se lo diga, que yo la echaré al momento.

–¿Y cómo se llama la tal mujer? –respondió don Antonio.

–Llámase Cornelia –respondió el paje.

El paje que había descubierto la celada, que no era muy amigo de Santisteban, ni se sabe si simplemente o con malicia, bajó donde estaban el duque, don Juan y Lorenzo, diciendo:

unable to give him news of her, he was the saddest and most bewildered man in the world, and when he saw that the housekeeper was missing he surmised that it was through her work that Cornelia too had disappeared. The pages told him that the housekeeper had gone away the same day that they had, and they had not seen the Cornelia for whom he was asking. Don Antonio was beside himself at this unexpected turn of events, fearing that the Duke would perhaps think they were deceiving him or telling lies, or perhaps imagine something even worse which might jeopardise Cornelia's honour and good name. He was pondering this when in came the Duke and Don Juan and Lorenzo who, having left the others outside the city, came to Don Juan's house through out-of-the-way and hidden streets, and they found Don Antonio sitting at a chair with his cheek resting on his hand and looking deathly pale.

Don Juan asked what was the matter with him and where Cornelia was.

Don Antonio replied:

"What isn't the matter with me? Cornelia is missing, for on the very day that we went away she too went away with the housekeeper whom we left to keep her company."

The Duke was almost struck dead by this news and Lorenzo was close to despair. In the end, they were all left confused, in suspense and wondering. Then a page approached Don Antonio and whispered in his ear:

"My master, Santisteban, Don Juan's page, has had a very beautiful woman shut away in his room since the day you left, and I think her name is Cornelia for I have heard him call her by that name."

Don Antonio became agitated again and he would have preferred it if Cornelia had not turned up at all rather than that she should be found in such a place, for he undoubtedly thought she was the woman in the page's room. Despite this, he did not say anything but, keeping quiet, he went to the page's room. He found the door locked and the page out; he approached the door and said in a low voice:

"Open, Lady Cornelia, and come out to welcome your brother and your husband, the Duke, who have come looking for you."

From inside came the reply:

"Are you making fun of me? Truly I am not so ugly nor so lowly that dukes and counts might not come after me, but this is what I get for having anything to do with pages."

From these words Don Antonio gathered that it was not Cornelia who was replying. In the midst of this, Santisteban the page arrived, went to his room and found Don Antonio there asking that all the keys in the house should be brought to him to see if any fitted the door. The page, on his knees and key in hand, said to him:

"Your absence, and even more so my wickedness, led me to bring a woman to spend the last three nights with me. I beg your lordship, Don Antonio de Isunza, by the good news you may receive from Spain, not to tell my lord, Don Juan de Gamboa, if he does not know of it, for I will send this woman away immediately."

"And what is this woman called?" Don Antonio asked.

"She is called Cornelia," the page answered.

The page who had uncovered the deceit and who was not very friendly with Santisteban, either through malice or innocence, went down to where the Duke, Don Juan and Lorenzo were, and said:

–Tómame paje, por Dios, que le han hecho gormar a la señora Cornelia; escondidita la tenía; a buen seguro que no quisiera él que hubieran venido los señores para alargar más el *gaudeamus* tres o cuatro días más.

Oyó esto Lorenzo, y preguntóle:

–¿Qué es lo que decís, gentilhombre? ¿Dónde está Cornelia?

–Arriba –respondió el paje.

Apenas oyó esto el duque, cuando como un rayo subió la escalera arriba a ver a Cornelia, que imaginó que había parecido, y dio luego con el aposento donde estaba don Antonio, y entrando, dijo:

–¿Dónde está Cornelia, dónde está la vida de la vida mía?

–Aquí está Cornelia –respondió una mujer que estaba envuelta en una sábana de la cama y cubierto el rostro, y prosiguió diciendo–: ¡Válamos Dios! ¿Es éste algún buey de hurto? ¿Es cosa nueva dormir una mujer con un paje, para hacer tantos milagrones?

Lorenzo, que estaba presente, con despecho y cólera tiró de un cabo de la sábana y descubrió una mujer moza y no de mal parecer, la cual, de vergüenza, se puso las manos delante del rostro y acudió a tomar sus vestidos, que le servían de almohada, porque la cama no la tenía, y en ellos vieron que debía de ser alguna pícara de las perdidas del mundo.

Preguntóle el duque que si era verdad que se llamaba Cornelia; respondió que sí y que tenía muy honrados parientes en la ciudad, y que nadie dijese "de esta agua no beberé". Quedó tan corrido el duque, que casi estuvo por pensar que si hacían los españoles burla de él; pero por no dar lugar a tan mala sospecha, volvió las espaldas, y sin hablar palabra, siguiéndole Lorenzo, subieron en sus caballos y se fueron, dejando a don Juan y a don Antonio harto más corridos que ellos iban, y determinaron de hacer las diligencias posibles y aun imposibles en buscar a Cornelia y satisfacer al duque de su verdad y buen deseo. Despidieron a Santisteban por atrevido, y echaron a la pícara Cornelia, y en aquel punto se les vino a la memoria que se les había olvidado de decir al duque las joyas del *agnus* y la cruz de diamantes que Cornelia les había ofrecido, pues con estas señas creería que Cornelia había estado en su poder y que si faltaba no había estado en su mano. Salieron a decirle esto, pero no le hallaron en casa de Lorenzo, donde creyeron que estaría. A Lorenzo sí, el cual les dijo que sin detenerse un punto se había vuelto a Ferrara, dejándole orden de buscar a su hermana.

Dijéronle lo que iban a decirle, pero Lorenzo les dijo que el duque se iba muy satisfecho de su buen proceder, y que entrambos habían echado la falta de Cornelia a su mucho miedo, y que Dios sería servido de que pareciese, pues no había de haber tragado la tierra al niño, y al ama, y a ella. Con esto se consolaron todos, y no quisieron hacer la inquisición de buscarla por bandos públicos, sino por diligencias secretas, pues de nadie sino de su prima se sabía su falta; y entre los que no sabían la intención del duque correría riesgo del crédito de su hermana si la pregonasen, y ser gran trabajo andar satisfaciendo a cada uno de las sospechas que una vehemente presunción les infunde.

Siguió su viaje el duque, y la buena suerte, que iba disponiendo su ventura, hizo que llegase a la aldea del cura, donde ya estaban Cornelia, y el niño, y el ama, y la

"Good, they've got the page, they have made him return Lady Cornelia. He had her well tucked away. For sure he did not want the gentlemen to come back so that he could have enjoyed his pleasures a few more days."

Lorenzo heard this and asked him:

"What are you saying, sir? Where is Cornelia?"

"Upstairs," replied the page.

Hardly had the Duke heard this than he dashed upstairs to see Cornelia whom he thought had turned up, found the room in which Don Antonio was and entering it, said:

"Where is Cornelia, where is the life of my life?"

"Here is Cornelia," came the reply from a woman who was enveloped in a white bed sheet and whose face was covered up, and she went on to say: "Good Heavens! Isn't this carrying things a bit far? Is it such a novelty for a woman to sleep with a page; does it call for so much fuss?"

Lorenzo, who was present, in anger and contempt pulled one end of the sheet and uncovered a young and not bad-looking woman who feeling embarrassed covered her face with her hands and then started to pick up her clothes which she had used as a pillow, for there was none on the bed, and by these clothes they saw that she must be one of those fallen streetwalkers.

The Duke asked her if it was true that she was called Cornelia. She replied that it was and that she had some very honourable relatives in the city, and that no one should feel entitled to look down on others. The Duke was so embarrassed that he was almost inclined to think that the Spaniards were making a fool of him; but so as not to encourage such evil suspicions, he turned round, and without saying a word, and with Lorenzo following, mounted his horse and went away, leaving Don Juan and Don Antonio much more embarrassed than they themselves were. Don Juan and Don Antonio determined to do everything possible, and even the impossible, in order to find Cornelia and assure the Duke of their true and good intent. They dismissed Santisteban for his rashness, and they sent the tart Cornelia away, and at that point they remembered that they had not thought to tell the Duke about the *agnus* jewels and the diamond cross that Cornelia had offered them, for through these he would realise that Cornelia had been in their power and that if she was missing, they had not been able to prevent it. They went out to tell him this but they did not find him at Lorenzo's house where they thought he would be. But they did find Lorenzo who told them that without any delay at all the Duke had returned to Ferrara instructing him to search for his sister.

They told him what they had come to tell him, but Lorenzo replied that the Duke had gone away highly satisfied with the way they had gone about things, and that they had both attributed Cornelia's absence to her great fear, and that God willing, she would turn up, for the earth could not have swallowed up the boy, the housekeeper and Cornelia. This comforted everyone, and they decided not to mount a public search for her but rather to do so by secret means, for her absence was known to no one except her cousin. If they announced it in public, his sister's reputation would be at risk amongst those who did not know of the Duke's intentions, and it would be a difficult task to go round one by one trying to allay the suspicions aroused in each one by hasty conclusions.

The Duke had continued on his way, and by good luck, which was guiding his destiny, he arrived at the priest's village. Cornelia, the boy and his nursemaid were already there, as was the housekeeper who had counselled Cornelia, and they had given

consejera; y ellas le habían dado cuenta de su vida y pedídole consejo de lo que harían. Era el cura grande amigo del duque, en cuya casa, acomodada a lo clérigo rico y curioso, solía el duque venirse desde Ferrara muchas veces, y desde allí salía a caza, porque gustaba mucho así de la curiosidad del cura como de su donaire, que le tenía en cuanto decía y hacía. No se alborotó por ver al duque en su casa, porque, como se ha dicho, no era la vez primera; pero descontentóle verle venir triste, porque luego echó de ver que con alguna pasión tenía ocupado el ánimo.

Entreoyó Cornelia que el duque de Ferrara estaba allí, y turbóse en extremo, por no saber con qué intención venía; torcíase las manos y andaba de una parte a otra, como persona fuera de sentido. Quisiera hablar Cornelia al cura, pero estaba entreteniendo al duque y no tenía lugar de hablarle.

El duque le dijo:

–Yo vengo, padre mío, tristísimo, y no quiero hoy entrar en Ferrara, sino ser vuestro huésped; decid a los que vienen conmigo que pasen a Ferrara y que sólo se quede Fabio.

Hízolo así el buen cura, y luego fue a dar orden como regalar y servir al duque, y con esta ocasión le pudo hablar Cornelia, la cual, tomándole de las manos, le dijo:

–¡Ay padre y señor mío! Y ¿qué es lo que quiere el duque? Por amor de Dios, señor, que le dé algún toque en mi negocio y procure descubrir y tomar algún indicio de su intención; en efecto, guíelo como mejor le pareciere y su mucha discreción le aconsejare.

A esto le respondió el cura:

–El duque viene triste; hasta ahora no me ha dicho la causa. Lo que se ha de hacer es que luego se aderece ese niño muy bien, y ponedle, señora, las joyas todas que tuviéredes, principalmente las que os hubiere dado el duque, y dejadme hacer, que yo espero en el cielo que hemos de tener hoy un buen día.

Abrazóle Cornelia, y besóle la mano, y retiróse a aderezar y componer al niño. El cura salió a entretener al duque en tanto que se hacía hora de comer, y en el discurso de su plática preguntó el cura al duque si era posible saberse la causa de su melancolía, porque sin duda de una legua se echaba de ver que estaba triste.

–Padre –respondió el duque–, claro está que las tristezas del corazón salen al rostro. En los ojos se lee la relación de lo que está en mi alma, y lo que peor es que por ahora no puedo comunicar mi tristeza con nadie.

–Pues en verdad, señor –respondió el cura–, que si estuviérades para ver cosas de gusto, que os enseñara yo una, que tengo para mí que os le causara y grande.

–Simple sería –respondió el duque– aquel que ofreciéndole el alivio de su mal no quisiese recibirle. Por vida mía, padre, que me mostréis eso que decís, que debe de ser alguna de vuestras curiosidades, que para mí son todas de grandísimo gusto.

Levantóse el cura, y fue donde estaba Cornelia, que ya tenía adornado a su hijo y puéstole las ricas joyas de la cruz y del *agnus*, con otras tres piezas preciosísimas, todas dadas del duque a Cornelia, y tomando al niño entre sus brazos, salió adonde el duque estaba, y diciéndole que se levantase y se llegase a la claridad de una ventana, quitó al niño de sus brazos y le puso en los del duque, el cual, cuando miró y reconoció las joyas

the priest an account of Cornelia's life and asked him for advice as to what they should do.

The priest was a great friend of the Duke who would come frequently from Ferrara to his house, which was furnished according to the means of a wealthy and careful priest, and from there go out hunting, for he greatly liked both the priest's careful approach to things and his liveliness, which manifested itself in all he said and did. The priest was not surprised to see the Duke in his house because, as has been said, it wasn't the first time he had gone there; but he was unhappy at seeing him so sad for he soon realised that his heart was burdened by some great sorrow.

When Cornelia realised that the Duke of Ferrara was there, she became extremely upset because she did not know with what intention he had come. She paced up and down wringing her hands as if out of her mind. She would have liked to speak to the priest but he was looking after the Duke and she did not have the chance to do so.

The Duke said to him:

"I come, dear father, in a state of great sadness, and I do not wish to enter Ferrara today but rather to be your guest; tell those who have come with me to go on into Ferrara and that Fabio alone should stay on here."

The good priest did this and then went to give instructions as to how the Duke should be served and regaled. This gave Cornelia the opportunity to speak to him, and holding both of his hands, she said:

"Oh, my lord and father! What is it the Duke wants? For the love of God, sound him out about me, my lord, and try to get some idea of his intentions, and direct him as you judge best and as your great discretion indicates."

To this the priest replied:

"The Duke is sad; so far he has not told me the cause. What we need to do is to dress the boy very well. My lady, put on him all the jewellery you have, especially that which the Duke has given to you, and leave the rest to me, for I trust in Heaven that today is going to be a good one for us."

Cornelia embraced him, kissed his hand, and went off to dress and get the boy ready. The priest went to keep the Duke company until it was time to eat, and in the course of their conversation the priest asked the Duke if he could possibly know the cause of his sadness because one could see a mile off that he was unhappy.

"Father," the Duke replied, "it's obvious that the sadness of the heart shows on one's face; through the eyes one can read the soul, but what's worse for me is that, for the time being, I can't share my sadness with anyone else."

"Well, truly, sir," the priest replied, "if you feel like seeing pleasant things, I can show you one which I think will give you great pleasure."

The Duke replied:

"Stupid indeed would be the person who on being offered a remedy for his malady should not wish to receive it. Upon my life, father, show me what you are referring to, for it must be one of your interesting pursuits, all of which give me great pleasure."

The priest stood up and went where Cornelia was with her son all dressed up and wearing the rich jewels of the cross and the *agnus*, with another three very beautiful pieces, all given by the Duke to Cornelia. Taking the boy from her arms he went out to where the Duke was and telling him to stand and approach the window where it was lighter, he placed the child in the arms of the Duke who was left in a state of amazement

y vio que eran las mismas que él había dado a Cornelia, quedó atónito; y mirando ahincadamente al niño, le pareció que miraba su mismo retrato, y lleno de admiración preguntó al cura cúya era aquella criatura que en su adorno y aderezo parecía hijo de algún príncipe.

–No sé –respondió el cura–; sólo sé que habrá no sé cuántas noches que aquí me le trajo un caballero de Bolonia, y me encargó mirase por él y le criase, que era hijo de un valeroso padre y de una principal y hermosísima madre. También vino con el caballero una mujer para dar leche al niño, a quien yo he preguntado si sabe algo de los padres de esta criatura, y responde que no sabe palabra; y en verdad que si la madre es tan hermosa como el ama, que debe ser la más hermosa mujer de Italia.

–¿No la veríamos? –preguntó el duque.

–Sí por cierto –respondió el cura–; veníos, señor, conmigo, que si os suspende el adorno y la belleza de esa criatura, como creo que os ha suspendido, el mismo efecto entiendo que ha de hacer la vista de su ama.

Quísole tomar la criatura el cura al duque, pero él no la quiso dejar, antes la apretó en sus brazos y le dio muchos besos. Adelantóse el cura un poco, y dijo a Cornelia que saliese sin turbación alguna a recibir al duque. Hízolo así Cornelia, y con el sobresalto le salieron tales colores al rostro, que sobre el modo mortal la hermosearon. Pasmóse el duque cuando la vio, y ella, arrojándose a sus pies, se los quiso besar. El duque, sin hablar palabra, dio el niño al cura, y volviendo las espaldas se salió con gran prisa del aposento. Lo cual visto por Cornelia, volviéndose al cura dijo:

–¡Ay señor mío! ¿Se ha espantado el duque de verme? ¿Si me tiene aborrecida? ¿Si le he parecido fea? ¿Si se le han olvidado las obligaciones que me tiene? ¿No me hablará siquiera una palabra? ¿Tanto le cansaba ya su hijo que así le arrojó de sus brazos?

A todo lo cual no respondía palabra el cura, admirado de la huida del duque, que así le pareció que fuese huida antes que otra cosa, y no fue sino que salió a llamar a Fabio y decirle:

–Corre, Fabio amigo, y a toda diligencia vuelve a Bolonia y di que al momento Lorenzo Bentibolli y los dos caballeros españoles don Juan de Gamboa y don Antonio de Isunza, sin poner excusa alguna, vengan luego a esta aldea. Mira, amigo, que vueles y no te vengas sin ellos, que me importa la vida el verlos.

No fue perezoso Fabio, que luego puso en efecto el mandamiento de su señor.

El duque volvió luego a donde Cornelia estaba derramando hermosas lágrimas. Cogióla el duque en sus brazos, y añadiendo lágrimas a lágrimas, mil veces le bebió el aliento de la boca, teniéndoles el contento atadas las lenguas; y así en silencio honesto y amoroso se gozaban los dos felices amantes y esposos verdaderos.

El ama del niño y la Cribela por lo menos, como ella decía, que por entre las puertas de otro aposento habían estado mirando lo que entre el duque y Cornelia pasaba, de gozo se daban de calabazadas por las paredes, que no parecía sino que habían perdido el juicio. El cura daba mil besos al niño, que tenía en sus brazos, y con la mano derecha, que desocupó, no se hartaba de echar bendiciones a los dos abrazados señores. El ama del cura, que no se había hallado presente al grave caso por estar ocupada aderezando la comida, cuando la tuvo en su punto entró a llamarlos que se sentasen a la mesa. Esto

when he recognised the jewels as the same ones that he had given to Cornelia. Looking intently at the boy, it seemed to him that he was looking at a portrait of himself, and full of wonder he asked the priest whose child it was that by the manner of his dress seemed to be the son of a prince.

"I don't know," the priest replied. "All I know is that a few nights ago he was brought here by a gentleman from Bologna who entrusted me with looking after him and bringing him up, saying he was the son of a brave father and of a beautiful mother of noble birth. The gentleman was accompanied by a lady to give the child milk. I asked her if she knew anything about the parents of the child, but she says she knows nothing; and in truth if the mother is as beautiful as the nurse, she must be the most beautiful woman in Italy."

"Couldn't we see her?" the Duke asked.

"Yes, of course," the priest replied, "come with me, sir, for if the adornment and beauty of that child fill you with wonder, as I think is the case, the same effect I think is likely to be produced by the sight of his nurse".

The priest tried to take the child from the Duke but he did not want to let go of it, and he held it more tightly in his arms and kissed it many times. The priest walked forward a little and told Cornelia to come out to welcome the Duke and not to get upset. Cornelia did this, and with the shock such colour came to her face that it gave her a beauty which covered her deathly appearance. The Duke was stunned when he saw her and she threw herself at his feet trying to kiss them. The Duke, without saying a word, gave the boy to the priest and turning around went out of the room in a great hurry. Seeing this Cornelia turned to the priest and said:

"Oh, my lord! Has the Duke taken fright at seeing me? Does he hate me? Do I seem ugly to him? Has he forgotten his obligations to me? Won't he say a single word to me? Is he so tired of his child that he has thrown him from his arms in this way?"

To all this there was not a word in reply from the priest who was amazed at the Duke's flight, for it seemed to him that he was indeed fleeing rather than anything else but, in fact, he was merely going to call Fabio and give him these instructions:

"Hurry, Fabio, my friend, and with all speed return to Bologna and tell Lorenzo Bentibolli and the two Spanish gentlemen, Don Juan de Gamboa and Don Antonio de Isunza, to come immediately to this village. Accept no excuses. See to it, my friend, that you fly there and that you do not return without them for, upon my life, I need to see them."

Fabio did not delay, and he straightaway put into effect his master's instructions.

The Duke then went back to where Cornelia was shedding beautiful tears. He took her in his arms and, adding tears to tears, a thousand times he drank the breath from her mouth, since their happiness had made them tongue-tied; and so, in chaste and loving silence the two happy lovers and true spouses enjoyed each other.

The boy's nursemaid and Cribela, at least this is how she called herself, who had been watching what had been happening between the Duke and Cornelia through a door from another room, were delirious with joy. The priest kissed the boy in his arms a thousand times and then, freeing his right hand, he continually blessed the couple who were embracing each other. The priest's housekeeper, who had not been present at the solemn event because she was preparing the meal, came in when it was ready to ask them to sit at the table. This brought apart the arms which were closely entwined, and

apartó los estrechos abrazos, y el duque desembarazó al cura del niño y le tomó en sus brazos, y en ellos le tuvo todo el tiempo que duró la limpia y bien sazonada más que suntuosa comida; y en tanto que comían dio cuenta Cornelia de todo lo que había sucedido hasta venir a aquella casa por consejo del ama de los dos caballeros españoles, que la habían servido, amparado y guardado con el más honesto y puntual decoro que pudiera imaginarse. El duque le contó asimismo a ella todo lo que por él había pasado hasta aquel punto. Halláronse presentes las dos amas, y hallaron en el duque grandes ofrecimientos y promesas. En todos se renovó el gusto con el feliz fin del suceso, y sólo esperaban a colmarle y a ponerle en estado mejor que acertara a desearse con la venida de Lorenzo, de don Juan y don Antonio, los cuales de allí a tres días vinieron desalados y deseosos por saber si alguna nueva sabía el duque de Cornelia; que Fabio, que los fue a llamar, no les pudo decir ninguna cosa de su hallazgo, pues no la sabía.

Saliólos a recibir el duque [a] una sala antes de donde estaba Cornelia, y esto sin muestras de contento alguno, de que los recién venidos se entristecieron. Hízolos sentar el duque, y él se sentó con ellos, y encaminando su plática a Lorenzo, le dijo:

–Bien sabéis, señor Lorenzo Bentibolli, que yo jamás engañé a vuestra hermana, de lo que es buen testigo el cielo y mi conciencia. Sabéis asimismo la diligencia con que la he buscado y el deseo que he tenido de hallarla para casarme con ella, como se lo tengo prometido; ella no parece y mi palabra no ha de ser eterna. Yo soy mozo, y no tan experto en las cosas del mundo que no me deje llevar de las que me ofrece el deleite a cada paso. La misma afición que me hizo prometer ser esposo de Cornelia me llevó también a dar antes que a ella palabra de matrimonio a una labradora de esta aldea, a quien pensaba dejar burlada por acudir al valor de Cornelia, aunque no acudiera a lo que la conciencia me pedía, que no fuera pequeña muestra de amor. Pero pues nadie se casa con mujer que no parece, ni es cosa puesta en razón que nadie busque la mujer que le deja por no hallar la prenda que le aborrece, digo que veáis, señor Lorenzo, qué satisfac[c]ión puedo daros del agravio que no os hice, pues jamás tuve intención de hacéroslo, y luego quiero que me deis licencia para cumplir mi primera palabra y desposarme con la labradora, que ya está dentro de esta casa.

En tanto que el duque esto decía, el rostro de Lorenzo se iba mudando de mil colores, y no acertaba a estar sentado de una manera en la silla, señales claras que la cólera le iba tomando posesión de todos sus sentidos. Lo mismo pasaba por don Juan y por don Antonio, que luego propusieron de no dejar salir al duque con su intención aunque le quitasen la vida. Leyendo, pues, el duque en sus rostros sus intenciones, dijo:

–Sosegaos, señor Lorenzo, que antes que me respondáis palabra quiero que la hermosura que veréis en la que quiero recibir por mi esposa os obligue a darme la licencia que os pido; porque es tal y tan extremada, que de mayores yerros será disculpa.

Esto dicho, se levantó y entró donde Cornelia estaba riquísimamente adornada, con todas los joyas que el niño tenía, y muchas más. Cuando el duque volvió las espaldas, se levantó don Juan, y puestas ambas manos en los dos brazos de la silla donde estaba sentado Lorenzo, al oído le dijo:

the Duke relieved the priest of the boy and took him in his own arms, and in his arms he held him all through the meal which was wholesome and well-seasoned rather than sumptuous. While they ate, Cornelia gave an account of all that had happened until she had come to that house on the advice of the housekeeper of the two Spanish gentlemen who had served, protected and guarded her with the most honourable and proper respect that could be imagined. The Duke likewise related to her all that he had been through up to then. The housekeeper and nurse were present, and they received great offers and promises from the Duke. They were all filled with joy again because of the happy way in which the matter was ending, and they now only awaited to crown it in the best possible manner with the arrival of Lorenzo, Don Juan and Don Antonio who, in fact, arrived three days later, anxious and eager to know if there was any news of the Duke and Cornelia, for Fabio, who had gone for them, had been unable to say anything about their having been found, for he was not aware of it.

The Duke came out to greet them in a room which adjoined the one where Cornelia was, and he did this without giving any sign of happiness, which saddened those who had just arrived. The Duke made them sit down, and he himself sat with them, and addressing Lorenzo, he said:

"You know full well, my Lord Lorenzo Bentibolli, that I never deceived your sister, and heaven and my conscience will bear witness to this. You know equally well how hard I looked for her and the desire I had to find her in order to marry her, as I promised her; but she has not turned up and my word is not eternal. I am a young man, and not so experienced in the ways of the world that I can afford to pass by those things which pleasure throws in my path at every turn. The same inclination which made me promise to be Cornelia's husband also led me to make an earlier promise of marriage to a peasant girl of this village whom I was intending to deceive in order to respond to Cornelia's worth, even though I might not respond to what my conscience dictated, and this would have been no small token of my love. But no one can marry a woman who is not there nor is it reasonable to expect that anyone should look for the woman who leaves him because he has not found the precious creature who detests him. My lord Lorenzo, what I mean is that you should ponder this: what redress can I give you for the injury I never did you, for I never had any intention of injuring you? And so I should like you to give me permission to keep the first promise I made and marry the peasant girl who is here in this house."

As the Duke was saying these things, Lorenzo's face changed colour a thousand times, and he could not sit calmly in the chair, clear signs that anger was taking hold of all his senses. The same was happening to Don Juan and Don Antonio who decided not to let the Duke have his way even though they might have to take his life. Reading their minds in their expressions, the Duke said:

"Calm yourself, Lorenzo, for before you utter a word in reply I want you to feel obliged to give me the permission I seek when you see the beauty of the woman I want to take as my wife; for it is such and so extreme that it will excuse greater mistakes."

Having said this, he got up and went into the room where Cornelia was waiting bedecked with all the jewels the boy had, and many more. When the Duke turned his back, Don Juan stood up, and placing both hands on the arms of the chair where Lorenzo was sitting, whispered in his ear:

–Por Santiago de Galicia, señor Lorenzo, y por la fe de cristiano y de caballero que tengo, que así deje yo salir con su intención al duque como volverme moro. ¡Aquí, aquí y en mis manos, ha de dejar la vida, o ha de cumplir la palabra que a la señora Cornelia, vuestra hermana, tiene dada, o a lo menos nos ha de dar tiempo de buscarla, y hasta que de cierto se sepa que es muerta, él no ha de casarse!

–Yo estoy de ese parecer mismo –respondió Lorenzo.

–Pues del mismo estará mi camarada don Antonio –replicó don Juan.

En esto entró por la sala delante Cornelia en medio del cura y del duque, que la traía de la mano, detrás de los cuales venían Sulpicia, la doncella de Cornelia, que el duque había enviado por ella a Ferrara, y las dos amas, [la] del niño y la de los caballeros.

Cuando Lorenzo vio a su hermana, y la acabó de refigurar y conocer, que al principio la imposibilidad, a su parecer, de tal suceso no le dejaba enterar en la verdad, tropezando en sus mismos pies fue a arrojarse a los del duque, que le levantó y le puso en los brazos de su hermana; quiero decir que su hermana le abrazó con las muestras de alegría posibles. Don Juan y don Antonio dijeron al duque que había sido la más discreta y más sabrosa burla del mundo. El duque tomó al niño, que Sulpicia traía, y dándosele a Lorenzo le dijo:

–Recibid, señor hermano, a vuestro sobrino y mi hijo, y ver si queréis darme licencia que me case con esta labradora, que es la primera a quien he dado palabra de casamiento.

Sería nunca acabar contar lo que respondió Lorenzo, lo que preguntó don Juan, lo que sintió don Antonio, el regocijo del cura, la alegría de Sulpicia, el contento de la consejera, el júbilo del ama, la admiración de Fabio y, finalmente, el general contento de todos.

Luego el cura los desposó, siendo su padrino don Juan de Gamboa; y entre todos se dio traza que aquellos desposorios estuviesen secretos hasta ver en qué paraba la enfermedad que tenía muy al cabo a la duquesa su madre, y en tanto la señora Cornelia se volviese a Bolonia con su hermano. Todo se hizo así; la duquesa murió, Cornelia entró en Ferrara, alegrando al mundo con su vista, los lutos se volvieron en galas, las amas quedaron ricas, Sulpicia por mujer de Fabio, don Antonio y don Juan contentísimos de haber servido en algo al duque, el cual les ofreció dos primas suyas por mujeres con riquísima dote. Ellos dijeron que los caballeros de la nación vizcaína por la mayor parte se casaban en su patria; y que no por menosprecio, pues no era posible, sino por cumplir su loable costumbre y la voluntad de sus padres, que ya los debían de tener casados, no aceptaban tan ilustre ofrecimiento.

El duque admitió su disculpa, y por modos honestos y honrosos, y buscando ocasiones lícitas, les envió muchos presentes a Bolonia, y algunos tan ricos y enviados a tan buena sazón y coyuntura, que aunque pudieran no admitirse por no parecer que recibían paga, el tiempo en que llegaban lo facilitaba todo; especialmente los que les envió al tiempo de su partida para España, y los que les dio cuando fueron a Ferrara a

"By St. James of Galicia,[15] Lorenzo, and by the faith I have as a Christian and a gentleman, there is as much chance of my letting the Duke get away with his plan as there is of my becoming a Moor. Here, here in my very hands, he will leave his life or he will fulfil the promise he made to Cornelia, your sister, or at least, he will have to give us time to find her, and until we know for certain whether or not she is dead he will not marry!"

"I agree," Lorenzo replied.

"And Don Antonio, my companion, is bound to have the same opinion," Don Juan added.

Then Cornelia entered from the room opposite walking between the priest and the Duke who was holding her by the hand; behind them came Sulpicia, Cornelia's maidservant, whom the Duke had sent for to Ferrara, and the two ladies, the boy's nurse and the gentlemen's housekeeper.

When Lorenzo saw his sister and finally recognised and understood that it was really her, for at first the impossibility, as it seemed to him, of such an event did not allow him to accept the truth, stumbling over his own feet he threw himself at the Duke's, but the Duke raised him and put him in his sister's arms; I wish to stress that his sister embraced him with all possible show of happiness. Don Juan and Don Antonio told the Duke that the joke had been the most clever and agreeable in the whole world. The Duke took the boy, whom Sulpicia was holding, and giving him to Lorenzo, said to him:

"My dear brother, take your nephew and my son, and see if you are prepared to give me permission to marry this peasant girl who is the one to whom I first made a promise of marriage."

It would be a story without end to relate what Lorenzo replied, what Don Juan asked, what Don Antonio felt, the joy of the priest, the happiness of Sulpicia, the satisfaction of the housekeeper, the jubilation of the nurse, the wonderment of Fabio and, finally, the general happiness of all.

Then the priest married them, Don Juan de Gamboa acting as the principal witness, and everyone agreed that the marriage should be kept secret until they should see the outcome of the illness which kept the Duchess, his mother, close to death, and that meanwhile Lady Cornelia should return to Bologna with her brother. Everything happened as follows: the Duchess died, Cornelia entered Ferrara, giving happiness to all who saw her, and mourning was turned into rejoicing, the housekeeper and nurse became rich, Sulpicia became Fabio's wife, Don Antonio and Don Juan were exceedingly pleased to have been able to be of some service to the Duke who offered them two of his cousins for their wives and large dowries. They replied that gentlemen from the Basque country usually married in their region, and that it was not out of contempt that they did not accept such a distinguished offer, for that was not possible, but in order to fulfil that laudable custom and comply with the wishes of their fathers, who felt their sons should be married already.

The Duke accepted their explanation, and through proper and honourable means, and on suitable occasions, sent them many presents to Bologna, some so valuable and at such opportune times and occasions that, although they could have rejected them so as not to appear to be receiving payment, the moment in which they arrived made it easy to accept them, especially those he sent when they left for Spain and the ones he gave them when they went to Ferrara to take their leave of him and found that Cornelia had given

despedirse de él, y hallaron a Cornelia con otras dos criaturas hembras, y al duque más enamorado que nunca. La duquesa dio la cruz de diamantes a don Juan y el *agnus* a don Antonio, que sin ser poderosos a hacer otra cosa las recibieron.

Llegaron a España y a su tierra, adonde se casaron con ricas, principales y hermosas mujeres, y siempre tuvieron correspondencia con el duque y la duquesa y con el señor Lorenzo Bentibolli, con grandísimo gusto de todos.

birth to two baby girls and that the Duke was more in love with her than ever. The Duchess gave the diamond cross to Don Juan and the *agnus* to Don Antonio, both of whom felt they could not refuse these gifts.

Don Juan and Don Antonio returned to their own region of Spain where they married wealthy, noble and beautiful ladies, and they always continued to write to the Duke and Duchess and Lorenzo Bentibolli, to the great delight of all concerned.

THE DECEITFUL MARRIAGE
and
THE DIALOGUE OF THE DOGS

Introduction

Although the two stories which close the collection of *Exemplary Novels* are capable of standing on their own, they are inextricably and cleverly interconnected in order to highlight and explore the art of story-telling, the nature of reality, the power of illusion and the complex relationships between all three. *The Deceitful Marriage*, as the title implies, deals with matrimony not in the idealized, harmonious context so often found in Cervantes as, for example, in *Lady Cornelia* and other works of Golden Age literature, but in a context of deception, self-interest and lust. This moral and spiritual disorder is reflected at the very beginning of the story in the physical description of the principal male character, the Ensign Campuzano, as he leaves the Hospital de la Resurrección, yellowish and weak having been treated for syphilis. His meeting with his friend, the Licentiate Peralta, provides the occasion for the narration of the story which explains how Campuzano has come to be in this sorry state: he had been enticed into a whirlwind relationship and marriage to a certain Doña Estefanía de Caicedo who tricked him into thinking that she had inherited wealth and owned a large house. For his part, Campuzano had similarly misled Doña Estefanía about his own wealth and status, and the mutual deceit had soon come to light when the real owner of Doña Estefanía's supposed house, Doña Clementa Bueso, had unexpectedly returned and precipitated a series of events which led to Campuzano finding out how he had been duped, but at a point when it was too late to do anything about it. He had been fleeced by Doña Estefanía who had got clean away leaving him, for his sins, suffering from the syphilis he had contracted from her, on account of which he had gone to the Hospital de la Resurrección when a free cure was on offer. The Licentiate Peralta has sympathy for Campuzano but reminds him that he who takes pleasure in deceiving should not complain at being deceived.

Campuzano's story illustrates in various ways the power of appearances and lies and the ease with which we can be deceived. In this way and in the penalty that Campuzano pays for his weakness, *The Deceitful Marriage* is one of the *Exemplary Novels* in which the moral lesson is clearest. Campuzano has allowed himself to succumb to appearances, he has been attracted by Doña Estefanía's apparent wealth and physical qualities only to find that they are very different from what they appear to be. The attraction Estefanía holds for him through the veil with which she initially covers up her face in order to entice him conceals not only physical beauty which is merely modest but hides physical corruption in the form of her syphilis which is symbolic of her moral and spiritual disorder, a correspondence of the physical and spiritual which is characteristic

of the devotional literature of the time. Of course, Doña Estefanía has similarly allowed herself to be misled by Campuzano's appearance and supposed riches, and the mutual deceit exemplifies, as Campuzano confesses, that all that glitters is not gold and that truth does not always correspond to appearances. The Ensign and Doña Estefanía enter marriage through greed in pursuit of money and pleasure, and indeed in the description of their honeymoon the emphasis is on eating and a life of luxury. In a more general sense, they are taken in by the world; their earthly paradise is a false one, and this is the real moral lesson of the story. In its picture of the world as an evil place, *The Deceitful Marriage* is akin to *The Dialogue of the Dogs,* and both share features of the literature of *desengaño* with its pessimistic vision of the human condition in which feelings and sensual impressions can hinder the proper exercise of reason and discretion, blinding us to reality. Campuzano himself reminds us of this when he admits that "I at that time had my judgement not in my head but in my heels"(p71),[1] and that he heeded no "arguments other than those dictated by my pleasure, which had my powers of reasoning in its grip"(p.71). The novel, however, also deals with Campuzano's enlightenment. By the time he emerges from the Hospital de la Resurrección, with the associations of rebirth and renewal this name carries, Campuzano is a man reborn who has seen the truth embodied in his own tale and in his account of the talking dogs that follows it. It must be noted that in terms of the structure of the last two exemplary novels, the beginning of *The Deceitful Marriage* is really the chronological end of events. On a thematic level, it could be said that the pessimistic narrative is partly offset by the positive nature of Campuzano and Peralta's friendship, the meal they share and their visit to the Church. It can therefore be said that, although the weight of *The Deceitful Marriage* and *The Dialogue of the Dogs* is on fallen human nature, Cervantes is never totally one-sided, and his faith in humanity is never wholly obscured. In this way, we may talk of the ambivalence of his vision which is embodied in a complex pattern of dualities and apparent contradictions between truth and falsehood, appearance and reality, good and evil, which underpin the principal dualities of Cervantes's works, namely, the relationship between words and truth, fiction and reality, art and life.

In this brief story Cervantes clearly exemplifies his concern with these questions. The interest in the use of language, in narrating, and in the possibilities for communication and deception that language allows is well illustrated in Campuzano's account of this case of deception in marriage. Here again, as we often find in Cervantes's works, we have this interest illustrated through the use of a surrogate narrator and reader, through a character who tells and one who listens, a situation which mirrors the relationship between Cervantes as author and his readers. Campuzano is an eager narrator who, as soon as he has been suitably refreshed by Peralta, responds to the latter's request to recount his story, not waiting to be asked twice but immediately proceeding to speak. The deception that he then describes highlights not only the misleading appearance of material things – jewellery, clothes, buildings – but more importantly the power of words to trick and deceive. Doña Estefanía listens to rather than believes the long, tender conversations with Campuzano because she knows that words can be emptied of meaning, that words can be used to manipulate people, as she does with Campuzano when she deceptively courts his sympathy making a sham

---

[1]   The references in brackets following quotations are to our translation below.

profession of honesty which ironically tells the truth about her: "Ensign Campuzano, it would be foolish of me to sell myself to you as a saint: I have been a sinner and even now I still am"(p.69). Similarly, at a later point in the story, she asks for his trust saying that "you only need to know that what happens here is pretence and has an aim and purpose which will become clear to you in time"(p73). In fact, Doña Estefanía completely manipulates Campuzano who continues to be the victim of her deceits until the lady of the house in which Estefanía and Campuzano are lodging decides to reveal the truth to him saying that "everything that Doña Estefanía told you is false"(p75). Campuzano is thus shown to be easy prey. He is seen to be incapable of detecting the truth or of being worthy of trust, for he has shown not only how he was easily misled but also how he deliberately deceived and lied. Even now, as he confesses to his weaknesses, he still leaves scope for doubt because he is not completely open since, he says, "although I am telling the truth, it is not the whole truth, and nothing but the truth, as in the case of confession"(p.71).

The question of Campuzano's unreliability as a character and a narrator is linked to Cervantes's purpose in developing the story of *The Dialogue of the Dogs*, for Campuzano not only tells Peralta the account of his disastrous marriage but he says he has even more interesting things to relate. When Peralta expresses his amazement at what Campuzano has narrated, the latter tells him that he has as yet heard nothing compared to the other things he still has to tell him which defy all imagination because they go beyond the bounds of nature. With this statement a process of preparation begins for the introduction and presentation of an event apparently witnessed by Campuzano in the hospital which, he says, "you will not be able to believe now or ever, nor is there anyone else in the world who will believe it"(p79). These preambles and embellishments arouse Peralta's interest and eagerness to find out what Campuzano has to tell, in a process which mirrors the effects Cervantes is attempting to produce in his readers. The event that Campuzano is preparing to introduce is none other than a conversation between two dogs which he claims to have overheard in the hospital. The credibility of this event is put in doubt not only by its extraordinary nature but also by the unreliability we have seen in Campuzano and by the fact that he had this experience when he was in the grip of a feverish delirium. Peralta loses his patience with him, for he thinks that Campuzano cannot be trusted. However, the latter persists and convinces the licentiate to read the account of what he heard which he has faithfully recorded "without any rhetorical embellishments and without adding or taking away anything to make it more pleasing"(p.81). Campuzano therefore lies back and falls asleep whilst Peralta opens the notebook and begins to read *The Dialogue of the Dogs*.

The full title of this last story contains factual elements of the event it describes, firmly linking it to specific places and to a specific character - the Hospital de la Resurrección, Valladolid, the Puerta del Campo and Mahudes and his dogs. These details and others contribute towards the creation of a familiar and realistic environment. But around these factual references Cervantes constructs the fiction of the conversation between Cipión and Berganza, describing the account in hybrid terms as a novel/dialogue for, indeed, the colloquy of the dogs follows the model of the Lucianesque dialogue which was popular in the Renaissance for satirical social comment but, at the same time, the experiences of the dogs embody elements of life and characterization which link the work more closely to the novel as it was then developing,

particularly the picaresque form. In fact, *The Dialogue of the Dogs* is often seen as a picaresque work, and, although there may be differences of opinion as to whether or not it constitutes a genuine picaresque novel, there is no doubt that it embodies clear features of the picaresque genre, as may be gauged from the following brief description of it.[2]

The conversation between Cipión and Berganza follows a pattern found in several satirical works of the Golden Age, namely, an exchange of opinions by two characters who have contrasting views of the world and reality so that from the interaction between the two there is a resulting process of seeing things for what they are, in other words, a process of *desengaño*. In Cervantes's tale, it is Berganza who narrates the events of his life and Cipión who provides corrective advice and guidance, often supplying a note of optimism which is absent from Berganza's dark view of society. Berganza's account follows the episodic pattern of the picaresque, describing how he has gone from one master to the next, quite often at the same time experiencing deteriorating fortunes and undergoing a parallel process of illumination. The description he provides of his different masters and experiences provides a pessimistic view of society in which deceit, corruption, violence, greed and other sins and crimes are rife. He gives us the typical picaresque, gutter view of the world and people as he recounts his passage through different areas of the life of the time and his experiences with different social types. Berganza's descriptions of the world provide a lively if gloomy picture of a society in which the contrast between truth and falsehood, honesty and deceit, reality and fantasy is illustrated by an accumulation of characters and incidents drawn from satirical literature and designed to show the all-pervasive nature of evil and man's lower instincts. These characters and incidents include the Seville slaughterhouse, shepherds, a rich merchant, a constable, a group of soldiers, the sorceress and witch, Cañizares, and a company of actors. Marginal social groups such as the gypsies and the *moriscos* similarly come in for attack and ridicule. In the Hospital de la Resurrección, we also come across the lunatic fringe represented by the alchemist, the mathematician, the poet and the political theorist. The repetition of incident after incident reinforces the idea of the prevalence of human folly and sinfulness. In fact, Berganza's account contains little positive reference to any section of society except perhaps for the young girl whose beauty he respects and the Jesuits whose qualities as teachers he extols. However, Berganza's account and Cipión's comments are not a mere social document cataloguing a series of social abuses but embody a universal vision of evil underpinned by a pattern of imagery and symbolic reference drawn from the religious writing of the age, and raise moral and philosophical issues which overwhelm any alleged realism.

By far the most unreal, if at the same time most illuminating, of Berganza's experiences is the encounter with the witch Cañizares. The importance of this episode may be gauged from the fact that it is centrally placed in the work, with everything leading to it and from it. It is an episode which could well come first since it purports to explain the mystery of the power of speech that Cipión and Berganza enjoy and which had been hinted at earlier. Cañizares reveals to Berganza how he and Cipión are human beings who were changed to puppies at birth by the witch Camacha who had a grudge

---

2   For further information on the picaresque see: Alexander A. Parker, *Literature and the Delinquent: the Picaresque Novel in Spain and Europe, 1599-1753* (Edinburgh, 1967); Peter N. Dunn, *The Spanish Picaresque Novel* (Boston, 1979).

against their mother, another witch called Montiela, and how they are condemned to the canine state until such time as they witness the events described in the verses she quotes concerning the fall of the haughty and the exaltation of the meek and lowly. This is a complex passage in the narrative. The mysterious birth of the hero is a feature of romance which Cervantes here sets out to parody; he had parodied the conventions of the pastoral novel in the episode of the shepherds. Indeed, the Bible itself provides material for the Cañizares episode, for a feature of this novel is the profanation of the sacred, as Forcione[3] has pointed out, and several parodistic parallels may be noted. The prophecy clearly echoes the Biblical words in Luke I, 51-2, and equates the birth of the dogs with the birth of Christ. Other associations include: the Last Supper/the witches' banquet, the Good Shepherd/the shepherds Berganza works for, divine grace/Cañizares's oils, mystical ecstacy/Cañizares's trance.

The Cañizares episode is significant because it marks the lowest point in the process of the presentation of the dark forces in society and life which Berganza's story exhibits. In introducing the subject of witchcraft and sorcery, Cervantes was, in fact, touching on a phenomenon which had provoked considerable debate and action at the time not only in Spain but more particularly in other parts of Europe where the witch craze had infused panic and provoked extreme and violent measures to curtail it. Cervantes saw the potential of this subject for exploring further aspects of the role of imagination and fantasy, a matter which as a writer concerned him deeply, but in this case he did it in an inverse way to how he had done it in other of the *Exemplary Novels* in which he depicts a romanticized, idealistic world which highlights the human potential for goodness. *The Dialogue of the Dogs*, and in particular the Cañizares episode, depict the dark side of humanity and its potential for evil. The repulsive description of Cañizares clearly aims to provoke disgust and revulsion in the reader. In this sense, the placing of this tale at the end of the collection is significant since it represents aspects of the role of imagination and fantasy which are far removed from those brought out in the more idealistic stories. The latter explore the role of the imagination in ways which aim to reassure readers and confirm established values of honour, trust, love, confidence and so on. In *The Dialogue of the Dogs*, Cervantes explores the imagination from the diametrically opposed perspective of the dark and the ugly. Instead of satisfying and confirming the readers' need for beauty and perfection Cervantes seeks to point to our hiddenmost fears and impulses drawing attention not to the positive, creative forces within us but to the destructive ones. The darkness and ugliness which we may find in the innermost recesses of the human mind are reflected in the scene in which Berganza is left watching over Cañizares after she has anointed herself with the witches' oils and falls into a death-like trance. Berganza's fear, the revulsion he feels at seeing her naked body, the details of physical ugliness he provides all illustrate the satanic darkness and evil which this whole episode embodies and which points to the central tensions and fundamental conflicts in human life between good and evil, beauty and ugliness, creation and destruction. These contrasts and conflicts are also reinforced by the use of animal imagery and the transference of human and animal attributes. The talking dogs display many human qualities whereas humans are shown to behave like beasts, notably

---

3   Alban K. Forcione, *Cervantes and the Mystery of Lawlessness: A Study of `El casamiento engañoso y El coloquio de los perros'* (Princeton, 1984).

in the Seville slaughter-house and also in the case of the shepherds. Similarly, Cañizares is depicted as wise, intelligent and perceptive yet she is the embodiment of evil itself. These and other apparent contradictions are part and parcel of the confused and confusing picture of life and the world which Cervantes depicts, a topsy-turvy world in which dogs can speak, a world in turmoil which challenges the reader to find meaning and truth. This is reflected in the image of the octopus that Cervantes provides as a symbol for the form or formlessness of his work, an image of shapelessness which, as Forcione has pointed out, "offers a striking inversion of the figure which nearly every literary theorist of the age invoked to describe the coherence of the perfect work of literature - the well-formed body, in which parts are perfectly proportioned to each other and to the whole so as to yield a single unified effect of beauty and harmony."[4] The reader naturally seeks form in what he or she reads, so that the novel is a kind of metaphor of the reader's desire to give shape and meaning to disparate experience. However, the text offers an image of the world as chaotic, confusing, difficult to interpret and apparently without order. The theme of *desengaño* and the structure are thus closely linked so as to give expression to underlying tensions of Cervantes's work, namely, the contrast between truth and falsehood, imagination and reality, the conscious and the subconscious, the spiritual and the material, all aspects of the central questions that concern him, the nature of truth in fiction and the relationship between art and life.

This is evident in the opening of *The Dialogue of the Dogs* which continues the concern expressed at the end of *The Deceitful Marriage* with the question of the credibility of the talking dogs. Cipión and Berganza show surprise at their own ability to speak, analysing the power that they have inexplicably acquired and defining it as the ability to speak using proper discourse and reason. The novel thus expresses Cervantes's preoccupation with the whole question of truth within fiction and the nature and role of fiction, a matter which he self-consciously highlights by directly raising the issues involved as part of the discourse itself. By so doing, he not only creates an awareness in the reader of the problems involved in composing a work of fiction but at the same time he also guides and coaxes the reader to suspend disbelief and enter into the spirit of the game of fiction. For example, it is hinted that the reader will get an explanation of the situation that is presented, and then Cañizares actually provides it, only to have it undermined by Cipión's reasoning. The reader thus experiences an increasing bewilderment in that meaning is promised but the promise is never fulfilled, for even more questions arise: are Cipión and Berganza merely Campuzano's dream? Are they dreaming, as they themselves think? They seek an explanation and look for a way out just as the reader searches for a path through this labyrinthine text. The uncertainty created is linked to the relativistic viewpoint which underlies *The Dialogue of the Dogs*, and which is related to Cervantes's concern with language and the ways in which he explores and undermines fixed ways of thinking.

In *The Deceitful Marriage* and *The Dialogue of the Dogs*, as in other exemplary novels, language is shown to be ambiguous, for there is no stable connection between words and things. This shifting relationship is illustrated in many different ways, for example, references to various styles of writing, Doña Estefanía's deceitful words, the use of Latin for show and effect, Cañizares's riddles. However, language is also

---

4   Forcione, pp.8-9.

portrayed in its most positive ways, as a gift which Cipión and Berganza are privileged to enjoy, as a mark of culture and education, as a quality that separates man from beast, as the most valuable tool of communication which both reader and writer need to use effectively. We thus find that throughout their dialogue Cipión and Berganza express opinions about story-telling which reflect Cervantes's preoccupation with how words are used and with the craft of fiction. Cipión continually exhorts Berganza to narrate briefly, to keep to the point, to relate events in a fitting manner and so on. For example, he interrupts Berganza's account of his experiences in the abattoir to recommend to him brevity in narrating: "Berganza, my friend, if you are going to take as long telling me about the circumstances of the masters you have had and the defects of their occupations as you have done this time, it will be necessary to ask heaven to give us the power of speech for a year..."(p.89). He goes on to explain to Berganza how different stories require different qualities in their narration: some embody pleasure in their content, others require a certain manner of narration, others demand fine words and accompanying gestures and expressions. Cipión's advice to Berganza here and elsewhere highlights and illustrates Cervantes's awareness of the importance of the author-reader relationship which is essential for the success of any work of fiction. Therefore, in these ways, Cervantes raises in a direct fashion the concerns which are at the bottom of all his work - the need to stimulate and capture the readers' interest, to encourage and facilitate the suspension of disbelief and to handle and structure his material so as to retain the readers' attention to the end. The ways in which Cervantes raises these matters before the readers' eyes prompt the readers to an awareness of the process of reading and writing and to reflecting on the nature of fiction and its relationship to experience and reality. The readers are provided with suspenseful entertainment which elicits wonder and admiration while instruction is imparted not only on a moral level but perhaps more importantly on an intellectual and literary level. Cervantes attempts to show the value of fiction in exposing human illusions, in communicating the elusive nature of reality and in depicting the difficulty of attaining the truth. He thus offers a pluralistic, tolerant view of the world which is seen in the inconclusive nature of the text and which is well illustrated by the important prophecy that cannot be explained and by the lunatic fringe depicted at the end, the four inmates of the hospital who are constantly seeking the impossible.

It is in this respect that the intimate relationship between *The Deceitful Marriage* and *The Dialogue of the Dogs* is best seen. The frame provided by Campuzano and Peralta, and the way the dogs' conversation springs from Campuzano's story, provide a clear stimulus to an awareness of the processes mentioned above and offer a major example of a typically Cervantine playing with narrative levels which reinforces the fictional illusion and exposes it at the same time. The narrator introduces Campuzano who then tells his story to Peralta who in turn listens to the text that the reader reads. Then Campuzano introduces Berganza who tells his story to Cipión as Peralta and the reader read the text of *The Dialogue of the Dogs*. The narrator thus fades out leaving the characters freedom, as it were, to tell their own stories. As Avalle-Arce and others have stated, Cervantes provides us here with a box-within-box technique in which one story grows out of another in a kind of playful conjuring trick. This fictional game begins and ends with the two friends Campuzano and Peralta, and in a parallel way to their comments at the end of *The Deceitful Marriage*, they exchange comments at the end of

The Dialogue of the Dogs which are important in the context of fiction and its relationship to reality. Despite his initial reservations, the Licentiate has read Campuzano's account, he has become immersed in what it relates and he has enjoyed it so much that he is moved to state that, even if the colloquy is made up and has never happened, it is so well contrived that Campuzano should proceed to write the promised second part relating Cipión's life, a comment which serves as sufficient encouragement to Campuzano to proceed to write it. Peralta no longer wishes to become involved in questions and doubts as to whether the dogs spoke or not. What matters now is not whether the story is true or false but whether the art and invention are effective and good. A work of art is valid in itself and not in its apparent similarity to everyday reality which is shown to be anything but simple. This is what Peralta has realized, and this is what Cervantes's readers should also appreciate. Literature that is skilfully composed and written will entertain and convey its own message, its own poetic truth; good literature will be convincing aesthetically and challenging intellectually, and that is sufficient.

Bibliography
The Deceitful Marriage and The Dialogue of the Dogs

Aylward, E.T., 'The Device of the Layered Commentary', *Cervantes*, 7 (1987), 57-69.

Cabrera, V., 'Nuevos valores de *El casamiento engañoso* y *El coloquio de los perros*' *Hispanófila*, 45 (1972), 49-58.

Carrasco, F., '*El coloquio de los perros*: veridicción y modelo narrativo', *Criticón*, 35 (1986), 119-33.

El Saffar, Ruth, '*El casamiento engañoso*' and '*El coloquio de los perros*' (London, 1976).

Forcione, Alban K., *Cervantes and the Mystery of Lawlessness: A Study of 'El casamiento engañoso y El coloquio de los perros*' (Princeton, 1984).

González Echevarría, Roberto, 'The Life and Adventures of Cipión: Cervantes and the Picaresque', *Diacritics*, 10 (1980), 15-26.

Hart, Thomas R., 'Cervantes's Sententious Dogs', *Modern Language Notes* 94 (1979), 377-85.

'Renaissance Dialogue into Novel: Cervantes's *Coloquio*', *Modern Language Notes* 105 (1990), 191-202.

Hutchinson, Steven, 'Counterfeit Chains of Discourse: a Comparison of Citation in Cervantes's *Casamiento/Coloquio* and in Islamic *Hadith*', *Cervantes*, 8 (1988), 139-58.

Lloris, Manuel, '*El casamiento engañoso*' *Hispanófila*, 39, (1970), 15-20.

Molho, Maurice, 'Antroponimia y cinonimia del *Casamiento engañoso* y *Coloquio de los perros*', in José Jesús de Bustos Tovar (coordinador), *Lenguaje, ideología y organización textual en las 'Novelas ejemplares*' (Madrid, 1983), 81-92.

Ricapito, Joseph V., 'Cervantes and the Picaresque: Redivivo', in *Hispanic Studies in Honour of Joseph J. Silverman*, ed. Joseph V. Ricapito (Newark, Delaware, 1988), 335 ff.

Riley, E.C., 'Cervantes and the Cynics (*El licenciado vidriera* and *El coloquio de los perros*)', *Bulletin of Hispanic Studies*, 53 (1976), 189-200.

Sobejano, Gonzalo, '*El coloquio de los perros* en la picaresca y otros apuntes', *Hispanic Review*, 43 (1975), 25-41.

Soons, Alan, 'An Interpretation of the Form of *El casamiento engañoso y El Coloquio de los perros*' *Anales cervantinos*, 9 (1961-62), 203-12.

Waley, Pamela, 'The Unity of *Casamiento engañoso* and the *Coloquio de los perros*', *Bulletin of Hispanic Studies*, 34 (1957), 201-12.

Woodward, L.J., '*El casamiento engañoso y El coloquio de los perros*' *Bulletin of Hispanic Studies*, 36 (1959), 80-7.

Williamson, E., 'Cervantes as Moralist and Trickster: the Critique of the Picaresque Autobiography in *El casamiento engañoso y El coloquio de los perros*' in Jennifer Lowe & Philip Swanson, eds., *Essays on Hispanic Themes in Honour of Edward C. Riley* (Edinburgh, 1989), 104-26.

Novela del Casamiento Engañoso

Salía del Hospital de la Resurrección, que está en Valladolid, fuera de la Puerta del Campo, un soldado que, por servirle su espada de báculo y por la flaqueza de sus piernas y amarillez de su rostro, mostraba bien claro que, aunque no era el tiempo muy caluroso, debía de haber sudado en veinte días todo el humor que quizá granjeó en una hora. Iba haciendo pinitos y dando traspiés, como convaleciente; y al entrar por la puerta de la ciudad, vio que hacia él venía un su amigo, a quien no había visto en más de seis meses; el cual, santigüándose, como si viera alguna mala visión, llegándose a él le dijo:

–¿Qué es esto, señor alférez Campuzano? ¿Es posible que está vuesa merced en esta tierra? ¡Como quien soy que le hacía en Flandes, antes terciando allá la pica que arrastrando aquí la espada! ¿Qué color, qué flaqueza es ésa?

A lo cual respondió Campuzano:

–A lo si estoy en esta tierra o no, señor licenciado Peralta, el verme en ella le responde; a las demás preguntas no tengo que decir sino que salgo de aquel hospital, de sudar catorce cargas de bubas que me echó a cuestas una mujer que escogí por mía, que non debiera.

–¿Luego casóse vuesa merced? –replicó Peralta.

–Sí, señor –respondió Campuzano.

–Sería por amores –dijo Peralta–, y tales casamientos traen consigo aparejada la ejecución del arrepentimiento.

–No sabré decir si fue por amores –respondió el Alférez–, aunque sabré afirmar que fue por dolores, pues de mi casamiento, o cansamiento, saqué tantos en el cuerpo y en el alma, que los del cuerpo, para entretenerlos, me cuestan cuarenta sudores, y los del alma no hallo remedio para aliviarlos siquiera. Pero porque no estoy para tener largas pláticas en la calle, vuesa merced me perdone; que otro día con más comodidad le daré cuenta de mis sucesos, que son los más nuevos y peregrinos que vuesa merced habrá oído en todos los días de su vida.

–No ha de ser así –dijo el Licenciado–, sino que quiero que venga conmigo a mi posada, y allí haremos penitencia juntos; que la olla es muy de enfermo, y aunque está tasada para dos, un pastel suplirá con mi criado; y si la convalecencia lo sufre, unas lonjas de jamón de Rute nos harán la salva, y, sobre todo, la buena voluntad con que lo ofrezco, no sólo esta vez, sino todas las que vuesa merced quisiere.

Agradecióselo Campuzano, y aceptó el convite y los ofrecimientos. Fueron a San Llorente, oyeron misa, llevóle Peralta a su casa, diole lo prometido y ofreciósele de nuevo, y pidióle, en acabando de comer, le contase los sucesos que tanto le había encarecido. No se hizo de rogar Campuzano; antes comenzó a decir de esta manera:

The Deceitful Marriage

Out of the Hospital of the Resurrection,[1] which is in Valladolid, beyond the Puerta del Campo, [2] hobbled a soldier using his sword as a walking stick. This, together with the weakness in his legs and the yellow colour of his face, showed clearly that, although the weather was not very hot, he must have sweated out in twenty days all the fluids[3] he had perhaps collected in a single hour. He staggered and stumbled as if not fully recovered from an illness; and as he passed through the city gate, he saw heading towards him a friend of his whom he had not seen for at least six months. This friend made the sign of the cross as if he had seen the devil himself and said as he approached him:

"What's this, my dear Ensign[4] Campuzano? Is it possible that you are here? I could have sworn you were shouldering your pike in Flanders[5] and not dragging your sword around here. But why are you such an awful colour and so weak?"

To which Campuzano replied:

"As to whether I am here or not, Licentiate[6] Peralta, you have your answer in seeing me; as to your other questions, suffice it to say that I have just come out of that hospital where I have sweated out a dozen or so sores from the clap given to me by a woman whom I took to be mine when I should not have done so."

"Did you marry her then?" asked Peralta.

"Yes, I did," responded Campuzano.

"It must have been passionate love then," said Peralta, "and marriages born of passion inevitably bring repentance in their wake."

"I could not say whether it was passion," the Ensign replied, "but it was certainly pain,[7] for that tying, or should I say tiring,[8] of myself caused me much suffering in body and soul. The pain in my body was only contained by sweating it out forty times, but as for the pain in my soul I find no relief at all. But I'm in no fit state to stand talking for long in the street, so please forgive me. Some other day when I'm feeling better I shall give you an account of these events which are likely to be the strangest and most incredible you have heard in all your life."

"We can't have that," the Licentiate said, "I would rather you came with me to my lodgings where we can do penance together; [9] stew is very good for a sick person and although there is only enough for two, my servant can make do with a pie instead; and if your delicate state allows it, a few slices of Rute ham[10] will make a good starter, and so will the good will with which I offer it to you not only on this occasion but each and every time you wish."

Campuzano thanked him and accepted the invitation and what was offered. They went to the Church of San Llorente and heard Mass and then Peralta took him home, gave him what he had promised, offered some more and when they had finished eating asked him to relate the events that he had extolled so much. Campuzano did not have to be asked twice but immediately proceeded to speak as follows:

–Bien se acordará vuesa merced, señor licenciado Peralta, como yo hacía en esta ciudad camarada con el capitán Pedro de Herrera, que ahora está en Flandes.

–Bien me acuerdo –respondió Peralta.

–Pues un día –prosiguió Campuzano– que acabábamos de comer en aquella Posada de la Solana, donde vivíamos, entraron dos mujeres de gentil parecer, con dos criadas; la una se puso a hablar con el Capitán en pie, arrimados a una ventana; y la otra se sentó en una silla junto a mí, derribado el manto hasta la barba, sin dejar ver el rostro más de aquello que concedía la raridad del manto; y aunque le supliqué que por cortesía me hiciese merced de descubrirse, no fue posible acabarlo con ella, cosa que me encendió más el deseo de verla. Y para acrecentarle más, o ya fuese de industria o acaso, sacó la señora una muy blanca mano, con muy buenas sortijas. Estaba yo entonces bizarrísimo, con aquella gran cadena que vuesa merced debió de conocerme, el sombrero con plumas y cintillo, el vestido de colores, a fuer de soldado, y tan gallardo a los ojos de mi locura, que me daba a entender que las podía matar en el aire. Con todo esto, le rogué que se descubriese, a lo que ella me respondió:

–No seáis importuno; casa tengo; haced a un paje que me siga, que aunque yo soy más honrada de lo que promete esta respuesta, todavía, a trueco de ver si responde vuestra discreción a vuestra gallardía, holgaré de que me veáis.

Beséle las manos por la grande merced que me hacía, en pago de la cual le prometí montes de oro. Acabó el Capitán su plática; ellas se fueron; siguiólas un criado mío. Díjome el Capitán que lo que la dama le quería era que le llevase unas cartas a Flandes a otro Capitán, que decía ser su primo, aunque él sabía que no era sino su galán. Yo quedé abrasado con las manos de nieve que había visto y muerto por el rostro que deseaba ver; y así, otro día, guiándome mi criado, dióseme libre entrada. Hallé una casa muy bien aderezada y una mujer de hasta treinta años, a quien conocí por las manos. No era hermosa en extremo; pero éralo de suerte que podía enamorar comunicada, porque tenía un tono de habla tan suave que se entraba por los oídos en el alma. Pasé con ella luengos y amorosos coloquios. Blasoné, hendí, rajé, ofrecí, prometí e hice todas las demonstraciones que me pareció ser necesarias para hacerme bienquisto con ella. Pero como ella estaba hecha a oír semejantes o mayores ofrecimientos y razones, parecía que les daba atento oído antes que crédito alguno. Finalmente, nuestra plática se pasó en flores cuatro días que continué en visitarla, sin que llegase a coger el fruto que deseaba.

En el tiempo que la visité siempre hallé la casa desembarazada, sin que viese visiones en ella de parientes fingidos ni de amigos verdaderos. Servíala una moza más taimada que simple. Finalmente, tratando mis amores como soldado que está en víspera de mudar, apuré a mi señora doña Estefanía de Caicedo (que éste es el nombre de la que así me tiene), y respondióme: "Señor Alférez Campuzano, simplicidad sería si yo quisiera venderme a vuesa merced por santa. Pecadora he sido, y aun ahora lo soy; pero no de manera que los vecinos me murmuren ni los apartados me noten; ni de mis padres ni de otro pariente heredé hacienda alguna, y con todo esto vale el menaje de mi casa, bien validos, dos mil y quinientos escudos; y éstos, en cosas que, puestas en almoneda, lo que se tardare en ponerlas se tardará en convertirse en dineros. Con esta hacienda

"You will no doubt remember, Licentiate Peralta, how in this city I served with Captain Pedro de Herrera, who is now in Flanders".

"I certainly do," replied Peralta.

"Well, one day," continued Campuzano, "we had just finished eating in the Solana Inn, where we were living, when two women of genteel appearance came in, accompanied by two maids. One began to speak with the Captain, both of them remaining standing and leaning on the window, and the other sat down on a chair next to me, with her cloak pulled round her chin so that one could only see that part of her face that the cloak did not reach and, although I begged her out of courtesy to kindly reveal her countenance, it was not possible to persuade her, and this only served to inflame further my desire to see her. And she inflamed it even more, I do not know whether on purpose or by accident, by showing a white hand, which wore very good rings. At that time, I myself was rather flash, wearing that big chain that you have seen on me, a hat with feathers and hatbands, a coloured jacket, as befits a soldier, and so splendid was I in the eyes of my own delusion, that I believed that I could have any woman I wanted. In this frame of mind, I asked her to show her face, to which she replied:

"Do not be in such a hurry; I own a house; have a page follow me, and although I am more honourable than this answer implies, nevertheless, to see if your discretion matches your gallantry, I shall be pleased to let you see me."

I kissed her hands in thanks for the great favour that she was doing me, in payment for which I promised her piles of gold. The captain finished his conversation; the women left and a servant of mine followed them. The captain told me that what the lady wanted was for him to take some letters to Flanders to another captain, who she said was her cousin, although he knew that he was none other than her beau. I was inflamed with the snow-white hands[11] I had seen, and consumed by the desire to see her face; and so, the next day, guided by my servant, I was admitted to her house. I found a beautifully kept house and a woman of about thirty years of age, whom I recognised by her hands. She was not outstandingly beautiful, but she was in the sense that she could enthrall with her speech, for she had a tone of voice so soft that it entered the ear and reached the soul. I held long, tender conversations with her; I boasted, bragged, chattered, offered, promised and said everything I thought necessary to win her affection; but as she was accustomed to hearing similar or better offers and arguments, it appeared that she listened to them attentively rather than believed them. In the end, our conversations remained trivial for the four days I continued to visit her, without my being able to pluck the fruit I desired.

In the time that I visited her, I always found the house empty, and I did not catch sight of either imaginary relatives or real friends. She was attended by a maid who was astute rather than simple. In the end, treating my passion like a soldier who is on the eve of departing, I put pressure on my lady Estefanía de Caicedo (for this is the name of the one who had me in her thrall), and she replied to me:

"Ensign Campuzano, it would be foolish of me to sell myself to you as a saint; I have been a sinner, and even now I still am; but not in the sense that my neighbours gossip about me and those further away have heard of me. Neither from my parents nor from other relatives have I inherited any wealth and yet my entire household is worth a good two thousand five hundred *escudos*, and this in things which, if put into an auction, would take no time at all to convert into money. With this I am seeking a husband to

busco marido a quien entregarme y a quien tener obediencia; a quien, juntamente con la enmienda de mi vida, le entregaré una increíble solicitud de regalarle y servirle; porque no tiene príncipe cocinero más goloso ni que mejor sepa dar el punto a los guisados que le sé dar yo, cuando, mostrando ser casera, me quiero poner a ello. Sé ser mayordomo en casa, moza en la cocina y señora en la sala; en efecto, sé mandar y sé hacer que me obedezcan. No desperdicio nada, y allego mucho; mi real no vale menos, sino mucho más cuando se gasta por mi orden. La ropa blanca que tengo, que es mucha y buena, no se sacó de tiendas ni lenceros; estos pulgares y los de mis criadas la hilaron. Y si pudiera tejerse en casa, se tejiera. Digo estas alabanzas mías porque no acarrean vituperio cuando es forzosa la necesidad de decirlas. Finalmente, quiero decir que yo busco marido que me ampare, me mande y me honre, y no galán que me sirva y me vitupere. Si vuesa merced gustare de aceptar la prenda que le ofrece, aquí estoy moliente y corriente, sujeta a todo aquello que vuesa merced ordenare, sin andar en venta, que es lo mismo andar en lenguas de casamenteros, y no hay ninguno tan bueno para concertar el todo como las mismas partes."

Yo, que tenía entonces el juicio, no en la cabeza, sino en los carcañares, haciéndoseme el deleite en aquel punto mayor de lo que en la imaginación le pintaba y ofreciéndoseme tan a la vista la cantidad de hacienda, que ya la contemplaba en dineros convertida, sin hacer discursos de aquellos a que daba lugar el gusto, que me tenía echados grillos al entendimiento, le dije que yo era el venturoso y bien afortunado en haberme dado el cielo, casi por milagro, tal compañera, para hacerla señora de mi voluntad y de mi hacienda, que no era tan poca que no valiese, con aquella cadena que traía al cuello y con otras joyuelas que tenía en casa, y con deshacerme de algunas galas de soldado, más de dos mil ducados, que juntos con los dos mil y quinientos suyos, eran suficiente cantidad para retirarnos a vivir a una aldea de donde yo era natural y adonde tenía algunas raíces; hacienda tal, que, sobrellevada con el dinero, vendiendo los frutos a su tiempo, nos podía dar una vida alegre y descansada. En resolución, aquella vez se concertó nuestro desposorio, y se dio traza cómo los dos hiciésemos información de solteros, y en los tres días de fiesta que vinieron luego juntos en una Pascua se hicieron las amonestaciones, y al cuarto día nos desposamos, hallándose presentes al desposorio dos amigos míos y un mancebo que ella dijo ser primo suyo, a quien yo me ofrecí por pariente con palabras de mucho comedimiento, como lo habían sido todas las que hasta entonces a mi nueva esposa había dado, con intención tan torcida y traidora, que la quiero callar; porque aunque estoy diciendo verdades, no son verdades de confesión, que no pueden dejar de decirse.

Mudó mi criado el baúl de la posada a casa de mi mujer; encerré en él, delante de ella, mi magnífica cadena; mostréle otras tres o cuatro, si no tan grandes, de mejor hechura, con otros tres o cuatro cintillos de diversas suertes; hícele patentes mis galas y mis plumas, y entreguéle para el gasto de casa hasta cuatrocientos reales que tenía. Seis días gocé del pan de la boda, espaciándome en casa como el yerno ruin en la del suegro rico. Pisé ricas alfombras, ajé sábanas de holanda, alumbréme con candeleros de plata; almorzaba en la cama, levantábame a las once, comía a las doce, y a las dos sesteaba en el estrado; bailábanme doña Estefanía y la moza el agua delante. Mi mozo, que hasta

give myself to and to obey; as well as mending my ways, I will devote an enormous effort to pleasing him and serving him; because no prince has a cook who can make more appetising dishes or can prepare a better stew than I can when, wanting to be a housewife, I put my mind to it. I can be a butler in the house, a servant in the kitchen and a lady in the drawing-room; in short, I know how to give orders and how to make myself obeyed. I waste nothing and I collect a lot; my coin is not worth less, but much more, when it is spent as I decree. My linen, of which there is much and of very good quality, was not bought in shops or from a draper; these fingers and those of my servants sewed them; if they could have been spun at home they would have been. I say these things in praise of myself because they do not bring censure when it is necessary to say them. Finally, I want to say that I am seeking a husband to look after me, to rule me and honour me, and not a beau to serve me and condemn me. If you would like to accept the gift which is offered to you, here I am ready and willing, subject to whatever you may decide, without putting myself up for sale, which is the same as putting myself in the hands of marriagebrokers, for there is no one as good at arranging the whole affair as the parties themselves."

I at that time had my judgement not in my head but in my heels,[12] so that my pleasure seemed greater than my imagination painted it, and with the amount of her property displayed before my eyes, which I could see converted into money, I listened to no arguments other than those dictated by my pleasure, which had my powers of reasoning in its grip. I told her that I was very lucky and fortunate in having been granted by Heaven, by a miracle, such a companion, to make her mistress of my will and belongings. These were not inconsiderable, taking into account that chain that I wore around my neck and other jewels which I had at home, and the possible sale of my soldier's full dress uniform worth more than two thousand ducats which, together with the two thousand five hundred of hers, were sufficient to go off and live in the village where I was born and where I had some roots. This property, with the money added on, and selling fruit in season, could provide us with a happy and peaceful life. The upshot was that we decided there and then to get married, and we set in train the procedure for both of us to be officially recognised as unmarried, the banns were read on three holy days which came together around Easter, and on the fourth day we were married, in the presence of two friends of mine and a lad she said was a cousin of hers, and whom I accepted as a relative of mine with words that were extremely polite, as had been all my words to my new wife up until then, although my intentions were so base and deceitful that I prefer not to mention them; for although I am telling the truth, it is not the whole truth, and nothing but the truth, as in the case of confession.

My servant moved my trunk from the inn where I was staying to my wife's house; in front of her I locked my magnificent chain in this trunk; I showed her three or four others which, though smaller, were better made, along with three or four hatbands of different kinds; I let her see my fine clothes and my feathers, and I gave her four hundred or so *reales* I had on me to cover her household expenses. For six days I enjoyed the fruits of marriage, making myself at home like a poor son-in-law in the house of his rich father-in-law. I trod on rich carpets, crumpled linen sheets, had my way lit up by the light from silver candlesticks; I had breakfast in bed, got up at eleven, had lunch at twelve, and at two I took a nap in the drawing-room; Doña Estefanía and the maid danced attendance on me. My servant, whom up till then I had assumed to be

allí le había conocido perezoso y lerdo, se había vuelto un corzo. El rato que doña Estefanía faltaba de mi lado, la habían de hallar en la cocina, toda solícita en ordenar guisados que me despertasen el gusto y me avivasen el apetito. Mis camisas, cuellos y pañuelos eran un nuevo Aranjuez de flores, según olían, bañados en el agua de ángeles y de azahar que sobre ellos se derramaba.

Pasáronse estos días volando, como se pasan los años, que están debajo de la jurisdicción del tiempo; en los cuales días, por verme tan regalado y tan bien servido, iba mudando en buena la mala intención con que aquel negocio había comenzado. Al cabo de los cuales, una mañana –que aun estaba con doña Estefanía en la cama– llamaron con grandes golpes a la puerta de la calle. Asomóse la moza a la ventana, y quitándose al momento dijo:

–¡Oh, que sea ella la bienvenida! ¿Han visto y cómo ha venido más presto de lo que escribió el otro día?

–¿Quién es la que ha venido, moza? –le pregunté.

–¿Quién? –respondió ella. –Es mi señora doña Clementa Bueso, y viene con ella el señor don Lope Meléndez de Almendárez, con otros dos criados, y Hortigosa, la dueña que llevó consigo.

–¡Corre, moza, bien haya yo, y ábreles! –dijo a este punto doña Estefanía–. Y vos, señor, por mi amor que no os alborotéis ni respondáis por mí a ninguna cosa que contra mí oyéredes.

–Pues ¿quién ha de deciros cosa que os ofenda, y más estando yo delante? Decidme: ¿qué gente es ésta, que me parece que os ha alborotado su venida?

–No tengo lugar de responderos –dijo doña Estefanía–; sólo sabed que todo lo que aquí pasare es fingido y que tira a cierto designio y efecto que después sabréis.

Y aunque quisiera replicarle a esto, no me dio lugar la señora doña Clementa Bueso, que se entró en la sala, vestida de raso verde prensado, con muchos pasamanos de oro, capotillo de lo mismo y con la misma guarnición, sombrero con plumas verdes, blancas y encarnadas, y con rico cintillo de oro, y con un delgado velo cubierta la mitad del rostro. Entró con ella el señor don Lope Meléndez de Almendárez, no menos bizarro que ricamente vestido de camino. La dueña Hortigosa fue la primera que habló, diciendo:

–¡Jesús! ¿Qué es esto? ¿Ocupado el lecho de mi señora doña Clementa, y más con ocupación de hombre? ¡Milagros veo hoy en esta casa! ¡A fe que se ha ido bien del pie a la mano la señora Estefanía, fiada en la amistad de mi señora!

–Yo te lo prometo, Hortigosa –replicó doña Clementa–; pero yo me tengo la culpa. ¡Que jamás escarmiente yo en tomar amigas que no lo saben ser si no es cuando les viene a cuento!

A todo lo cual respondió doña Estefanía:

–No reciba vuesa merced pesadumbre, mi señora doña Clementa Bueso, y entienda que no sin misterio ve lo que ve en esta su casa; que cuando lo sepa, yo sé que quedaré disculpada y vuesa merced sin ninguna queja.

En esto ya me había puesto yo en calzas y en jubón, y tomándome doña Estefanía por la mano me llevó a otro aposento, y allí me dijo que aquella su amiga quería hacer una burla a aquel don Lope que venía con ella, con quien pretendía casarse, y que la burla era darle a entender que aquella casa y cuanto estaba en ella era todo suyo, de lo

lazy and sluggish, had become as fast-moving as a deer. On the rare occasions when Doña Estefanía was not at my side, she would be found in the kitchen, totally taken up in preparing dishes that would whet my appetite and stimulate my tastebuds. My shirts, collars and handkerchiefs smelt like Aranjuez in bloom,[13] bathed as they were in the orange-blossom and other scented water she sprinkled on them.

Those days flew by, as do the years which are ruled by the laws of time; during that time, finding myself so well looked after and attended, the bad intentions with which the affair had begun were changing to good ones. One morning, however, when I was still in bed with Doña Estefanía, there was a loud knocking at the front door. The maid stuck her head out of the window and pulled it in at once saying:

"What a time to turn up! She's come much sooner than she said the other day in her letter."

"Who is it that's come, girl?" I asked.

"Who?" she replied. "My lady Doña Clementa Bueso, and she's accompanied by Don Lope Meléndez de Almendárez and two servants, and Hortigosa, the lady-in-waiting she took with her."

"Hurry up, girl, for goodness sake, and let them in!" said Doña Estefanía at this point. "And you, sir, if you love me do not get excited and do not reply on my behalf to anything you may hear said against me."

"But who would say anything against you, especially when I'm there? Tell me, who are these people, whose arrival seems to have startled you?"

"I haven't time to tell you now," said Doña Estefanía. "You only need to know that what happens here is pretence and has an aim and purpose which will become clear to you in time."

And although I wanted to reply to this, Doña Clementa Bueso did not give me the opportunity for she came into the room, dressed in green satin lustre with many gold edgings, a cape of the same material and trimmings, a hat with green, white and red feathers, and a rich gold band, and a fine veil which covered half of her face. With her was Don Lope Meléndez de Almendárez, equally resplendent in his rich, showy clothes. Hortigosa was the first to speak:

"Heavens above! What is this? Someone in the bed of my lady Doña Clementa, and that someone is a man? I can't believe my eyes. Lady Estefanía has overdone it this time, taking advantage of my lady's friendship."

"You can say that again," replied Doña Clementa, "but the fault is mine. I'll never learn not to have as friends the kind of people who are only friends when it is to their advantage!"

To all of which Doña Estefanía replied:

"Don't be upset, my lady, and please understand that what you are seeing in your own house is not what it seems; and when you learn the truth I know that I will be forgiven and that you will have no cause for complaint."

By this time I had already put on my breeches and doublet, and Doña Estefanía took me by the hand and led me to another room, and there she told me that her friend wanted to play a trick on don Lope who had come with her, and whom she intended to marry, and that the trick was to pretend that that house and all in it were hers, and that it would

cual pensaba hacerle carta de dote, y que hecho el casamiento se le daba poco que se descubriese el engaño, fiada en el grande amor que el don Lope la tenía.

–Y luego se me volverá lo que es mío, y no se le tendrá a mal a ella ni a otra mujer alguna de que procure buscar marido honrado, aunque sea por medio de cualquier embuste.

Yo le respondí que era grande extremo de amistad el que quería hacer, y que primero se mirase bien en ello, porque después podría ser tener necesidad de valerse de la justicia para cobrar su hacienda. Pero ella me respondió con tantas razones, representando tantas obligaciones que la obligaban a servir a doña Clementa, aun en cosas de más importancia, que, mal de mi grado, y con remordimiento de mi juicio, hube de condescender con el gusto de doña Estefanía, asegurándome ella que solos ocho días podía durar el embuste, los cuales estaríamos en casa de otra amiga suya. Acabámonos de vestir ella y yo, y luego, entrándose a despedir de la señora doña Clementa Bueso y del señor don Lope Meléndez de Almendárez, hizo a mi criado que se cargase el baúl y que la siguiese, a quien yo también seguí, sin despedirme de nadie.

Paró doña Estefanía en casa de una amiga suya, y antes que entrásemos dentro estuvo un buen espacio hablando con ella, al cabo del cual salió una moza y dijo que entrásemos yo y mi criado. Llevónos a un aposento estrecho, en el cual había dos camas tan juntas que parecían una, a causa de que no había espacio que las dividiese, y las sábanas de entrambas se besaban. En efecto, allí estuvimos seis días, y en todos ellos no se pasó hora que no tuviésemos pendencia diciéndole la necedad que había hecho en haber dejado su casa y su hacienda, aunque fuera a su misma madre.

En esto iba yo y venía por momentos, tanto, que la huéspeda de casa, un día que doña Estefanía dijo que iba a ver en qué término estaba su negocio, quiso saber de mí qué era la causa que me movía a reñir tanto con ella, y qué cosa había hecho que tanto se la afeaba diciéndole que había sido necedad notoria más que amistad perfecta. Contéle todo el cuento, y cuando llegué a decir que me había casado con doña Estefanía, y la dote que trajo, y la simplicidad que había hecho en dejar su casa y hacienda a doña Clementa, aunque fuese con tan sana intención como era alcanzar tan principal marido como don Lope, se comenzó a santiguar y hacerse cruces con tanta prisa y con tanto "¡Jesús, Jesús, de la mala hembra!", que me puso en gran turbación, y al fin me dijo:

–Señor Alférez, no sé si voy contra mi conciencia en descubriros lo que me parece que también la cargaría si lo callase; pero, a Dios y a ventura sea lo que fuere, ¡viva la verdad y muera la mentira! La verdad es que doña Clementa Bueso es la verdadera señora de la casa y de la hacienda de que os hicieron la dote; la mentira es todo cuanto os ha dicho doña Estefanía; que ni ella tiene casa, ni hacienda, ni otro vestido del que trae puesto. Y el haber tenido lugar y espacio para hacer este embuste fue que doña Clementa fue a visitar unos parientes suyos a la ciudad de Plasencia, y de allí fue a tener novenas en Nuestra Señora de Guadalupe, y en este entretanto dejó en su casa a doña Estefanía, que mirase por ella, porque, en efecto, son grandes amigas; aunque, bien mirado, no hay que culpar a la pobre señora, pues ha sabido granjear a una tal persona como la del señor Alférez por marido.

serve as a dowry, and that once the marriage was contracted she didn't care if the deceit was discovered, as she was confident of the extent of Don Lope's love for her.

"And then what's mine will be given back to me, and no one will hold it against her or any other woman who is trying to find an honourable husband, even though it is by trickery."

I replied that this was to carry friendship to a great extreme, and that she should first consider it very carefully, because afterwards it could be that she needed to go to court to get her property back. But she replied with so many arguments, adducing the many ways in which she was indebted to Doña Clementa and had obligations towards her in matters of even greater importance that, very much against my will and better judgement, I had to accede to Doña Estefanía's wishes, with the assurance that the deception would last only eight days during which we would be in the house of another friend of hers. We both finished dressing and then, after going in to take her leave of Doña Clementa Bueso and Don Lope Meléndez de Almendárez, she instructed my servant to take the trunk and to follow her, which I also did without saying good-bye to anybody.

Doña Estefanía stopped at the house of a friend of hers, and before we went in she spent a long time speaking to her, until eventually a maid came out and told my servant and myself to go in. She led us to a narrow room, in which there were two beds so close together that they appeared to be only one, since there was no dividing space between them, and the sheets of both beds touched each other. In fact, we were there for six days, and on all of them not an hour went past without our having an argument and my telling her that it was really stupid to have left her house and belongings, even if it had been to her own mother.

I kept this up so much that one day when Doña Estefanía said that she was going to see how her affairs were going, the lady of the house wanted to know why I quarrelled so much with her, and what had she done for me to criticise her so much and say that what she had done was crass stupidity rather than an act of sincere friendship. I told her the whole story, and when I reached the point where I recounted how I had married Doña Estefanía, and told her about the dowry she had brought with her, and the foolishness with which she had given over her house and property to Doña Clementa, even though it was with the good intention of getting such a suitable husband as Don Lope, she made the sign of the cross and repeated again and again:

"My God, my God, what a wicked woman she is!"

This caused me great anxiety and confusion until at last she said:

"Ensign, I do not know if I am acting against my conscience in telling you what I think but it would also trouble me if I kept silent. Anyway, I'll put my trust in God and fate, so long live truth and let falsehood be damned. The truth is that Doña Clementa is the true owner of the house and property which was given to you as a dowry; everything that Doña Estefanía told you is false, for she neither has a house, nor property, nor any clothes other than those she wears. And the reason why she was able to play this trick was because Doña Clementa went to visit some relatives of hers in Plasencia, and from there she went to pray for nine days at the convent of Our Lady of Guadalupe, during which time she left her house to Doña Estefanía, for her to look after, as in fact they are great friends; at the same time, who can blame the poor woman, for she has been able to get such a fine person as the Ensign for her husband."

Aquí dio fin a su plática y yo di principio a desesperarme, y sin duda lo hiciera si tantico se descuidara el ángel de mi guarda en socorrerme acudiendo a decirme en el corazón que mirase que era cristiano y que el mayor pecado de los hombres era el de la desesperación, por ser pecado de demonios. Esta consideración o buena inspiración me confortó algo; pero no tanto que dejase de tomar mi capa y espada y salir a buscar a doña Estefanía, con prosupuesto de hacer de ella un ejemplar castigo; pero la suerte, que no sabré decir si mis cosas empeoraba o mejoraba, ordenó que en ninguna parte donde pensé hallar a doña Estefanía la hallase. Fuime a San Llorente, encomendéme a Nuestra Señora, sentéme sobre un escaño, y con la pesadumbre me tomó un sueño tan pesado, que no despertara tan presto si no me despertaran.

Fui lleno de pensamientos y congojas a casa de doña Clementa, y halléla con tanto reposo como señora de su casa; no le osé decir nada porque estaba el señor don Lope delante; volví en casa de mi huéspeda, que me dijo haber contado a doña Estefanía como yo sabía toda su maraña y embuste, y que ella le preguntó qué semblante había yo mostrado con tal nueva, y que le había respondido que muy malo, y que, a su parecer, había salido yo con mala intención y peor determinación a buscarla. Díjome, finalmente, que doña Estefanía se había llevado cuanto en el baúl tenía, sin dejarme en él sino un solo vestido de camino.

¡Aquí fue ello! ¡Aquí me tuvo de nuevo Dios de su mano! Fui a ver mi baúl, y halléle abierto y como sepultura que esperaba cuerpo difunto, y a buena razón había de ser el mío, si yo tuviera entendimiento para saber sentir y ponderar tamaña desgracia.

–Bien grande fue –dijo a esta sazón el licenciado Peralta– haberse llevado doña Estefanía tanta cadena y tanto cintillo; que, como suele decirse, todos los duelos..., etc.

–Ninguna pena me dio esa falta –respondió el Alférez–, pues también podré decir: "Pensóse don Simueque que me engañaba con su hija la tuerta, y por el Dío, contrecho soy de un lado."

–No sé a qué propósito pueda vuesa merced decir eso –respondió Peralta.

–El propósito es –respondió el Alférez– de que toda aquella balumba y aparato de cadenas, cintillos y brincos podía valer hasta diez o doce escudos.

–Eso no es posible –replicó el Licenciado–; porque la que el señor Alférez traía al cuello mostraba pesar más de doscientos ducados.

–Así fuera –respondió el Alférez– si la verdad respondiera al parecer; pero como no es todo oro lo que reluce, las cadenas, cintillos, joyas y brincos, con sólo ser de alquimia se contentaron; pero estaban tan bien hechas, que sólo el toque o el fuego podía descubrir su malicia.

–De esa manera –dijo el Licenciado–, entre vuesa merced y la señora Estefanía, pata es la traviesa.

–Y tan pata –respondió el Alférez–, que podemos volver a barajar; pero el daño está, señor Licenciado, en que ella se podrá deshacer de mis cadenas y yo no de la falsía de su término; y, en efecto, mal que me pese, es prenda mía.

–Dad gracias a Dios, señor Campuzano –dijo Peralta–, que fue prenda con pies, y que se os ha ido, y que no estáis obligado a buscarla.

–Así es –respondió el Alférez–; pero, con todo eso, sin que la busque, la hallo siempre en la imaginación, y adondequiera que estoy, tengo afrenta presente.

–No sé qué responderos –dijo Peralta–, si no es traeros a la memoria dos versos de Petrarca, que dicen:

Here she ended her speech and I began to despair, and no doubt I would have done so if my guardian angel had not interceded to help me by reminding me that I was a Christian and that the greatest sin is despair, as it is the sin of devils. This thought or inspiration brought me some comfort, but not enough to stop me fetching my cape and sword and going out in search of Doña Estefanía, with the intention of meting out to her an exemplary punishment. But fate, I don't know whether for better or worse, decreed that I should not be able to find her anywhere. I went to San Llorente, I commended myself to Our Lady, I sat down on a pew, and in my grief I slept so soundly that I would not have woken up so soon if I had not been awakened.

With my mind full of thoughts and anxieties I went to Doña Clementa's house and I found her relaxed and at ease as the lady of her own house. I didn't dare say anything to her as Don Lope was there. I returned to my hostess's house and she told me that she had told Doña Estefanía that I knew all about her tricks and deceits and that she had asked how I had reacted to this news, and that she had replied very badly, and that in her opinion I had gone out in search of her in a bad frame of mind and with even worse intentions. She told me, finally, that Doña Estefanía had carried off everything in the trunk without leaving me a single item of clothing.

What a mess! Here again God came to my aid! I went to see my trunk and I found it open and like a grave awaiting a corpse, which might well have been mine had I been sufficiently clear-minded to understand and reflect on the magnitude of my misfortune.

"It was indeed a great misfortune," said Licentiate Peralta at this point, for Doña Estefanía to have taken so many chains and hatbands for, as they say, nothing consoles as much as etc..."[14]

"That loss didn't cause me any sorrow", replied the Ensign, "for I can also say: `Don Simueque thought he was deceiving me with his squint-eyed daughter, but by God, I'm crooked on one side myself'."[15]

"I don't know quite what point you are making," replied Peralta.

"The point is," replied the Ensign, "that all that display and show of chains, hatbands and baubles could only be worth about ten or twelve *escudos*."

"That's not possible," replied the Licentiate, "because the one you wore around your neck looked to be worth more than two hundred ducats."

"That would be so," replied the Ensign, "if truth corresponded to appearances; but as all that glitters is not gold, the chains, hatbands, jewels and baubles, are in fact only imitation; but they were so well made that only proper examination or fire could reveal the deceit."

"So," said the Licentiate, "between you and the lady Doña Estefanía, it's quits."

"And so much so," replied the Ensign, "that we can shuffle the pack again; but the trouble is, my dear Licentiate, that she can dispose of my chains but I cannot so easily be rid of her treachery; like it or not, I'm stuck with her."

"Give thanks to God, Señor Campuzano," said Peralta, "that she's got feet and gone off and that you're not obliged to look for her."

"That's right," replied the Ensign, "but, the fact is that, without looking for her, she's always in my mind, and wherever I am, I always see my disgrace."

"I don't know what to say to you," replied Peralta, "other than to bring to your mind a couple of verses of Petrarch, which go:

Ché, chi prende diletto di far frode;
Non si de' lamentar s'altri lo 'nganna.

Que responden en nuestro castellano: "Que el que tiene costumbre y gusto de engañar a otro no se debe quejar cuando es engañado."

–Yo no me quejo –respondió el Alférez–, sino lastímome; que el culpado no por conocer su culpa deja de sentir la pena del castigo. Bien veo que quise engañar y fui engañado, porque me hirieron por mis propios filos; pero no puedo tener tan a raya el sentimiento que no me queje de mí mismo. Finalmente, por venir a lo que hace más al caso a mi historia (que este nombre se le puede dar al cuento de mis sucesos), digo que supe que se había llevado a doña Estefanía el primo que dije que se halló a nuestros desposorios, el cual de luengos tiempos atrás era su amigo a todo ruedo. No quise buscarla, por no hallar el mal que me faltaba. Mudé posada y mudé el pelo dentro de pocos días, porque comenzaron a pelárseme las cejas y las pestañas, y poco a poco me dejaron los cabellos, y antes de edad me hice calvo, dándome una enfermedad que llaman *lupicia*, y por otro nombre más claro, *la pelarela*. Halléme verdaderamente hecho pelón, porque ni tenía barbas que peinar ni dineros que gastar. Fue la enfermedad caminando al paso de mi necesidad, y como la pobreza atropella a la honra, y a unos lleva a la horca y a otros al hospital, y a otros les hace entrar por las puertas de sus enemigos con ruegos y sumisiones, que es una de las mayores miserias que puede suceder a un desdichado. Por no gastar en curarme los vestidos que me habían de cubrir y honrar en salud, llegado el tiempo en que se dan los sudores en el Hospital de la Resurrección, me entré en él, donde he tomado cuarenta sudores. Dicen que quedaré sano si me guardo; espada tengo, lo demás, Dios lo remedie.

Ofreciósele de nuevo el Licenciado, admirándose de las cosas que le había contado.

–Pues de poco se maravilla vuesa merced, señor Peralta –dijo el Alférez–; que otros sucesos me quedan por decir que exceden a toda imaginación, pues van fuera de todos los términos de naturaleza: no quiera vuesa merced saber más sino que son de suerte que doy por bien empleadas todas mis desgracias, por haber sido parte de haberme puesto en el hospital donde vi lo que ahora diré, que es lo que ahora ni nunca vuesa merced podrá creer, ni habrá persona en el mundo que lo crea.

Todos estos preámbulos y encarecimientos que el Alférez hacía antes de contar lo que había visto, encendían el deseo de Peralta de manera que, con no menores encarecimientos, le pidió que luego luego le dijese las maravillas que le quedaban por decir.

–Ya vuesa merced habrá visto –dijo el Alférez– dos perros que con dos linternas andan de noche con los hermanos de la Capacha, alumbrándoles cuando piden limosna.

–Sí he visto –respondió Peralta.

–También habrá visto u oído vuesa merced –dijo el Alférez– lo que de ellos se cuenta: que si acaso echan limosna de las ventanas y se cae en el suelo, ellos acuden luego a alumbrar y a buscar lo que se cae, y se paran delante de las ventanas donde saben que tienen costumbre de darles limosna; y con ir allí con tanta mansedumbre que más parecen corderos que perros, en el hospital son unos leones, guardando la casa con grande cuidado y vigilancia.

–Yo he oído decir –dijo Peralta– que todo es así; pero eso no me puede ni debe causar maravilla.

Ché, chi prende diletto di far frode;
Non si de' lamentar s'altri lo'nganna,

which when translated mean: "He who takes pleasure in deceiving others should not complain when he himself is deceived."

"I don't complain," replied the Ensign, "but I feel sorry for myself; the guilty man does not cease to feel the pain of his punishment because he is aware of his guilt. I can see that I wanted to deceive and I was deceived, because I was caught in my own net; but I cannot have my feelings so under control that I do not feel sorry for myself. Finally, to come to the main point of my story,[16] (for I can give this name to the account of what happened to me), I discovered that Doña Estefanía had been taken away by the cousin I told you was at our wedding, who had stuck with her through thick and thin. I had no desire to go looking for her because I did not want any more trouble than I had. I changed my lodgings and I changed my hair within a few days, because my eyebrows and my eyelashes began to thin out, and gradually my hair fell out, so that I became prematurely bald, due to a complaint called *alopetia*, or more commonly, 'hair loss'. I was completely 'fleeced', having neither hair to comb nor money to spend. My illness kept pace with my needs, for poverty destroys honour, and leads some to the gallows and others to the hospital, and makes others go through their enemies' doors begging and asking favours, which is one of the greatest misfortunes which can befall a man who is down on his luck. In order not to have to pay for a cure by selling the clothes which would cover me and ensure my honour when I was healthy again, when the time arrived for them to offer sweat treatment in the Hospital of the Resurrection, I went into it, and was sweated forty times. They say I'll be fine if I look after myself; I have a sword; as for the rest, it's in God's hands."

The Licentiate, amazed at the things he had told him, offered to help him.

"You're surprised at very little, Peralta," said the Ensign, "for I've still got other things to tell which defy all imagination for they go beyond the bounds of nature; suffice it to say that they are of such a kind that I consider all my misfortunes to have been valuable to me in that they brought me to the hospital where I witnessed what I shall now recount to you, which you will not be able to believe now or ever, nor is there anyone else in the world who will believe it."

All these preambles and embellishments which the Ensign used before beginning his account so aroused the interest of Peralta that, with no less embellishment, he asked him to tell him at once of the marvellous things he had yet to tell.

"You will have seen," said the Ensign, "two dogs with lanterns that go around at night with the Capacha[17] friars to light their way when they beg for alms."

"Yes, I've seen them," replied Peralta.

"You will also have seen or heard," said the Ensign, "what is said of them: that if by chance alms are thrown from a window and fall on the ground, they run and light up the place to find what has fallen, and they stop under the windows where they know that alms are usually given; and that although in these circumstances they are so gentle that they are more like lambs than dogs, in the hospital they are more like lions, guarding the house with great care and vigilance."

"I have heard," said Peralta, "that this is so, but that is no cause for amazement."

–Pues lo que ahora diré de ellos es razón que la cause, y que sin hacerse cruces, ni alegar imposibles ni dificultades, vuesa merced se acomode a creerlo; y es que yo oí y casi vi con mis ojos a estos dos perros, que el uno se llama Cipión y el otro Berganza, estar una noche, que fue la penúltima que acabé de sudar, echados detrás de mi cama en unas esteras viejas, y a la mitad de aquella noche, estando a oscuras y desvelado, pensando en mis pasados sucesos y presentes desgracias, oí hablar allí junto, y estuve con atento oído escuchando, por ver si podía venir en conocimiento de los que hablaban y de lo que hablaban, y a poco rato vine a conocer, por lo que hablaban, los que hablaban, y eran los dos perros Cipión y Berganza.

Apenas acabó de decir esto Campuzano, cuando, levantándose el Licenciado, dijo:

–Vuesa merced quede mucho en buena hora, señor Campuzano; que hasta aquí estaba en duda si creería o no lo que de su casamiento me había contado, y esto que ahora me cuenta de que oyó hablar los perros me ha hecho declarar por la parte de no creerle ninguna cosa. Por amor de Dios, señor Alférez, que no cuente estos disparates a persona alguna, si ya no fuere a quien sea tan su amigo como yo.

–No me tenga vuesa merced por tan ignorante –replicó Campuzano– que no entienda que si no es por milagro no pueden hablar los animales; que bien sé que si los tordos, picazas y papagayos hablan, no son sino las palabras que aprenden y toman de memoria, y por tener la lengua estos animales cómoda para poder pronunciarlas; mas no por esto pueden hablar y responder con discurso concertado, como estos perros hablaron; y así, muchas veces, después que los oí, yo mismo no he querido dar crédito a mí mismo, y he querido tener por cosa soñada lo que realmente estando despierto, con todos mis cinco sentidos, tales cuales nuestro Señor fue servido de dármelos, oí, escuché, noté y, finalmente, escribí, sin faltar palabra por su concierto; de donde se puede tomar indicio bastante que mueva y persuada a creer esta verdad que digo. Las cosas de que trataron fueron grandes y diferentes, y más para ser tratadas por varones sabios que para ser dichas por bocas de perros; así que, pues yo no las pude inventar de mío, a mi pesar y contra mi opinión vengo a creer que no soñaba y que los perros hablaban.

–¡Cuerpo de mí! –replicó el Licenciado–. ¡Si se nos ha vuelto el tiempo de Maricastaña, cuando hablaban las calabazas, o el de Isopo, cuando departía el gallo con la zorra y unos animales con otros!

–Uno de ellos sería yo, y el mayor –replicó el Alférez–, si creyese que ese tiempo ha vuelto, y aun también lo sería si dejase de creer lo que oí, y lo que vi, y lo que me atreveré a jurar con juramento que obligue, y aun fuerce, a que lo crea la misma incredulidad. Pero puesto caso que me haya engañado, y que mi verdad sea sueño, y el porfiarla disparate, ¿no se holgará vuesa merced, señor Peralta, de ver escritas en un coloquio las cosas que estos perros, o sean quien fueren, hablaron?

–Como vuesa merced –replicó el Licenciado– no se canse en persuadirme que oyó hablar a los perros, de muy buena gana oiré ese coloquio, que por ser escrito y notado del bueno ingenio del señor Alférez, ya le juzgo por bueno.

–Pues hay en esto otra cosa –dijo el Alférez–: que, como yo estaba tan atento y tenía delicado el juicio, delicada, sutil y desocupada la memoria (merced a las muchas pasas y almendras que había comido), todo lo tomé de coro, y casi por las mismas palabras que había oído lo escribí otro día, sin buscar colores retóricas para adornarlo, ni qué añadir

"But what I am now going to tell you about them certainly is, and without making the sign of the cross, nor alleging that it is unlikely or impossible, prepare yourself to believe it; the fact is that I heard and virtually saw with my own eyes these two dogs, one of which is called Cipión[18] and the other Berganza, one night, the one before my last sweat treatment, lying behind my bed on some old mats, and in the middle of the night, when I was lying awake in the dark, thinking about my past life and my present misfortune, I heard voices nearby. I listened carefully to see if I could make out who was speaking and what they were saying, and I soon came to realise from what they were saying that the speakers were the two dogs Cipión and Berganza."

No sooner had Campuzano said this, than the Licentiate stood up and said:

"You may say what you like, Señor Campuzano; up to now I was in doubt as to whether to believe or not to believe all you told me about your wedding, but what you have now told me about hearing dogs talk has convinced me that I shouldn't believe anything you say. For the love of God, Ensign, don't tell this nonsense to anyone else, unless it's to someone who is as good a friend of yours as I am."

"Don't think I'm so ignorant," replied Campuzano, "that I do not understand that only by a miracle can animals speak; for I know that if thrushes, magpies and parrots talk, it's only with words they pick up and learn by heart, and because they have a tongue which is able to pronounce them; but that is not the same as speaking and replying in coherent speech, such as those dogs used. And so, many times after I heard them, I myself was unwilling to believe it, and I wanted to assume to be a dream that which in reality and while awake, with all my five senses, which the Lord saw fit to give me, I heard, listened to, noted and finally wrote down without missing a word; all of which you can take as proof which should incline and persuade you to believe the truth of what I am telling you. The things they talked about were many and varied, and more appropriate to the discourse of wise men than of dogs. And so, since I could not invent them myself, despite everything and against my better judgement, I have come to the conclusion that I was not dreaming and that the dogs were speaking."

"My goodness!" replied the Licentiate. "We have gone back to the time of Maricastaña,[19] when pumpkins talked, or of Aesop when the cock conversed with the fox and all the animals talked to one another."

"I would be one such animal, and the greatest of all," replied the Ensign, "if I believed that those times had returned, but I would also be one if I stopped believing what I heard, what I saw, and what I will dare to swear on an oath which will oblige and force incredulity itself to believe it. But assuming I was mistaken, and that my truth was a dream, and to trust it were madness, would you not take pleasure, Señor Peralta, in seeing written in a colloquy the things that those dogs, or whatever they were, said?"

"As long as you do not persist in persuading me that you heard the dogs speak," replied the Licentiate, "I shall listen to the colloquy very willingly, for since it was written and noted down by the talent of the Ensign himself, I already consider it to be good."

"Well, there's something else," said the Ensign. "Since I was so alert and my mind was sharp, and my memory clear, lucid, and free of other concerns (thanks to the many raisins and almonds I had eaten), I learnt it all by heart and I wrote it all down the next day using almost the same words, without any rhetorical embellishments and without adding or taking away anything to make it more pleasing. The conversation did not take

ni quitar para hacerle gustoso. No fue una noche sola la plática, que fueron dos consecutivamente, aunque yo no tengo escrita más de una, que es la vida de Berganza, y la del compañero Cipión pienso escribir (que fue la que se contó la noche segunda) cuando viere, o que ésta se crea, o, a lo menos, no se desprecie. El coloquio traigo en el seno; púselo en forma de coloquio por ahorrar de *dijo Cipión, respondió Berganza*, que suele alargar la escritura.

Y en diciendo esto, sacó del pecho un cartapacio y le puso en las manos del Licenciado, el cual le tomó riéndose y como haciendo burla de todo lo que había oído y de lo que pensaba leer.

–Yo me recuesto –dijo el Alférez– en esta silla en tanto que vuesa merced lee, si quiere, esos sueños o disparates, que no tienen otra cosa de bueno si no es el poderlos dejar cuando enfaden.

–Haga vuesa merced su gusto –dijo Peralta–, que yo con brevedad me despediré de esta lectura.

Recostóse el Alférez, abrió el Licenciado el cartapacio, y en el principio vio que estaba puesto este título:

place all on one night, but on two consecutive nights, although I have only written one, which is the life of Berganza. I intend to write the life-story of his companion Cipión (which was recounted the second night) when I have seen that this first one is believed, or at least not scorned. I am carrying the colloquy on my person; I wrote it in the form of a dialogue to avoid having to write "Cipión said", "Berganza replied", which tends to lengthen the account."

And saying this, he took a notebook out of his shirt and put it into the hands of the Licentiate, who took it and laughed as if he were making fun of all that he had heard and expected to read.

"I shall lie back in this chair," said the Ensign, "while you read, if you please, these dreams and absurdities, whose only merit is that they can be put down when one gets fed up with them."

"You make yourself comfortable," said Peralta, "for it shall not take me long to read this through."

The Ensign lay back, the Licentiate opened the notebook, and at the beginning he saw that it bore this title:

El coloquio de los perros

Novela y coloquio que pasó entre
Cipión y Berganza,
Perros del Hospital de la Resurrección,
Que está en la ciudad de Valladolid,
Fuera de la Puerta del Campo,
A quien comúnmente llaman los perros
de Mahudes

CIPIÓN. –Berganza amigo, dejemos esta noche el Hospital en guarda de la confianza y retirémonos a esta soledad y entre estas esteras, donde podremos gozar sin ser sentidos de esta no vista merced que el cielo en un mismo punto a los dos nos ha hecho.

BERGANZA. –Cipión hermano, óigote hablar y sé que te hablo, y no puedo creerlo, por parecerme que el hablar nosotros pasa de los términos de naturaleza.

CIPIÓN. –Así es la verdad, Berganza, y viene a ser mayor este milagro en que no solamente hablamos, sino en que hablamos con discurso, como si fuéramos capaces de razón, estando tan sin ella que la diferencia que hay del animal bruto al hombre es ser el hombre animal racional, y el bruto, irracional.

BERGANZA. –Todo lo que dices, Cipión, entiendo, y el decirlo tú y entenderlo yo me causa nueva admiración y nueva maravilla. Bien es verdad que en el discurso de mi vida diversas y muchas veces he oído hablar grandes prerrogativas nuestras; tanto, que parece que algunos han querido sentir que tenemos un natural distinto, tan vivo y tan agudo en muchas cosas, que da indicios y señales de faltar poco para mostrar que tenemos un no sé qué de entendimiento capaz de discurso.

CIPIÓN. –Lo que yo he oído alabar y encarecer es nuestra mucha memoria, el agradecimiento y gran fidelidad nuestra; tanto, que nos suelen pintar por símbolo de la amistad; y así, habrás visto (si has mirado en ello) que en las sepulturas de alabastro, donde suelen estar las figuras de los que allí están enterrados, cuando son marido y mujer, ponen entre los dos, a los pies, una figura de perro, en señal que se guardaron en la vida amistad y fidelidad inviolable.

BERGANZA. –Bien sé que ha habido perros tan agradecidos que se han arrojado con los cuerpos difuntos de sus amos en la misma sepultura. Otros han estado sobre las sepulturas donde estaban enterrados sus señores, sin apartarse de ellas, sin comer, hasta que se les acababa la vida. Sé también que, después del elefante, el perro tiene el primer lugar de parecer que tiene entendimiento; luego, el caballo, y el último, la simia.

CIPIÓN. –Así es; pero bien confesarás que ni has visto ni oído decir jamás que haya hablado ningún elefante, perro, caballo o mona; por donde me doy a entender que este nuestro hablar tan de improviso cae debajo del número de aquellas cosas que llaman

The Dialogue of the Dogs

Novel and Dialogue which took place between
Cipión and Berganza
Dogs of the Hospital of the Resurrection
which is in the city of Valladolid
outside the Puerta del Campo
and who are commonly called the dogs
of Mahudes [1]

CIPIÓN: Berganza, my friend, tonight let us leave the hospital to be guarded by trust and let us repair to peace and quiet between these mats where we can enjoy undisturbed this unique gift which heaven has bestowed upon both of us at one and the same time.

BERGANZA: Cipión, my brother, I hear you speak and I know that I am speaking to you and I cannot believe it, for it seems to me that for us to speak is to proceed beyond the bounds of nature.

CIPIÓN: That's true, Berganza, and the miracle is even greater in that we not only speak but we speak using proper discourse, as if we were endowed with the power of reason, and yet we are so lacking in it that the difference between man and animal is that man is a rational being and the animal an irrational creature.

BERGANZA: Everything that you say, Cipión, I understand, and the fact that you say it and I understand it causes me amazement and wonder. It is true that on many occasions in the course of my life I have heard people speak of our great qualities; so much so that it appears that some have been inclined to think that we have a natural instinct, so keen and sharp in many respects that there are indications and signs that we are not far from having an understanding which is capable of rational discourse.

CIPIÓN: What I have heard praised and extolled is our exceptional memory, our gratitude and our fidelity; so much so that we are often portrayed as a symbol of friendship; and so you will have seen (if you have troubled to notice) that on alabaster tombs, where the effigies of those who are buried within are represented, when they are man and wife, they place between the two of them the figure of a dog, as a sign that in life their friendship and fidelity to one another was inviolate.

BERGANZA: I know for a fact that there have been dogs so loyal that they have thrown themselves into the very tomb with the dead bodies of their masters. Others have remained on the tombs where their masters were buried, not leaving them and not eating, until they themselves passed away. I also know that, after the elephant, it appears that the dog is next in understanding; then the horse and finally the ape.

CIPIÓN: That is so; but you must admit that you have never seen or heard it said that an elephant has spoken, or a dog, or a horse, or a monkey; from which I deduce that our speaking so unexpectedly falls into the category of what are called portents which

portentos, las cuales, cuando se muestran y parecen, tiene averiguado la experiencia que alguna calamidad grande amenaza a las gentes.

BERGANZA. –De esa manera no haré yo mucho en tener por señal portentosa lo que oí decir los días pasados a un estudiante, pasando por Alcalá de Henares.

CIPIÓN. –¿Qué le oíste decir?

BERGANZA. –Que de cinco mil estudiantes que cursaban aquel año en la Universidad, los dos mil oían Medicina.

CIPIÓN. –Pues, ¿qué vienes a inferir de eso?

BERGANZA. –Infiero, o que estos dos mil médicos han de tener enfermos que curar (que sería harta plaga y mala ventura), o ellos se han de morir de hambre.

CIPIÓN. –Pero sea lo que fuere, nosotros hablamos, sea portento o no; que lo que el cielo tiene ordenado que suceda, no hay diligencia ni sabiduría humana que lo pueda prevenir; y así, no hay para qué ponernos a disputar nosotros cómo o por qué hablamos; mejor será que este buen día, o buena noche, la metamos en nuestra casa, y pues la tenemos tan buena en estas esteras y no sabemos cuánto durará esta nuestra ventura, sepamos aprovecharnos de ella y hablemos toda esta noche, sin dar lugar al sueño que nos impida este gusto, de mí por largos tiempos deseado.

BERGANZA. –Y aun de mí, que desde que tuve fuerzas para roer un hueso tuve deseo de hablar, para decir cosas que depositaba en la memoria, y allí, de antiguas y muchas, o se enmohecían o se me olvidaban. Empero ahora, que tan sin pensarlo me veo enriquecido de este divino don del habla, pienso gozarle y aprovecharme de él lo más que pudiere, dándome prisa a decir todo aquello que se me acordare, aunque sea atropellada y confusamente, porque no sé cuándo me volverán a pedir este bien, que por prestado tengo.

CIPIÓN. –Sea ésta la manera, Berganza amigo: que esta noche me cuentes tu vida y los trances por donde has venido al punto en que ahora te hallas, y si mañana en la noche estuviéremos con habla, yo te contaré la mía; porque mejor será gastar el tiempo en contar las propias que en procurar saber las ajenas vidas.

BERGANZA. –Siempre, Cipión, te he tenido por discreto y por amigo, y ahora más que nunca, pues como amigo quieres decir tus sucesos y saber los míos, y como discreto has repartido el tiempo donde podamos manifestarlos. Pero advierte primero si nos oye alguno.

CIPIÓN. –Ninguno, a lo que creo, puesto que aquí cerca está un soldado tomando sudores; pero en esta sazón más estará para dormir que para ponerse a escuchar a nadie.

BERGANZA. –Pues si puedo hablar con ese seguro, escucha; y si te cansare lo que te fuere diciendo, o me reprende o manda que calle.

CIPIÓN. –Habla hasta que amanezca, o hasta que seamos sentidos; que yo te escucharé de muy buena gana, sin impedirte sino cuando viere ser necesario.

BERGANZA. –Paréceme que la primera vez que vi el sol fue en Sevilla, y en su Matadero, que está fuera de la Puerta de la Carne; por donde imaginara (si no fuera por lo que después te diré) que mis padres debieron de ser alanos de aquellos que crían los ministros de aquella confusión, a quien llaman jiferos. El primero que conocí por amo fue uno llamado Nicolás el Romo, mozo robusto, doblado y colérico, como lo son todos aquellos que ejercitan la jifería. Este tal Nicolás me enseñaba a mí y a otros cachorros a

manifest themselves or appear, as is attested through experience, when some great calamity is about to strike.

BERGANZA: If that is so then what I heard a student say a few days ago, as I passed through Alcalá de Henares,[2] must be a portentous sign.

CIPIÓN: What did you hear him say?

BERGANZA: That of the five thousand students in the university that year, two thousand were studying medicine.

CIPIÓN: And what do you deduce from that?

BERGANZA: I deduce either that these two thousand doctors must have patients to cure (which would be a mighty plague and great misfortune), or else that they will die of hunger.[3]

CIPIÓN: But the fact is that we are speaking, whether it's a portent or not; whatever heaven has ordained should happen, no precaution or human wisdom can prevent it. So there is no reason for us to discuss how and why we speak; it is better that we make the most of this good day, or good night; since it's so good here on our mats and we don't know how long our good fortune will last, let us take advantage of it and talk all night, and not give in to sleep which will rob us of this pleasure, which I have wanted for so long.

BERGANZA: I too, ever since I was strong enough to gnaw at a bone, had the desire to speak in order to say the many things I had deposited in my memory where so many lay for so long that they grew mouldy and were forgotten. But now that so unexpectedly I find myself enriched with this divine gift of speech, I intend to enjoy it and take advantage of it to the full, and hasten to say all I can remember, even if it's all muddled and confused, for I do not know when I shall be asked to give back this gift, which is only on loan.

CIPIÓN: Let's make an agreement, Berganza my friend, that tonight you will tell me the story of your life and the events that led you to the point where you are now, and if tomorrow night we still have speech, I will tell you mine; for it's better to spend the time telling one's own life than trying to find out about other people's.

BERGANZA: Cipión, I have always regarded you as a friend possessed of discretion, and now more than ever, since as a friend you want to know of my life and to tell me about your own, and in your discretion you have divided the time in order to enable us to do so. But first make sure that no one is listening to us.

CIPIÓN: No one is, as far as I can see, for nearby is a soldier undergoing sweat treatment, but at this hour he will be more in the mood to sleep than to listen to anyone.

BERGANZA: Well, if I can speak with that assurance, listen; and if what I am telling you wearies you, reproach me and tell me to be silent.

CIPIÓN: Speak until dawn, or until someone hears us; I will listen to you very willingly, only stopping you when it becomes necessary.

BERGANZA: I think that I first saw the light of day in Seville, and in its abattoir, outside the Puerta de la Carne,[4] from which I assume (were it not for what I will tell you later) that my parents must have been mastiffs of the sort reared by those who preside over this awful butchery, and are called knifemen.[5] My first master was a certain Nicolás el Romo, a strong lad, stocky and bad-tempered, like all of those whose trade is slaughtering animals. This Nicolás taught me and other pups, together with

que, en compañía de alanos viejos, arremetiésemos a los toros y les hiciésemos presa de las orejas. Con mucha facilidad salí un águila en esto.

CIPIÓN. –No me maravillo, Berganza; que como el hacer mal viene de natural cosecha, fácilmente se aprende el hacerle.

BERGANZA. –¿Qué te diría, Cipión hermano, de lo que vi en aquel Matadero y de las cosas exorbitantes que en él pasan? Primero, has de presuponer que todos cuantos en él trabajan, desde el menor hasta el mayor, es gente ancha de conciencia, desalmada, sin temer al Rey ni a su justicia; los más, amancebados; son aves de rapiña carniceras; mantiénense ellos y sus amigas de lo que hurtan. Todas las mañanas que son días de carne, antes que amanezca están en el Matadero gran cantidad de mujercillas y muchachos, todos con talegas que, viniendo vacías, vuelven llenas de pedazos de carne, y las criadas, con criadillas y lomos medio enteros. No hay res alguna que se mate de quien no lleve esta gente diezmos y primicias de lo más sabroso y bien parado. Y como en Sevilla no hay obligado de la carne, cada uno puede traer la que quisiere, y la que primero se mata, o es la mejor, o la de más baja postura, y con este concierto hay siempre mucha abundancia. Los dueños se encomiendan a esta buena gente que he dicho, no para que no les hurten (que esto es imposible), sino para que se moderen en las tajadas y socaliñas que hacen en las reses muertas, que las escamondan y podan como si fuesen sauces o parras. Pero ninguna cosa me admiraba más ni me parecía peor que el ver que estos jiferos con la misma facilidad matan a un hombre que a una vaca; por quítame allá esa paja, a dos por tres, meten un cuchillo de cachas amarillas por la barriga de una persona, como si acogotasen un toro. Por maravilla se pasa día sin pendencias y sin heridas, y a veces sin muertes; todos se pican de valientes, y aun tienen sus puntas de rufianes; no hay ninguno que no tenga su ángel de guarda en la plaza de San Francisco, granjeado con lomos y lenguas de vaca. Finalmente, oí decir a un hombre discreto que tres cosas tenía el Rey por ganar en Sevilla: la calle de la Caza, la Costanilla y el Matadero.

CIPIÓN. –Si en contar las condiciones de los amos que has tenido y las faltas de sus oficios te has de estar, amigo Berganza, tanto como esta vez, menester será pedir al cielo nos conceda el habla siquiera por un año, y aun temo que, al paso que llevas, no llegarás a la mitad de tu historia. Y quiérote advertir de una cosa, de la cual verás la experiencia cuando te cuente los sucesos de mi vida; y es que los cuentos unos encierran y tienen la gracia en ellos mismos; otros, en el modo de contarlos; quiero decir que algunos hay que aunque se cuenten sin preámbulos y ornamentos de palabras, dan contento; otros hay que es menester vestirlos de palabras, y con demostraciones del rostro y de las manos y con mudar la voz se hacen algo de nonada, y de flojos y desmayados se vuelven agudos y gustosos; y no se te olvide este advertimiento, para aprovecharte de él en lo que te queda por decir.

BERGANZA. –Yo lo haré así, si pudiere y si me da lugar la grande tentación que tengo de hablar; aunque me parece que con grandísima dificultad me podrá ir a la mano.

CIPIÓN. –Vete a la lengua, que en ella consisten los mayores daños de la humana vida.

BERGANZA. –Digo, pues, que mi amo me enseñó a llevar una espuerta en la boca y a defenderla a quien quitármela quisiese. Enseñóme también la casa de su amiga, y con

older mastiffs, to charge at the bulls and hold them by the ears. It didn't take me long to become a master at this art.

CIPIÓN: That doesn't surprise me, Berganza; for doing wrong comes naturally and is thus easily learned.

BERGANZA: What shall I tell you, Cipión my brother, about what I saw in that slaughterhouse and of the extraordinary things that go on in it? First, you have to realise that all those who work in it, from the lowest to the highest, are people with little conscience, without mercy, with no fear of the King nor of his justice; most of them have mistresses; they are like devouring birds of prey, keeping themselves and their mistresses with what they steal. Before dawn, on those mornings when meat arrives, the slaughter-house is full of young girls and boys, all with bags which, although empty when they arrive, end up full of chunks of meat, and the maids go off with sweetbreads and almost complete shoulders of meat. No animal is killed without these people carrying off their tithes and the best and tastiest cuts, and as in Seville there is no official supplier of meat, everyone can bring what he likes, and the first animal killed is either the best or the cheapest, and with this arrangement there is always plenty. The owners entrust themselves to these fine people, not so that they won't steal from them (it would be impossible to avoid that), but so that they do not go too far in the cuts and slices they take from the dead animals, which they clean and prune as if they were willows or creeping-vines. But nothing shocked me more than to see that these knifemen could kill a man with the same ease as they kill a cow; for hardly any reason, and quick as a flash, they put a bone-handled knife into a man's stomach as if they were killing a bull. Rarely does a day pass without a fight and somebody being wounded, and sometimes being killed; they all fancy themselves as hard men, and boast of being ruffians. There isn't one of them without a guardian angel in the Plaza de San Francisco,[6] bought with shoulders of meat and ox tongues. Finally, I heard a wise man say that the King still has three things to get control of in Seville: the Calle de la Caza,[7] the Costanilla[8] and the slaughter-house.

CIPIÓN: Berganza, my friend, if you are going to take as long telling me about the circumstances of the masters you have had and the defects of their occupations as you have done this time, it will be necessary to ask heaven to give us the power of speech for a year, and even then I fear that, given the pace at which you are going, you will not get halfway through your story. And I want to point something out to you, and you will see the truth of it when I recount the events of my life, and it is that some stories embody and contain their pleasure within themselves, and others in the manner of their narration; what I mean is that there are some which, even if they are told without preambles and polished language, give pleasure. There are others which need to be dressed up in fine words, and accompanied by facial expressions and gestures of the hands and with changes in the tone of voice so that something is made out of very little, and from being weak and insipid they become witty and entertaining; don't forget this and bear it in mind for the remainder of what you have to say.

BERGANZA: So I will, if I am able and the great urge I have to speak allows me; but I fear I will have great difficulty in controlling myself.

CIPIÓN: Control your tongue, which is the greatest source of human misfortune.

BERGANZA: I will tell you then that my master showed me how to carry a basket in my mouth and to defend it from anyone who wanted to take it from me. He also showed

esto se excusó la venida de su criada al Matadero, porque yo le llevaba las madrugadas lo que él había hurtado las noches. Y un día que, entre dos luces, iba yo diligente a llevarle la porción, oí que me llamaban por mi nombre desde una ventana; alcé los ojos y vi una moza hermosa en extremo; detúveme un poco, y ella bajó a la puerta de la calle, y me tornó a llamar. Lleguéme a ella, como si fuera a ver lo que me quería, que no fue otra cosa que quitarme lo que llevaba en la cesta y ponerme en su lugar un chapín viejo. Entonces dije entre mí: "La carne se ha ido a la carne." Díjome la moza en habiéndome quitado la carne: "Andad Gavilán, o como os llamáis, y decid a Nicolás el Romo, vuestro amo, que no se fíe de animales, y que del lobo, un pelo, y ése, de la espuerta." Bien pudiera yo volver a quitar lo que me quitó; pero no quise, por no poner mi boca jifera y sucia en aquellas manos limpias y blancas.

CIPIÓN. –Hiciste muy bien, por ser prerrogativa de la hermosura que siempre se la tenga respeto.

BERGANZA. –Así lo hice yo; y así, me volví a mi amo sin la porción y con el chapín. Parecióle que volví presto, vio el chapín, imaginó la burla, sacó uno de cachas y tiróme una puñalada que, a no desviarme, nunca tú oyeras ahora este cuento, ni aun otros muchos que pienso contarte. Puse pies en polvorosa, y tomando el camino en las manos y en los pies, por detrás de San Bernardo, me fui por aquellos campos de Dios adonde la fortuna quisiese llevarme. Aquella noche dormí al cielo abierto, y otro día me deparó la suerte un hato o rebaño de ovejas y carneros. Así como le vi, creí que había hallado en él el centro de mi reposo, pareciéndome propio y natural oficio de los perros guardar ganado, que es obra donde se encierra una virtud grande, como es amparar y defender de los poderosos y soberbios los humildes y los que poco pueden. Apenas me hubo visto uno de los tres pastores que el ganado guardaban, cuando diciendo: "¡To, to!" me llamó y yo, que otra cosa no deseaba, me llegué a él bajando la cabeza y meneando la cola. Trájome la mano por el lomo, abrióme la boca, escupióme en ella, miróme las presas, conoció mi edad, y dijo a otros pastores que yo tenía todas las señales de ser perro de casta. Llegó a este instante el señor del ganado sobre una yegua rucia a la jineta, con lanza y adarga, que más parecía atajador de la costa que señor de ganado. Preguntó al pastor "¿Qué perro es éste, que tiene señales de ser bueno?" "Bien lo puede vuesa merced creer –respondió el pastor–, que yo le he cotejado bien y no hay señal en él que no muestre y prometa que ha de ser un gran perro. Ahora se llegó aquí, y no sé cúyo sea, porque sé que no es de los rebaños de la redonda." "Pues así es – respondió el señor–, ponle luego el collar de *Leoncillo*, el perro que se murió, y denle la ración que a los demás, y acaríciale, porque tome cariño al hato y se quede en él." En diciendo esto se fue, y el pastor me puso luego al cuello unas carlancas llenas de puntas de acero, habiéndome dado primero en un dornajo gran cantidad de sopas en leche. Y asimismo me puso nombre, y me llamó Barcino. Vime harto y contento con el segundo amo y con el nuevo oficio; mostréme solícito y diligente en la guarda del rebaño, sin apartarme de él sino las siestas, que me iba a pasarlas, o ya a la sombra de algún árbol, o de algún ribazo o peña, o a la de alguna mata, a la margen de algún arroyo de los muchos que por allí corrían. Y estas horas de mi sosiego no las pasaba ociosas, porque en ellas ocupaba la memoria en acordarme de muchas cosas, especialmente en la vida

me his mistress's house, and thereby avoided his maid coming to the slaughterhouse, for I brought to her in the morning what he had stolen at night. And once when, at daybreak, I was dutifully delivering her share, I heard my name being called from a window; I looked up and saw an extremely beautiful girl; I slowed down a little, and she came down to the front door and called me again. I went up to her to see what she wanted, which was in fact to take what I had in the basket and put an old shoe in its place. Then I said to myself: "Flesh to flesh". The girl said to me on taking away the meat:

"Off you go, Gavilán, or whatever your name is, and tell your master, Nicolás el Romo, not to trust animals, and that one must take whatever one can get from a skinflint."

I could easily have taken back what she took from me, but I didn't want to, so as not to put my bloody and dirty mouth in those clean, white hands.

CIPIÓN: You did well, since it is the prerogative of beauty always to be respected.

BERGANZA: That's what I did, and so I returned to my master without the rations and with the shoe. He thought I had returned quickly, he saw the shoe, guessed what had happened, took out a knife and took a lunge at me and, had I not jumped to avoid it, you would not now be hearing this tale, nor the many others I intend to tell you.

I headed out to the street and taking to my heels as fast as I could behind San Bernardo I set off to wherever God and luck decided to take me. That night I slept in the open air, and the following day I had the good fortune to stumble across a herd or flock of sheep and lambs. As soon as I saw it, I thought that I had found my ideal abode, thinking it was the right and natural occupation of dogs to look after flocks, which is a work of great virtue involving the protection and defence of the poor and the weak from the powerful and mighty. As soon as one of the three shepherds who were tending the flock saw me, he called me saying "Oy! Oy!" and I, wanting nothing better, went up to him with my head down and my tail wagging. He ran his hand over my back, opened my mouth and spat in it,[9] looked at my teeth, assessed my age, and said to the other shepherds that I had all the signs of being a thoroughbred dog. At this moment, the owner of the herd rode up African style[10] on a grey mare, carrying a lance and shield, looking more like a coastguard than a sheepfarmer. He asked the shepherd:

"Whose dog is this? It has all the signs of being a good one."

"You can well believe it," replied the shepherd, "I have examined him closely and there is nothing to suggest that he will not turn out be a great dog. He's just turned up here and I don't know whose he is, but I do know that he's not from any flock around here."

"Well then," replied the owner, "put Leoncillo's collar on him, the dog that died, and give him the same food as the others, and stroke him so that he takes to the flock and stays with it."

On saying this, he went off, and the shepherd put a strong collar, with steel studs, around my neck, but not before giving me a bowlful of bread and milk. And he gave me the name of Barcino. I was delighted with my second master and with the new job; I showed myself to be attentive and careful in guarding the flock, never leaving it except for my siesta, which I took either in the shade of a tree or of some bank or rock, or of some bush, beside one of the many streams which flowed through that area. And I did not spend those hours of rest in idleness for I used them to commit many things to

que había tenido en el Matadero, y en la que tenía mi amo y todos los como él, que están sujetos a cumplir los gustos impertinentes de sus amigas. ¡Oh, qué cosas te pudiera decir ahora de las que aprendí en la escuela de aquella jifera dama de mi amo. Pero habrélas de callar, por que no me tengas por largo y por murmurador.

CIPIÓN. –Por haber oído decir que un gran poeta de los antiguos que era difícil cosa el no escribir sátiras, consentiré que murmures un poco de luz y no de sangre; quiero decir que señales y no hieras ni des mate a ninguno en cosa señalada; que no es buena la murmuración, aunque haga reír a muchos, si mata a uno; y si puedes agradar sin ella, te tendré por muy discreto.

BERGANZA. –Yo tomaré tu consejo, y esperaré con gran deseo que llegue el tiempo en que me cuentes tus sucesos; que de quien tan bien sabe conocer y enmendar los defectos que tengo en contar los míos, bien se puede esperar que contará los suyos de manera que enseñen y deleiten a un mismo punto. Pero, anudando el roto hilo de mi cuento, digo que en aquel silencio y soledad de mis siestas, entre otras cosas, consideraba que no debía de ser verdad lo que había oído contar de la vida de los pastores; a lo menos, de aquellos que la dama de mi amo leía en unos libros cuando yo iba a su casa, que todos trataban de pastores y pastoras, diciendo que se les pasaba toda la vida cantando y tañendo con gaitas, zampoñas, rabeles y chirumbelas, y con otros instrumentos extraordinarios. Deteníame a oírla leer, y leía cómo el pastor de Anfriso cantaba extremada y divinamente, alabando a la sin par Belisarda, sin haber en todos los montes de Arcadia árbol en cuyo tronco no se hubiese sentado a cantar desde que salía el sol en los brazos de la Aurora hasta que se ponía en los de Tetis; y aun después de haber tendido la negra noche por la faz de la tierra sus negras y oscuras alas, él no cesaba de sus bien cantadas y mejor lloradas quejas. No se le quedaba entre renglones el pastor Elicio, más enamorado que atrevido, de quien decía que, sin atender a sus amores ni a su ganado, se entraba en los cuidados ajenos. Decía también que el gran pastor de Fílida, único pintor de un retrato, había sido más confiado que dichoso. De los desmayos de Sireno y arrepentimiento de Diana decía que daba gracias a Dios y a la sabia Felicia, que con su agua encantada deshizo aquella máquina de enredos y aclaró aquel laberinto de dificultades. Acordábame de otros muchos libros que de este jaez la había oído leer; pero no eran dignos de traerlos a la memoria.

CIPIÓN. –Aprovechándote vas, Berganza, de mi aviso; murmura, pica y pasa, y sea tu intención limpia, aunque la lengua no lo parezca.

BERGANZA. –En estas materias nunca tropieza la lengua si no cae primero la intención, pero si acaso por descuido o por malicia murmurare, responderé a quien me reprendiere lo que respondió Mauleón, poeta tonto y académico de burla de la Academia de los Imitadores, a uno que le preguntó que qué quería decir *Deum de Deo*; y respondió que *dé donde diere*.

CIPIÓN. –Esa fue una respuesta de un simple; pero tú, si eres discreto o lo quieres ser, nunca has de decir cosa de que debas dar disculpa. Di adelante.

BERGANZA. –Digo que todos los pensamientos que he dicho, y muchos más, me causaron ver los diferentes tratos y ejercicios que mis pastores y todos los demás de aquella marina tenían de aquellos que había oído leer que tenían los pastores de los libros; porque si los míos cantaban, no eran canciones acordadas y bien compuestas,

memory, especially the life I had in the slaughterhouse and the life my master and all those like him had, having to satisfy the whims of their mistresses. Oh, how many things I could tell you now which I learned in the school of my master's lady at the slaughterhouse! But I will have to keep quiet about them so that you do not consider me long-winded and a gossip.

CIPIÓN: As I've heard that a great poet in ancient times said it was difficult not to write satire,[11] I will allow you to gossip a little, but to enlighten and not to harm;[12] by which I mean that you can point things out but not wound or kill anyone in what you point out. Although it makes many people laugh, gossip is not good if it kills; and if you can please without it, I shall consider you very discreet.

BERGANZA: I shall take your advice, and I shall wait eagerly for the time when you will tell me your story, for one can expect that someone who can recognise and correct the deficiencies I show in telling mine will tell his own in a way that will instruct and delight at the same time. But, picking up the broken thread of my own account, I will say that in the silence and solitude of my siestas, among other things, I reckoned that what I had heard about the life of shepherds could not be true; at least, what I heard about the ones that my master's lady read about in books[13] when I went to her house, that were all about shepherds and shepherdesses, saying that they spent the whole day singing and playing bagpipes, whistles, flutes, and shawms, and other extraordinary instruments. I used to stop to hear her read, and she read about how the shepherd Anfrisa sang divinely praising Belisarda of unsurpassed beauty and of how there was not in the whole countryside of Arcadia a single treetrunk where he did not sit and sing from the moment the sun came out in the arms of Aurora[14]until it set in those of Thetys,[15]and even after black night spread over the face of the earth its black dark wings, he did not cease his well sung laments, which were even better when accompanied by tears. She did not omit to mention the shepherd Elicio, more lovestruck than daring, of whom it was said that, neglectful both of his love and his flock, he got involved in the cares of others. She also told how the great shepherd of Filida, the renowned portrait painter, had been more trusting than fortunate. Of the fainting fits of Sireno and the repentance of Diana she said that she gave thanks to God and the wise Felicia who with her enchanted water undid that web of entanglements and showed the way out of that maze of difficulties. I remembered many other books of this type that I had heard her read; but they were not worthy of being recalled.

CIPIÓN: Berganza, you are heeding my advice; gossip, sting and pass on, and let your intention be pure, even if your tongue does not appear to be.

BERGANZA: In these matters the tongue never stumbles if the intention does not falter first, but if by chance through carelessness or malice I should gossip, I shall reply to whoever reproaches me with the words Mauleon, the stupid poet and ridiculous academician of the Academy of the Imitators,[16] used in response to one who asked him what *Deum de Deo* meant; he replied "Give as you shall give".

CIPIÓN: That was the reply of a simpleton; but you, if you are discreet or wish so to be, must never say anything for which you must apologise. Carry on.

BERGANZA: I tell you that all the thoughts I have revealed, and many more, enabled me to see how the practices and habits of my shepherds and of all the others from that land by the sea differed from those I had heard about from books about shepherds, because if mine sang, their songs were not tuneful and beautifully composed, but "Watch

sino un "*Cata el lobo dó va, Juanica*" y otras cosas semejantes; y esto no al son de chirumbelas, rabeles o gaitas, sino al que hacía el dar un cayado con otro o al de algunas tejuelas puestas entre los dedos; y no con voces delicadas, sonoras y admirables, sino con voces roncas, que, solas o juntas, parecía, no que cantaban, sino que gritaban, o gruñían. Lo más del día se les pasaba espulgándose o remendando sus abarcas; ni entre ellos se nombraban Amarilis, Fílidas, Galateas y Dianas, ni había Lisardos, Lausos, Jacintos ni Riselos; todos eran Antones, Domingos, Pablos o Llorentes; por donde vine a entender lo que pienso que deben de creer todos: que todos aquellos libros son cosas soñadas y bien escritas para entretenimiento de los ociosos, y no verdad alguna; que a serlo, entre mis pastores hubiera alguna reliquia de aquella felicísima vida, y de aquellos amenos prados, espaciosas selvas, sagrados montes, hermosos jardines, arroyos claros y cristalinas fuentes, y de aquellos tan honestos cuanto bien declarados requiebros, y de aquel desmayarse aquí el pastor, allí la pastora, acullá resonar la zampoña del uno, acá el caramillo del otro.

CIPIÓN. –Basta, Berganza; vuelve a tu senda y camina.

BERGANZA. –Agradézcotelo, Cipión amigo; porque si no me avisaras, de manera se me iba calentando la boca que no parara hasta pintarte un libro entero de estos que me tenían engañado; pero tiempo vendrá en que lo diga todo con mejores razones y con mejor discurso que ahora.

CIPIÓN. –Mírate a los pies, y desharás la rueda, Berganza: quiero decir que mires que eres un animal que carece de razón, y si ahora muestras tener alguna, ya hemos averiguado entre los dos ser cosa sobrenatural y jamás vista.

BERGANZA. –Eso fuera así si yo estuviera en mi primera ignorancia; mas ahora que me ha venido a la memoria lo que había de haber dicho al principio de nuestra plática, no sólo no me maravillo de lo que hablo, pero espántome de lo que dejo de hablar.

CIPIÓN. –Pues ¿ahora no puedes decir lo que ahora se te acuerda?

BERGANZA. –Es una cierta historia que me pasó con una grande hechicera, discípula de la Camacha de Montilla.

CIPIÓN. –Digo que me la cuentes antes que pases más adelante en el cuento de tu vida.

BERGANZA. –Eso no haré yo, por cierto, hasta su tiempo; ten paciencia, y escucha por su orden mis sucesos, que así te darán más gusto, si ya no te fatiga querer saber los medios antes de los principios.

CIPIÓN. –Sé breve, y cuenta lo que quisieres y como quisieres.

BERGANZA. –Digo, pues, que yo me hallaba bien con el oficio de guardar ganado, por parecerme que comía el pan de mi sudor y trabajo, y que la ociosidad, raíz y madre de todos los vicios, no tenía que ver conmigo, a causa que si los días holgaba, las noches no dormía, dándonos asaltos a menudo y tocándonos a arma los lobos; y apenas me habían dicho los pastores: "¡Al lobo, Barcino!", cuando acudía, primero que los otros perros, a la parte que me señalaban que estaba el lobo; corría los valles, escudriñaba los montes, desentrañaba las selvas, saltaba barrancos, cruzaba caminos, y a la mañana volvía al hato, sin haber hallado lobo ni rastro de él, anhelando, cansado, hecho pedazos y los pies abiertos de los garranchos, y hallaba en el hato, o ya una oveja muerta, o un carnero degollado y medio comido del lobo. Desesperábame de ver cuán poco servía mi mucho cuidado y diligencia. Venía el señor del ganado; salían los pastores a

out for the wolf, Joanica" and others of that ilk; and these were not sung to the sound of shawms, pipes and whistles, but to the sound of crooks being knocked together or of a few tiles clicking between their fingers; and not with delicate, melodious and admirable voices, but rather rough ones which, either solo or together, sounded not like singing but shouting, or indeed grunting. Most of the day they spent removing fleas or mending their sandals; none of them had names like Amarilis, Filida, Galatea or Diana, nor were there any Lisardos, Lausos, Jacintos or Riselos: all of them were Antons, Domingos, Pablos or Llorentes; from which I came to understand what I think everyone must believe: that all those books are imagined and written for the entertainment of the idle, and are not true at all. If they were, there would be some vestige among my shepherds of that blissful life, of those pleasant meadows, spacious woods, sacred mounts, beautiful gardens, clear streams and crystalline fountains, and of those pure and beautifully declaimed verses, and of that shepherd who faints here, and shepherdess there, and the sound of the one's pipe and the other's flute.

CIPIÓN: That's enough, Berganza. Return to your path and continue.

BERGANZA: I am grateful to you, Cipión, my friend, for if you had not warned me, I would have got so carried away that I would not stop until I had portrayed for you a whole book of the type that had taken me in; but a time will come when I tell everything more coherently and in better language than now.

CIPIÓN: Look at your feet, and you will come out of your spin, Berganza; I mean, bear in mind that you are an animal lacking in reason, and if you appear to have some, we have already worked out between the two of us that it is something supernatural and never seen before.

BERGANZA: That would be so if I were in a state of innocence; but now that I have remembered what I should have said at the beginning of our conversation, not only am I not amazed at what I am saying, but I am astonished at what I am leaving out.

CIPIÓN: But can you not tell what you remember now?

BERGANZA: It's a true story which happened to me with a great sorceress, a disciple of Camacha de Montilla.[17]

CIPIÓN: I want you to tell it to me before you carry on with the story of your life.

BERGANZA: That I shall not do, you can be sure, until the right moment; be patient, and listen to these events in the order in which they come, for in this way you will have greater pleasure, unless wanting to know the middle before the beginning tires you out.

CIPIÓN: Be brief, and narrate whatever you wish and however you wish.

BERGANZA: Well then, I can tell you that I was happy with my job of guarding sheep, as I felt I was earning my bread by the sweat of my brow and my labour, and that idleness, the root and mother of all vices, formed no part of me, for if I rested by day, I did not sleep at night, for the wolves frequently attacked us and spurred us to action; and no sooner did the shepherds shout: "Barcino! Wolf!" than I would run up, the first of all the dogs, to the place they indicated the wolf was; I would run through valleys, scour the hills, search the woods, jump over ravines, cross roads, and return to the flock in the morning, without finding any trace of the wolf, panting, worn out, exhausted, and with my feet torn by running over broken branches, and I would find in the flock either a dead sheep or a lamb slaughtered and half-eaten by the wolf. I was in despair seeing how little use my care and diligence were to me. The owner of the herd would arrive; the shepherds would go out to meet him with the skin of the dead animal; he would

recibirle con las pieles de la res muerta; culpaba a los pastores por negligentes y mandaba castigar a los perros por perezosos; llovían sobre nosotros palos, y sobre ellos represiones; y así, viéndome un día castigado sin culpa y que mi cuidado, ligereza y braveza no eran de provecho para coger el lobo, determiné de mudar de estilo, no desviándome a buscarle, como tenía de costumbre, lejos del rebaño, sino estarme junto a él: que pues el lobo allí venía, allí sería más cierta la presa. Cada semana nos tocaban a rebato, y en una oscurísima noche tuve yo vista para ver los lobos, de quien era imposible que el ganado se guardase. Agachéme detrás de una mata, pasaron los perros, mis compañeros, adelante, y desde allí oteé, y vi que dos pastores asieron de un carnero de los mejores del aprisco, y le mataron, de manera que verdaderamente pareció a la mañana que había sido su verdugo el lobo. Pasméme, quedé suspenso cuando vi que los pastores eran los lobos y que despedazaban el ganado los mismos que le habían de guardar. Al punto hacían saber a su amo la presa del lobo, dábanle el pellejo y parte de la carne, y comíanse ellos lo más y lo mejor. Volvía a reñirles el señor, y volvía también el castigo de los perros. No había lobos; menguaba el rebaño; quisiera yo descubrirlo; hallábame mudo. Todo lo cual me traía lleno de admiración y de congoja. "¡Válame Dios! –decía entre mí–. ¿Quién podrá remediar esta maldad? ¿Quién será poderoso a dar a entender que la defensa ofende, que las centinelas duermen, que la confianza roba y el que os guarda os mata?"

CIPIÓN. –Y decías muy bien, Berganza; porque no hay mayor ni más sutil ladrón que el doméstico, y así, mueren muchos más de los confiados que de los recatados; pero el daño está en que es imposible que puedan pasar bien las gentes en el mundo si no se fía y se confía. Mas quédese aquí esto, que no quiero que parezcamos predicadores. Pasa adelante.

BERGANZA. –Paso adelante, y digo que determiné dejar aquel oficio, aunque parecía tan bueno, y escoger otro donde por hacerle bien, ya que no fuese remunerado, no fuese castigado. Volvíme a Sevilla, y entré a servir a un mercader muy rico.

CIPIÓN. –¿Qué modo tenías para entrar con amo? Porque, según lo que se usa, con gran dificultad el día de hoy halla un hombre de bien señor a quien servir. Muy diferentes son los señores de la tierra del Señor del cielo; aquéllos, para recibir un criado, primero le espulgan el linaje, examinan la habilidad, le marcan la apostura, y aun quieren saber los vestidos que tiene; pero entrar a servir a Dios, el más pobre es más rico; el más humilde, de mejor linaje; y con sólo que se disponga con limpieza de corazón a querer servirle, luego le manda poner en el libro de sus gajes, señalándoselos tan aventajados, que, de muchos y de grandes, apenas pueden caber en su deseo.

BERGANZA. –Todo eso es predicar, Cipión amigo.

CIPIÓN. –Así me lo parece a mí, y así callo.

BERGANZA. –A lo que me preguntaste del orden que tenía para entrar con amo, digo que ya tú sabes que la humildad es la base y fundamento de todas las virtudes, y que sin ella no hay alguna que lo sea. Ella allana inconvenientes, vence dificultades, y es un medio que siempre a gloriosos fines nos conduce; de los enemigos hace amigos, templa la cólera de los airados y menoscaba la arrogancia de los soberbios; es madre de la modestia y hermana de la templanza; en fin, con ella no pueden atravesar triunfo que

blame the shepherds for being negligent and would order the dogs to be punished for being lazy; they would be heavily reproached and we would be beaten with sticks. And so, seeing myself one day punished unjustly and realizing that my zeal, speed and bravery were to no avail in catching the wolf, I decided to change tactics and not set off to find him, as was my custom, far from the flock, but to stay close to it, for since the wolf came there, that was where I would be more certain of catching him. Every week they called us out, and on a very dark night I caught sight of wolves against which it would be impossible to guard the flock. I crouched down behind a bush as the dogs, my companions, passed by and went ahead, and from there I observed and saw two shepherds taking hold of one of the best lambs in the flock and kill it so that the next morning it really looked as if it were a wolf's handiwork. I was dumbstruck and totally amazed when I saw that the shepherds were the wolves and that those who were supposed to guard the flock were the ones who were destroying it. Immediately, they brought the news of the wolf's attack to the master, gave him the skin and some of the meat and kept the biggest and best bits for themselves. The master reprimanded them again, and the dogs were punished again. There were no wolves; the flock was getting smaller; I wanted to tell all, but was unable to speak. All this filled me with amazement and anguish.

"Good Lord!" I said to myself, "Who can put an end to this wrong-doing? Who is able to reveal that the defence is attacking, that the sentries sleep, that trust steals and that the guard is the killer?"

CIPIÓN: Well said, Berganza, because there is no greater or cleverer thief than the one which is from within the household itself; so it is that the trusting die more often than the careful, but the trouble is that people cannot get on well in the world if they do not have confidence and trust in others. But let's leave it there, for I do not want us to appear to be preaching. Carry on.

BERGANZA: I shall carry on and tell you that I resolved to abandon that occupation, even though it seemed so good, and find another where if I did it well, even if I didn't get rewarded, at least I wouldn't get punished. I returned to Seville and entered into the service of a very rich merchant.

CIPIÓN: How did you manage to enter his service, because, as things stand, a good man has great difficulty these days finding a master to serve? The lords of the earth are very different from the lords of heaven; the former, in order to take on a servant, first check out his lineage, examine his skills, look at his appearance, and even want to know what clothes he has; but to serve God, the poorest is the richest, the most humble, of noblest birth; and being willing to serve him with a pure heart is enough for him to order one's name to be entered in the book which records the wages, which are so favourable, abundant and generous, that they go beyond one's wildest expectations.

BERGANZA: All this is preaching, Cipión, my friend.

CIPIÓN: I think so too, so I will be silent.

BERGANZA: In reply to what you asked me about how I came to enter the service of my master, I can only say that you know that humility is the basis and foundation of all the virtues, for without it they cannot exist. Humility removes obstacles, overcomes difficulties, and it is a means which always leads us to glorious ends; it makes friends of enemies, it assuages the anger of the irate and brings down the arrogance of the haughty; it is the mother of modesty and sister of moderation; in short, with humility, vices can

les sea de provecho los vicios, porque en su blandura y mansedumbre se embotan y despuntan las flechas de los pecados. De ésta, pues, me aprovechaba yo cuando quería entrar a servir en alguna casa, habiendo primero considerado y mirado muy bien ser casa que pudiese mantener y donde pudiese entrar un perro grande. Luego arrimábame a la puerta y cuando, a mi parecer, entraba algún forastero, le ladraba, y cuando venía el señor bajaba la cabeza y, moviendo la cola, me iba a él, y con la lengua le limpiaba los zapatos. Si me echaban a palos, sufríalos, y con la misma mansedumbre volvía a hacer halagos al que me apaleaba, que ninguno segundaba viendo mi porfía y mi noble término. De esta manera, a dos porfías me quedaba en casa; servía bien, queríanme luego bien, y nadie me despidió, si no era que yo me despidiese, o, por mejor decir, me fuese; y tal vez hallé amo que éste fuera el día que yo estuviera en su casa, si la contraria suerte no me hubiera perseguido.

CIPIÓN. –De la misma manera que has contado entraba yo con los amos que tuve, y parece que nos leímos los pensamientos.

BERGANZA. –Como en esas cosas nos hemos encontrado, si no me engaño, y yo te las diré a su tiempo, como tengo prometido; y ahora escucha lo que me sucedió después que dejé el ganado en poder de aquellos perdidos. Volvíme a Sevilla, como dije, que es amparo de pobres y refugio de desechados; que en su grandeza no sólo caben los pequeños, pero no se echan de ver los grandes. Arriméme a la puerta de una gran casa de un mercader, hice mis acostumbradas diligencias, y a pocos lances me quedé en ella. Recibiéronme para tenerme atado detrás de la puerta de día y suelto de noche; servía con gran cuidado y diligencia; ladraba a los forasteros y gruñía a los que no eran muy conocidos; no dormía de noche, visitando los corrales, subiendo a los terrados, hecho universal centinela de la mía y de las casas ajenas. Agradóse tanto mi amo de mi buen servicio, que mandó que me tratasen bien y me diesen ración de pan y los huesos que se levantasen o arrojasen de su mesa, con las sobras de la cocina, a lo que yo me mostraba agradecido, dando infinitos saltos cuando veía a mi amo, especialmente cuando venía de fuera; que eran tantas las muestras de regocijo que daba y tantos los saltos, que mi amo ordenó que me desatasen y me dejasen andar suelto de día y de noche. Como me vi suelto corrí a él, rodéele todo, sin osar llegarle con las manos, acordándome de la fábula de Isopo, cuando aquel asno, tan asno que quiso hacer a su señor las mismas caricias que le hacía una perrilla regalada suya, que le granjearon ser molido a palos. Parecióme que en esta fábula se nos dio a entender que las gracias y donaires de algunos no están bien en otros; apode el truhán, juegue de manos y voltee el histrión, rebuzne el pícaro, imite el canto de los pájaros y los diversos gestos y acciones de los animales y los hombres el hombre bajo que se hubiere dado a ello, y no lo quiera hacer el hombre principal, a quien ninguna habilidad de éstas le puede dar crédito ni nombre honroso.

CIPIÓN. –Basta; adelante, Berganza, que ya estás entendido.

BERGANZA. –¡Ojalá que como tú me entiendes me entendiesen aquellos por quien lo digo; que no sé qué tengo de buen natural, que me pesa infinito cuando veo que un caballero se hace chocarrero y se precia que sabe jugar los cubiletes y las agallas y que no hay quien como él sepa bailar la chacona! Un caballero conozco yo que se alababa que, a ruegos de un sacristán, había cortado de papel treinta y dos florones para poner en un monumento sobre paños negros, y de estas cortaduras hizo tanto caudal, que así

never come up trumps, for the arrows of sin are blunted and dulled in its softness and gentleness. I took advantage of this quality, then, when I wanted to enter service in any house, having first made sure and verified that the house was one which could take in a large dog and maintain it. Then I placed myself near the door and when what appeared to me to be a stranger went in, I barked at him, and when the master came out I lowered my head and, wagging my tail, went up to him and licked his boots. If I got a beating and was thrown out, I put up with it, and with the same meekness I made up to the person who beat me, for no one did it again seeing my persistence and noble behaviour. In this manner, after two attempts I stayed in the house. I gave good service, they grew fond of me, and nobody dismissed me, unless I myself took leave or, more accurately, went off. And perhaps I had found a master in whose house I would have stayed until this day, if ill fortune had not dogged me.

CIPIÓN: I also entered the service of the masters I had in just the way you have described, and you would think we had read each other's thoughts.

BERGANZA: As we have coincided in these matters, if I'm not mistaken, I will tell you about them in due course, as I have promised, and now listen to what happened to me after I left the flock in the power of those rogues. I returned to Seville, as I said, which is a shelter for the poor and a refuge for outcasts; in its greatness not only do the poor find a home, but the great are also not out of place there. I went up to the door of the house of a great merchant, made the usual obsequies, and in no time at all was installed. They took me on to keep me tied behind the door during the day and to let me loose at night; I carried out my duties carefully and diligently; I barked at strangers and growled at those who were not very well known to me; I did not sleep at night, visiting the yards, going up to the terraces, having become the sentry of both my own and other people's houses. My excellent service pleased my master so much that he ordered me to be well treated and given a ration of bread and the bones which were taken or thrown away from his table, along with the left-overs from the kitchen, for which I showed my gratitude, jumping up and down at the sight of my master, especially when he had been away for a while. My expressions of joy were such and my jumping so frantic that my master ordered me to be untied and allowed to run around free day and night. As I saw myself free I ran to him, and ran around him, but without daring to touch him with my hands, remembering Aesop's fable, in which that ass, which was such an ass that he wanted to caress his master in the same way as his little spoiled dog did, got a beating as his reward. It seemed to me that in this fable we are given to understand that what is graceful and elegant in some people is not necessarily so in others; let the jester tell jokes, let the clown do tricks with his hands and do somersaults, let the rogue rant and rave, and let the common man imitate the song of the birds and the actions and gestures of animals and men if he has such talent, but let not the man of distinction do these things, for none of these skills bestows credit or an honourable name.

CIPIÓN: That's enough. Get on with it, Berganza, for we get your point.

BERGANZA: Would that those for whom I say these things got my point as well as you do, for I am so good-natured that it pains me immensely to see a gentleman act the fool and be proud of being able to play tricks like `find the ball' or claim that nobody can dance the chaconne like he does. I know a gentleman who used to boast that, at the request of a sacristan, he had cut out thirty-two paper flowers to place on the black hangings on a monument, and that he was so taken with these cuttings that he took his

llevaba a sus amigos a verlas como si los llevara a ver las banderas y despojos de enemigos que sobre la sepultura de sus padres y abuelos estaban puestas. Este mercader, pues, tenía dos hijos, el uno de doce y el otro de hasta catorce años, los cuales estudiaban gramática en el estudio de la Compañía de Jesús; iban con autoridad, con ayo y con pajes, que les llevaban los libros y aquel que llaman *vademecum*. El verlos ir con tanto aparato, en sillas si hacía sol, en coche si llovía, me hizo considerar y reparar en la mucha llaneza con que su padre iba a la Lonja a negociar sus negocios, porque no llevaba otro criado que un negro, y algunas veces se desmandaba a ir en un machuelo aun no bien aderezado.

CIPIÓN. –Has de saber, Berganza, que es costumbre y condición de los mercaderes de Sevilla, y aun de las otras ciudades, mostrar su autoridad y riqueza, no en sus personas, sino en las de sus hijos; porque los mercaderes son mayores en su sombra que en sí mismos. Y como ellos por maravilla atienden a otra cosa que a sus tratos y contratos, trátanse modestamente; y como la ambición y la riqueza muere por manifestarse, revienta por sus hijos, y así los tratan y autorizan como si fuesen hijos de algún príncipe; algunos hay que les procuran títulos y ponerles en el pecho la marca que tanto distingue la gente principal de la plebeya.

BERGANZA. –Ambición es, pero ambición generosa, la de aquel que pretende mejorar su estado sin perjuicio de tercero.

CIPIÓN. –Pocas o ninguna vez se cumple con la ambición que no sea con daño de tercero.

BERGANZA. –Ya hemos dicho que no hemos de murmurar.

CIPIÓN. –Sí, que yo no murmuro de nadie.

BERGANZA. –Ahora acabo de confirmar por verdad lo que muchas veces he oído decir. Acaba un maldiciente murmurador de echar a perder diez linajes y de calumniar veinte buenos, y si alguno le reprende por lo que ha dicho, responde que él no ha dicho nada, y que si ha dicho algo, no lo ha dicho por tanto, y que si pensara que alguno se había de agraviar, no lo dijera. A la fe, Cipión, mucho ha de saber, y muy sobre los estribos ha de andar el que quisiere sustentar dos horas de conversación sin tocar los límites de la murmuración; porque yo veo en mí que, con ser un animal, como soy, a cuatro razones que digo me acuden palabras a la lengua como mosquitos al vino, y todas maliciosas y murmurantes; por lo cual vuelvo a decir lo que otra vez he dicho: que el hacer y decir mal lo heredamos de nuestros primeros padres y lo mamamos en la leche. Vése claro en que apenas ha sacado el niño el brazo de las fajas cuando levanta la mano con muestras de querer vengarse de quien, a su parecer, le ofende; y casi la primera palabra articulada que habla es llamar puta a su ama o a su madre.

CIPIÓN. –Así es verdad, y yo confieso mi yerro, y quiero que me le perdones, pues te he perdonado tantos; echemos pelillos a la mar, como dicen los muchachos, y no murmuremos de aquí adelante; y sigue tu cuento, que le dejaste en la autoridad con que los hijos del mercader tu amo iban al estudio de la Compañía de Jesús.

BERGANZA. –A Él me encomiendo en todo acontecimiento; y aunque el dejar de murmurar lo tengo por dificultoso, pienso usar de un remedio que oí decir que usaba un gran jurador, el cual, arrepentido de su mala costumbre, cada vez que después de un arrepentimiento juraba, se daba un pellizco en el brazo, o besaba la tierra, en pena de su

friends to see them as if he were taking them to see the flags and spoils of his enemies placed on the tomb of his parents and grandparents. This merchant, then, had two sons, one of twelve and another of about fourteen years, who were studying grammar in the Jesuit school;[18] they were imposing in their manner, going about with their tutor and pages who carried their books and what are known as portfolios. Seeing them go about with such ostentation, in sedan chairs if it was sunny and in carriages if it was raining, made me consider and reflect upon the great simplicity with which their father went to the Exchange[19] to carry out his business, because he had no servant other than a negro, and sometimes he even went on a mule, and not a particularly fine one at that.

CIPIÓN: You should know, Berganza, that it is the custom and practice of the merchants of Seville, and of other cities too, to show off their riches, not on themselves, but on their sons; because the merchants are greater by virtue of the shadow they cast than because of their own persons. And as they never attend to anything other than their dealings and contracts, they live modestly; and as ambition and riches long to be displayed, they burst forth in the children, and so they treat them and invest them with authority as if they were the sons of some prince; there are some who arrange titles for them and put on their chest some insignia or cross which clearly sets distinguished people apart from the plebs.

BERGANZA: It is ambition, but a noble ambition, to aim to improve one's position without harming anyone else.

CIPIÓN: Rarely if ever does ambition succeed without harming someone else.

BERGANZA: We have already said that we will not gossip.

CIPIÓN: That's right, and I'm not gossiping about anyone.

BERGANZA: Now I have just had confirmed as true what I have often heard said. A malicious slanderer has just ruined ten families and destroyed the reputation of twenty good persons, and if anyone reproaches him for what he has said, he replies that he has said nothing, and that if he has said something, it wasn't intentional, and that if he had known that someone would be offended, he would not have said it. In truth, Cipión, anyone who wants to sustain two hours' conversation without getting to the borders of gossip has to be very wise and very prudent; for I can see in myself that, although I am an animal, no sooner do I utter a few phrases than words come to the tip of my tongue like flies around wine, and all of them malicious and slanderous; wherefore I say again what I have already said: that saying and doing wrong is something we inherit from our first parents and drink with our mother's milk. This can clearly be seen in the fact that the child no sooner takes its arm out of its blankets than it raises its hand as if to seek to exact vengeance on whoever he thinks has offended him; and almost the first word he says is to call his nurse or mother a whore.

CIPIÓN: That's true, and I confess my error and ask you to forgive me mine as I have forgiven many of yours. Pax,[20] as children say, and let us not gossip from here on; continue your story, which you left at the point where you were describing the os'entation of the sons of your master, the merchant, as they went to the school run by the Jesuits.

BERGANZA: I commend myself to Him in everything, and although I find it difficult to desist from gossiping, I intend to use a remedy which I heard was used by a man greatly given to swearing who, repenting of this bad habit, every time he swore after having repented, pinched his arm, or kissed the ground, as penance for his sin; but,

culpa; pero, con todo esto, juraba. Así yo, cada vez que fuere contra el precepto que me has dado de que no murmure, y contra la intención que tengo de no murmurar, me morderé el pico de la lengua de modo que me duela, y me acuerde de mi culpa para no volver a ella.

CIPIÓN. –Tal es ese remedio, que si usas de él espero que te has de morder tantas veces que has de quedar sin lengua, y así, quedarás imposibilitado de murmurar.

BERGANZA. –A lo menos, yo haré de mi parte mis diligencias, y supla las faltas el cielo. Y así, digo que los hijos de mi amo se dejaron un día un cartapacio en el patio, donde yo a la sazón estaba; y como estaba enseñado a llevar la esportilla del jifero mi amo, así del *vademecum* y fuime tras ellos, con intención de no soltarle hasta el estudio. Sucedióme todo como lo deseaba: que mis amos, que me vieron venir con el *vademecum* en la boca, asido sutilmente de las cintas, mandaron a un paje me le quitase; mas yo no lo consentí ni le solté hasta que entré en el aula con él, cosa que causó risa a todos los estudiantes. Lleguéme al mayor de mis amos, y, a mi parecer, con mucha crianza se le puse en las manos, y quedéme sentado en cuclillas a la puerta del aula, mirando de hito en hito al maestro que en la cátedra leía. No sé qué tiene la virtud, que, con alcanzárseme a mí tan poco, o nada, de ella, luego recibí gusto de ver el amor, el término, la solicitud y la industria con que aquellos benditos padres y maestros enseñaban a aquellos niños, enderezando las tiernas varas de su juventud, porque no torciesen ni tomasen mal siniestro en el camino de la virtud, que justamente con las letras les mostraban. Consideraba cómo los reñían con suavidad, los castigaban con misericordia, los animaban con ejemplos, los incitaban con premios y los sobrellevaban con cordura, y, finalmente, cómo les pintaban la fealdad y horror de los vicios y les dibujaban la hermosura de las virtudes, para que, aborrecidos ellos y amadas ellas, consiguiesen el fin para que fueron criados.

CIPIÓN. –Muy bien dices, Berganza; porque yo he oído decir de esa bendita gente que para repúblicos del mundo no los hay tan prudentes en todo él, y para guiadores y adalides del camino del cielo, pocos les llegan. Son espejos donde se mira la honestidad, la católica doctrina, la singular prudencia, y, finalmente, la humildad profunda, basa sobre quien se levanta todo el edificio de la bienaventuranza.

BERGANZA. –Todo es así como lo dices. Y, siguiendo mi historia, digo que mis amos gustaron de que les llevase siempre el *vademecum*, lo que hice de muy buena voluntad; con lo cual tenía una vida de rey, y aun mejor, porque era descansada, a causa que los estudiantes dieron en burlarse conmigo, y domestiquéme con ellos de tal manera que me metían la mano en la boca y los más chiquillos subían sobre mí. Arrojaban los bonetes o sombreros, y yo se los volvía a la mano limpiamente y con muestras de grande regocijo. Dieron en darme de comer cuanto ellos podían, y gustaban de ver que cuando me daban nueces o avellanas las partía como mona, dejando las cáscaras y comiendo lo tierno. Tal hubo que, por hacer prueba de mi habilidad, me trajo en un pañuelo gran cantidad de ensalada, la cual me comí como si fuera persona. Era tiempo de invierno, cuando campean en Sevilla los molletes y mantequillas, de quien era tan bien servido, que más de dos *Antonios* se empeñaron o vendieron para que yo almorzase. Finalmente, yo pasaba una vida de estudiante sin hambre y sin sarna, que es lo más que se puede encarecer para decir que era buena; porque si la sarna y el hambre no fuesen tan unas con los estudiantes, en las vidas no habría otra de más gusto y

despite this, he continued to swear. And so I, every time I go against your exhortation not to gossip, and against my own intention not to gossip, will bite the end of my tongue so that it hurts, and I shall remember my sin so as not to commit it again.

CIPIÓN: Such is your remedy that if you use it I expect you will have to bite yourself so many times that you will end up without a tongue and thus will be quite unable to gossip.

BERGANZA: At least I for my part will make an effort and let heaven supply whatever is lacking. And so let me recount how one day my master's sons left a folder in the patio, where I happened to be at the time; and as I had been taught by my slaughterman master to carry a basket, I picked up the portfolio with the intention of not letting go of it until I reached the school. Everything turned out as I wished: my masters, seeing me come with the portfolio lightly held by the ribbons, sent a page to take it from me. But I did not allow him to do so and did not let go of it until I went into the classroom holding it, which made all the students laugh. I went up to the elder of my masters and showing, as I thought, great breeding, I put it in his hands, and went and squatted at the door of the classroom, looking intently at the teacher who was giving his class from the lectern. I don't know what it is about virtue, having none or very little of it, but I was very pleased to see the love, care, dedication and effort with which those blessed fathers and teachers taught those children, straightening up and stiffening the tender branches that were these youngsters, so that they should not be deflected or deviate from the path of virtue, which they taught them together with the study of letters. I observed how they gently scolded them, punished them with mercy, inspired them by example, encouraged them with prizes and calmly endured them and, finally, how they painted for them the horrors of vice and described the beauties of virtue so that, hating the one and loving the other, they should achieve the end for which they were created.

CIPIÓN: Very well said, Berganza, for I have heard it said of those blessed people that as benefactors of the world there are none in it as wise as they, and that as guides and leaders on the way to heaven, few can touch them. They are mirrors which reflect honesty, Catholic doctrine, rare prudence and, finally, profound humility, the foundation on which the whole edifice of human happiness is built.

BERGANZA: It is just as you say. And carrying on with my story, my masters wanted me always to carry their portfolio, which I did willingly and lived the life of a king, or even better, because it was one of relaxation, for the students took to playing with me and I was so tame with them that they put their hands in my mouth and the smallest of them climbed on to my back. They threw their caps or hats and I fetched them and put them back into their hands neatly and with obvious pleasure. They began to feed me with whatever they had, and they liked to see when they gave me walnuts or hazelnuts that I broke them open like a monkey, casting aside the shells and eating the soft bit. There was one who, wanting to test my skill, brought a handkerchief containing a large amount of salad, which I ate as if I were a human being. It was winter, when in Seville you get buttered muffins, and I was so well looked after that more than one Nebrija Latin grammar[21] was sold or pawned so that I could eat my fill of them. The fact is that I lived the life of a student, suffering neither hunger nor itching, which is as much as one need say to show how good it was, for if itching and hunger were not part and parcel of student life, there could be none more agreeable and enjoyable, in which

pasatiempo, corren parejas en ella la virtud y el gusto, y se pasa la mocedad aprendiendo y holgándose. De esta gloria y de esta quietud me vino a quitar una señora que, a mi parecer, llaman por ahí razón de estado, que cuando con ella se cumple, se ha de descumplir con otras razones muchas. Es el caso que a aquellos señores maestros les pareció que la media hora que hay de lección la ocupaban los estudiantes, no en repasar las lecciones, sino en holgarse conmigo, y así, ordenaron a mis amos que no me llevasen más al estudio; obedecieron, volviéronme a casa y a la antigua guarda de la puerta y, sin acordarse señor el viejo de la merced que me había hecho de que de día y de noche anduviese suelto, volvía a entregar el cuello a la cadena y el cuerpo a una esterilla que detrás de la puerta me pusieron. ¡Ay, amigo Cipión, si supieses cuán dura cosa es sufrir el pasar de un estado feliz a un desdichado! Mira: cuando las miserias y desdichas tienen larga la corriente y son continuas, o se acaban presto, con la muerte, o la continuación de ellas hace un hábito y costumbre en padecerlas, que suele en su mayor rigor servir de alivio; mas cuando de la suerte desdichada y calamitosa, sin pensarlo y de improviso, se sale a gozar de otra suerte próspera, venturosa y alegre, y de allí a poco se vuelve a padecer la suerte primera y a los primeros trabajos y desdichas, es un dolor tan riguroso que si no acaba la vida es por atormentarla más viviendo. Digo, en fin, que volví a mi ración perruna y a los huesos que una negra de casa me arrojaba, y aun éstos me diezmaban dos gatos romanos que, como sueltos y ligeros, érales fácil quitarme lo que no caía debajo del distrito que alcanzaba mi cadena. Cipión hermano, así el cielo te conceda el bien que deseas, que, sin que te enfades, me dejes ahora filosofar un poco; porque si dejase de decir las cosas que en este instante me han venido a la memoria de aquellas que entonces me ocurrieron, me parece que no sería mi historia cabal ni de fruto alguno.

CIPIÓN. –Advierte, Berganza, no sea tentación del demonio esa gana de filosofar que dices te ha venido; porque no tiene la murmuración mejor velo para paliar y encubrir su maldad disoluta que darse a entender el murmurador que todo cuanto dice son sentencias de filósofos y que el decir mal es represión y el descubrir los defectos ajenos buen celo. Y no hay vida de ningún murmurante que, si la consideras y escudriñas, no la halles llena de vicios y de insolencias. Y debajo de saber esto, filosofea ahora cuanto quisieres.

BERGANZA. –Seguro puedes estar, Cipión, de que más murmure, porque así lo tengo prosupuesto. Es, pues, el caso, que como me estaba todo el día ocioso y la ociosidad sea madre de los pensamientos, di en repasar con la memoria algunos latines que me quedaron en ella de muchos que oí cuando fui con mis amos al estudio, con que, a mi parecer, me hallé algo más mejorado de entendimiento, y determiné, como si hablar supiera, aprovecharme de ellos en las ocasiones que se me ofreciesen; pero en manera diferente de la que se suelen aprovechar algunos ignorantes. Hay algunos romancistas que en las conversaciones disparan de cuando en cuando con algún latín breve y compendioso, dando a entender a los que no lo entienden que son grandes latinos, y apenas saben declinar un nombre ni conjugar un verbo.

CIPIÓN. –Por menor daño tengo ése que el que hacen los que verdaderamente saben latín, de los cuales hay algunos tan imprudentes que hablando con un zapatero o con un sastre arrojan latines como agua.

BERGANZA. –De eso podremos inferir que tanto peca el que dice latines delante de quien los ignora como el que los dice ignorándolos.

pleasure and virtue go hand in hand, and one's youth is spent learning and enjoying oneself.

I was taken out of this blissful and quiet situation by a lady who, I think, is called in these parts reasons of state,[22] with which one can only comply by failing to comply with lots of other reasons. The fact is that the masters thought that the students spent the half hour between lessons not going over their work but playing with me, and so they ordered my masters not to take me to school any more. They obeyed and took me home to my old job as guard dog at the door, and the old master, forgetting the favour he had done me by letting me run about day and night, put the chain back around my neck and laid my body on a mat which they placed for me behind the door. Oh! Cipión, my friend, if you only knew how hard it is to go from a happy state to a miserable one! Look, when miseries and misfortunes are of long duration and are continuous, or are suddenly ended by death, or their continuation becomes a habit and one is accustomed to putting up with them, even when they are harshest, this can offer relief; but when from a state of calamitous and dreadful misfortune, suddenly and unexpectedly, one emerges to enjoy another prosperous, happy and joyful fate, and then shortly afterwards returns to suffer one's former fate with its travails and hardships, the pain is so intense that if life does not end, living becomes a torment. So, as I say, I returned to my dog's ration and the bones which a negress in the house threw to me, and even these were reduced by two tabby cats which, being free and swift, easily took away whatever did not fall within the range of my chain. Cipión, my brother, may God give you all you desire if, without getting angry, you let me philosophise a little, because if I did not say the things which have come into my mind at this instant and which happened at that time, I fear my story would not be complete or of any benefit to anyone.

CIPIÓN: Take care, Berganza, that this urge to philosophise that has come over you is not the temptation of the devil, for gossiping has no better veil to cover up and disguise its dissolute malice than for the slanderer to give the impression that all that he says are the wise pronouncements of philosophers and that to speak ill is a reproach and to reveal the defects of others is to be good and zealous. And you will not find any slanderer's life, if you examine and inspect it closely, that is not full of vice and insolence. And now that you know this, philosophise as much as you like.

BERGANZA: You can be sure, Cipión, that I shall gossip no more, for it is my intention not to. The fact is that, as I was idle all day long and idleness gives rise to thinking, I began to go through in my mind all the Latin phrases I remembered from hearing them when I went to school with my masters and which, it seemed to me, had improved my mind, and I resolved, as if I could talk, to use them whenever the occasion arose, but not in the manner in which they are used by ignorant people. There are those who when speaking Spanish let fly from time to time in conversation some little piece of Latin, pretending to those who do not understand it that they are great Latin scholars, when they barely know how to decline a noun or conjugate a verb.

CIPIÓN: I find that less harmful than that which those who really know Latin do, for there are some so foolish that when speaking to a cobbler or a tailor they sprinkle Latin phrases like water.

BERGANZA: From which we can infer that equally wrong are those who use Latin to those who do not know it, as are those who use it in ignorance.

CIPIÓN. –Pues otra cosa puedes advertir, y es que hay algunos que no les excusa el ser latinos de ser asnos.

BERGANZA. –Pues ¿quién lo duda? La razón está clara, pues cuando en tiempo de los romanos hablaban todos latín, como lengua materna suya, algún majadero habría entre ellos, a quien no excusaría el hablar latín de ser necio.

CIPIÓN. –Para saber callar en romance y hablar en latín, discreción es menester, hermano Berganza.

BERGANZA. –Así es, porque también se puede decir una necedad en latín como en romance, y yo he visto letrados tontos, y gramáticos pesados, y romancistas vareteados con sus listas de latín, que con mucha facilidad pueden enfadar al mundo no una, sino muchas veces.

CIPIÓN. –Dejemos esto, y comienza a decir tus filosofías.

BERGANZA. –Ya las he dicho: éstas son que acabo de decir.

CIPIÓN. –¿Cuáles?

BERGANZA. –Estas de los latines y romances, que yo comencé y tú acabaste.

CIPIÓN. –¿Al murmurar llamas filosofar? ¡Así va ello! Canoniza, Berganza, a la maldita plaga de la murmuración, y dale el nombre que quisieres, que ella dará a nosotros el de cínicos, que quiere decir perros murmuradores; y por tu vida que calles ya y sigas tu historia.

BERGANZA. –¿Cómo la tengo de seguir si callo?

CIPIÓN. –Quiero decir que la sigas de golpe, sin que la hagas que parezca pulpo, según la vas añadiendo colas.

BERGANZA. –Habla con propiedad: que no se llaman colas las del pulpo.

CIPIÓN. –Ese es el error que tuvo el que dijo que no era torpedad ni vicio nombrar las cosas por sus propios nombres, como si fuese mejor, ya que sea forzoso nombrarlas, decirlas por circunloquios y rodeos que templen la asquerosidad que causa el oírlas por sus mismos nombres. Las honestas palabras dan indicio de la honestidad del que las pronuncia o las escribe.

BERGANZA. –Quiero creerte; y digo que, no contenta mi fortuna de haberme quitado de mis estudios y de la vida que en ellos pasaba, tan regocijada y compuesta, y haberme puesto atraillado tras de una puerta, y de haber trocado la liberalidad de los estudiantes en la mezquindad de la negra, ordenó de sobresaltarme en lo que ya por quietud y descanso tenía. Mira, Cipión, ten por cierto y averiguado, como yo lo tengo, que al desdichado las desdichas le buscan y le hallan, aunque se esconda en los últimos rincones de la tierra. Dígolo porque la negra de casa estaba enamorada de un negro, asimismo esclavo de casa, el cual negro dormía en el zaguán, que es entre la puerta de la calle y la de en medio, detrás de la cual yo estaba, y no se podían juntar sino de noche, y para esto habían hurtado o contrahecho las llaves; y así, las más de las noches bajaba la negra, y, tapándome la boca con algún pedazo de carne o queso, abría al negro, con quien se daba buen tiempo, facilitándolo mi silencio, y a costa de muchas cosas que la negra hurtaba. Algunos días me estragaron la conciencia las dádivas de la negra, pareciéndome que sin ellas se me apretarían las ijadas y daría de mastín en galgo. Pero, en efecto, llevado de mi buen natural, quise responder a lo que a mi amo debía, pues tiraba sus gajes y comía su pan, como lo deben hacer no sólo los perros honrados, a quien se les da renombre de agradecidos, sino todos aquellos que sirven.

CIPIÓN: And there is something else you should know, and that is that there are people who know Latin and are still asses.

BERGANZA: Who can doubt that? The reason is clear, for at the time when the Romans all spoke Latin as their native tongue, there must have been some idiot among them who, though speaking Latin, was still a fool.

CIPIÓN: In order to know how to be silent in romance and to speak in Latin, discretion is necessary, Berganza my brother.

BERGANZA: That is so, for one can say something foolish in both Latin and romance, and I have seen educated men who are stupid, and grammarians who are boring, and people whose speech is speckled with Latin which can easily annoy everyone, not just once but frequently.

CIPIÓN: Let's leave this now and start hearing your philosophical ideas.

BERGANZA: I've said them: I've just been telling them.

CIPIÓN: What were they?

BERGANZA: Those ideas about Latin and romance which I began and you finished.

CIPIÓN: You call gossiping philosophy? That's great! Dress up the accursed plague known as gossiping and give it whatever name you like, it will call us cynics,[23] which means gossiping dogs; for heaven's sake keep quiet and carry on with your story.

BERGANZA: How can I carry on if I keep quiet?

CIPIÓN: I mean that you should carry on straightaway, without adding tails to it which makes it seem like an octopus.

BERGAN2A: Speak properly: you don't talk of an octopus having tails.

CIPIÓN: That's the mistake made by the man who said that it was not inappropriate or wrong to call things by their proper names, as if it were better, since it is necessary to name them, to refer to them by circumlocutions and in a roundabout manner so as to temper the repulsion which hearing their right name causes. Honest words bear witness to the honesty of the one who utters them or writes them.

BERGANZA: I can believe you; and I will say that my fortune, not content to have taken me away from my studies and the happy and ordered life I had when undertaking them, and to have left me tethered behind a door, and to have exchanged the generosity of the students for the meanness of the negress, ordained that I should be jolted out of such peace and quiet as I had. Look, Cipión, and know for certain, as I do, that the unfortunate man is sought out and found by misfortune, even if he tries to hide in the furthest corners of the earth. I say this because the negress in the house was in love with a negro, also a slave in the house, who slept in the porch between the front door and the middle door, behind which I was, and they could only get together at night, and for this they had stolen or forged the keys; and so most nights the negress came down, and shutting my mouth with a piece of meat or cheese, let the negro in and had a good time with him, helped by my silence and at the cost of the many things she had stolen. On some days the gifts of the negress wreaked havoc with my conscience, since I thought that without them I'd be all skin and bone and change from a mastiff into a greyhound. But, in fact, led by my good nature, I decided to give back what I owed to my master, since I took his wages and ate his bread, as not only honourable dogs who have the reputation for being grateful ought to do, but also all those who serve.

CIPIÓN. –Esto sí, Berganza, quiero que pase por filosofía, porque son razones que consisten en buena verdad y en buen entendimiento; y adelante y no hagas soga, por no decir cola, de tu historia.

BERGANZA. –Primero te quiero rogar me digas, si es que lo sabes, qué quiere decir filosofía; que aunque yo la nombro, no sé lo que es; sólo me doy a entender que es cosa buena.

CIPIÓN. –Con brevedad te lo diré. Este nombre se compone de dos nombres griegos, que son *filos* y *sofía*; *filos* quiere decir *amor*, y *sofía*, la *ciencia*; así que *filosofía* significa *amor de la ciencia*, y *filósofo*, *amador de la ciencia*.

BERGANZA. –Mucho sabes, Cipión. ¿Quién diablos te enseñó a ti nombres griegos?

CIPIÓN. –Verdaderamente, Berganza, que eres simple, pues de esto haces caso; porque éstas son cosas que las saben los niños de la escuela, y también hay quien presuma saber la lengua griega, sin saberla, como la latina, ignorándola.

BERGANZA. –Eso es lo que yo digo, y quisiera que a estos tales los pusieran en una prensa, y a fuerza de vueltas les sacaran el jugo de lo que saben, porque no anduviesen engañando el mundo con el oropel de sus gregüescos rotos y sus latines falsos, como hacen los portugueses con los negros de Guinea.

CIPIÓN. –Ahora sí, Berganza, que te puedes morder la lengua, y tarazármela yo; porque todo cuanto decimos es murmurar.

BERGANZA. –Sí, que no estoy obligado a hacer lo que he oído decir que hizo uno llamado Corondas, tirio, el cual puso ley que ninguno entrase en el ayuntamiento de su ciudad con armas, so pena de la vida. Descuidóse de esto, y otro día entró en el cabildo ceñida la espada; advirtiéronselo, y acordáronse de la pena por él puesta; al momento desenvainó su espada y se pasó con ella el pecho, y fue el primero que puso y quebrantó la ley y pagó la pena. Lo que yo dije no fue poner ley, sino prometer que me mordería la lengua cuando murmurase; pero ahora no van las cosas por el tenor y rigor de las antiguas; hoy se hace una ley, y mañana se rompe, y quizá conviene que así sea. Ahora promete uno de enmendarse de sus vicios, y de allí a un momento cae en otros mayores. Una cosa es alabar la disciplina y otra el darse con ella, y, en efecto, del dicho al hecho hay gran trecho. Muérdase el diablo, que yo no quiero morderme ni hacer finezas detrás de una estera, donde de nadie soy visto que pueda alabar mi honrosa determinación.

CIPIÓN. –Según eso, Berganza, si tú fueras persona, fueras hipócrita, y todas las obras que hicieras fueran aparentes, fingidas y falsas, cubiertas con la capa de la virtud, sólo porque te alabaran, como todos los hipócritas hacen.

BERGANZA. –No sé lo que entonces hiciera; esto sé que quiero hacer ahora, que es no morderme, quedándome tantas cosas por decir que no sé cómo ni cuándo podré acabarlas, y más estando temeroso que al salir del sol nos hemos de quedar a oscuras, faltándonos el habla.

CIPIÓN. –Mejor lo hará el cielo. Sigue tu historia y no te desvíes del camino carretero con impertinentes digresiones; y así, por larga que sea, la acabarás presto.

BERGANZA. –Digo, pues, que habiendo visto la insolencia, ladrocinio y deshonestidad de los negros, determiné, como buen criado, estorbarlo, por los mejores medios que pudiese; y pude tan bien, que salí con mi intento. Bajaba la negra como has oído, a refocilarse con el negro, fiada en que me enmudecían los pedazos de carne, pan

CIPIÓN: Now this, Berganza, I will admit does pass for philosophy, since it involves reasoning which is true and full of sense. Continue and don't add any strings, or indeed tails, to your story.

BERGANZA: First I want you to tell me what philosophy is, for although I talk about it, I don't know what it is; I only know that it is something good.

CIPIÓN: I will tell you briefly. The noun is made up of two Greek nouns, *filos* and *sofia*; *filos* means "love" and *sofia* "knowledge", so that "philosophy" means "love of knowledge" and "philosopher" "lover of knowledge".

BERGANZA: You are very learned, Cipión. Who the devil taught you Greek words?

CIPIÓN: You are indeed very simple, Berganza, if you are impressed by that; these are things that every schoolboy knows, and there are also those who pretend to know Greek, without knowing it, like some do Latin, even though they are ignorant of it.

BERGANZA: That's what I say, and I should like such people to be put in a press and it turned until the juice of all they know is squeezed out of them so that they do not go around deceiving everyone with their threadbare Greek and their false Latin, as the Portuguese with the negroes in Guinea.

CIPIÓN: Now, Berganza, you can bite your tongue, and so can I, for everything that we are saying is gossip.

BERGANZA: Yes, but I am not obliged to do what I heard a certain Corondas from Thurium did.[24] He promulgated a law preventing anyone from entering the town hall bearing arms, under threat of death. He himself forgot this and one day entered the council wearing his sword; this was pointed out to him and he was reminded of the punishment he had decreed; he immediately took out his sword and plunged it into his chest, and he was the first one to break the law and pay the penalty. What I said was not promulgating a law but promising that I would bite my tongue whenever I gossiped; but now things are not as strict as they were in ancient times; today a law is passed, tomorrow it is broken, and perhaps this is how it should be. Now one promises to mend one's ways, and a moment later one is committing even greater sins. It is one thing to praise discipline and another to submit to it, and in fact there's many a slip between cup and lip. Let the devil bite himself, but I don't want to bite myself or perform heroics behind a mat, where no one can see me and praise my honour and determination.

CIPIÓN: According to what you say, Berganza, if you were a person, you would be a hypocrite, and all the works you performed would merely be appearance, falsehood and sham, covered with the cloak of virtue to attract the praise of others, as all hypocrites do.

BERGANZA: I don't know what I would do then, but I know what I want to do now, which is not bite myself, leaving so many things still unsaid that I do not know how or when I shall be able to finish them, the more so as I fear that when the sun comes out we shall remain in darkness, lacking the power of speech.

CIPIÓN: Heaven will arrange things better than that. Continue your story and do not go off the beaten track with irrelevant digressions, and, however long the story is, you will soon get to the end of it.

BERGANZA: Well, then, having seen the insolence, thieving and dishonesty of the two negroes, I resolved, as a good servant, to put an end to it by the best means at my disposal; and I was well able to carry out my intention. The negress would come down, as I've explained already, to have fun with the negro, confident that the pieces of meat,

o queso que me arrojaba... ¡Mucho pueden las dádivas, Cipión!

CIPIÓN. –Mucho. No te diviertas, pasa adelante.

BERGANZA. –Acuérdome que cuando estudiaba oí decir al preceptor un refrán latino, que ellos llaman adagio, que decía: *Habet bovem in lingua.*

CIPIÓN. –¡Oh, que en hora mala hayáis encajado vuestro latín! ¿Tan presto se te ha olvidado lo que poco ha dijimos contra los que entremeten latines en las conversaciones de romance?

BERGANZA. –Este latín viene aquí de molde; que has de saber que los atenienses usaban, entre otras, de una moneda sellada con la figura de un buey, y cuando algún juez dejaba de decir o hacer lo que era razón y justicia, por estar cohechado, decían: "Este tiene el buey en la lengua."

CIPIÓN. –La aplicación falta.

BERGANZA. –¿No está bien clara, si las dádivas de la negra me tuvieron muchos días mudo, que ni quería ni osaba ladrarla cuando bajaba a verse con su negro enamorado? Por lo que vuelvo a decir que pueden mucho las dádivas.

CIPIÓN. –Ya te he respondido que pueden mucho, y si no fuera por no hacer ahora una larga digresión, con mil ejemplos probara lo mucho que las dádivas pueden; mas quizá lo diré, si el cielo me concede tiempo, lugar y habla para contarte mi vida.

BERGANZA. –Dios te dé lo que deseas, y escucha. Finalmente, mi buena intención rompió por las malas dádivas de la negra; a la cual, bajando una noche muy oscura a su acostumbrado pasatiempo, arremetí sin ladrar, por que no se alborotasen los de casa, y en un instante le hice pedazos toda la camisa y le arranqué un pedazo de muslo; burla que fue bastante a tenerla de veras más de ocho días en la cama, fingiendo para con sus amos no sé qué enfermedad. Sanó, volvió otra noche, y yo volví a la pelea con mi perra, y, sin morderla, la arañé todo el cuerpo como si la hubiera cardado como manta. Nuestras batallas eran a la sorda, de las cuales salía siempre vencedor, y la negra, malparada y peor contenta. Pero sus enojos se parecían bien en mi pelo y en mi salud; alzóseme con la ración y los huesos, y los míos poco a poco iban señalando los nudos del espinazo. Con todo esto, aunque me quitaron el comer, no me pudieron quitar el ladrar. Pero la negra, por acabarme de una vez, me trajo una esponja frita con manteca; conocí la maldad; vi que era peor que comer zarazas, porque a quien la come se le hincha el estómago y no sale de él sin llevarse tras sí la vida. Y pareciéndome ser imposible guardarme de las asechanzas de tan indignados enemigos, acordé de poner tierra en medio, quitándomeles delante de los ojos. Halléme un día suelto, y sin decir adiós a ninguno de casa, me puse en la calle, y a menos de cien pasos me deparó la suerte al alguacil que dije al principio de mi historia, que era grande amigo de mi amo Nicolás el Romo; el cual, apenas me hubo visto, cuando me conoció y me llamó por mi nombre; también le conocí yo y al llamarme me llegué a él con mis acostumbradas ceremonias y caricias; asióme del cuello y dijo a dos corchetes suyos: "Éste es famoso perro de ayuda, que fue de un grande amigo mío; llevémosle a casa." Holgáronse los

bread or cheese that she tossed to me would keep me quiet ... Gifts can achieve a lot, Cipión!

CIPIÓN: Indeed they can! Don't get distracted. Carry on.

BERGANZA: I remember that when I was studying I heard from the teacher a Latin proverb, which they call an adage, which went: *Habet bovem in lingua.*

CIPIÓN: What a bad time to let drop some of your Latin! Have you forgotten already what we said a short time ago about those who slip Latin into conversation in Spanish?

BERGANZA: This piece of Latin fits perfectly here, for you should know that the Athenians used a coin stamped with the figure of an ox and when a judge failed to say or do what was right and just, because he had been bribed, they used to say: "This judge has an ox on his tongue."

CIPIÓN: I don't see the relevance.

BERGANZA: Isn't it clear, if the negress's gifts kept me quiet for many days, that I did not want or dare to bark when she came down to rendezvous with her lover? For which reason I say again that gifts can achieve a lot.

CIPIÓN: And I have replied that so they can, and if it were not to lead to a long digression, I would prove with a thousand examples that gifts can achieve a lot; but perhaps I will, if heaven gives me time, a place and the power of speech to tell you my life-story.

BERGANZA: May God grant you whatever you desire, and listen. In the end, my good intention overcame the wicked gifts of the negress, and one very dark night as she was coming down to indulge in her usual pastime, I jumped at her without barking, so as not to disturb the whole house, and in a second ripped her nightdress to shreds amd tore out a piece of her calf, a stunt that was sufficient to keep her in bed for more than a week, pretending to her master and mistress that she had some sickness or other. She got better, she came back again on another night, and I attacked her again and, without biting her, I scratched her whole body as though I were carding wool for a blanket. Our battles were waged in silence, and I always emerged victorious from them, and the negress ended up in poor shape and pretty angry. But her anger soon had consequences for my coat and the state of my health; my rations and bones were taken away, and my bones were soon sticking out through my skin. Nevertheless, even though they could take away my food they could not take away my bark. But the negress, to finish me off once and for all, brought me a sponge fried in butter; I saw her evil intent and knew that I might as well swallow poison, for if you eat it your stomach swells up and you never survive. So I came to the conclusion that I would never be able to protect myself against the wiles of those wicked enemies, and I decided to get away to somewhere out of their sight. One day I was off the leash and, without saying goodbye to anyone, I headed out into the street, and less than a hundred yards down the road I was lucky to meet the police officer[25] I mentioned at the beginning of my tale, who was a great friend of my master, Nicolás el Romo, and who recognised me as soon as he saw me and called out my name. I also recognised him and when he called me I went up to him with my usual courtesy and display of affection. He caught me by the collar and said to two of his men:

"This is a very famous guard dog who belonged to a great friend of mine. Let's take him home."

corchetes, y dijeron que si era de ayuda a todos sería de provecho. Quisieron asirme para llevarme, y mi amo dijo que no era menester asirme, que yo me iría, porque le conocía. Háseme olvidado decirte que las carlancas con puntas de acero que saqué cuando me desgarré y ausenté del ganado me las quitó un gitano en una venta, y ya en Sevilla andaba sin ellas; pero el alguacil me puso un collar tachonado todo de latón morisco. Considera, Cipión, ahora esta rueda variable de la fortuna mía: ayer me vi estudiante, y hoy me ves corchete.

CIPIÓN. –Así va el mundo, y no hay para qué te pongas ahora a exagerar los vaivenes de fortuna, como si hubiera mucha diferencia de ser mozo de un jifero a serlo de un corchete. No puedo sufrir ni llevar en paciencia oír las quejas que dan de la fortuna algunos hombres que la mayor que tuvieron fue tener premisas y esperanzas de llegar a ser escuderos. ¡Con qué maldiciones la maldicen!. ¡Con cuántos improperios la deshonran! Y no por más de que porque piense el que los oye que de alta, próspera y buena ventura han venido a la desdichada y baja en que los miran.

BERGANZA. –Tienes razón; y has de saber que este alguacil tenía amistad con un escribano, con quien se acompañaba; estaban los dos amancebados con dos mujercillas, no de poco más a menos, sino de menos en todo; verdad es que tenían algo de buenas caras, pero mucho de desenfado y de taimería putesca. Estas les servían de red y de anzuelo para pescar en seco, en esta forma: vestíanse de suerte que por la pinta descubrían la figura, y a tiro de arcabuz mostraban ser damas de la vida libre; andaban siempre a caza de extranjeros, y cuando llegaba la vendeja a Cádiz y a Sevilla llegaba la huella de su ganancia, no quedando bretón con quien no embistiesen; y en cayendo el grasiento con alguna de estas limpias, avisaban al alguacil y al escribano adónde y a qué posada iban, y en estando juntos les daban asalto y los prendían por amancebados; pero nunca los llevaban a la cárcel, a causa de que los extranjeros siempre redimían la vejación con dineros.

"Sucedió, pues, que la Colindres, que así se llamaba la amiga del alguacil, pescó un bretón unto y bisunto; concertó con él cena y noche en su posada; dio el cañuto a su amigo; y apenas se habían desnudado, cuando el alguacil, el escribano, dos corchetes y yo dimos con ellos. Alborotáronse los amantes; exageró el alguacil el delito; mandólos vestir a toda prisa para llevarlos a la cárcel; afligióse el bretón; terció, movido de caridad, el escribano, y a puros ruegos redujo la pena a solos cien reales. Pidió el bretón unos follados de gamuza que había puesto en una silla a los pies de la cama, donde tenía dineros para pagar su libertad, y no parecieron los follados, ni podían parecer; porque así como yo entré en el aposento, llegó a mis narices un olor de tocino que me consoló todo; descubríle con el olfato, y halléle en una faltriquera de los follados. Digo que hallé en ella un pedazo de jamón famoso, y por gozarle y poderle sacar sin rumor saqué los follados a la calle, y allí me entregué en el jamón a toda mi voluntad, y cuando volví al aposento hallé que el bretón daba voces diciendo en lenguaje adúltero y bastardo, aunque se entendía, que le volviesen sus calzas, que en ellas tenía cincuenta *escuti d'oro in oro*. Imaginó el escribano o que la Colindres o los corchetes se los habían robado; el

The constables were pleased, and said that if I were a guard dog I'd be of great benefit to all of them. They wanted to grab hold of me and take me, but my master said that that was not necessary, that I would go willingly because I knew him. I forgot to tell you that the steel-studded collar I took when I fled from the flock was removed by a gypsy in an inn and that I no longer wore it in Seville. But the police officer put a collar studded with Moorish brass around my neck. See, Cipión, how the wheel of fortune turns: yesterday I was a student, today I am a police constable.

CIPIÓN: That's the way of the world, and there's no need for you to exaggerate the ups and downs of fate, as if there were much difference between being the servant of a slaughterhouse man or of a constable. I cannot stand or put up with the complaints made against fate by some men when their greatest hope and expectation was to reach the level of squire. And how they curse their accursed fate! How they rant and rail against it! And only so that whoever is listening to them will think that they have fallen from the heights of good fortune and prosperity into the sorry state in which they now see them.

BERGANZA: You are right. And you should know that this police officer was friendly with a notary, with whom he went around. They had as mistresses two women, who were more bad than good in all things; the truth is that they were not bad-looking, but they had all the brashness and slyness that one associates with tarts. These women acted as a net and hook for their catches in this manner: they dressed in such a way that there was no mistaking what they were, and you could see from a mile off that they were loose women; they were always chasing foreigners and when the merchant fleet came to Cadiz and Seville for the autumn fair they could smell profit and no foreigner was immune from their attacks. When one of these greasy fellows fell in with these fair ladies, they told the police officer and the notary where they were going and where their lodgings were, and when they were together they would pounce and arrest them for consorting with prostitutes; but they never took them to prison because the foreigners always redeemed the offence with money.

It happened, then, that Colindres, for that was the police officer's girlfriend's name, caught a slimy, greasy foreigner. She agreed to have dinner and spend the night with him at his inn and informed her friend; and no sooner had they taken their clothes off than the police officer, the notary, and two constables and myself all came upon them. The lovers were alarmed; the officer exaggerated the offence and ordered them to get dressed at once to be taken away to prison. The foreigner became very upset and the notary, moved by compassion, in response to his pleading reduced the punishment to a fine of only one hundred *reales*. The foreigner asked for his chamois leather breeches which he had put on a chair at the foot of the bed and in which he had the money to buy his freedom, but they did not appear, nor could they; because as soon as I entered the room the smell of bacon reached my nostrils, which cheered me up no end. I followed the scent to one of the pockets of the breeches, and there I found a fine piece of ham, and in order to enjoy it and remove it without making a noise, I took the breeches out to the street and settled down to feast heartily on the ham, and when I returned to the room I found that the foreigner was shouting in some strange and grotesque language, although one could understand him, asking for his breeches to be returned, for he had fifty golden *escudos* in them. The notary imagined that either Colindres or the constables had stolen them, the officer thought the same; he called them to one side but none of them

alguacil pensó lo mismo; llamólos aparte, no confesó ninguno, y diéronse al diablo todos. Viendo yo lo que pasaba, volví a la calle donde había dejado los follados, para volverlos, pues a mí no me aprovechaba nada el dinero; no los hallé, porque ya algún venturoso que pasó se los había llevado. Como el alguacil vio que el bretón no tenía dinero para el cohecho, se desesperaba, y pensó en sacar de la huéspeda de la casa lo que el bretón no tenía; llamóla, y vino medio desnuda, y como oyó las voces y quejas del bretón, y a la Colindres desnuda y llorando, el alguacil en cólera y al escribano enojado y a los corchetes despabilando lo que hallaban en el aposento, no le plugo mucho. Mandó el alguacil que se cubriese y se viniese con él a la cárcel, porque consentía en su casa hombres y mujeres de mal vivir. ¡Aquí fue ello! ¡Aquí sí que fue cuando se aumentaron las voces y creció la confusión!; porque dijo la huéspeda: "Señor alguacil y señor escribano no conmigo tretas, que entrevo toda costura; no conmigo dijes ni poleos; callen la boca y váyanse con Dios; si no, por mi santiguada que arroje el bodegón por la ventana, y que saque a plaza toda la chirinola de esta historia; que bien conozco a la señora Colindres, y sé que ha muchos meses que es su cobertor el señor alguacil; y no hagan que me aclare más, sino vuélvase el dinero a este señor, y quedemos todos por buenos; porque yo soy mujer honrada y tengo un marido con su carta de ejecutoria, y con *a perpenan rei de memoria*, con sus colgaderos de plomo, Dios sea loado, y hago este oficio muy limpiamente y sin daño de barras. El arancel tengo clavado donde todo el mundo le vea; y no conmigo cuentos, que, por Dios, que sé despolvorearme. ¡Bonita soy yo para que por mi orden entren mujeres con los huéspedes! Ellos tienen las llaves de sus aposentos, y yo no soy quince, que tengo de ver tras siete paredes."

"Pasmados quedaron mis amos de haber oído la arenga de la huéspeda y de ver cómo les leía la historia de sus vidas; pero como vieron que no tenían de quién sacar dinero si de ella no, porfiaban en llevarla a la cárcel. Quejábase ella al cielo de la sinrazón y justicia que la hacían, estando su marido ausente y siendo tan principal hidalgo. El bretón bramaba por sus cincuenta *escuti*. Los corchetes porfiaban que ellos no habían visto los follados, ni Dios permitiese lo tal. El escribano, por lo callado, insistía al alguacil que mirase los vestidos de la Colindres, que le daba sospecha que ella debía de tener los cincuenta *escuti*, por tener de costumbre visitar los escondrijos y faltriqueras de aquellos que con ella se envolvían. Ella decía que el bretón estaba borracho y que debía de mentir en lo del dinero. En efecto, todo era confusión, gritos y juramentos, sin llevar modo de apaciguarse, ni se apaciguaran si al instante no entrara en el aposento el teniente de Asistente, que viniendo a visitar aquella posada, las voces le llevaron adonde era la grita. Preguntó la causa de aquellas voces; la huéspeda se la dio muy por menudo: dijo quién era la ninfa Colindres, que ya estaba vestida; publicó la pública amistad suya y del alguacil; echó en la calle sus tretas y modo de robar; disculpóse a sí misma de que con su consentimiento jamás había entrado en su casa mujer de mala sospecha; canonizóse por santa y a su marido por un bendito, y dio voces a una moza que fuese corriendo y trajese de un cofre la carta ejecutoria de su marido, para que la viese el señor Teniente, diciéndole que por ella echaría de ver que mujer de tan honrado marido no podía hacer cosa mala, y que si tenía aquel oficio de casa de camas era a no poder más; que Dios sabía lo que le pesaba, y si quisiera ella tener alguna renta y pan cuotidiano para pasar la vida que tener aquel ejercicio. El Teniente,

confessed and all swore that they didn't do it. Seeing what was going on, I went back out to the street where I had left the breeches to give them back, for the money was of no use to me. I couldn't find them, for some lucky chap had come across them and kept them. As the officer saw that the foreigner had no money to pay the bribe, he went berserk, and thought of getting from the landlady what the foreigner owed him; he called her, and she came half-naked, and as she heard the shouts and complaints of the foreigner, and saw Colindres naked and crying, the police officer in a rage, the notary angry and the constables pilfering what was in the room, she was not best pleased. The officer told her to get dressed and accompany him to the prison for allowing immoral men and women in her establishment. What an uproar! Now voices really were raised and there was even more confusion, for the landlady said:

"My dear Police Officer and Notary, don't play around with me for I can see through your tricks. Don't try to intimidate or threaten me; just shut up and clear off. If you don't, I swear I'll raise the roof and spill the beans about this little affair; I know Madam Colindres well, and I know that for months now you, Mr. Police Officer, have been her pimp; don't make me spell it out any more and give this gentleman back his money and we'll say no more about it; for I am an honest woman and I have a husband with a patent of nobility and his *a perpenan rei de memoria*[26] and his lead seal, praise God, and I carry out my profession decently and do no harm to anyone. I have my prices displayed where everyone can see them. So don't come to me with these stories for, by God, I know how to look after myself. I'm not fool enough to allow guests to bring women in with them? They have the keys to their rooms and I am no quinx[27] and cannot see through walls."

My masters were flabbergasted hearing the way the landlady harangued them and seeing how she was able to tell them all about the lives they led; but as they could see that they had only her to get money from, they still persisted in wanting to take her away to prison. She complained to high heaven about the unreasonableness and injustice of what they were doing when her husband, who was such a distinguished gentleman, was away. The foreigner was roaring for his fifty *escudos*. The constables were insisting that they, God forbid, had not seen the breeches. The notary, in a whisper, was pressing the constable to look at Colindres' clothes, for he suspected that she had the fifty *escudos*, since she usually looked into the hidingplaces and pockets of those she got involved with. She was saying that the foreigner was drunk and must have been lying about the money. In short, everything was confusion, shouting and swearing, with no sign of abating, and things would not have calmed down if at that moment the magistrate's lieutenant, who had come to visit that inn, had not entered the room drawn by the shouts emanating from it. He asked what all the shouting was about and the landlady told him in minute detail. She told him all about the nymph Colindres, who was now dressed; she revealed her public liaison with the police officer; she exposed their tricks and methods for stealing from others; she exonerated herself saying that no woman of ill-repute had ever entered her house with her consent; she proclaimed herself a saint and her husband the next best thing, and she called to a servant girl to run and fetch from a chest her husband's patent of nobility, so that the lieutenant could see it, saying that it would show that the wife of such an honourable husband could not do anything evil, and that if she kept a guesthouse it was because she had no choice; for God knew how much it grieved her, and she wished she had some income and enough to

enfadado de su mucho hablar y presumir de ejecutoria, le dijo: "Hermana camera, yo quiero creer que vuestro marido tiene carta de hidalguía con que vos me confeséis que es hidalgo mesonero." "Y con mucha honra –respondió la huéspeda–. Y ¿qué linaje hay en el mundo, por bueno que sea, que no tenga algún dime y direte?" "Lo que yo os digo, hermana, es que os cubráis, que habéis de venir a la cárcel." La cual nueva dio con ella en el suelo; arañóse el rostro; alzó el grito; pero, con todo eso, el Teniente, demasiadamente severo, los llevó a todos a la cárcel, conviene a saber: al bretón, a la Colindres y a la huéspeda. Después supe que el bretón perdió sus cincuenta *escuti*, y más diez, en que le condenaron en las costas; la huéspeda pagó otro tanto, y la Colindres salió libre por la puerta afuera. Y el mismo día que la soltaron pescó a un marinero, que pagó por el bretón, con el mismo embuste del soplo; porque veas, Cipión, cuántos y cuán grandes inconvenientes nacieron de mi golosina.

CIPIÓN. –Mejor dijeras de la bellaquería de tu amo.

BERGANZA. –Pues escucha, que aun más adelante tiraban la barra, puesto que me pesa de decir mal de alguaciles y de escribanos.

CIPIÓN. –Sí, que decir mal de uno no es decirlo de todos; sí, que muchos y muy muchos escribanos hay buenos, fieles y legales, y amigos de hacer placer sin daño de tercero; sí, que no todos entretienen los pleitos, ni avisan a las partes, ni todos llevan más de sus derechos, ni todos van buscando e inquiriendo las vidas ajenas para ponerlas en tela de juicio, ni todos se aúnan con el juez para "hácheme la barba y hacerte he el copete", ni todos los alguaciles se conciertan con los vagamundos y fulleros, ni tienen todos las amigas de tu amo para sus embustes. Muchos y muy muchos hay hidalgos por naturaleza y de hidalgas condiciones; muchos no son arrojados, insolentes, ni mal criados, ni rateros, como los que andan por los mesones midiendo las espadas a los extranjeros, y hallándolas un pelo más de la marca destruyen a sus dueños. Sí, que no todos como prenden sueltan y son jueces y abogados cuando quieren.

BERGANZA. –Más alto picaba mi amo; otro camino era el suyo; presumía de valiente y de hacer prisiones famosas; sustentaba la valentía sin peligro de su persona, pero a costa de su bolsa. Un día acometió en la Puerta de Jerez él solo a seis famosos rufianes, sin que yo le pudiese ayudar en nada porque llevaba con un freno de cordel impedida la boca; que así me traía de día, y de noche me lo quitaba. Quedé maravillado de ver su atrevimiento, su brío y su denuedo; así se entraba y salía por las seis espadas de los rufos como si fueran varas de mimbre: era cosa maravillosa ver la ligereza con que acometía, las estocadas que tiraba, los reparos, la cuenta, el ojo alerta porque no le tomasen las espaldas. Finalmente, él quedó en mi opinión y en la de todos cuantos la pendencia miraron y supieron por un nuevo Rodamonte, habiendo llevado a sus enemigos desde la Puerta de Jerez hasta los mármoles del Colegio de Mase Rodrigo, que hay más de cien pasos. Dejólos encerrados, y volvió a coger los trofeos de la batalla, que fueron tres vainas, y luego se las fue a mostrar al Asistente, que, si mal no me acuerdo, lo era entonces el licenciado Sarmiento de Valladares, famoso por la destrucción de La Sauceda. Miraban a mi amo por las calles do pasaba, señalándole con el dedo, como si dijeran: "Aquél es el valiente que se atrevió a reñir solo con la flor de

eat so as not to have to engage in that trade. The lieutenant, angered by her endless chatter and her pretensions to nobility, said to her:

"My dear landlady, I will believe that your husband has a patent of nobility if you admit that he is a nobleman who runs an inn".

"He does, and very honourably", replied the landlady. "And what dynasty is there in the world, however good, that hasn't got something to hide?"

"What I'm telling you, my dear, is to get dressed and accompany me to the prison."

This news did for her; she scratched her face, screamed at the top of her voice, but the lieutenant, despite this, showed himself to be very severe and took them all off to prison, that is, the foreigner, Colindres and the landlady. I later learned that the foreigner lost his fifty *escudos*, and ten more in payment of costs; the landlady paid as much again, and Colindres was let off scot free. And on the very day she was let out she caught a sailor, who made up for the foreigner, with the same trick. I tell you this, Cipión, so that you can see how much misery was caused by my greed.

CIPIÓN: Rather by your master's wickedness.

BERGANZA: Well listen, for they even went further, although I do not like to speak ill of police officers and notaries.

CIPIÓN: Quite right, but to speak ill of one of them is not to speak ill of all of them, for there are many, very many notaries who are good, trustworthy and honest, and who want to please without harming a third party; not all of them bring lawsuits, or represent all sides, or take more than they are entitled to, or go inquiring and poking their noses into other people's lives to cast aspersions on them, and not all of them team up with the Judge in the spirit of "you scratch my back and I'll scratch yours", nor do all police officers consort with vagabonds and rogues, nor do they all have mistresses for their con tricks like your master. Very many of them are gentlemen by nature and by birth; many are not arrogant, insolent, nor ill-bred, nor thieves, like those who go around inns measuring foreigners' swords and if they find them a fraction longer than is legal they ruin their owners. Indeed, not all of them catch people and let them go, and act as lawyers and judges when they feel like it.

BERGANZA: My master had higher ambitions; his route was a different one; he thought himself tough and that he could make spectacular catches. He showed his toughness without running any risks to himself, but at the cost of his purse. One day at the Puerta de Jerez[28] he attacked six well-known ruffians, without my being able to give him any help because I had a muzzle on my mouth: he kept it on me during the day, and took it off at night. I was astonished at his daring, his courage and his dash; he dodged in and out of the six ruffians' swords as if they were wicker wands; it was a marvel to see how swiftly he attacked, his thrusting and parrying, the way he weighed up the situation and kept his eye out for his back. In the end, in my opinion and in that of all the others who witnessed the fight, he emerged as a new Rodamonte,[29] having driven his enemies from the Puerta de Jerez to the marble columns of the Colegio de Mase Rodrigo,[30] which is more than a hundred feet away. He left them locked up and went back to collect the trophies of battle, which were three scabbards, and then he went to show them to the Magistrate who, if I am not mistaken, was at that time Licentiate Sarmiento de Valladares,[31] famous for the destruction of La Sauceda.[32] People looked at my master as he went through the streets pointing him out as if to say: "That's the brave man who dared to fight with the hardest men of all Andalusia." He spent the

los bravos de Andalucía." En dar vueltas a la ciudad, para dejarse ver, se pasó lo que quedaba del día, y la noche nos halló en Triana, en una calle junto al Molino de la Pólvora; y habiendo mi amo avizorado (como en la jácara se dice) si alguien le veía, se entró en una casa, y yo tras él, y hallamos en un patio a todos los jayanes de la pendencia, sin capas ni espadas, y todos desabrochados; y uno, que debía de ser el huésped, tenía un gran jarro de vino en la una mano y en la otra una copa grande de taberna, la cual, colmándola de vino generoso y espumante, brindaba a toda la compañía. Apenas hubieron visto a mi amo, cuando todos se fueron a él con los brazos abiertos, y todos le brindaron, y él hizo la razón a todos, y aun la hiciera a otros tantos si le fuera algo en ello, por ser de condición afable y amigo de no enfadar a nadie por pocas cosas. Quererte yo contar ahora lo que allí se trató, la cena que cenaron, las peleas que se contaron, los hurtos que se refirieron, las damas que de su trato se calificaron y las que se reprobaron, las alabanzas que los unos a los otros se dieron, los bravos ausentes que se nombraron, la destreza que allí se puso en su punto, levantándose en mitad de la cena a poner en práctica las tretas que se les ofrecían, esgrimiendo con las manos, los vocablos tan exquisitos de que usaban, y, finalmente, el talle de la persona del huésped, a quien todos respetaban como a señor y padre, sería meterme en un laberinto donde no me fuese posible salir cuando quisiese. Finalmente, vine a entender con toda certeza que el dueño de la casa, a quien llamaban Monipodio, era encubridor de ladrones y pala de rufianes, y que la gran pendencia de mi amo había sido primero concertada con ellos, con las circunstancias del retirarse y de dejar las vainas, las cuales pagó mi amo allí, luego, de contado, con todo cuanto Monipodio dijo que había costado la cena, que se concluyó casi al amanecer, con mucho gusto de todos. Y fue su postre dar soplo a mi amo de un rufián forastero que, nuevo y flamante, había llegado a la ciudad: debía de ser más valiente que ellos, y de envidia le soplaron. Prendióle mi amo la siguiente noche, desnudo en la cama; que si vestido estuviera, yo vi en su talle que no se dejara prender tan a mansalva. Con esta prisión, que sobrevino sobre la pendencia, creció la fama de mi cobarde, que lo era mi amo más que una liebre, y a fuerza de meriendas y tragos sustentaba la fama de ser valiente, y todo cuanto con su oficio y con sus inteligencias granjeaba se le iba y desaguaba por la canal de la valentía.

"Pero ten paciencia, y escucha ahora un cuento que le sucedió, sin añadir ni quitar de la verdad una tilde. Dos ladrones hurtaron en Antequera un caballo muy bueno; trajéronle a Sevilla, y para venderle sin peligro usaron de un ardid que, a mi parecer, tiene del agudo y del discreto. Fuéronse a posar a posadas diferentes, y el uno se fue a la justicia y pidió por una petición que Pedro de Losada le debía cuatrocientos reales prestados, como parecía por una cédula firmada de su nombre, de la cual hacía presentación. Mandó el Teniente que el tal Losada reconociese la cédula, y que si la reconociese, le sacasen prendas de la cantidad o le pusiesen en la cárcel; tocó hacer esta diligencia a mi amo y al escribano su amigo; llevóles el ladrón a la posada del otro, y al punto reconoció su firma, y confesó la deuda, y señaló por prenda de la ejecución el caballo, el cual visto por mi amo, le creció el ojo; y le marcó por suyo si acaso se vendiese. Dio el ladrón por pasados los términos de la ley, y el caballo se puso en venta y se remató en quinientos reales en un tercero que mi amo echó de manga para que se le comprase. Valía el caballo tanto y medio más de lo que dieron por él. Pero como el bien del vendedor estaba en la brevedad de la venta, a la primer postura remató su mercadería. Cobró el un ladrón la deuda que no le debían, y el otro la carta de pago que

remainder of the day walking around the city, to let himself be seen, and at nightfall we were in Triana,[33] in a street near the gunpowder mill. Having had a dekko (as they say in slang) to check if anyone could see him, he went into a house, with me following him, and there in a patio were all the thugs from the fight, without cloaks or swords, and with their tunics undone; and one, who must have been the host, held a large jar of wine in one hand and in the other a large glass with which, having filled it with fine, sparkling wine, he toasted the company present. No sooner had they seen my master than they all rushed towards him with open arms and all toasted him, and he responded in kind, and he would have done so again and again if there had been something in it for him, since he was of a friendly disposition and not the kind to offend others for something trivial. I want to tell you now what went on there, the supper they had, the fights they talked about, the robberies they described, the women they had had and which ones were up to standard and which not, the praise they heaped on one another, toughs who were not there that they talked about, the skill with which they fenced, with some of them getting up in the middle of supper to demonstrate moves, fencing with their hands, the choice language they used and finally the fine figure cut by the host, whom all respected as their lord and father, but to do so would take me into a labyrinth from which I could not escape if I wanted to. Eventually, I came to realise that the owner of the house, who was called Monipodio, was a protector of criminals and a leader of a gang and that my master's great fight had first been agreed with them, including the details of fleeing and leaving the scabbards, which my master paid for there and then in cash and the full amount that Monipodio said it cost to put on the meal, which lasted until daybreak and which they all enjoyed. And as a dessert they gave my master the word about a new ruffian, an outsider who had arrived in the city: he must have been tougher than they were, and they fingered him out of envy. My master caught him the following night, naked in bed; if he had been dressed, I could see from his build that he would not have been taken so easily. With this arrest, which came on top of the fight, my cowardly master's fame grew, and he was as cowardly as a hare, and through meals and drinks he kept up his reputation as a hard man, and everything he earned from his job and his wit leaked away down the drain of his toughness.

But be patient and listen now to a tale of what happened to him, which has had nothing added or taken away. Two thieves stole a very fine horse in Antequera; they brought it to Seville and in order to sell it without any risk they used a stratagem which, to my mind, was very clever and resourceful. They went to stay at different inns, and one of them went to court and petitioned that Pedro de Losada owed him four hundred *reales*, as testified by a certificate signed in his name, which he presented. The magistrate ordered the said Losada to acknowledge the certificate and, if he did so, either to guarantee to pay the amount owed or be put in prison. This task was entrusted to my master and his friend the notary; the thief took them to the other's inn, and immediately he acknowledged his signature, confessed the debt, and offered the horse as a guarantee of payment. When my master saw it, he coveted it and marked it down for himself in the event of its being sold. The thief let the time fixed by the law pass by, and the horse was put up for sale and knocked down for five hundred *reales* through a third party which my master contracted to buy it for him. The horse was worth half as much again as what they paid for it, but as a quick sale was in the vendor's interest, he accepted the first bid. One thief collected a debt that was not owed to him, and the other a receipt

no había menester, y mi amo se quedó con el caballo, que para él fue peor que el Seyano lo fue para sus dueños. Mondaron luego la haza los ladrones, y de allí a dos días, después de haber trastejado mi amo las guarniciones y otras faltas del caballo, pareció sobre él en la plaza de San Francisco, más hueco y pomposo que aldeano vestido de fiesta. Diéronle mil parabienes de la buena compra, afirmándole que valía ciento y cincuenta escudos como un huevo un maravedí, y él, volteando y revolviendo el caballo, representaba su tragedia en el teatro de la referida plaza. Y estando en sus caracoles y rodeos, llegaron dos hombres de buen talle y de mejor ropaje, y el uno dijo: "¡Vive Dios, que éste es Piedehierro, mi caballo, que ha pocos días que me le hurtaron en Antequera!" Todos los que venían con él, que eran cuatro criados, dijeron que así era la verdad: que aquél era Piedehierro, el caballo que le habían hurtado. Pasmóse mi amo, querellóse el dueño, hubo pruebas, y fueron las que hizo el dueño tan buenas, que salió la sentencia en su favor y mi amo fue desposeído del caballo. Súpose la burla y la industria de los ladrones, que por manos e intervención de la misma justicia vendieron lo que habían hurtado, y casi todos se holgaban de que la codicia de mi amo le hubiese rompido el saco.

"Y no paró en esto su desgracia; que aquella noche, saliendo a rondar el mismo Asistente, por haberle dado noticia que hacia los barrios de San Julián andaban ladrones, al pasar de una encrucijada vieron pasar un hombre corriendo, y dijo a este punto el Asistente, asiéndome por el collar y zuzándome: "¡Al ladrón, Gavilán! ¡Ea, Gavilán, hijo, al ladrón, al ladrón!" Yo, a quien ya tenían cansado las maldades de mi amo, por cumplir lo que el señor Asistente me mandaba sin discrepar en nada, arremetí con mi propio amo, y sin que pudiese valerse, di con él en el suelo; y si no me lo quitaran, yo hiciera a más de a cuatro vengados; quitáronme con mucha pesadumbre de entrambos. Quisieran los corchetes castigarme, y aun matarme a palos, y lo hicieran si el Asistente no les dijera: "No le toque nadie, que el perro hizo lo que yo le mandé." Entendióse la malicia, y yo, sin despedirme de nadie, por un agujero de la muralla salí al campo, y antes que amaneciese me puse en Mairena, que es un lugar que está cuatro leguas de Sevilla. Quiso mi buena suerte que hallé allí una compañía de soldados que, según oí decir, se iban a embarcar a Cartagena. Estaban en ella cuatro rufianes de los amigos de mi amo, y el atambor era uno que había sido corchete, y gran chocarrero, como lo suelen ser los más atambores. Conociéronme todos, y todos me hablaron, y así me preguntaban por mi amo como si les hubiera de responder; pero el que más afición me mostró fue el atambor, y así, determiné de acomodarme con él, si él quisiese, y seguir aquella jornada, aunque me llevase a Italia o a Flandes; porque me parece a mí, y aun a ti te debe parecer lo mismo, que puesto que dice el refrán: "Quien necio es en su villa, necio es en Castilla", el andar tierras y comunicar con diversas gentes hace a los hombres discretos.

CIPIÓN. —Es eso tan verdad, que me acuerdo haber oído decir a un amo que tuve de bonísimo ingenio que al famoso griego llamado Ulises le dieron renombre de prudente por sólo haber andado muchas tierras y comunicado con diversas gentes y varias naciones; y así, alabo la intención que tuviste de irte donde te llevasen.

which he did not need, and my master got the horse, which turned out to be worse for him than Sejanus's horse[34] was for its owners. The thieves then moved on, and two days later when he had put in order the horse's harness and other trappings, my master appeared on it in the Plaza de San Francisco, looking more conceited and pompous than a country bumpkin in his Sunday best. He was congratulated warmly on his excellent buy and was told that it was worth one hundred and fifty *escudos* as sure as an egg was worth a *maravedí*, while he, turning and parading the horse, acted out his tragedy in the theatre provided by the aforementioned square. And as he was turning and prancing about, two men with good looks and even better clothes appeared and one of them said:

"My God, it's Piedehierro, my horse, which was stolen a few days ago in Antequera!"

All four servants who were accompanying him said it was true, that that was Piedehierro, the horse that had been stolen from him. My master was dumbfounded, the owner complained, supported his claim with proofs which were so good that judgement came down on his side and my master was dispossessed of the horse. The trickery and resourcefulness of the thieves were recognised, for they had sold what they had stolen through the medium and intervention of the courts, and almost everyone was delighted that my master's covetousness had brought him down.

And his misfortune did not stop there, for that night as the magistrate himself was going his rounds having heard that there were thieves in the San Julian district,[35] as they passed a crossroads they saw a man running by, whereupon the magistrate said, catching hold of my collar and urging me on:

"Thief, Gavilán! Go on, Gavilán, get him, good boy! Thief! Thief!"

I, who by now was fed up with my master's wrong-doing, in order to carry out the magistrate's orders to the full, attacked my own master and brought him to the ground before he could do anything about it. And if they hadn't taken me off him, I'd have wreaked vengeance for quite a few; they pulled me off, much to the regret of both of us. The constables wanted to punish me, and even beat me to death, and they would have done so if the magistrate had not said to them:

"Nobody touch him, for the dog did what I told him."

Everyone understood, and I headed off to the countryside through a hole in the wall, without saying goodbye to anyone, and before dawn was in Mairena,[36] a place about four leagues from Seville. Fortune had it that there I met a company of soldiers who, as I heard, were going to board ship at Cartagena. In the company were four rough friends of my master and the drummer was one who had been a constable, and a great exhibitionist, as drummers usually are. They all recognised me, and all spoke to me, and asked me about my master as if I could reply; but the one who showed me most affection was the drummer, and so I resolved to attach myself to him, if he were willing, and follow them, even if this took me to Italy or Flanders, for I think, and you should think likewise, that since the proverb says : "If someone is a fool in his home town, he'll be a fool in his own country," visiting other lands and communicating with different people makes men wise.

CIPIÓN: That's so true that I remember a very clever master of mine saying that Ulysses, the famous Greek, had the reputation for being wise simply because he had visited many lands and communicated with different peoples and various nations; so I praise your intention in going wherever they took you.

BERGANZA. –Es, pues, el caso que el atambor, por tener con qué mostrar más sus chocarrerías, comenzó a enseñarme a bailar al son del atambor y a hacer otras monerías, tan ajenas de poder aprenderlas otro perro que no fuera yo como las oirás cuando te las diga. Por acabarse el distrito de la comisión, se marchaba poco a poco; no había comisario que nos limitase; el capitán era mozo, pero muy buen caballero y gran cristiano; el alférez no había muchos meses que había dejado la Corte y el tinelo; el sargento era matrero y sagaz, y grande harriero de compañías, desde donde se levantaban hasta el embarcadero. Iba la compañía de rufianes churrulleros, los cuales hacían algunas insolencias por los lugares do pasábamos, que redundaban en maldecir a quien no lo merecía; infelicidad es del buen príncipe ser culpado de sus súbditos por la culpa de sus súbditos, a causa que los unos son verdugos de los otros, sin culpa del señor; pues aunque quiera y lo procure no puede remediar estos daños, porque todas o las más cosas de la guerra traen consigo aspereza, riguridad y desconveniencia. En fin, en menos de quince días, con mi buen ingenio y con la diligencia que puso el que había escogido por patrón, supe saltar por el Rey de Francia y no saltar por la mala tabernera. Enseñóme a hacer corvetas como caballo napolitano y a andar a la redonda como mula de atahona, con otras cosas que, si yo no tuviera cuenta en no adelantarme a mostrarlas, pusiera en duda si era algún demonio en figura de perro el que las hacía. Púsome nombre del "perro sabio", y no habíamos llegado al alojamiento cuando, tocando su atambor, andaba por todo el lugar pregonando que todas las personas que quisiesen venir a ver las maravillosas gracias y habilidades del perro sabio, en tal casa, o en tal hospital, las mostraban, a ocho, o a cuatro maravedís, según era el pueblo grande o chico. Con estos encarecimientos no quedaba persona en todo el lugar que no me fuese a ver, y ninguno había que no saliese admirado y contento de haberme visto. Triunfaba mi amo con la mucha ganancia, y sustentaba seis camaradas como unos reyes. La codicia y la envidia despertó en los rufianes voluntad de hurtarme, y andaban buscando ocasión para ello; que esto del ganar de comer holgando tiene muchos aficionados y golosos; por esto hay tantos titereros en España, tantos que muestran retablos, tantos que venden alfileres y coplas, que todo su caudal, aunque le vendiesen todo, no llega a poderse sustentar un día; y con esto los unos y los otros no salen de los bodegones y tabernas en todo el año; por do me doy a entender que de otra parte que de la de sus oficios sale la corriente de sus borracheras. Toda esta gente es vagamunda, inútil y sin provecho; esponjas del vino y gorgojos del pan.

CIPIÓN. –No más, Berganza; no volvamos a lo pasado; sigue, que se va la noche, y no querría que al salir del sol quedásemos a la sombra del silencio.

BERGANZA. –Tenle, y escucha. Como sea cosa fácil añadir a lo ya inventado, viendo mi amo cuán bien sabía imitar el corcel napolitano, hízome unas cubiertas de guadamecí y una silla pequeña, que me acomodó en las espaldas, y sobre ella puso una figura liviana de un hombre con una lancilla de correr sortija, y enseñóme a correr derechamente a una sortija que entre los dos palos ponía; y el día que había de correrla pregonaba que aquel día corría sortija el perro sabio, y hacía otras nuevas y nunca vistas galanterías, las cuales de mi santiscario, como dicen, las hacía, por no sacar mentiroso a mi amo. Llegamos, pues, por nuestras jornadas contadas a Montilla, villa del famoso y

BERGANZA: The fact is that the drummer, in order to be able to show off even more, taught me to dance to the sound of the drum and perform other tricks that no other dog but I could master, as you will hear as I go on. As they were nearly out of the district where they were recruited, they marched slowly on; there was no recruiting-officer to control us; the captain was young, but a gentleman and a good Christian; the ensign had left the Court and the dining-hall only a few months before; the sergeant was wise and experienced, and was good at hurrying a company from where it was raised to the point of embarcation. The company was made up of thugs and deserters who sometimes behaved badly in the places we passed through, causing those who did not deserve it to be cursed; the good prince has the misfortune to be blamed for his subjects and for the harm they inflict on one another, though it is no fault of his; and even if he wants and tries to remedy this, he cannot, because most things to do with war involve hardship, suffering and unpleasantness. So, in less than a fortnight, with my own ability and the effort put in by the man I had chosen as master, I knew how to jump for the King of France and how not to for the innkeeper's bad wife.[37] He taught me to trot like a Neapolitan steed and how to go round in circles like a miller's mule, as well as other turns which, if I had not been careful not to show them off prematurely, people would wonder if they were being performed by some devil in the form of a dog. He named me "wise dog" and no sooner would we arrive at our lodgings than, beating his drum, he would go around announcing that all those who wanted to see the wonderful skills and feats of the wise dog, in such and such a house, or such and such a hospital, could see them for eight or four *maravedis,* according to the size of the village. With this advance publicity, there was no one in the place who didn't want to see me, and no one who didn't come out amazed and well pleased with what they had seen. My master was delighted with the large profit, and with it he kept six comrades in a style fit for kings. Greed and envy put the thugs in a mind to steal me, and they looked out for a good opportunity to do so; for many people are keen supporters of the idea of earning one's keep by doing next to nothing; for this reason there are so many puppeteers in Spain, so many who put on shows, so many who sell pins and couplets, for all their belongings, even if they sold them all, would not keep them for a single day; and so some of them frequent taverns and inns all the year round; which inclines me to think that the bill for their drinking is paid for by some source other than their occupations. All these people are idle, useless and worthless, people who drink up wine like sponges and gobble down food like grubs.

CIPIÓN: That's enough, Berganza. What's past is past; carry on, for the night is drawing to an end and I don't want us to be in the darkness of silence when the sun comes up.

BERGANZA: Be quiet and listen. As it is easy to add more to what has already been invented, since my master saw how well I imitated the Neapolitan steed, he made some coverings of embossed leather and a little saddle which he put on my back and on it he placed a dummy figure of a man holding a little lance like those used to pick up a ring and he taught me to run straight at a ring which was suspended between two poles; and on the day I had to do it, he announced that the wise dog would tilt at a ring and would do other stunts never before seen, which I made up out of my own head, as they say, so as not to make my master appear a liar. We arrived, after a few days' march, at Montilla, where the famous and great Christian Marqués de Priego, lord of the house of Aguilar

gran cristiano Marqués de Priego, señor de la casa de Aguilar y de Montilla. Alojaron a mi amo, porque él lo procuró, en un hospital; echó luego el ordinario bando, y como ya la fama se había adelantado a llevar las nuevas de las habilidades y gracias del perro sabio, en menos de una hora se llenó el patio de gente. Alegróse mi amo viendo que la cosecha iba de guilla, y mostróse aquel día chocarrero en demasía. Lo primero en que comenzaba la fiesta era en los saltos que yo daba por un aro de cedazo, que parecía de cuba: conjurábame por las ordinarias preguntas, y cuando él bajaba una varilla de membrillo que en la mano tenía era señal del salto; y cuando la tenía alta, de que me estuviese quedo. El primer conjuro de este día (memorable entre todos los de mi vida) fue decirme: "Ea, Gavilán amigo, salta por aquel viejo verde que tú conoces que se escabecha las barbas; y si no quieres, salta por la pompa y el aparato de doña Pimpinela de Plafagonia, que fue compañera de la moza gallega que servía en Valdeastillas. ¿No te cuadra el conjuro, hijo Gavilán? Pues salta por el bachiller Pasillas, que se firma licenciado sin tener grado alguno. ¡Oh perezoso estás! ¿Por qué no saltas? Pero ya entiendo y alcanzo tus marrullerías: ahora salta por el licor de Esquivias, famoso al par del de Ciudad Real, San Martín y Ribadavia. Bajó la varilla, y salté yo, y noté sus malicias y malas entrañas. Volvióse luego al pueblo, y en voz alta dijo: "No piense vuesa merced, senado valeroso, que es cosa de burla lo que este perro sabe: veinte y cuatro piezas le tengo enseñadas, que por la menor de ellas volaría un gavilán; quiero decir que por ver la menor se pueden caminar treinta leguas. Sabe bailar la zarabanda y chacona mejor que su inventora misma; bébese una azumbre de vino sin dejar gota; entona un *sol fa mi re* tan bien como un sacristán; todas estas cosas, y otras muchas que me quedan por decir, las irán viendo vuesas mercedes en los días que estuviese aquí la compañía; y por ahora dé otro salto nuestro sabio, y luego entraremos en lo grueso. Con esto suspendió el auditorio que había llamado senado, y les encendió el deseo de no dejar de ver todo lo que yo sabía. Volvióse a mí mi amo y dijo: "Volved, hijo Gavilán, y con gentil agilidad y destreza deshaced los saltos que habéis hecho; pero ha de ser a devoción de la famosa hechicera que dicen que hubo en este lugar." Apenas hubo dicho esto, cuando alzó la voz la hospitalera, que era una vieja, al parecer, de más de sesenta años, diciendo: "¡Bellaco, charlatán, embaidor e hijo de puta, aquí no hay hechicera alguna! Si lo decís por la Camacha, ya ella pagó su pecado, y está donde Dios se sabe; si lo decís por mí, chocarrero, ni yo soy ni he sido hechicera en mi vida; y si he tenido fama de haberlo sido, merced a los testigos falsos, y a la ley del encaje, y al juez arrojadizo y mal informado; ya sabe todo el mundo la vida que hago, en penitencia, no de los hechizos que no hice, sino de otros muchos pecados, otros que como pecadora he cometido. Así que, socarrón tamborilero, salid del hospital: si no, por vida de mi santiguada que os haga salir más que de paso." Y con esto comenzó a dar tantos gritos y a decir tantas y tan atropelladas injurias a mi amo, que le puso en confusión y sobresalto; finalmente, no dejó que pasase adelante la fiesta en ningún modo. No le pesó a mi amo del alboroto, porque se quedó con los dineros y aplazó para otro día y en otro hospital lo que en aquél había faltado. Fuese la gente maldiciendo a la vieja, añadiendo al nombre de hechicera el de bruja, y el de barbuda sobre vieja. Con todo

and Montilla, had his residence. They put my master up in a hospital, as he had requested. He did the usual advertising and as the reputation and news of the skill and tricks of the wise dog had gone before us, the patio filled with people in less than an hour. My master, seeing that there was a bumper harvest, exceeded himself in his showmanship that day. The show began with some jumps through the hoop of a sieve which looked as if it had come from a barrel; he got me going with the usual questions and when he lowered a wicker wand he had in his hand that was the signal for me to jump, and when he held it aloft, for me to stay where I was. The first instruction that day (the most memorable of my life) was:

"Right, boy. Gavilán, jump for that dirty old man you know dyes his beard, and if you don't want to do that, then jump for the pomp and show of Doña Pimpenela de Plafagonia, who was the friend of that Galician girl who was servant in Valdeastillas. Don't you like that order, Gavilán, my boy? Well then jump for Pasillas, the student who signs himself as a licentiate when he has no degree at all. Oh, but you're lazy! Why don't you jump? But I can see what you're up to. Now jump for the wine of Esquivias, as famous as that of Ciudad Real, San Martín and Ribadavia."

He lowered the wand and I jumped and was well aware of his evil trickery. Then he turned to the crowd and said in a loud voice:

"Do not think, distinguished public, that what this dog knows is not serious. I have taught him twenty-four tricks, and a sparrow-hawk would fly miles to see the least good of them; I mean to say that it would be worth travelling thirty leagues to see it; he can dance the saraband and the chaconne better than those men who invented them; he can drink a flagon of wine without leaving a drop; he can sing *so, fa, mi re*, as well as a sacristan; all these things, and many more besides, your lordships will see in the days the company is here, and let our wise dog do another jump now and we'll come to the real stuff."

At this point he left the audience, which he had called "distinguished public", in suspense and left them not wanting to miss anything I could do. My master turned to me and said:

"Come back, Gavilán, and skilfully and gracefully go through the jumps you did, but as ordered by the famous sorceress who is said to have inhabited this place."

No sooner had he said this than the hospitaler, an old woman who looked over sixty years old, stood up and said:

"Rogue, charlatan, trickster, bastard, there's no sorceress here! If you're talking about Camacha, she paid for her sins and is God knows where; if you mean me, you swine, I am not and never have been a sorceress in my life, and if I was reputed to be one, it was either because of false witnesses, or because of a law which is arbitrary or a hasty and ill-informed judge; everybody knows the life I lead, as penance, not for spells I didn't cast, but for many other sins, which I as a sinner committed. So, you sly drummer, get out of this hospital; if you do not, by God, I'll make you get out double quick."

Whereupon she began to shout and to hurl so much abuse at my master that he was taken aback and alarmed; in the end the show was not allowed to proceed at all. My master was not bothered by the uproar because he had the money, and he put off the remainder for another day and another hospital. The people went away cursing the old woman, calling her a witch as well as a sorceress, and an old hag as well as an old

esto, nos quedamos en el hospital aquella noche; y encontrándome la vieja en el corral solo, me dijo: "¿Eres tú, hijo Montiel? ¿Eres tú, por ventura, hijo?" Alcé la cabeza y miréla muy despacio; lo cual visto por ella, con lágrimas en los ojos se vino a mí, y me echó los brazos al cuello, y si la dejara me besara en la boca; pero tuve asco y no lo consentí.

CIPIÓN. –Bien hiciste; porque no es regalo, sino tormento, el besar ni dejar besarse de una vieja.

BERGANZA. –Esto que ahora te quiero contar te lo había de haber dicho al principio de mi cuento, y así excusáramos la admiración que nos causó el vernos con habla. Porque has de saber que la vieja me dijo: "Hijo Montiel, vente tras mí, y sabrás mi aposento, y procura que esta noche nos veamos a solas en él, que yo dejaré abierta la puerta; y sabe que tengo muchas cosas que decirte de tu vida y para tu provecho." Bajé yo la cabeza en señal de obedecerla, por lo cual ella se acabó de enterar en que yo era el perro Montiel que buscaba, según después me lo dijo. Quedé atónito y confuso, esperando la noche, por ver en lo que paraba aquel misterio o prodigio de haberme hablado la vieja; y cómo había oído llamarla de hechicera, esperaba de su vista y habla grandes cosas. Llegóse, en fin, el punto de verme con ella en su aposento, que era oscuro, estrecho y bajo, y solamente claro con la débil luz de un candil de barro que en él estaba; atizóle la vieja, y sentóse sobre una arquilla, y llegóme junto a sí, y, sin hablar palabra, me volvió a abrazar, y yo volví a tener cuenta con que no me besase. Lo primero que me dijo fue:

"Bien esperaba yo en el cielo que antes que estos mis ojos se cerrasen con el último sueño te había de ver, hijo mío, y ya que te he visto, venga la muerte y lléveme de esta cansada vida. Has de saber, hijo, que en esta villa vivió la más famosa hechicera que hubo en el mundo, a quien llamaron la Camacha de Montilla; fue tan única en su oficio, que las Eritos, las Circes, las Medeas, de quien he oído decir que están las historias llenas, no la igualaron. Ella congelaba las nubes cuando quería, cubriendo con ellas la faz del sol, y cuando se le antojaba, volvía sereno el más turbado cielo; traía los hombres en un instante de lejas tierras; remediaba maravillosamente las doncellas que habían tenido algún descuido en guardar su entereza; cubría a las viudas que con honestidad fuesen deshonestas; descasaba las casadas, y casaba las que ella quería. Por diciembre tenía rosas frescas en su jardín y por enero segaba trigo. Esto de hacer nacer berros en una artesa era lo menos que ella hacía, ni el hacer ver en un espejo, o en la uña de una criatura, los vivos o los muertos que le pedían que mostrase. Tuvo fama que convertía los hombres en animales, y que se había servido de un sacristán seis años, en forma de asno, real y verdaderamente, lo que yo nunca he podido alcanzar cómo se haga, porque lo que se dice de aquellas antiguas magas, que convertían los hombres en bestias, dicen los que más saben que no era otra cosa sino que ellas, con su mucha hermosura y con sus halagos, atraían los hombres de manera a que las quisiesen bien, y los sujetaban de suerte, sirviéndose de ellos en todo cuanto querían, que parecían bestias. Pero en ti, hijo mío, la experiencia me muestra lo contrario: que sé que eres persona racional y te veo en semejanza de perro, si ya no es que esto se hace con aquella ciencia que llaman *tropelía*, que hace parecer una cosa por otra. Sea lo que fuere, lo que me pesa es que yo ni tu madre, que fuimos discípulas de la buena Camacha, nunca

woman. Despite everything, we stayed in the hospital that night, and when the old woman found me alone in the patio, she said:

"Is it you, Montiel my boy? Is it you, by any chance?"

I raised my head and looked at her very slowly; when she saw this, she came to me with tears in her eyes and threw her arms around my neck, and if I had let her she would have kissed me on the mouth; but the idea repelled me and I wouldn't allow it.

CIPIÓN: You did well, because it's not a treat, but a torment, to be kissed by an old woman.

BERGANZA: What I am going to tell you now I should have told you at the beginning of my tale, and that way we wouldn't have been so surprised at finding ourselves with the power of speech. For what the old lady said to me was this:

"Montiel, that's a good boy, come with me and you will see where my room is, and try to come to it tonight so we can be alone, and I shall leave the door open, for I have many things to tell you about your life which will be to your benefit."

I lowered my head as a sign of obedience, from which she knew for certain that I was the dog Montiel that she was seeking, according to what she told me afterwards. I was surprised and confused, waiting for the night to come, to see what the mysterious and portentous words of the old woman would lead to, and as I had heard her called a sorceress, I expected great things from seeing her and speaking to her. The moment arrived for seeing her in her room, which was dark, narrow and with a low ceiling, lit only by the feeble light of an earthenware lamp. The old woman trimmed it and sat down on a little chest and drew me towards her and, without saying a word, embraced me again, and I took care again lest she try to kiss me. The first thing she said was this:

"I hoped in heaven that these eyes of mine would see you again before closing for the final sleep, my boy, and now that I have seen you, let death come and carry me away from this wearisome life. You must know, dear boy, that in this town lived the most famous sorceress in all the world, called Camacha la Montilla.[38] She was unique in her profession so that the Ericthos, Circes and Medeas[39] of whom I have heard that the history books are full, could not match her. She froze clouds when she wanted to, and covered the face of the sun with them, and when it took her fancy she made the most unsettled sky calm again; in a moment she would bring men from faraway lands; she marvellously restored virgins who had been careless and had not kept themselves intact; she provided a cloak of propriety for widows who wanted to behave improperly; she undid marriages and arranged any others she wanted. In December she had fresh roses in her garden and in January she reaped wheat. Growing watercress in a trough was the least of what she could do, or making the image of a person, whether living or dead, appear on demand in a mirror or in the fingernail of a child. She had the reputation of being able to change men into animals, and that she had used a sacristan as an ass, really and truly, for six years, and I have never found out how it was done, for it is said of those old magicians who turn men into beasts by those who know about these things that they simply attract men by their great beauty and charm and make them fall in love with them and keep them so subjugated, doing whatever is asked of them, that they appear to be animals. But in you, my boy, experience shows the opposite, for I know that you are a rational person and I see you in the form of a dog, unless it is being done by that science they call *eutrapely* that is making one thing seem another. Whatever the case may be, what grieves me is that neither I nor your mother, who were disciples of the

llegamos a saber tanto como ella; y no por falta de ingenio, ni de habilidad, ni de ánimo, que antes nos sobraba que faltaba, sino por sobra de su malicia, que nunca quiso enseñarnos las cosas mayores, porque las reservaba para ella.

"Tu madre, hijo, se llamó la Montiela, que después de la Camacha fue famosa; yo me llamo la Cañizares, y si no tan sabia como las dos, a lo menos de tan buenos deseos como cualquiera de ellas. Verdad es que al ánimo que tu madre tenía de hacer y entrar en un cerco y encerrarse en él con una legión de demonios no le hacía ventaja la misma Camacha. Yo fui siempre algo medrosilla; con conjurar media legión me contentaba; pero, con paz sea dicho de entrambas, en esto de confeccionar las unturas con que las brujas nos untamos, a ninguna de las dos diera ventaja, ni la daré a cuantas hoy siguen y guardan nuestras reglas. Que has de saber, hijo, que como yo he visto y veo que la vida, que corre sobre las ligeras alas del tiempo, se acaba, he querido dejar todos los vicios de la hechicería en que estaba engolfada muchos años había, y sólo me he quedado con la curiosidad de ser bruja, que es un vicio dificultosísimo de dejar. Tu madre hizo lo mismo: de muchos vicios se apartó; muchas buenas obras hizo en esta vida; pero al fin murió bruja, y no murió de enfermedad alguna, sino de dolor de que supo que la Camacha, su maestra, de envidia que la tuvo porque se le iba subiendo a las barbas en saber tanto como ella, o por otra pendenzuela de celos, que nunca pude averiguar, estando tu madre preñada, y llegándose la hora del parto; fue su comadre la Camacha, la cual recibió en sus manos lo que tu madre parió, y mostróle que había parido dos perritos; y así como los vio dijo: "¡Aquí hay maldad, aquí hay bellaquería!" "Pero, hermana Montiela, tu amiga soy; yo encubriré este parto, y atiende tú a estar sana, y haz cuenta que esta tu desgracia queda sepultada en el mismo silencio; no te dé pena alguna este suceso, que ya sabes tú que puedo yo saber que si no es con Rodríguez, el ganapán tu amigo, días ha que no tratas con otro; así que este perruno parto de otra parte viene y algún misterio contiene." Admiradas quedamos tu madre y yo, que me hallé presente a todo, del extraño suceso. La Camacha se fue y se llevó a los cachorros; yo me quedé con tu madre para asistir a su regalo, la cual no podía creer lo que le había sucedido. Llegóse el fin de la Camacha, y estando en la última hora de su vida llamó a tu madre y le dijo cómo ella había convertido a sus hijos en perros por cierto enojo que con ella tuvo; pero que no tuviese pena: que ellos volverían a su ser cuando menos lo pensasen; mas que no podía ser primero que ellos por sus mismos ojos viesen lo siguiente:

> *Volverán en su forma verdadera*
> *cuando vieren con presta diligencia*
> *derribar los soberbios levantados,*
> *y alzar a los humildes abatidos*
> *por poderosa mano para hacerlo.*

"Esto dijo la Camacha a tu madre al tiempo de su muerte, como ya te he dicho. Tomólo tu madre por escrito y de memoria, y yo lo fijé en la mía para si sucediese tiempo de poderlo decir a alguno de vosotros; y para poder conoceros, a todos los perros que veo de tu color los llamo con el nombre de tu madre, no por pensar que los perros han de saber el nombre, sino por ver si respondían a ser llamados tan diferentemente como se llaman los otros perros. Y esta tarde, como te vi hacer tantas cosas, y que te llaman *el*

good Camacha, ever managed to know as much as she did; and not through lack of talent, or skill, or enthusiasm, for we had too much rather than too little of that, but because she was really wicked and did not want to teach us the best things, but preferred to keep them for herself.

"Your mother, my boy, was called Montiela, and in fame was second only to Camacha; I am called Cañizares, and if I didn't know as much as those two, at least I was every bit as willing. The truth is that your mother's eagerness to create, enter and remain enclosed within a circle with a legion of devils was not surpassed even by Camacha herself. I was always a little timid; I was happy conjuring up half a legion; but with all due respect to the two of them, when it came to making up the oils with which we witches anoint ourselves, neither of them could touch me, nor can any of those who today practise our craft. Well, my boy, as I have seen and can see that my life, which flies on the wings of time, is drawing to an end, I wanted to leave behind all the vices of sorcery in which I was immersed for many years, and all I have left is the expertise of a witch, which is very difficult indeed to pass on. Your mother did the same: she abandoned many vices, and did many good works in this life, but in the end she died a witch, and she did not die of any illness, but of the pain of knowing that her mentor, Camacha, was jealous of her because she was getting to know as much as she did, or because of some other jealous quarrel, which I never fully discovered, when your mother was pregnant and about to give birth. Camacha was the midwife, and took into her hands what your mother gave birth to, and showed her that she had given birth to two pups. As soon as she saw them, she said:

`There is some evil, some trickery going on here!' But Montiela, my sister, I am your friend. I will hide this offspring, and you concentrate on getting well. This misfortune of yours will be buried in silence; don't let this occurrence upset you for you know that I know for sure that you have been with no one else for days except your friend, that scruff Rodríguez; so this canine offspring must come from somewhere else, and there's something mysterious about it.'

"Your mother and I, who witnessed the whole strange business, were astonished. Camacha took off the pups and I stayed with your mother to look after her, for she could not believe what had happened. Camacha's end drew near and when she was about to expire she called for your mother and told her that she had changed her sons into dogs because she had been annoyed with her about something, but she wasn't to worry for they would return to normal when it was least expected; but that this could not take place until they themselves had seen the following with their own eyes:

> they will return to their true form
> when they see how quickly and surely
> the haughty are brought down
> and the meek exalted
> by the hand that has the power to do it.

Camacha said this to your mother as she was dying, as I have said. Your mother wrote it down and committed it to memory, and I fixed it in mine in case a time should come when I could say it to one of you; and in order to be able to recognise you, I call every dog of your colour by your mother's name, not because I think that the dogs will know the name, but to see if they reply when they are called by names that are so different from those of other dogs. And this afternoon, as I saw you do so many things, and that

perro sabio, y también cómo alzaste la cabeza a mirarme cuando te llamé en el corral, he creído que tú eres hijo de la Montiela, a quien con grandísimo gusto doy noticia de tus sucesos y del modo con que has de cobrar tu forma primera; el cual modo quisiera yo que fuera tan fácil como el que se dice de Apuleyo en *El asno de oro*, que consistía en sólo comer una rosa. Pero este tuyo va fundado en acciones ajenas, y no en tu diligencia. Lo que has de hacer, hijo, es encomendarte a Dios allá en tu corazón, y espera que éstas, que no quiero llamarlas profecías, sino adivinanzas, han de suceder presto y prósperamente; que pues la buena de la Camacha las dijo, sucederán sin duda alguna, y tú y tu hermano, si es vivo, os veréis como deseáis.

"De lo que a mí me pesa es que estoy tan cerca de mi acabamiento que no tendré lugar de verlo. Muchas veces he querido preguntar a mi cabrón qué fin tendrá vuestro suceso; pero no me he atrevido, porque nunca a lo que le preguntamos responde a derechas, sino con razones torcidas y de muchos sentidos. Así, que a este nuestro amo y señor no hay que preguntarle nada, porque con una verdad mezcla mil mentiras; y a lo que yo he colegido de sus respuestas, él no sabe nada de lo por venir ciertamente, sino por conjeturas. Con todo esto, nos trae tan engañadas a las que somos brujas, que, con hacernos mil burlas, no le podemos dejar. Vamos a verle muy lejos de aquí, a un gran campo, donde nos juntamos infinidad de gente, brujos y brujas, y allí nos da de comer desabridamente, y pasan otras cosas que en verdad y en Dios y en mi ánima que no me atrevo a contarlas, según son sucias y asquerosas, y no quiero ofender tus castas orejas. Hay opinión que no vamos a estos convites sino con la fantasía en la cual nos representa el demonio las imágenes de todas aquellas cosas que después contamos que nos han sucedido. Otros dicen que no, sino que verdaderamente vamos en cuerpo y en ánima; y entrambas opiniones tengo para mí que son verdaderas, puesto que nosotras no sabemos cuándo vamos de una o de otra manera, porque todo lo que nos pasa en la fantasía es tan intensamente que no hay diferenciarlo de cuando vamos real y verdaderamente. Algunas experiencias de esto han hecho los señores inquisidores con algunas de nosotras que han tenido presas, y pienso que han hallado ser verdad lo que digo.

"Quisiera yo, hijo, apartarme de este pecado, y para ello he hecho mis diligencias: heme acogido a ser hospitalera; curo a los pobres, y algunos se mueren que me dan a mí la vida con lo que me mandan o con lo que se les queda entre los remiendos, por el cuidado que yo tengo de espulgarlos los vestidos; rezo poco, y en público; murmuro mucho, y en secreto; vame mejor con ser hipócrita que con ser pecadora declarada: las apariencias de mis buenas obras presentes van borrando en la memoria de los que me conocen las malas obras pasadas. En efecto: la santidad fingida no hace daño a ningún tercero, sino al que la usa. Mira, hijo Montiel, este consejo te doy: que seas bueno en todo cuanto pudieres; y si has de ser malo, procura no parecerlo en todo cuanto pudieres. Bruja soy, no te lo niego; bruja y hechicera fue tu madre, que tampoco te lo puedo negar; pero las buenas apariencias de las dos podían acreditarnos en todo el mundo. Tres días antes que muriese habíamos estado las dos en un valle de los Montes Perineos en una gran gira; y con todo eso, cuando murió fue con tal sosiego y reposo, que si no fueron algunos visajes que hizo un cuarto de hora antes que rindiese el alma, no parecía sino que estaba en aquella hora como en un tálamo de flores. Llevaba atravesados en el corazón sus dos hijos, y nunca quiso, aun en el artículo de la muerte, perdonar a la Camacha: tal era ella de entera y firme en sus cosas. Yo le cerré los ojos;

you are called the wise dog, and as you also raised your head to look at me when I called you in the yard, I thought that you were Montiela's son, and I am really pleased to be able to inform you of what happened to you and of how you can recover your original form. I wish it were as easy as it was said to be for Apuleius in *The Golden Ass*,[40] just eating a rose. But in your case it depends on the actions of others and not on your own efforts. What you must do, my son, is to commend yourself to God with all your heart, and wait for these divinations, which I'd rather not call prophecies, to be fulfilled quickly and happily, for since the good Camacha said them, they will come about without fail and you and your brother, if he is alive, will see each other as you desire.

"What grieves me is that I am so near to my end that I will not have the opportunity to see it. I have often wanted to ask my demon how your affair will turn out, but I have not dared, for he never replies directly to what we ask him, but always in enigmatic phrases with different possible meanings. So one must not ask my lord and master anything, for he mixes the truth with a thousand lies; and from what I have gathered from his replies, he does not know anything for certain about the future, and can only guess. Despite this, he has us witches so fooled that, even though he's always tricking us, we cannot leave him. We go to see him very far from here, in the open country, where a large group of us, wizards and witches, gather, and he gives us rotten food to eat, and other things happen which in truth and for God's sake and the good of my soul I dare not recount, so dirty and disgusting are they, that I do not wish to offend your chaste ears. There are those who think we only go to these gatherings in our imagination and that we imagine through the power of the devil all the things we say afterwards have happened. Others disagree and say that we really go in body and soul. I think both opinions are correct, since we do not know when we go in one way or in the other, for everything that takes place in our fantasies is so vivid that we cannot distinguish it from when we really and truly go. The gentlemen of the Inquisition have done some experiments about this on some of us they have arrested, and I think they have found that what I am saying is true.[41]

"Son, I should like to give up these sinful ways, and with this in mind I have done several things: I have become a hospitaler, and I look after the poor, whose death quite often provides a living for me either because of what they leave me or leave hidden amongst their ragged clothes which I make sure I pick clean; I say few prayers and in public; I gossip a great deal and in secret; I do better by being a hypocrite than a declared sinner. The good works I openly do now are gradually wiping away the memory of the evil ones I did in the past from the minds of those who know me. In short, feigning holiness does no harm to anyone except the person who indulges in it. Look, Montiel, my child, this is the advice I give you: be good as far as you can, but if you have to be bad, try as far as possible not to appear to be so. I am a witch, I do not deny it; your mother too was a witch and a sorceress, I cannot deny that either; but the appearance of goodness in both of us made us well thought of everywhere. Three days before she died we had both been at a big gathering in a valley near the Pyrenees; and even so, when she died it was with such calm and repose that if it had not been for a few grimaces a quarter of an hour before she yielded up her soul, one would have thought that she was lying on a bed of roses.[42] Her heart grieved for her two sons, and not even in the throes of death could she bring herself to pardon Camacha, that's how determined and firm she could be when she set her mind to it. It was I who closed her

y fui con ella hasta la sepultura; allí la dejé para no verla más, aunque no tengo perdida la esperanza de verla antes que me muera, porque se ha dicho por el lugar que la han visto algunas personas andar por los cementerios y encrucijadas en diferentes figuras, y quizá alguna vez la toparé yo, y le preguntaré si manda que haga alguna cosa en descargo de su conciencia."

"Cada cosa de estas que la vieja me decía en alabanza de la que decía ser mi madre era una lanzada que me atravesaba el corazón, y quisiera arremeter a ella y hacerla pedazos entre los dientes; y si lo dejé de hacer fue porque no le tomase la muerte en tan mal estado. Finalmente, me dijo que aquella noche pensaba untarse para ir a uno de sus usados convites, y que cuando allá estuviese pensaba preguntar a su dueño algo de lo que estaba por sucederme. Quisiérale yo preguntar qué unturas eran aquellas que decía, y parece que me leyó el deseo, pues respondió a mi intención como si se lo hubiera preguntado, pues dijo:

"Este ungüento con que las brujas nos untamos es compuesto de jugos de yerbas en todo extremo fríos, y no es, como dice el vulgo, hecho con la sangre de los niños que ahogamos. Aquí pudieras también preguntarme qué gusto o provecho saca el demonio de hacernos matar las criaturas tiernas, pues sabe que estando bautizadas, como inocentes y sin pecado, se van al cielo, y él recibe pena particular con cada alma cristiana que se le escapa; a lo que no te sabré responder otra cosa sino lo que dice el refrán: "que tal hay que se quiebra dos ojos porque su enemigo se quiebre uno"; y por la pesadumbre que da a sus padres matándoles los hijos, que es la mayor que se puede imaginar. Y lo que más le importa es hacer que nosotras cometamos a cada paso tan cruel y perverso pecado; y todo esto lo permite Dios por nuestros pecados, que sin su permisión yo he visto por experiencia que no puede ofender el diablo a una hormiga; y es tan verdad esto, que rogándole yo una vez que destruyese una viña de un mi enemigo, me respondió que ni aun tocar a una hoja de ella no podía, porque Dios no quería; por lo cual podrás venir a entender cuando seas hombre que todas las desgracias que vienen a las gentes, a los reinos, a las ciudades y a los pueblos; las muertes repentinas, los naufragios, las caídas, en fin, todos los males que llaman de daño, vienen de la mano del Altísimo y de su voluntad permitente; y los daños y males que llaman de culpa, vienen y se causan por nosotros mismos. Dios es impecable; de do se infiere que nosotros somos autores del pecado, formándole en la intención, en la palabra y en la obra, todo permitiéndolo Dios, por nuestros pecados, como ya he dicho. Dirás tú ahora, hijo, si es que acaso me entiendes, que quién me hizo a mí teóloga, y aun quizá dirás entre ti: "Cuerpo de tal con la puta vieja! ¿Por qué no deja de ser bruja, pues sabe tanto, y se vuelve a Dios, pues sabe que está más pronto a perdonar pecados que a permitirlos?" A esto te respondo, como si me lo preguntaras, que la costumbre del vicio se vuelve en naturaleza, y éste de ser brujas se convierte en sangre y carne, y en medio de su ardor, que es mucho, trae un frío que pone en el alma tal, que la resfría y entorpece aun en la fe, de donde nace un olvido de sí misma, y ni se acuerda de los temores con que Dios la amenaza ni de la gloria con que la convida; y, en efecto, como es pecado de carne y de deleites, es fuerza que amortigüe todos los sentidos, y los embelese y absorte, sin dejarlos usar sus oficios como deben; y así, quedando el alma inútil, floja y desmazalada, no puede levantar la consideración siquiera a tener algún buen pensamiento; y así, dejándose estar sumida en la profunda sima de su miseria, no quiere alzar la mano a la de Dios, que se la está dando, por sola su misericordia, para que se

eyes and I who went with her to her grave. There I left her, never to set eyes on her again, although I have not lost hope that I may see her again before I die, for people are saying round here that she has been seen walking the cemeteries and highways in different forms. Perhaps I myself will come across her some time, and will be able to ask her if she wants me to do anything to soothe her conscience."

Each of the things that the old woman told me in praise of my so-called mother was like a lance that pierced my heart, and I felt like charging at her and tearing her to pieces with my teeth; and if I did not do so it was because I did not want her to die in such a state. Finally, she told me that that evening she would apply her oils to go to one of her usual gatherings where she would ask her master for information as to what was to happen to me. I wanted to ask about the oils she mentioned, and she seemed to read my mind, for she responded to my thoughts as if I had actually asked the question, saying:

"The oils that we witches apply to ourselves are made up of herbal juices which are extremely cold and not, as people say, of the blood of children that we strangulate. If you ask what pleasure or profit the devil derives from making us kill such young children, for he knows that since they are baptized they are innocent and sinless and go straight to Heaven, and every Christian soul that escapes his clutches fills him with great sorrow, I can only reply what the proverb says: `some people are prepared to lose one eye provided their enemy loses both.' The devil does it because of the suffering he causes parents by killing their children, for it is the greatest suffering imaginable. And what he wants most is that we should constantly fall into such a cruel and perverse sin, and God allows all this precisely because of our sins, for without God's permission I know from experience that the devil cannot harm even an ant. I saw the truth of this once when I entreated him to destroy the vineyard of an enemy of mine and he replied that he could not touch a single leaf because God would not allow him to do so. This will make you realise when you are a man that all the disasters which befall peoples and kingdoms, cities and towns, such as sudden deaths, shipwrecks, the fall of the mighty, in short, all the evil woes which are said to befall us, all come from the hand of the Most High and with the consent of His Will; and the evils and woes which are said to be brought about through our fault, come from and are caused by ourselves. God cannot sin, therefore, we ourselves are the authors of sin, giving shape to it in our intentions, words and works, and God allows all this, as I have already said, because of our sins. You will probably ask yourself, son, if you are able to follow me, who made me a theologian and you may even say to yourself: `Damn the old whore! Why doesn't she give up being a witch, since she knows so much, and turn to God, for she knows that He is quicker to forgive sin than to allow it?' To this I would reply, were you to ask, that habitual vice becomes second nature, and being a witch is part of our flesh and blood, and with all its ardour, which can be very strong, it brings such a coldness to the soul that it weakens and hinders its faith, from whence there arises such a forgetfulness of itself that it neither remembers the punishment which God threatens nor the glory He invites it to share and, as it is a sin of the pleasures of the flesh, it is bound to deaden all the senses, lulling and charming them and not allowing them to be employed as they are meant to be. The soul is therefore left weak, useless and discouraged, so that it cannot even begin to entertain any good thoughts, and so, allowing itself to be plunged in the lowest depths of its misery, it refuses to reach out to take God's hand, which He offers in

levante. Yo tengo una de estas almas que te he pintado: todo lo veo y todo lo entiendo, y como el deleite me tiene echados grillos a la voluntad, siempre he sido y seré mala.

"Pero dejemos esto y volvamos a lo de las unturas; y digo que son tan frías, que nos privan de todos los sentidos en untándonos con ellas, y quedamos tendidas y desnudas en el suelo, y entonces dicen que en la fantasía pasamos todo aquello que nos parece pasar verdaderamente. Otras veces, acabadas de untar, a nuestro parecer, mudamos forma, y convertidas en gallos, lechuzas o cuervos, vamos al lugar donde nuestro dueño nos espera, y allí cobramos nuestra primera forma y gozamos de los deleites que te dejo de decir, por ser tales que la memoria se escandaliza en acordarse de ellos, y así la lengua huye de contarlos; y con todo esto soy bruja, y cubro con la capa de la hipocresía todas mis muchas faltas. Verdad es que si algunos me estiman y honran por buena, no faltan muchos que me dicen, no dos dedos del oído, el nombre de las fiestas, que es el que les imprimió la furia de un juez colérico que en los tiempos pasados tuvo que ver conmigo y con tu madre, depositando su ira en las manos de un verdugo que, por no estar sobornado, usó de toda su plena potestad y rigor con nuestras espaldas. Pero esto ya pasó, y todas las cosas se pasan; las memorias se acaban, las vidas no vuelven, las lenguas se cansan, los sucesos nuevos hacen olvidar los pasados. Hospitalera soy; buenas muestras doy de mi proceder; buenos ratos me dan mis unturas; no soy tan vieja que no pueda vivir un año, puesto que tengo setenta y cinco; y ya que no puedo ayunar, por la edad; ni rezar, por los vaguidos; ni andar romerías, por la flaqueza de mis piernas; ni dar limosna, porque soy pobre; ni pensar en bien, porque soy amiga de murmurar, y para haberlo de hacer es forzoso pensarlo primero, así que siempre mis pensamientos han de ser malos; con todo esto sé que Dios es bueno y misericordioso y que Él sabe lo que ha de ser de mí, y basta. Y quédese aquí esta plática, que verdaderamente me entristece. Ven, hijo, verásme untar; que todos los duelos con pan son buenos; el buen día, meterle en casa, pues mientras se ríe no se llora; quiero decir que aunque los gustos que nos da el demonio son aparentes y falsos, todavía nos parecen gustos, y el deleite mucho mayor es imaginado que gozado, aunque en los verdaderos gustos debe de ser al contrario."

Levantóse en diciendo esta larga arenga, y tomando el candil se entró en otro aposentillo más estrecho; seguíla combatido de mil varios pensamientos y admirado de lo que había oído y de lo que esperaba ver. Colgó la Cañizares el candil de la pared, y con mucha prisa se desnudó hasta la camisa, y sacando de un rincón una olla vidriada, metió en ella la mano, y murmurando entre dientes, se untó desde los pies a la cabeza, que tenía sin toca. Antes que se acabase de untar me dijo que, ora se quedase su cuerpo en aquel aposento, sin sentido; ora desapareciese de él, que no me espantase, ni dejase de aguardar allí hasta la mañana, porque sabría las nuevas de lo que me quedaba por pasar hasta ser hombre. Díjele bajando la cabeza que sí haría, y con esto acabó su untura, y se tendió en el suelo como muerta. Llegué mi boca a la suya, y vi que no respiraba poco ni mucho.

Una verdad te quiero confesar, Cipión amigo: que me dio gran temor verme encerrado en aquel estrecho aposento con aquella figura delante, la cual te la pintaré como mejor supiere. Ella era larga de más de siete pies; toda era notomía de huesos,

all His mercy to enable the soul to rise. I possess one of these souls I have described to you. I see and understand all this, but as pleasure has gripped my will, I am and will always be evil.

"But let's leave this and return to the oils. As I said, they are so cold that they deprive us of all our senses when we apply them, and as we lie on the ground without any clothes on, we are said to experience in our imagination all that we think we are actually experiencing. Other times when we apply the oils, it seems that we change form, and turning into cockerels, owls or crows, we go to the spot where our master is waiting for us and there, recovering our original forms, we enjoy pleasures which I shall not recount, for they are such that the memory is scandalized to recall them and the tongue flees from telling them. But despite all this, I am a witch and, with the cloak of hypocrisy, I cover up all my many faults. It's true enough that if some people think highly of me and honour me as a good person, there are many who call me to my face all kinds of names[43] which have stuck ever since an enraged judge dealt with your mother and me in the past and we felt his fury at the hands of the executioner who, since he was not bribed, beat our backs as hard and severely as he could. But all this is past, as everything passes; memories fade away, life does not come back, tongues become tired, new events make us forget old ones. I am a hospitaler now; I give plenty of signs of my good behaviour, my oils provide me with many enjoyable moments, and I am not so old that I cannot look forward to another year, for I am seventy-five. I cannot fast because of my age, nor pray because of my dizzy spells, nor go on pilgrimages because my legs are so weak, nor give alms because I am poor, nor think good thoughts because I am given to gossip, and in order to do good it's necessary to be able to think it first, but my thoughts are always bad. Despite all this, I am aware that God is good and merciful and He knows what is to become of me, and that is enough for me. But let's leave this kind of talk now, for it makes me sad. Come, son, and see how I anoint myself; difficulties can be borne on a full stomach so let's make the most of it while we can, for whilst we are laughing we are not crying. What I mean is that, although the pleasures the devil gives us are false and deceptive, they still appear as pleasures to us, and pleasures can be enjoyed more in the imagination than in actual experience, although with true pleasure the opposite must be the case."

She got up after having made this harangue, took the lamp and went into a smaller room. I followed her, assailed by a thousand different thoughts and full of wonder at what I had heard and what I hoped to see. Cañizares hung up the wall lamp, and quickly undressed herself down to her shift, took a glass dish from a corner, put her hand in it, muttered something, and anointed herself from her feet right up to her head which was not covered up in any way. Before she finished anointing herself she told me that whether her body remained in that room unconscious, or whether it disappeared from there, I should not be frightened but should continue to wait there until morning, because then I should learn what I still had to go through in the process of becoming a man. I lowered my head in agreement and at that point she finished anointing herself and stretched herself out on the floor as though dead. I brought my face close to hers and saw that she was not breathing at all.

One thing I must tell you, Cipión, my friend, I was really frightened to find myself shut up in that small room with that figure in front of me which I shall describe to you as best I can. She was more than seven feet long; she was all bone, covered in a black,

cubiertos con una piel negra, vellosa y curtida; con la barriga, que era de badana, se cubría las partes deshonestas, y aun le colgaba hasta la mitad de los muslos; las tetas semejaban dos vejigas de vaca secas y arrugadas; denegridos los labios, traspillados los dientes, la nariz corva y entablada, desencasados los ojos, la cabeza desgreñada, las mejillas chupadas, angosta la garganta y los pechos sumidos; finalmente, toda era flaca y endemoniada. Púseme de espacio a mirarla, y aprisa comenzó a apoderarse de mí el miedo, considerando la mala visión de su cuerpo y la peor ocupación de su alma. Quise morderla, por ver si volvía en sí, y no hallé parte en toda ella que el asco no me lo estorbase; pero, con todo esto, la así de un carcaño y la saqué arrastrando al patio; mas ni por esto dio muestras de tener sentido. Allí, con mirar el cielo y verme en parte ancha, se me quitó el temor; a lo menos, se templó de manera que tuve ánimo de esperar a ver en lo que paraba la ida y vuelta de aquella mala hembra y lo que me contaba de mis sucesos. En esto me preguntaba yo a mí mismo: "¿Quién hizo a esta mala vieja tan discreta y tan mala? ¿De dónde sabe ella cuáles son males de daño y cuáles de culpa? ¿Cómo entiende y habla tanto de Dios y obra tanto del diablo? ¿Cómo peca tan de malicia no excusándose con ignorancia?"

En estas consideraciones se pasó la noche y se vino el día, que nos halló a los dos en mitad del patio, ella no vuelta en sí y a mí junto a ella, en cuclillas, atento, mirando su espantosa y fea catadura. Acudió la gente del hospital, y viendo aquel retablo, unos decían: "Ya la bendita Cañizares es muerta; mirad cuán desfigurada y flaca la tenía la penitencia"; otros, más considerados, la tomaron el pulso, y vieron que le tenía, y que no era muerta, por do se dieron a entender que estaba en éxtasis y arrobada, de puro buena. Otros hubo que dijeron: "Esta puta vieja, sin duda debe de ser bruja, y debe de estar untada; que nunca los santos hacen tan deshonestos arrobos, y hasta ahora, entre los que la conocemos, más fama tiene de bruja que de santa." Curiosos hubo que se llegaron a hincarle alfileres por las carnes, desde la punta hasta la cabeza; ni por eso recordaba la dormilona, ni volvió en sí hasta las siete del día; y como se sintió acribada de los alfileres, y mordida de los carcañares, y magullada del arrastramiento fuera de su aposento, y a vista de tantos ojos que la estaban mirando, creyó, y creyó la verdad, que yo había sido el autor de su deshonra; y así, arremetió a mí, y echándome ambas manos a la garganta, procuraba ahogarme, diciendo: "¡Oh bellaco, desagradecido, ignorante y malicioso! Y ¿es éste el pago que merecen las buenas obras que a tu madre hice y de las que te pensaba hacer a ti?" Yo, que me vi en peligro de perder la vida entre las uñas de aquella fiera arpía, sacudíme y asiéndole de las luengas faldas de su vientre la zamarreé y arrastré por todo el patio: ella daba voces que la librasen de los dientes de aquel maligno espíritu.

Con estas razones de la mala vieja creyeron los más que yo debía de ser algún demonio de los que tienen ojeriza continua con los buenos cristianos, y unos acudieron a echarme agua bendita, otros no osaban llegar a quitarme, otros daban voces que me conjurasen; la vieja gruñía; yo apretaba los dientes; crecía la confusión, y mi amo, que

hairy, hard skin; her stomach, which was like sheepskin, covered her private parts, and hung down to her thighs; her teats looked like two bladders of dried up and wrinkled cows; her lips were blackened, her teeth closed tight, her nose was hooked and misshapen and her eyes protruded; her hair was disshevelled, her cheeks sunken, her neck thin and her breasts flaccid; in short, she was thin as a rake and like the devil himself. I began to look at her carefully, and suddenly I was gripped by fear, seeing the evil appearance of her body and, even worse, considering the occupation of her soul. I decided to bite her to see if she would come to, but I could not find a part of her which did not repel me; even so, I grabbed her by her heels and dragged her into the yard, but not even this made her give any sign of recovering her senses. Then, seeing the open sky and having space to breathe, I felt no fear at all, or at least very little, so that I was able to wait and see how the going and coming of this evil woman would turn out and what she would tell me of the events which awaited me. Meanwhile, I was asking myself these questions: Who made this old woman so discreet and so evil? Where has she learned the difference between the evils which befall us and those that we bring on ourselves? How does she understand and talk so much about God and yet does so much work for the devil? How does she sin with so much malice and does not even excuse herself on grounds of ignorance?"

Pondering these matters, night passed and day came, finding us both still in the middle of the yard, she not having regained consciousness yet and I lying next to her and watching carefully her frightening and ugly appearance. The people from the hospital came and, witnessing that scene, some of them said:

"The Blessed Cañizares is dead; see how disfigured and skinny her penances left her." Others, who thought further, felt her pulse, and seeing that she still had one and that she was not dead, assumed that she was in a trance or state of ecstasy because she was so good. Others said:

"This old whore is doubtless a witch who has been anointed, for saints never undergo such shameless states of trance, and up to now, amongst those of us who know her, she has more fame as a witch than a saint."

There were some curious people who went up to her and stuck pins in her body from her toes up to her head, but not even that roused her from her sleep, and she did not come to until seven o'clock. As she felt riddled by the pinpricks, bitten in her heels and bruised from being dragged out of her room, and there were so many eyes peering at her, she thought, and she thought correctly, that I had been the author of her dishonour; and so, charging at me, and grabbing me by the throat with both hands, she tried to strangle me, saying:

"You scoundrel, you ungrateful, ignorant and malicious creature! Is this the way you repay all the good I did your mother and the good I intended to do you?"

Seeing that I was in danger of losing my life at the hands of that fierce harpy, I shook myself free and grabbing her by the flaps of her stomach I shook her and dragged her all over the yard whilst she screamed, asking to be released from the teeth of that evil spirit.

These comments of the evil old woman made most of the bystanders think that I must be one of those devils who constantly have it in for good Christians, and some came to sprinkle holy water over me, others did not dare to come to remove me, others called at the top of their voices that I should be exorcised. The old woman growled, and I pressed my teeth together. The confusion increased and my master who had come because of

ya había llegado al ruido, se desesperaba oyendo decir que yo era demonio. Otros, que no sabían de exorcismos, acudieron a tres o cuatro garrotes, con los cuales comenzaron a santiguarme los lomos; escocióme la burla, solté la vieja, y en tres saltos me puse en la calle, y en pocos más salí de la villa, perseguido de una infinidad de muchachos, que iban a grandes voces diciendo: "¡Apártense, que rabia el perro sabio!" Otros decían: "¡No rabia, sino que es demonio en figura de perro!" Con este molimiento, a campana herida salí del pueblo, siguiéndome muchos que indudablemente creyeron que era demonio, así por las cosas que me habían visto hacer como por las palabras que la vieja dijo cuando despertó de su maldito sueño. Dime tanta prisa a huir y a quitarme delante de sus ojos, que creyeron que me había desaparecido como demonio; en seis horas anduve doce leguas, y llegué a un rancho de gitanos que estaba en un campo junto a Granada. Allí me reparé un poco, porque algunos de los gitanos me conocieron por el perro sabio, y con no pequeño gozo me acogieron y escondieron en una cueva, por que no me hallasen si fuese buscado, con intención, a lo que después entendí, de ganar conmigo como lo hacía el atambor mi amo. Veinte días estuve con ellos, en los cuales supe y noté su vida y costumbres, que por ser notables es forzoso que te las cuente.

CIPIÓN. –Antes, Berganza, que pases adelante, es bien que reparemos en lo que te dijo la bruja y averigüemos si puede ser verdad la grande mentira a quien das crédito. Mira, Berganza, grandísimo disparate sería creer que la Camacha mudase los hombres en bestias y que el sacristán en forma de jumento la sirviese los años que dicen que la sirvió. Todas estas cosas y las semejantes son embelecos, mentiras o apariencias del demonio; y si a nosotros nos parece ahora que tenemos algún entendimiento y razón, pues hablamos siendo verdaderamente perros, o estando en su figura, ya hemos dicho que éste es caso portentoso y jamás visto, y que aunque le tocamos con las manos, no le habemos de dar crédito hasta tanto que el suceso de él nos muestre lo que conviene que creamos. ¿Quiéreslo ver más claro? Considera en cuán vanas cosas y en cuán tontos puntos dijo la Camacha que consistía nuestra restauración; y aquellas que a ti te deben parecer profecías no son sino palabras de consejas o cuentos de viejas, como aquellos del caballo sin cabeza y de la varilla de virtudes, con que se entretienen al fuego las dilatadas noches del invierno, porque, a ser otra cosa, ya estaban cumplidas, si no es que sus palabras se han de tomar en un sentido que he oído decir se llama alegórico, el cual sentido no quiere decir lo que la letra suena, sino otra cosa que, aunque diferente, le haga semejanza, y así, decir:

> Volverán a su forma verdadera
> cuando vieren con presta diligencia
> derribar los soberbios levantados
> y alzar a los humildes abatidos
> por mano poderosa para hacerlo.

tomándolo en el sentido que he dicho, paréceme que quiere decir que cobraremos nuestra forma cuando viéremos que los que ayer estaban en la cumbre de la rueda de fortuna, hoy están hollados y abatidos a los pies de la desgracia y tenidos en poco de aquellos que más los estimaban. Y asimismo, cuando viéremos que otros que no ha dos

the noise, was in despair hearing people say that I was a devil. Others, who did not know about exorcisms, came armed with three or four sticks with which they started to hit me on my back. I certainly felt it and I let go of the old woman, and in no time at all I was in the street and out of the village, pursued by a host of young boys who were shouting:

"Run away, the wise dog has gone mad!"

Others were saying:

"No, he is not mad, he is the devil in the shape of a dog!"

Having received this beating, I went out of the town as fast as I could as though the alarm bells were ringing, followed by many who undoubtedly thought I was a devil, both because of the things they had seen me do and because of the words uttered by the old woman when she woke up from her wretched sleep. I took flight and got out of their sight so quickly that they thought I had disappeared like a devil. In six hours I walked twelve leagues and arrived at a gypsy camp in a field near Granada.[44] There I was able to recover a little because some of the gypsies recognised me as the wise dog, and with not a little joy they welcomed me and hid me in a cave, so that if anyone searched for me I should not be found, and with the intention too, as I later found out, of making some money through me as my master, the drummer, had done. I was with them twenty days, during which I got to know and observed their life and customs which since they are worthy of note I must relate to you.

CIPIÓN: Before you proceed, Berganza, we had better ponder what the witch told you in order to ascertain whether this big lie which you believe can possibly be true. Look, Berganza, it would be crass stupidity to believe that Camacha turned men into beasts and that the sacristan served her all those years that people say in the form of a donkey. All these things and similar ones are deceits, lies and make-believe on the part of the devil, and if it seems to us now that we have some powers of understanding and reasoning since we speak even though we are dogs, or at least have the form of dogs, we have already established that this is a portentous thing which has never been seen, and that even though we can, as it were, touch it with our hands, we must reserve judgement until we see how it turns out and then see what we think. Do you want me to make it clearer? Consider the vain and stupid things on which Camacha said our restoration depends; those things which to you probably seem to be prophesies are merely proverbs and old wives' tales, like that of the headless horse and the magic wand[45] with which people keep each other amused round the fire during long winter evenings for, if they were anything else, they would already be fulfilled, unless her words have to be taken in what I have heard called an allegorical sense that does not mean what the words seem to say but something else which, although different, is similar. And so, if you say

> they will return to their true form
> when they see how quickly and surely
> the haughty are brought down
> and the meek exalted
> by the hand with the power to do it,

taking it in the sense I have said, I think means that we shall recover our form when we see that those who yesterday were at the top of the wheel of fortune are today humiliated and fallen at the feet of misfortune and held in low esteem by those who thought most highly of them. And likewise, when we see that others who not two hours ago did

horas que no tenían de este mundo otra parte que servir en él de número que acrecentase el de las gentes, y ahora están tan encumbrados sobre la buena dicha que los perdemos de vista; y si primero no parecían por pequeños y encogidos, ahora no los podemos alcanzar por grandes y levantados. Y si en esto consistiera volver nosotros a la forma que dices, ya lo hemos visto y lo vemos a cada paso; por do me doy a entender que no en el sentido alegórico, sino en el literal, se han de tomar los versos de la Camacha; ni tampoco en éste consiste nuestro remedio, pues muchas veces hemos visto lo que dicen y nos estamos tan perros como ves; así, que la Camacha fue burladora falsa, y la Cañizares embustera, y la Montiela tonta, maliciosa y bellaca, con perdón sea dicho, si acaso es nuestra madre, de entrambos o tuya, que yo no la quiero tener por madre. Digo, pues, que el verdadero sentido es un juego de bolos, donde con presta diligencia derriban los que están en pie y vuelven a alzar los caídos, y esto por la mano de quien lo puede hacer. Mira, pues, si en el discurso de nuestra vida habremos visto jugar a los bolos, y si hemos visto por esto haber vuelto a ser hombres, si es que lo somos.

BERGANZA. –Digo que tienes razón, Cipión hermano, y que eres más discreto de lo que pensaba; y de lo que has dicho vengo a pensar y creer en todo lo que hasta aquí hemos pasado y lo que estamos pasando es sueño, y que somos perros; pero no por esto dejemos de gozar de este bien del habla que tenemos y de la excelencia tan grande de tener discurso humano todo el tiempo que pudiéremos, y así, no te canse el oírme contar lo que me pasó con los gitanos que me escondieron en la cueva.

CIPIÓN. –De buena gana te escucho, por obligarte a que me escuches cuando te cuente, si el cielo fuere servido, los sucesos de mi vida.

BERGANZA. –La que tuve con los gitanos fue considerar en aquel tiempo sus muchas malicias, sus embaimientos y embustes, los hurtos en que se ejercitan así gitanas como gitanos, desde el punto casi que salen de las mantillas y saben andar. ¿Ves la multitud que hay de ellos esparcida por España? Pues todos se conocen y tienen noticia los unos de los otros, y trasiegan y trasponen los hurtos de éstos en aquéllos y los de aquéllos en éstos. Dan la obediencia, mejor que a su rey, a uno que llaman Conde al cual, y a todos los que de él suceden, tienen el sobrenombre de Maldonado; y no porque vengan del apellido de este noble linaje, sino porque un paje de un caballero de este nombre se enamoró de una gitana, la cual no le quiso conceder su amor si no se hacía gitano y la tomaba por mujer. Hízolo así el paje, y agradó tanto a los demás gitanos, que le alzaron por señor y le dieron la obediencia; y como en señal de vasallaje, le acuden con parte de los hurtos que hacen, como sean de importancia. Ocúpanse, por dar color a su ociosidad, en labrar cosas de hierro, haciendo instrumentos con que facilitan sus hurtos; y así, los verás siempre traer a vender por las calles tenazas, barrenas, martillos, y ellas trébedes y badiles. Todas ellas son parteras, y en esto llevan ventaja a las nuestras, porque sin costa ni adherentes sacan sus partos a luz, y lavan las criaturas con agua fría en naciendo; y desde que nacen hasta que mueren se curten y muestran a sufrir las inclemencias y rigores del cielo; y así verás que todos son alentados, volteadores, corredores y bailadores. Cásanse siempre entre ellos, por que no salgan sus malas costumbres a ser conocidas de otros; ellas guardan el decoro a sus maridos, y

nothing else in this world except add to the number of people that live in it, are now so exalted by good fortune that they have risen out of sight; and if previously they could not be seen because they were so small and insignificant, now we cannot keep up with them because they are so great and lofty. And if our return to the form you mention depends on this, we have already seen it and we continue to see it everywhere we go, whence I am inclined to believe that it is not in the allegorical sense but in the literal that the verses of Camacha have to be understood. But not even in this sense is our remedy to be found for many times we have witnessed what they say and we are still very much dogs, as you can see. And so Camacha was a deceptive trickster, Cañizares a liar, and Montiela a stupid, malicious scoundrel, begging her pardon if she should turn out to be our mother, or rather yours, for I do not wish to have her for a mother. In my opinion, the true meaning of the verses is to be found in a game of ninepins in which pins are knocked down and promptly raised again by the hand that is ready to do so. Consider, then, how often in the course of our lives we have witnessed a game of ninepins, and whether as a result we have become men again, if indeed we are men.

BERGANZA: Cipión, my brother, I admit that you are right and that you have more discretion than I thought. From what you say, I am inclined to think and believe that all that we have experienced up to now and what we are now experiencing is a dream, and that after all we are mere dogs. But let's not on that account cease to enjoy this gift of speech and the excellence of human discourse for as long as we can and so, don't give up listening to the account of what happened to me with the gypsies who hid me in their cave.

CIPIÓN: I will listen to you very willingly so that you will be obliged to listen to me when, please God, I relate to you the events of my life.

BERGANZA: My life with the gypsies at that time made me ponder their malice, lies and deceits, the thefts which both men and women amongst them practise almost from the moment they leave their cradles and begin to walk. Have you seen how many of them are scattered all over Spain? Well, they all know each other and what they are up to, and they move about and exchange in one place what one of them has stolen somewhere else, and so forth. They obey, more readily than they obey the king, one whom they call Conde[46] to whom, as with all who succeed him, they give the nickname of Maldonado. This is not because they come from the noble line that bears this name but because the page of a gentleman with this name fell in love with a gypsy girl who refused to return his love if he refused to become a gypsy and take her as his wife. The page did this, which pleased the other gypsies so much that they made him their leader and promised to obey him, and as a sign of allegiance they bring their leader part of what they steal if it is of any value. They while away their leisure time making iron objects, many of them instruments for their thefts. And so you will often see the men in the streets selling pliers, drills and hammers, and the women selling trivets and pokers. All the women are midwives. In this they have an advantage over ours because at no cost and without any other help they can bring their children into the world, washing them with cold water as soon as they are born. And so, from that moment until they die they become hardened and are able to endure the inclemency and severity of the elements so that you will notice that they are all strong, and good jumpers, runners and dancers. They always intermarry so that their bad habits will not become known to others; the women respect their husbands, and few women give them any cause for

pocas hay que les ofendan con otros que no sean de su generación. Cuando piden limosna, más la sacan con invenciones y chocarrerías que con devociones; y a título que no hay quien se fíe de ellas, no sirven, y dan en ser holgazanas; y pocas o ninguna vez he visto, si mal no me acuerdo, ninguna gitana a pie de altar comulgando, puesto que muchas veces he entrado en las iglesias. Son sus pensamientos imaginar cómo han de engañar y dónde han de hurtar; confieren sus hurtos, y el modo que tuvieron en hacerlos; y así, un día contó un gitano delante de mí a otros un engaño y hurto que un día había hecho a un labrador, y fue que el gitano tenía un asno rabón, y en el pedazo de la cola que tenía sin cerdas le ingirió otra peluda, que parecía ser suya natural. Sacóle al mercado, comprósele un labrador por diez ducados, y en habiéndosele vendido y cobrado el dinero, le dijo que si quería comprarle otro asno hermano del mismo, y tan bueno como el que llevaba, que se le vendería por más buen precio. Respondióle el labrador que fuese por él y le trajese, que él se le compraría, y que en tanto que volviese llevaría el comprado a su posada. Fuese el labrador, siguióle el gitano, y sea como sea, el gitano tuvo maña de hurtar al labrador el asno que le había vendido, y al mismo instante le quitó la cola postiza, y quedó con la suya pelada; mudóle la albarda y jáquima, y atrevióse a ir a buscar al labrador para que se le comprase y hallóle antes que hubiese echado menos el asno primero, y a pocos lances compró el segundo. Fuésele a pagar a la posada, donde halló menos la bestia a la bestia; y aunque lo era mucho, sospechó que el gitano se le había hurtado, y no quería pagarle. Acudió el gitano por testigos, y trajo a los que habían cobrado la alcabala del primer jumento, y juraron que el gitano había vendido al labrador un asno con una cola muy larga y muy diferente del asno segundo que vendía. A todo esto se halló presente un alguacil, que hizo las partes del gitano con tantas veras que el labrador hubo de pagar el asno dos veces. Otros muchos hurtos contaron, y todos, o los más, de bestias, en quien son ellos graduados y en los que más se ejercitan. Finalmente, ella es mala gente, y aunque muchos y muy prudentes jueces han salido contra ellos, no por eso se enmiendan.

A cabo de veinte días me quisieron llevar a Murcia; pasé por Granada, donde ya estaba el capitán cuyo atambor era mi amo; como los gitanos lo supieron, me encerraron en un aposento del mesón donde vivían; oíles decir la causa, no me pareció bien el viaje que llevaban, y así, determiné soltarme, como lo hice, y saliéndome de Granada di en una huerta de un morisco, que me acogió de buena voluntad, y yo quedé con mejor, pareciéndome que no me querría para más de para guardarle la huerta, oficio, a mi cuenta, de menos trabajo que el de guardar ganado; y como no había allí altercar sobre tanto más cuanto al salario, fue cosa fácil hallar el morisco criado a quien mandar y yo amo a quien servir. Estuve con él más de un mes, no por el gusto de la vida que tenía, sino por el que me daba saber la de mi amo, y por ella la de todos cuantos moriscos viven en España. ¡Oh cuántas y cuáles cosas te pudiera decir, Cipión amigo, de esta morisca canalla, si no temiera no poderlas dar fin en dos semanas! Y si las hubiera de particularizar, no acabara en dos meses; mas, en efecto, habré de decir algo; y así, oye

offence with outsiders. When they beg for alms they secure them more through stories and crude jokes than through prayers; and with the excuse that no one trusts them they never go into service and are given to idleness; and only once or twice, or perhaps never, if I remember rightly, have I seen a gypsy woman at the foot of the altar receiving communion, and I have gone into churches many times. The Gypsies' thoughts are all about how they are going to trick and where they are going to steal; they compare their thefts and how they carry them out.

One day a gypsy told some others in my presence of a trick and theft that he had once carried out on a peasant. The gypsy had a short-tailed donkey to which he attached a hairy tail with hair which seemed to be its own. He took the donkey to the market, a peasant bought it from him for ten ducats, and having sold it and taken his money, he told the peasant that if he wanted to buy another ass which was the brother of the one he had sold him and every bit as good, he would sell it to him at a cheaper price. The peasant asked him to fetch it, for he would buy it from him, and said that whilst the gypsy was gone he would take the one he had bought to his lodgings. The peasant left, the gypsy followed him and, somehow or other, found a way of stealing from him the ass he had already sold him. He straightaway removed the false tail, leaving the ass with its short, hairless one. He exchanged its saddle and bridle and he then had the cheek to go and look for the peasant to sell it to him. He found him before he had become aware of the loss of the first ass, and with little ado the peasant bought the second. He went to his lodgings to get money to pay the gypsy and there the silly fool found that his first ass was missing; and realizing that he himself had been an ass, he suspected that the gypsy had stolen it from him, and he refused to pay him. The gypsy went in search of witnesses and brought the people who had received the *alcabala* tax[47] on the first donkey who swore that the gypsy had sold the peasant an ass with a very long tail and very different from the second ass he was selling. All this was witnessed by a bailiff [48] who defended the gypsy so forcefully that the peasant ended up paying for the same ass twice. They related many other tales, all, or most of them, involving animals, for this is the area in which they are most skilled. In short, they are a bad breed, and despite the fact that many very wise judges have pronounced against them, they do not change their ways.

After twenty days, they decided to take me to Murcia. I went through Granada where the captain of my master, the drummer, happened to be living already. As soon as the gypsies found out, they shut me up in a room at the inn where they were staying; I heard them say why they had done this, and since I did not like the sound of things, I decided to try and set myself free, which I did, and, having left Granada, I came to an orchard that belonged to a *morisco*, who took me into his service willingly.[49] I was then in a better situation, for it seemed to me that he would want me for nothing else except guarding his orchard, a job, by my reckoning, which involved less work than guarding flocks; and as there was no question of salary involved, it was easy for the *morisco* to have a servant to order and for me a master to serve. I stayed with him more than a month, not because I particularly liked the life I led but because of the pleasure it gave me to find out about my master's life and through his about the life of all the *moriscos* of Spain. Oh, my friend Cipión, the things I could tell you about this *morisco* riff-raff if it were not for the fact that I am afraid I might be unable to finish them in two weeks! And if I were to go into detail, I would certainly not finish in two months; but, in fact, I

en general lo que yo vi y noté en particular de esta buena gente.

Por maravilla se hallará entre tantos uno que crea derechamente en la sagrada ley cristiana; todo su intento es acuñar y guardar dinero acuñado, y para conseguirle trabajan y no comen; en entrando el real en su poder, como no sea sencillo, le condenan a cárcel perpetua y a oscuridad eterna; de modo que ganando siempre y gastando nunca, llegan y amontonan la mayor cantidad de dinero que hay en España. Ellos son su hucha, su polilla, sus picazas y sus comadrejas; todo lo llegan, todo lo esconden y todo lo tragan. Considérese que ellos son muchos y que cada día ganan y esconden poco o mucho, y que una calentura lenta acaba la vida como la de un tabardillo; y como van creciendo, se van aumentando los escondedores, que crecen y han de crecer en infinito, como la experiencia lo muestra. Entre ellos no hay castidad, ni entran en religión ellos ni ellas; todos se casan, todos multiplican, porque el vivir sobriamente aumenta las causas de la generación. No los consume la guerra, ni ejercicio que demasiadamente los trabaje; róbannos a pie quedo, y con los frutos de nuestras heredades, que nos revenden, se hacen ricos. No tienen criados, porque todos lo son de sí mismos; no gastan con sus hijos en los estudios, porque su ciencia no es otra que la del robarnos. De los doce hijos de Jacob que he oído decir que entraron en Egipto, cuando los sacó Moisés de aquel cautiverio, salieron seiscientos mil varones, sin niños y mujeres; de aquí se podrá inferir lo que multiplicarán las de éstos, que, sin comparación, son en mayor número.

CIPIÓN. —Buscado se ha remedio para todos los daños que has apuntado y bosquejado en sombra: que bien sé que son más y mayores los que callas que los que cuentas, y hasta ahora no se ha dado con el que conviene; pero celadores prudentísimos tiene nuestra república, que considerando que España cría y tiene en su seno tantas víboras como moriscos, ayudados de Dios hallarán a tanto daño cierta, presta y segura salida. Di adelante.

BERGANZA. —Como mi amo era mezquino, como lo son todos los de su casta, sustentábame con pan de mijo y con algunas sobre de zahinas, común sustento suyo; pero esta miseria me ayudó a llevar el cielo por un modo tan extraño como el que ahora oirás. Cada mañana, juntamente con el alba, amanecía sentado al pie de un granado, de muchos que en la huerta había, un mancebo, al parecer estudiante, vestido de bayeta, no tan negra ni tan peluda que no pareciese parda y tundida. Ocupábase en escribir en un cartapacio, y de cuando en cuando se daba palmadas en la frente y se mordía las uñas, estando mirando al cielo; y otras veces se ponía tan imaginativo, que no movía ni pie ni mano, ni aun las pestañas; tal era su embelesamiento. Una vez me llegué junto a él sin que me echase de ver; oíle murmurar entre dientes, y al cabo de un buen espacio dio una gran voz, diciendo: "¡Vive el Señor que es la mejor octava que he hecho en todos los días de mi vida!" Y escribiendo aprisa en su cartapacio, daba muestras de gran contento; todo lo cual me dio a entender que el desdichado era poeta. Hícele mis acostumbradas caricias, por asegurarle de mi mansedumbre; echéme a sus pies, y él, con esta seguridad, prosiguió en sus pensamientos y tornó a rascarse la cabeza, y a sus arrobos, y a volver a escribir lo que había pensado. Estando en esto entró en la huerta otro mancebo, galán y bien aderezado, con unos papeles en la mano, en los cuales de

will say something, so listen to what I saw in general and noted in particular about these people.

It would be a wonder to find amongst so many of them a single individual who believes properly in the sacred laws of Christianity; all that concerns them is piling up money and stacking the piles they amass, and to achieve this they work and don't eat; as soon as a coin of any worth comes into their hands, they condemn it to life imprisonment and perpetual darkness; and so, always earning and never spending, they pile up and stack the biggest quantity of money you can find in Spain. They are money-box, moth, magpie and weasel; they get at everything, hide everything and swallow everything. Just remember that there are many of them and that each day they manage to put something away; remember too that a slow, steady fever can end life just as surely as a quick, sudden one does; and as they increase in number, so there are more of them who hoard, for they grow and grow *ad infinitum*, as experience shows. Chastity has no place amongst them and neither men nor women enter the religious life; they all marry, they all multiply, because sober living helps the propagation of their race. War does not consume them, nor any occupation unduly tire them; they steal from us with the greatest ease and with the fruits of our property which they sell back to us they become rich. They have no need of servants because they act as their own; they spend nothing on their childrens' education because all they need to learn is how to steal from us. I have heard it said that of the twelve sons of Jacob that went into Egypt, Moses brought out of captivity six hundred thousand men, leaving aside women and children; from this you can imagine how their wives will multiply since they are incomparably more in number.

CIPIÓN: Remedies have been sought for all the evils you have pointed to and outlined in general, for I know full well that the ones you are keeping quiet are more and greater than the ones you are talking about, but up to now the appropriate remedy has not been found. Our republic, however, has very wise guardians who, aware that Spain is breeding in its bosom as many *moriscos* as there are vipers, will find, with God's help, a sure, prompt and effective solution for so great an evil. Go on.

BERGANZA: Since my master was mean, as all of his breed are, he used to feed me on millet bread and some left-over soup, which was his basic fare; Heaven helped me, in a very strange way, to bear this misery as you will presently hear. Every morning as the new day dawned a young man was sitting at the foot of a pomegranate tree, one of the many in that orchard. His appearance was that of a student; he wore a flannel cloak which was no longer plush and black but discoloured and threadbare. He would be writing in a notebook and from time to time he would slap his forehead, bite his nails and look up to Heaven; other times he became so pensive that he moved neither hand nor foot, nor even his eyelashes, so absorbed was he in what he was doing. One day I went up to him without his noticing me, I heard him mutter something to himself and, after a good while, he gave a big shout and said:

"God be praised, this is the best eight-line poem I have written in my life!"

And writing hurriedly in his notebook, he gave signs of great happiness, all of which gave me to understand that the wretched fellow was a poet. I rubbed up against him in my usual way so as to reassure him of my tameness, and I lay at his feet, and he, with this assurance, continued thinking, scratched his head again, returned to his trance-like state and continued to write down what he had thought up. In the midst of this, there came into the orchard another young man, elegant and well dressed, carrying some

cuando en cuando leía; llegó donde estaba el primero y díjole: "¿Habéis acabado la primera jornada?" "Ahora le di fin –respondió el poeta–, la más gallardamente que imaginarse puede." "¿De qué manera?", preguntó el segundo. "De ésta –respondió el primero–: sale Su Santidad el Papa vestido de pontifical, con doce cardenales, todos vestidos de morado, porque cuando sucedió el caso que cuenta la historia de mi comedia era tiempo de *mutatio caparum*, en el cual los cardenales no se visten de rojo, sino de morado; y así, en todas maneras conviene, para guardar la propiedad, que estos mis cardenales salgan de morado; y éste es un punto que hace mucho al caso para la comedia, y a buen seguro dieran en él, y así hacen a cada paso mil impertinencias y disparates. Yo no he podido errar en esto, porque he leído todo el ceremonial romano, por sólo acertar en estos vestidos." "Pues ¿de dónde queréis vos –replicó el otro– que tenga mi autor vestidos morados para doce cardenales?" "Pues si me quita uno tan sólo –respondió el poeta–, así le daré yo mi comedia como volar. ¡Cuerpo de tal! ¿Esta apariencia tan grandiosa se ha de perder? Imaginad vos desde aquí lo que parecerá en un teatro un Sumo Pontífice con doce graves cardenales y con otros ministros de acompañamiento que forzosamente han de traer consigo. ¡Vive el cielo que sea uno de los mayores y más altos espectáculos que se haya visto en comedia, aunque sea la del *Ramillete de Daraja!*"

Aquí acabé de entender que el uno era poeta y el otro comediante. El comediante aconsejó al poeta que cercenase algo de los cardenales, si no quería imposibilitar al autor el hacer la comedia. A lo que dijo el poeta que le agradeciesen que no había puesto todo el cónclave que se halló junto al acto memorable que pretendía traer a la memoria de las gentes en su felicísima comedia. Rióse el recitante, y dejóle en su ocupación por irse a la suya, que era estudiar un papel de una comedia nueva. El poeta, después de haber escrito algunas coplas de su magnífica comedia, con mucho sosiego y espacio sacó de la faldriquera algunos mendrugos de pan y obra de veinte pasas, que, a mi parecer, entiendo que se las conté, y aun estoy en duda si eran tantas, porque juntamente con ellas hacían bulto ciertas migajas de pan que las acompañaban. Sopló y apartó las migajas, y una a una se comió las pasas y los palillos, porque no le vi arrojar ninguno, ayudándolas con los mendrugos, que morados con la borra de la faldriquera, parecían mohosos, y eran tan duros de condición, que aunque él procuró enternecerlos paseándolos por la boca una y muchas veces, no fue posible moverlos de su terquedad; todo lo cual redundó en mi provecho, porque me los arrojó, diciendo: "¡To, to! Toma, que buen provecho te hagan". "¡Mirad –dije entre mí– qué néctar o ambrosía me da este poeta, de los que ellos dicen que se mantienen los dioses y su Apolo allá en el cielo!" En fin, por la mayor parte, grande es la miseria de los poetas; pero mayor era mi necesidad, pues me obligó a comer lo que él desechaba. En tanto que duró la composición de su comedia no dejó de venir a la huerta ni a mí me faltaron mendrugos, porque los repartía conmigo con mucha liberalidad, y luego nos íbamos a la noria, donde, yo de bruces y él con un cangilón, satisfacíamos la sed como unos monarcas. Pero faltó el poeta, y sobró en mí el hambre tanto, que determiné dejar al morisco y

papers in his hand, from which he read from time to time. Going up to the first young man, he said to him:

"Have you finished the first act?"

"I have just done so," the poet replied, "it is the most elegant you can imagine."

"How ?" the second man asked.

"In this way," the first one replied. "There is a scene in which His Holiness the Pope, dressed in pontifical clothes, enters with twelve cardinals, all dressed in purple, because the events related in my play occurred at the time of *mutatio caparum*[50] when cardinals dress not in red but in purple; and so it is entirely fitting, for the sake of propriety, that these cardinals appear in purple; and this is a point which is very important for my play, and it would certainly be noticed, for inaccuracies and errors of this kind are often made. I have been saved from error in this because I have read the complete manual of Roman ceremonial just to get this matter of dress right."

"And where do you think," replied the other, "my producer[51] is going to find purple cloaks for twelve cardinals?"

"If he so much as removes one only," the poet replied, "I'd be as likely to give him my play as I am to fly. Good Heavens! Is this grand spectacle going to be wasted? Just imagine the scene in the theatre with the Supreme Pontiff and his twelve solemn cardinals and other ministers who have to be in attendance. In God's name, it would be one of the best and greatest spectacles to be seen in any play, even including *Ramillete de Daraja.*"[52]

From this I finally realized that one was a poet and the other an actor. The actor advised the poet to cut out the bit about the cardinals if he didn't want to make it impossible for the producer to stage the play. To which the poet replied that they should be thankful he had not included the whole conclave which assembled for the memorable ceremony about which he sought to remind his audience in his most entertaining play. The actor laughed and left the poet to his business so that he himself could continue his, which was studying the script of a new play. After having written some more lines for his magnificent play, the poet very calmly and slowly took out of his bag some chunks of bread and about twenty currants, for that's the number I think I counted, but I still have some doubt if there were as many as twenty because they were mixed with some breadcrumbs which added to their bulk. He blew the crumbs away and one by one he ate up the currants, stalks and all, for I did not see him throw any away, helping them down with the chunks of bread which, covered in purple fluff from the bag, seemed to be mouldy, and they were so hard that although he tried to soften them a little in his mouth they would not soften; all of which turned out to my advantage because he threw them over to me, saying:

"Here, boy, here, take this and enjoy it!"

"Just look at the nectar or ambrosia that this poet gives me," I said to myself. "On this they say the Gods and their Apollo feed up there in Heaven!"

In short, for the greater part, the poet's lot is a miserable one; but mine was even more so for I was obliged to eat what he threw away. All the while he was writing his play he did not fail to come to the orchard nor was I short of chunks of bread, for he shared them with me with great generosity, and then we used to go to the well where, in my case, flat on my belly and in his with the aid of a scoop, we quenched our thirst like Kings. But eventually the poet did not rewturn, I had more than enough of hunger, and I determined

entrarme en la ciudad a buscar ventura, que la halla el que se muda. Al entrar de la ciudad vi que salía del famoso monasterio de San Jerónimo mi poeta, que como me vio se vino a mí con los brazos abiertos, y yo me fui a él con nuevas muestras de regocijo por haberle hallado. Luego al instante comenzó a desembaular pedazos de pan, más tiernos de los que solía llevar a la huerta, y a entregarlos a mis dientes sin repasarlos por los suyos, merced que con nuevo gusto satisfizo mi hambre. Los tiernos mendrugos y el haber visto salir a mi poeta del monasterio dicho me pusieron en sospecha de que tenía las musas vergonzantes como otros muchos las tienen. Encaminóse a la ciudad, y yo le seguí, con determinación de tenerle por amo si él quisiese, imaginando que de las sobras de su castillo se podía mantener mi real; porque no hay mayor ni mejor bolsa que la de la caridad, cuyas liberales manos jamás están pobres, y así, no estoy bien con aquel refrán que dice: "Más da el duro que el desnudo", como si el duro y avaro diese algo, como lo da el liberal desnudo, que, en efecto, da el buen deseo cuando más no tiene. De lance en lance, paramos en la casa de un autor de comedias que, a lo que me acuerdo, se llamaba Angulo el Malo, de otro Angulo, no autor, sino representante, el más gracioso que entonces tuvieron y ahora tienen las comedias. Juntóse toda la compañía a oír la comedia de mi amo, que ya por tal le tenía, y a la mitad de la jornada primera, uno a uno y dos a dos se fueron saliendo todos, excepto el autor y yo, que servíamos de oyentes. La comedia era tal, que con ser yo un asno en esto de la poesía me pareció que la había compuesto el mismo Satanás, para total ruina y perdición del mismo poeta, que ya iba tragando saliva viendo la soledad en que el auditorio le había dejado; y no era mucho, si el alma, présaga, le decía allá dentro la desgracia que le estaba amenazando, que fue volver todos los recitantes, que pasaban de doce, y sin hablar palabra asieron de mi poeta, y si no fuera porque la autoridad del autor, llena de ruegos y voces, se puso de por medio, sin duda le mantearan. Quedé yo del caso pasmado; el autor, desabrido; los farsantes, alegres, y el poeta, mohino; el cual con mucha paciencia, aunque algo torcido el rostro, tomó su comedia, y encerrándosela en el seno, medio murmurando, dijo: "No es bien echar las margaritas a los puercos." Y con esto se fue con mucho sosiego. Yo, de corrido, ni pude ni quise seguirle; y acertélo, a causa que el autor me hizo tantas caricias que me obligaron a que con él me quedase, y en menos de un mes salí grande entremesista y gran farsante de figuras mudas. Pusiéronme un freno de orillos y enseñáronme a que arremetiese en el teatro a quien ellos querían; de modo que como los entremeses solían acabar por la mayor parte a palos, en la compañía de mi amo acababan en zuzarme, y yo derribaba y atropellaba a todos, con que daba que reír a los ignorantes y mucha ganancia a mi dueño. ¡Oh Cipión, quién te pudiera contar lo que vi en ésta y en otras dos compañías de comediantes en que anduve! Mas por no ser posible reducirlo a narración sucinta y breve, lo habré de dejar para otro día, si es que ha de haber otro día en que nos comuniquemos. ¿Ves cuán larga ha sido mi plática? ¿Ves mis muchos y diversos sucesos? ¿Consideras mis caminos y mis amos tantos? Pues todo lo que has oído es nada comparado a lo que te pudiera contar de lo que noté,

to leave the *morisco* and go into the city to seek better fortune, for he who ventures forth finds it. As I entered the city, I saw that my poet was coming out of the Monastery of St. Jerome,[53] and as soon as he saw me he came towards me with open arms, and I headed towards him happy at finding him again. Then he started to take out pieces of bread, softer than the ones he used to take to the orchard, and he put them in my mouth without first putting them in his, a gift which with renewed pleasure satisfied my hunger. The soft pieces of bread and the fact that the poet had come out of the monastery I've mentioned made me suspect that, in common with many others, he had gone to the monastery for something to eat.[54] He headed towards the city, and I followed him, determined to serve him if he were willing to be my master, thinking that I would be able to have the little bits I needed from what my great master had left over; because there isn't a bigger or kinder purse than that of charity whose generous hands are never empty, and so I do not agree with the proverb which says: "The hard-hearted man gives more than the poor man," as if a hard-hearted and avaricious man gives anything at all. It is the poor but generous man who, in fact, will at least give you his best wishes if he doesn't have anything else to give. Going from one place to another, we ended up at the house of a producer of plays who, if I remember rightly, was called Angulo el Malo,[55] a different one to Angulo the actor who is the funniest that has ever appeared or is currently appearing in any play. All the company gathered to listen to my master's play, for I already looked on him as my master, and half way through the first act, one by one and two by two they all started to leave except the producer and myself who continued to listen. The play was such that even though I am as stupid as an ass in poetic matters of this kind it seemed to me that Satan himself had written it for the total ruin and perdition of the poet who was having to swallow hard now, seeing the splendid solitude in which his public had left him; very probably his soul, sensing what was about to happen, communicated to his innermost self the impending misfortune which was, in fact, that all the actors, of whom there were more than twelve, returned and without saying a word seized my poet and, had it not been for the authority of the producer who intervened pleading and shouting, they would undoubtedly have given him a good tossing. I was amazed by what happened; the producer was bitter, the actors were happy and the poet angry. Showing great patience, although with a somewhat displeased face, he took his play, hid it away in his bosom, and half-muttering, said: "One should not cast pearls before swine."[56] And having said this, he left very calmly. I was so ashamed that I was unable to follow him, nor did I want to do so; but I did right because the producer stroked me so much that he forced me to stay with him, and in less than a month I was having great success with my walk-on parts in *entremeses*.[57] They put on me a fine muzzle and taught me to attack whomsoever they wished in the theatre so that, as the *entremeses* usually ended up in blows, in my master's company they tended to end up with my being let loose on people whom I brought down and tripped, to the amusement of the ignorant masses and my master's profit. Oh, Cipión, I wish I could tell you what I saw in this and another two actors' companies that I joined! But, since I cannot cut it down to a brief and succinct account, I will leave it for another occasion, if indeed there is to be another occasion on which we can communicate with each other. Do you see how long my discourse has been? Do you see my many and diverse experiences? Do you see the many masters I've had and the many paths I've walked? Well, all that you have heard is nothing compared to what I could tell you of what I

averigüé y vi de esta gente, su proceder, su vida, sus costumbres, sus ejercicios, su trabajo, su ociosidad, su ignorancia y su agudeza, con otras infinitas cosas, unas para decirse al oído y otras para aclamarlas en público, y todas para hacer memoria de ellas y para desengaño de muchos que idolatran en figuras fingidas y en bellezas de artificio y de transformación.

CIPIÓN. –Bien se me trasluce, Berganza, el largo campo que se te descubría para dilatar tu plática, y soy de parecer que la dejes para cuento particular y para sosiego no sobresaltado.

BERGANZA. –Sea así, y escucha. Con una compañía llegué a esta ciudad de Valladolid, donde en un entremés me dieron una herida que me llegó casi al fin de la vida; no pude vengarme, por estar enfrenado entonces, y después, a sangre fría, no quise: que la venganza pensada arguye crueldad y mal ánimo. Cansóme aquel ejercicio, no por ser trabajo, sino porque veía en él cosas que juntamente pedían enmienda y castigo; y como a mí estaba más el sentirlo que el remediarlo, acordé de no verlo, y así, me acogí a sagrado, como hacen aquellos que dejan los vicios cuando no pueden ejercitarlos, aunque más vale tarde que nunca. Digo, pues, que viéndote una noche llevar la linterna con el buen cristiano Mahudes, te consideré contento y justa y santamente ocupado; y lleno de buena envidia quise seguir tus pasos, y con esta loable intención me puse delante de Mahudes, que luego me eligió para tu compañero y me trajo a este hospital. Lo que en él me ha sucedido no es tan poco que no haya menester espacio para contarlo, especialmente lo que oí a cuatro enfermos que la suerte y la necesidad trajo a este hospital y a estar todos cuatro juntos en cuatro camas apareadas. Perdóname, porque el cuento es breve, y no sufre dilación, y viene aquí de molde.

CIPIÓN. –Sí perdono. Concluye, que, a lo que creo, no debe de estar lejos el día.

BERGANZA. –Digo que en las cuatro camas que están al cabo de esta enfermería, en la una estaba un alquimista, en la otra un poeta, en la otra un matemático y en la otra uno de los que llaman arbitristas.

CIPIÓN. –Ya me acuerdo haber visto a esa buena gente.

BERGANZA. –Digo, pues, que una siesta de las del verano pasado, estando cerradas las ventanas y yo cogiendo el aire debajo de la cama del uno de ellos, el poeta se comenzó a quejar lastimosamente de su fortuna, y preguntándole el matemático de qué se quejaba, respondió que de su corta suerte. "¿Cómo y no será razón que me queje –prosiguió–, que habiendo yo guardado lo que Horacio manda en su *Poética*, que no salga a luz la obra que después de compuesta no hayan pasado diez años por ella, y que tengo yo una de veinte años de ocupación y doce de pasante, grande en el sujeto, admirable y nueva en la invención, grave en el verso, entretenida en los episodios, maravillosa en la división, porque el principio responde al medio y al fin, de manera que constituyen el poema alto, sonoro, heroico, deleitable y sustancioso, y que, con todo esto, no hallo un príncipe a quien dirigirle? Príncipe, digo, que sea inteligente, liberal y magnánimo. ¡Mísera edad y depravado siglo nuestro!" "¿De qué trata el libro?", preguntó el alquimista. Respondió el poeta: "Trata de lo que dejó de escribir el

noted, ascertained and saw of these people, their way of life, their customs, their occupations, their work, their leisure, their ignorance and their astuteness, with an infinite number of other things, some fitting only to be whispered in the ear, others to be proclaimed in public, and all of them to be remembered in order to open the eyes of many who idolize fictitious figures and the illusory beauties born of artifice.

CIPIÓN: I can see clearly, Berganza, that you have great scope to extend your discourse, but I think that you should leave it for a separate account when you can take your time relating it without fear of interruption.

BERGANZA: So be it, but listen. I arrived in this city of Valladolid with a company in which in one of their *entremeses* I was wounded so badly that I nearly died. I could not take revenge because I was muzzled at the time, and later I did not want to do so in cold blood, for premeditated vengeance is a sign of cruelty and an evil spirit. I got tired of that occupation, not because of the work, but because in it I saw things that called both for reform and punishment; and as I had strong feelings about them but could not stop them, I decided not to witness them any more, and took safe refuge, as do those who leave their vices when they cannot indulge them any more, although it's better to do so late than never. What I mean is that, seeing you one night carrying the torch with the good brother Mahudes, it seemed that you were happy and occupied in a just and holy task and, full of a healthy envy, I decided to follow your steps, and with this laudable intention I stood in front of Mahudes who straightaway chose me for your companion and brought me to this hospital. What has happened to me here is not so insignificant that it doesn't deserve some time in which it may be related, especially what I heard from four patients whom fortune and necessity brought together in this hospital in four beds which were next to each other. Forgive me, but the story is brief and cannot be extended and fits in here perfectly.

CIPIÓN: Yes, all right. Get to the end for I think daybreak is not far off.

BERGANZA: In the four beds which are at the end of this ward, there was an alchemist in one, in the next a poet, in the next a mathematician and in the last bed, one of those so called political theorists.[58]

CIPIÓN: I remember having seen these good people.

BERGANZA: Well, during a siesta last summer, when the windows were closed and I was lying under one of the beds in the cool, the poet started to complain pitifully about his fortune and when the mathematician asked what he was complaining about he replied that it was about the small amount of good luck that he had.

"Am I not justified in complaining," he continued, "for having kept to what Horace demands in his *Poetics*, namely, that a work should not see the light of day until ten years after it's been written,[59] I have one in my possession which took me twenty years to complete, not to mention another twelve which have since gone by;[60] it is lofty in its subject-matter, admirable and new in its invention, measured in its verses, entertaining in its episodes, and marvellous in its structure, for the beginning corresponds to the middle and the middle to the end. It is therefore a lofty poem, sonorous, heroic, pleasing and substantial, and yet, despite all this, can I find a prince to whom I may dedicate it, a prince, that is, who is intelligent, generous and magnanimous? Miserable and depraved age of ours!"

"What is the book about?" the alchemist asked.

The poet replied:

Arzobispo Turpín del Rey Artús de Inglaterra, con otro suplemento de la *Historia de la demanda del Santo Brial*, y todo en verso heroico, parte en octavas y parte en verso suelto; pero todo esdrújulamente, digo, en esdrújulos de nombres sustantivos, sin admitir verbo alguno." "A mí –respondió el alquimista– poco se me entiende de poesía; y así, no sabré poner en su punto la desgracia de que vuesa merced se queja, puesto que, aunque fuera mayor, no se igualaba a la mía, que es que, por faltarme instrumento, o un príncipe que me apoye y me dé a la mano los requisitos que la ciencia de la alquimia pide, no estoy ahora manando en oro y con más riquezas que los Midas, que los Crasos y Cresos." "¿Ha hecho vuesa merced –dijo a esta sazón el matemático–, señor alquimista, la experiencia de sacar plata de otros metales?" "Yo –respondió el alquimista– no la he sacado hasta ahora; pero realmente sé que se saca, y a mí no me faltan dos meses para acabar la piedra filosofal, con que se puede hacer plata y oro de las mismas piedras." "Bien han exagerado vuesas mercedes sus desgracias –dijo a esta sazón el matemático–; pero, al fin, el uno tiene libro que dirigir y el otro está en potencia propincua de sacar la piedra filosofal; mas ¿qué diré yo de la mía, que es tan sola que no tiene donde arrimarse? Veintidós años ha que ando tras de hallar el punto fijo, y aquí lo dejo y allí lo tomo, y pareciéndome que ya lo he hallado y que no se me puede escapar en ninguna manera, cuando no me cato, me hallo tan lejos de él, que me admiro. Lo mismo me acaece con la cuadratura del círculo: que he llegado tan al remate de hallarla, que no sé ni puedo pensar cómo no la tengo ya en la faldriquera; y así, es mi pena semejante a las de Tántalo, que está cerca del fruto y muere de hambre, y propincuo al agua, y perece de sed. Por momentos pienso dar en la coyuntura de la verdad, y por minutos me hallo tan lejos de ella, que vuelvo a subir el monte que acabé de bajar, con el canto de mi trabajo a cuestas, como otro nuevo Sísifo."

Había hasta este punto guardado silencio el arbitrista, y aquí le rompió, diciendo: "Cuatro quejosos tales que lo pueden ser del Gran Turco ha juntado en este hospital la pobreza, y reniego yo de oficios y ejercicios que ni entretienen ni dan de comer a sus dueños. Yo, señores, soy arbitrista, y he dado a Su Majestad en diferentes tiempos muchos y diferentes arbitrios, todos en provecho y sin daño del reino; y ahora tengo hecho un memorial donde le suplico me señale persona con quien comunique un nuevo arbitrio que tengo, tal que ha de ser la total restauración de sus empeños; pero por lo que me ha sucedido con otros memoriales, entiendo que éste también ha de parar en el carnero. Mas porque vuesas mercedes no me tengan por mentecato, aunque mi arbitrio quede desde este punto público, le quiero decir que es éste. Hase de pedir en Cortes que todos los vasallos de Su Majestad, desde edad de catorce a sesenta años, sean obligados a ayunar una vez en el mes a pan y agua, y esto ha de ser el día que se escogiere y señalare, y que todo el gasto que en otros condumios de fruta, carne y pescado, vino, huevos y legumbres que han de gastar aquel día, se reduzca a dinero, y se dé a Su Majestad, sin defraudarle un ardite, so cargo de juramento; y con esto, en veinte años queda libre de socaliñas y desempeñado. Porque si se hace la cuenta, como yo la tengo hecha, bien hay en España más de tres millones de personas de la dicha edad, fuera de

"It deals with what Archbishop Turpin left unsaid about King Arthur of England, with a supplement, the *Historia de la demanda del Santo Brial*,[61] all in heroic verse, part in eight-syllable lines and part in blank verse; but all in dactylic stress, that is to say, in dactylic nouns, without including any verbs."

"As far as I'm concerned," the alchemist replied, "I know next to nothing about poetry; and so I am unable to appreciate properly the misfortune of which you complain, which, even if it is a major one, cannot equal mine which is that, through lack of instruments or a prince to support me and provide what I require for my science of alchemy, I am not already rolling in money and richer than Midas, Crassus and Croesus."[62]

"Have you, my dear alchemist," the mathematician asked at this point, "experimented in how to extract silver from other metals?"

"I have not done so up to now," the alchemist replied, "but I know for a fact that it can be extracted, and I am less than two months away from having the philosopher's stone with which silver and gold can be obtained even from stones."[63]

"You have exaggerated your misfortunes a great deal," the mathematician said at this juncture, "but when all is said and done, one of you has a book to dedicate to someone and the other is very close to finding the philosopher's stone. What can I say about my misfortune which is so unique that I can find help nowhere? For twenty-two years I have been trying to locate the fixed point, and I have tried here, there and everywhere, and thinking that I have found it and that I have got it in my grasp, I have been amazed by how far away it has suddenly seemed. It's been the same with squaring the circle; I have been so close to achieving it that I can't understand or work out how I haven't got it in the bag by now. And so I suffer like Tantalus, who though near to fruit is dying of hunger, and though near to water is dying of thirst.[64] One minute I think I am going to hit upon the truth, the next I find myself so far from it that I have to begin to climb again the mountain from which I have just descended, with the burden of my work on my back like a modern Sisyphus."[65]

The political theorist had been silent all this while but he now said:

"Poverty has brought together in this hospital four of the most querulous persons imaginable. In fact, one would think they were complaining about the Grand Turk.[66] For my part, I renounce jobs or occupations that neither please nor provide a living for those who practise them. Gentlemen, I am a political theorist, and at different times I have put forward to His Majesty many different theories, all of which would benefit and not harm our kingdom. I have now written a petition in which I entreat him to tell me of a person to whom I may communicate a new theory I have worked out, which is so good that it is totally in his interest; but judging by what has happened to previous petitions I fear this one is also going to be buried in oblivion.[67] But, gentlemen, so that you will not think me a fool, even though my theory will become public from now on, I want to explain what it is. The Cortes[68] is to require all His Majesty's subjects between the ages of fourteen and sixty to fast once a month on bread and water on a particular day, and all the money that would have been spent that day on other food such as fruit, meat, fish, wines, eggs and vegetables to be given to His Majesty, under oath, without doing him out of a single *real*. If this is done, in twenty years, he would need no further contributions and would owe no money for, if we add it all up, as I have done, there are in Spain more than three million people of those ages, leaving aside the sick and those

los enfermos, más viejos o más muchachos, y ninguno de éstos dejará de gastar, y esto contado al menorete, cada día real y medio; y yo quiero que sea no más de un real, que no puede ser menos aunque coma alholvas. Pues ¿paréceles a vuesas mercedes que sería barro tener cada mes tres millones de reales como ahechados? Y esto antes sería provecho que daño a los ayunantes, porque con el ayuno agradarían al cielo y servirían a su Rey; y tal podría ayunar que le fuese conveniente para su salud. Este es arbitrio limpio de polvo y de paja, y podríase coger por parroquias, sin costa de comisarios, que destruyesen la república." Riéronse todos del arbitrio y del arbitrante, y él también se rió de sus disparates, y yo quedé admirado de haberlos oído y de ver que, por la mayor parte, los de semejantes humores venían a morir en los hospitales.

CIPIÓN. –Tienes razón, Berganza. Mira si te queda más que decir.

BERGANZA. –Dos cosas no más, con que daré fin a mi plática, que ya me parece que viene el día. Yendo una noche mi mayor a pedir limosna en casa del Corregidor de esta ciudad, que es un gran caballero y muy gran cristiano, hallámosle solo, y parecióme a mí tomar ocasión de aquella soledad para decirle ciertos advertimientos que había oído decir a un viejo enfermo de este hospital acerca de cómo se podía remediar la perdición tan notoria de las mozas vagamundas, que por no servir dan en malas, y tan malas, que pueblan los veranos todos los hospitales de los perdidos que las siguen: plaga intolerable y que pedía presto y eficaz remedio. Digo que queriendo decírselo, alcé la voz, pensando que tenía habla, y en lugar de pronunciar razones concertadas ladré con tanta prisa y con tan levantado tono, que, enfadado el Corregidor, dio voces a sus criados que me echasen de la sala a palos; y un lacayo que acudió a la voz de su señor, que fuera mejor que por entonces estuviera sordo, asió de una cantimplora de cobre que le vino a la mano, y diómela tal en mis costillas, que hasta ahora guardo las reliquias de aquellos golpes.

CIPIÓN. –¿Y quéjaste de eso, Berganza?

BERGANZA. –Pues ¿no me tengo de quejar, si hasta ahora me duele como he dicho, y si me parece que no merecía tal castigo mi buena intención?

CIPIÓN. –Mira, Berganza, nadie se ha de meter donde no le llaman, ni ha de querer usar del oficio que por ningún caso le toca. Y has de considerar que nunca el consejo del pobre, por bueno que sea, fue admitido, ni el pobre humilde ha de tener presunción de aconsejar a los grandes y a los que piensan que lo saben todo. La sabiduría en el pobre está asombrada; que la necesidad y miseria son las sombras y nubes que la oscurecen, y si acaso se descubre, la juzgan por tontedad y la tratan con menosprecio.

BERGANZA. –Tienes razón, y escarmentando en mi cabeza, de aquí adelante seguiré tus consejos. Entré asimismo otra noche en casa de una señora principal, la cual tenía en los brazos una perrilla de estas que llaman de falda, tan pequeña, que la pudiera esconder en el seno; la cual, cuando me vio, saltó de los brazos de su señora y arremetió a mí ladrando, y con tan gran denuedo, que no paró hasta morderme de una pierna. Volvíla a mirar con respecto y con enojo, y dije entre mí: "Si yo os cogiera, animalejo ruin, en la calle, o no hiciera caso de vos, u os hiciera pedazos entre los dientes." Consideré en ella que hasta los cobardes y de poco ánimo son atrevidos e insolentes cuando son favorecidos, y se adelantan a ofender a los que valen más que ellos.

who are older or younger, none of whom spends less than a *real* and a half at least each day on food, and I am asking for no more than a *real*, for you can't exist on less than this unless you eat hay. Well, it's not to be sneezed at, is it, a clear three million *reales* a month just like that? And what's more, this would be to the benefit rather than harm of those who fast, for by so doing they would please both God and King; and each would be able to fast in a way that was good for his health. There are no drawbacks to this theory,[69] and the money could be collected through parishes without need of collectors who might wreck the state."

They all laughed at the theory and the theorist, and he himself laughed at his way-out ideas. I was amazed to hear them and to see that such men spend their last days in these hospitals.

CIPIÓN. Yes, that's right, Berganza. Do you have anything else to say?

BERGANZA. Two things and no more, and then I'll stop talking for I think daybreak is approaching. One night when my master went to ask for alms to the house of the Corregidor[70] of this city, who is a great Christian gentleman, we found him all alone, and it therefore seemed a good moment to tell him of some advice I had heard an old patient of the hospital give as to how a solution might be found to the well-known problem of the street girls who, rather than go into service, take up this evil life, so evil that every summer the hospitals are full of the wretched men who have gone with them. This is an intolerable plague which calls for prompt and effective action. As I said, wanting to tell him this, I raised my voice thinking that I could speak but instead of uttering meaningful statements I barked so much and so loudly that the Corregidor got annoyed and called to his servants to beat me and throw me out. One of the servants who answered his master's call, – I wish he had been deaf – seized a copper jar which was to hand, and hit me so hard with it on my back that I still have the bruises.

CIPIÓN: And did you complain, Berganza?

BERGANZA: Of course I did, for it was such a beating that I still feel the pain of those blows which were no fit recompense for my worthy intentions.

CIPIÓN: Look, Berganza, no one should poke his nose in where it is not wanted nor try to do a job which is not his. And remember that the advice of a poor man, no matter how good it is, is never accepted, and a poor, humble person should not presume to give advice to the great and to those who think they know it all. Wisdom in the poor man is hidden in the shadows and mists of want and misery, and if by chance it comes out in the open it is said to be stupidity and treated with contempt.

BERGANZA: You are right, and knowing where I went wrong, I shall follow your advice from now on. One night also I went into the house of a noble lady who was cuddling a little dog, one of those so-called lap-dogs, so small that it could be hidden in her bosom; and the little bitch, on seeing me, jumped off the arms of her mistress and ran at me barking so boldly that she did not stop until she had bitten one of my legs. I looked at her with some caution and annoyance and said to myself:

"If I could get hold of you in the street, you wretched little creature, I would either ignore you altogether or I would tear you to pieces with my teeth."

Seeing her reminded me that even cowards and the faint-hearted become daring and insolent when they enjoy some favour, and they are quick to offend those who are better than them.

CIPIÓN. –Una muestra y señal de esa verdad que dices nos dan algunos hombrecillos que a la sombra de sus amos se atreven a ser insolentes; y si acaso la muerte u otro accidente de fortuna derriba el árbol donde se arriman, luego se descubre y manifiesta su poco valor, porque, en efecto, no son de más quilates sus prendas que los que les dan sus dueños y valedores. La virtud y el buen entendimiento siempre es una y siempre es uno: desnudo o vestido, solo o acompañado. Bien es verdad que puede padecer acerca de la estimación de las gentes, mas no en la realidad verdadera de lo que merece y vale. Y con esto pongamos fin a esta plática, que la luz que entra por estos resquicios muestra que es muy entrado el día, y esta noche que viene, si no nos ha dejado este grande beneficio del habla, será la mía, para contarte mi vida.

BERGANZA. –Sea así, y mira que acudas a este mismo puesto.

El acabar el *Coloquio* el Licenciado y el despertar el Alférez fue todo a un tiempo, y el Licenciado dijo:

–Aunque este coloquio sea fingido y nunca haya pasado, paréceme que está tan bien compuesto que puede el señor Alférez pasar adelante con el segundo.

–Con ese parecer –respondió el Alférez– me animaré y dispondré a escribirle, sin ponerme más en disputas con vuesa merced si hablaron los perros o no.

A lo que dijo el Licenciado:

–Señor Alférez, no volvamos más a esa disputa. Yo alcanzo el artificio del *Coloquio* y la invención, y basta. Vámonos al Espolón a recrear los ojos del cuerpo, pues ya he recreado los del entendimiento.

–Vamos –dijo el Alférez.

Y con esto, se fueron.

El Fin

CIPIÓN: A good example of that truth you mention is provided by those paltry men who in the shadow of their masters dare to be insolent but if by chance death or some other accident of fortune brings down the tree under which they shelter, then their lack of courage becomes clear for all to see because, in fact, their claim to worth rests entirely on their masters and protectors. Virtue and understanding are always one and the same, naked or dressed up, alone or accompanied. It may well be that they might suffer a loss of esteem by the people but not of their true worth and merit. And with this let us bring to an end this conversation, for the light which is coming in through these gaps shows that we're well into the new day, and tonight, if we have not lost this great gift of speech, it will be my turn to tell you about my life.

BERGANZA: So be it, and make sure you come to this same spot.

The Licentiate finished the Colloquy and the Ensign woke up at the same time. The Licentiate said:

"Even if this colloquy is made up and has never happened, it seems to me that it is so well composed, dear Ensign, that you may proceed with the second."

"That comment," the Ensign replied, "is sufficient encouragement for me to proceed to write it without arguing with you any more as to whether the dogs spoke or not."

To this the Licentiate replied:

"Ensign, sir, let's not get involved in that again. I see the art of the Colloquy and its invention and that is enough. Let's repair to the Espolón[71] to entertain our eyes for we have already entertained our minds."

"Let's go," the Ensign said.

And with this, they left.

The End

Notes

Notes to *Lady Cornelia*

1   Flanders was one of the provinces of the Low Countries or Netherlands but it was also the term often used in the sixteenth century to denote the entire area of the seventeen provinces of the Low Countries which were then under Spanish rule. The developing process towards independence by the various peoples of the Netherlands created constant tensions and conflicts for the Spanish Crown, particularly between the first Dutch Revolt (1565) and the Peace of Munster (1648) which recognized the independence of the seven northern Dutch provinces.

2   The ancient University of Bologna was renowned in the sixteenth century for a range of studies. After Philip II's measures in 1559 to protect Spain against heresy, it was the only foreign university at which Spaniards were allowed to study. The university contained a Spanish College which dated from 1369. It should be noted too that Don Juan and Don Antonio's own University of Salamanca was one of the leading Spanish universities of the time.

3   Although Cornelia and Lorenzo are fictional characters, Cervantes links them to the real Bentivoglio family which became powerful in Bologna through Giovanni I in 1401-02 and continued with varying fortunes until 1506 when Giovanni II fled in the face of Pope Julius II's attacks.

4   The Spanish *'vais'* instead of *'vayais'* reflects an old standard form of the subjunctive.

5   Various references are made in the course of the story to characteristic qualities of sixteenth- and seventeenth-century Spaniards. Pride and arrogance are alluded to at the beginning of the story. We now have this reference to the more positive qualities of courtesy and politeness. On the subject of national and regional characteristics in sixteenth- and seventeenth-century Spain, see Miguel Herrero García, *Ideas de los españoles del siglo XVII* (Madrid, 1966).

6   The nobility of Ferrara was dominated from 1332 by the Este family who from 1471 were Dukes of Ferrara. Under this dynasty, Ferrara developed into a thriving, prosperous and cultured city. Although Cervantes's duke is fictional, there was a real Alfonso II d'Este (1533-97) who from 1559 became the fifth and last Duke of Ferrara. On his death, his territory reverted to the Papacy.

7   The reference here is to melancholia, a state of mind associated with bile, one of the four humours or body fluids (the others being blood, phlegm and choler) which were thought to determine the physical and mental make-up of a person. Melancholia, if untreated, was thought to be potentially fatal.

8   As an Italian, Lorenzo uses *vuestra señoría,* the ordinary polite form of address in Italy at the time which, however, in Spain was reserved only for grandees and titled nobility.

9   The term Argos was used as a symbol of constant vigilance after the mythical figure of a hundred eyes.

10 The massive forces of the Persian King Xerxes who in 480 B.C. attacked Greece winning the famous victory at Thermopylae but eventually being forced to retreat after his defeat at Salamis.

11 A holy relic blessed by the Pope. *Agnus* (lamb) is used as a symbol of Christ in the phrase *agnus Dei* (lamb of God).

12 The reference to *higa* is difficult to translate, although the phrase 'to give someone the fig' is recorded in English. Cf. 'I don't care a fig!'. The term denoted a dismissive gesture

which consisted of clenching the fist with the thumb protruding through the middle and index finger.

13   This was the distinguished Milan family which produced Pope Urban III and Cardinal Alessandro Crivelli, Papal Nuncio to Spain where he died in 1574.

14   Vizcayan was used to denote people from the Basque region who were as renowned for their down-to-earth sense of honour and nobility as for their sharp temper. The surnames Gamboa and Isunza would identify these two characters as Basque. The reference to the Galicians reflects the contemporary prejudice which made these people the butt of jokes in which they figured as lowly, simple characters.

15   St. James, the patron saint of Spain whose remains are supposed to be in Santiago de Compostela, named after the saint and one of the most famous centres of pilgrimage since the Middle Ages.

Notes to *The Deceitful Marriage*

1   The Hospital of the Resurrection, which in Cervantes's time was run by the friars of St. John of God, was built around 1579 and demolished in 1890.

2   One of the main gates to the city, near which Cervantes himself lived during his time in Valladolid.

3   The original Spanish, *humor*, refers to the theory of the humours. See *Lady Cornelia*, n.6. This and the subsequent reference are to the contemporary cure for syphilis.

4   The officer responsible for carrying a company's flag or ensign.

5   References to the wars in the Netherlands are common in the *Exemplary Novels*. See *Lady Cornelia*, n.1.

6   A person who has a University degree at graduate level.

7   There is a sound similarity in Spanish: *amores* (love) and *dolores* (pain). Cervantes's phrase echoes certain proverbial expressions.

8   There is a pun in Spanish which is difficult to render in English: *casamiento* (marriage) and *cansamiento* (tiredness).

9   A formula used in *Don Quixote*, II, 3, as an invitation to eat.

10   Rute, near Córdoba, was famous for its hams.

11   A common Petrarchan conceit linking fire and snow.

12   This is a formulation of the traditional conception of sin overthrowing the normal hierarchy in man.

13   The famous royal gardens near Madrid which date from the reign of Philip II.

14   The original Spanish `todos los dolores' is the beginning of a saying which, loosely translated, means `All sorrows are better with bread.' The basic idea, namely, that if she had left him some of her riches he would have felt better, would be apparent from the opening words of the Spanish phrase.

15   A Jewish proverb implying that, although one appeared to be deceived, the reality was rather different.

16   The original Spanish *historia* means both history and story, and therefore is a double-edged reference to the ensign's narrative as being both fictional and factual.

17   Popular name for the friars of the Holy Religion of St. John of God who collected alms in baskets which in Andalusia, where the Order originated, are called *capachas*.

18   Cipión is the Spanish for Scipio. We have left it in the original for the sake of consistency, but its associations of wisdom and learning would naturally strike a chord in the mind of the educated reader.

19   A popular way of referring to a mythical time in the distant past when incredible events occurred, such as animals and plants being able to talk. The expression is a way of reinforcing incredulity.

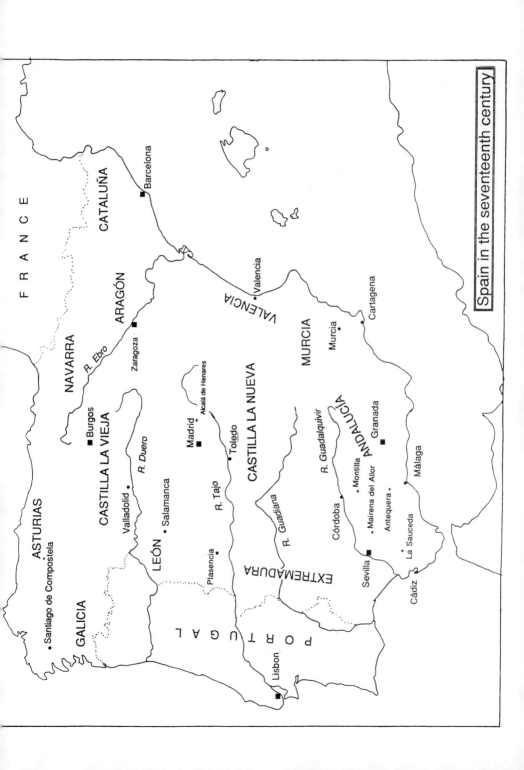

Spain in the seventeenth century

164

Notes to *The Dialogue of the Dogs*

1   Alonso de Mahudes was a real person who was in charge of collecting alms for the upkeep of the Hospital de la Resurrección, a task to which he devoted himself in thanksgiving for the cure he had received at the hospital many years before. Together with his two dogs, which provide the models for Cipión and Berganza, Mahudes was a well-known figure in Valladolid at the time. For further information, see A.G. de Amezúa y Mayo, *Cervantes, creador de la novela corta española*, 2 vols. (Madrid, 1958), II, 409 ff.

2   The city in which the famous university of Alcalá de Henares was founded by Cardinal Cisneros as the Colegio Mayor de San Ildefonso and built between 1499 and 1508. In the sixteenth century it was the centre of humanist learning during the Spanish Renaissance. The Complutense Bible (from the Latin name for Alcalá de Henares, *Complutum*), in Greek, Hebrew and Latin, was printed here around 1522.

3   Doctors, along with lawyers, were frequently the object of satire in the Golden Age. Good examples are to be found in *Don Quixote* and Mateo Alemán's *Guzmán de Alfarache*.

4   Literally Meat Gate, so called because the cattle going to the slaughter-house entered by it.

5   The Spanish term *jifero* refers to the large knife used by the slaughtermen and came to refer to the men themselves, and was used more generally as an adjective denoting anything dirty or unpleasant.

6   In the square, stand the *Cabildo* and *Audiencia* (Town Hall and Magistrate's Court) of Seville. The suggestion is that criminal types bribe corrupt officials who are therefore their "guardian angels."

7   Two streets really, one *(la grande)* which led to the Plaza de la Alfalfa, and another *(la chica)* which led to the Square of San Isidoro.

8   A small square near the Church of San Isidoro.

9   Reference to the superstitious belief that spitting guarded against the evil eye.

10 A style of riding, different from the European, essentially involving the drawing up of the rider's knees by the use of short stirrups.

11 Juvenal, *Satire* I, 1.30: *"Difficile est satyram non scribere."*

12 The Spanish makes a distinction between *de sangre* and *de luz*. This is apparently an allusion to penitents in religious processions, those *de luz* (of light) carrying candles and those *de sangre* (of blood) punishing themselves.

13 Reference to pastoral literature, the features of which are subsequently described and criticised. The most famous was Jorge de Montemayor's *La Diana* (1559). Cervantes himself wrote a pastoral novel, *La Galatea* (1585). The names of the characters which follow are taken from these and other pastoral novels.

14 Goddess of the dawn.

15 Goddess of the sea.

16 The Academy did exist, but who Mauleón was is not known. Cervantes recounts the same anecdote in *Don Quixote*, II, 71

17 A witch from Córdoba, alive in Cervantes's time.

18 The Jesuits had been teaching in Seville since 1557 and established the College of San Hermenegildo there in 1580.

19 The famous Seville Exchange, designed by Juan de Herrera, architect of the Escorial, was opened in 1598.

20 The Spanish phrase means literally to throw little hairs to the sea. The idea is that the hairs float away never to come back, and thus the phrase was used by children to make peace. It could be translated as "Let bygones be bygones," or "It's all water under the bridge."

21 Referred to in the Spanish text by the author's first name. Antonio de Nebrija's *Introductiones latinae* was first published in Salamanca in 1481 and became a standard text for the teaching of Latin.

22 A term popularised by Giovanni Botero's *Ragione di Stato* (1589) and first appearing in Spanish in 1593. The reference is to a superior consideration which overrides all others, and is ironical by virtue of its use in this context.

23 From the Greek *knyos* meaning dog.

24 The source of this story is Valerius Maximus, *Facta et dicta memorabilia*. Cervantes erroneously refers to Charondas as Corondas. See Amezúa y Mayo, II, 513.

25 The police officer is not, in fact, mentioned earlier in the story.

26 Patents of nobility were issued *ad perpetuam rei memoriam,* which is the formula the landlady is trying to say.

27 A further linguistic error on the part of the landlady who says *quince* (fifteen) for *lince* (lynx).

28 This was situated between the *Puerta de la Carne* and the *Torre del Oro*. It was the gate through which carts carrying South American silver and gold unloaded off the New World fleets approached the building of the *Casa de Contratación,* the organization established by the Spanish government to control trade with the newly-discovered territories.

29 Saracen warrior, appearing in several epic poems, endowed with exceptional strength, courage and pride.

30 Former name of the University of Seville, founded by Maese Rodríguez Fernández de Santaella, and originally called the Colegio Mayor de Santa María.

31 Succeeded Juan Hurtado de Mendoza, Count of Orgaz, as Magistrate (Asistente) of Seville in 1589.

32 A district near Cortes de la Frontera in the province of Málaga which in the late sixteenth century provided a refuge for criminals and bandits who were pardoned by Philip II in 1590. It was not therefore destroyed by Sarmiento de Valladares.

33 A suburb of Seville known at the time for its pottery and gypsy population.

34 Ownership of Sejanus's horse signified death for the owner.

35 An old district of Seville near the Macarena Gate.

36 Refers to *Mairena del Alcor*.

37 Simply, he was trained to jump when his master asked him to do it for the King of France, but when he was told to jump for the innkeeper's bad wife, he would not.

38 There were two famous witches of this name whose activities must have been known to Cervantes.

39 All were witches from Classical literature and mythology.

40 The famous Latin romance by Lucius Apuleius which provides realistic elements of the life of the time.

41 The Inquisition concerned itself with the problem of witchcraft and burned convicted witches at the stake. However, the witch-craze and the extreme reactions to curb it provoked in other parts of Europe were kept in check in Spain through the influence of men such as Alonso de Salazar Frías, who reported on the events which led to the *auto de fe* in Logroño in 1610, and of Philip III's *cronista,* Pedro de Valencia, who wrote the important *Discurso de las bruxas.* See Gustav Henningsen, *The Witches' Advocate: Basque Witchcraft and the Spanish Inquisition* (1609-1614) (Res. Nev., 1980).

42   For a discussion of the literary tradition associating roses with pleasure and happiness, see
     María Rosa Lida de Malkiel, 'Estar en (un) baño, estar en un lecho de rosas,' *Revista de
     Filología Hispánica*, III (1943), 263-70.

43   The Spanish phrase simply means to shower someone with insults. It is related to an old
     saying used to give vent to one's feelings when bad weather either at Christmas or Easter
     prevented the wearing of new clothes specially made for the occasion.

44   *Rancho* is used in the original seventeenth-century meaning of a temporary, mobile home.

45   These elements of universal folklore are associated with the devil and witches. See Stith
     Thompson, *Motif-Index of Folk Literature: A Classification of Narrative Elements in Folk
     Tales* (Copenhagen, 1955), G211, 1.1.1 *Witch in form of headless horse*, G 303, 7.3.3, *Devil
     in coach drawn by headless horses*, D 1254, *Magic staff*, D 1254.1. *Magic wand.*

46   *Conde* ('Count') was the term used by gypsies to refer to their leader.

47   This was a sales tax levied on commercial transactions and was one main form of indirect
     taxation of the period, having been in existence since the Middle Ages.

48   The *alguaciles*, seventeenth-century bailiffs or constables, frequently appear in the satirical
     literature of the time as dishonest and disreputable individuals when they should be upright
     guardians of the law. See, for example, the fifth *tratado* of *Lazarillo de Tormes* and
     Quevedo's *El alguacil endemoniado*.

49   *Moriscos* or converted Moors had constituted a marginalised social group in Spain since the
     beginning of the sixteenth century when Cardinal Cisneros embarked on a policy of forced
     conversions. They were eventually expelled from Spain in 1609. As with the bailiffs above,
     the *moriscos* often appear in satirical literature of the Golden Age as suspect individuals and
     as the butt of ridicule and attack. The historical literature on the subject is extensive but
     brief, succinct accounts of the issues may be found in: John Lynch, *Spain under the
     Hapsburgs* 2 vols, (Oxford, 1981), I, 218-33; Henry Kamen, *Spain, 1469-1714: A Society of
     Conflict* (London & New York, 1983), 172-77.

50   The changing of heavier winter cloaks for lighter summer ones was carried out by Cardinals
     on Easter Sunday at the ceremony known as *mutatio caparum*.

51   The Spanish term *autor* is here used in the seventeenth-century meaning of manager or
     producer of plays.

52   This play, which probably dealt with a Moorish subject, has been lost, but its existence is
     confirmed by references to it made by Quevedo and Jerónimo de Alcalá in *La hora de todos*
     and *El donado hablador* respectively.

53   The famous Hieronymite Monastery in Granada founded by the Catholic Monarchs.

54   The Spanish phrase refers to the shame experienced by those who are secretly obliged to beg
     for their living. Berganza has therefore here noted that the poet had gone to the monastery to
     obtain a free meal.

55   *Angulo el Malo* was a real theatrical manager.

56   Latin proverb: *Ne mittatis margaritas vestras ante porcos*. It was used by St. Matthew, VII,
     6: *Nolite dare sanctum canibus, neque mittatis margaritas vestras ante porcos*.

57   These were short plays usually performed between the three acts of Golden Age plays in
     order to provide comic relief. They often depicted low-life customs and characters, and they
     became very popular in the seventeenth century. There are also later examples of the genre.

58   *Arbitristas* provided one channel of expression of public opinion in the seventeenth century
     through the tracts they wrote on a broad range of public issues. Some, addressed to the
     government, offered solutions, *arbitrios*, for economic and political problems. *Arbitristas*
     were usually ecclesiastics, civil servants, businessmen and professional men or members of
     the army. The term came to have a pejorative connotation associated with wild, impractical
     schemes and ideas. For further information, see Kamen, 230-35.

59   Horace, *Poetics*, v. 388, refers to a period of nine years.
60   The term *pasante* denoted a type of assistantship in university faculties which aspiring
      doctors, lawyers, etc., needed to complete before becoming established in their professions.
      The reference here indicates that his work is now fully matured.
61   Refers to *La demanda del Santo Grial* (Toledo, 1515), but he confuses *brial*, "skirt" and
      grial, "grail."
62   Three names associated with great riches: Midas, the legendary King of Phrygia who was
      granted the wish that all he touched should turn to gold; Marcus Licinius Crassus who died
      in 53 B.C. and according to Plutarch's *Lives* owned silver mines and eventually also the
      greater part of Rome; Croesus, the last King of Lydia, 560-46 B.C., a man of renowned
      wealth.
63   The philosopher's stone was the highest substance in alchemy and was supposed to turn
      other metals into silver or gold.
64   Tantalus, who in Greek mythology was punished in Hades by being placed in a pool of
      water under fruit trees but was unable to satisfy either his hunger or his thirst, for the water
      receded whenever he tried to drink and the wind blew away the branches of the fruit tree
      whenever he attempted to pick fruit.
65   Sisyphus, punished in Hades by being made to roll a large rock to the top of a hill only for it
      to roll back down when he got to the summit. His punishment was therfore endless.
66   The reference to *Gran Turco* was an expression of exaggeration. There were parallel
      phrases referring to the Pope: *podía ser del Papa*, or *podían presentarse al Papa*.
67   The *carnero* denoted a type of public grave in which the bodies of those who did not own a
      private sepulchre were buried.
68   The term still used for the Spanish parliament.
69   *Ahechar* meant to clean corn by sieving it, and thus clearing it of dust, stones and hay, hence
      the word-play between *ahechados* and *limpio de polvo y de paja*.
70   *Corregidores* dated from the fourteenth century and were civil governors sent by the Crown
      to administer justice in towns. By the beginning of the sixteenth century, there were two
      types in existence in Castile, *letrados*,who had studied law at university, and *capa y espada*
      officials drawn from the army. See Kamen, 25-6.
71   A square overlooking the river in Valladolid.

MORE BOOKS FROM
Aris & Phillips Hispanic Classics

Medieval History

Fernão Lopes THE ENGLISH IN PORTUGAL 1383-1387
edited and translated by D. W. Lomax and R. J. Oakley
(Birmingham)

CHRISTIANS AND MOORS IN SPAIN
General Editor, C. C. Smith *(St. Catharine's, Cambridge)*

Vol I (711-1150)
Vol II (1195-1614)
Vol III Arabic Sources (711-1501)

Irene Lancaster
THE GOLDEN AGE OF THE JEWS IN SPAIN
(900-1200 CE)

In addition to the *Hispanic Classics* series Aris & Phillips also publish a
Classical Text series (Latin & Greek) and books on Ancient Egypt and
the Ancient Near East, Classical archaeology and Central Asia.

For further information and catalogues please write to

ARIS & PHILLIPS Ltd,
Teddington House, Warminster, BA12 8PQ

MORE BOOKS FROM
Aris & Phillips Hispanic Classics

Medieval Literature

Juan Manuel COUNT LUCANOR *(El Conde Lucanor)*
edited and translated by J. P. England, *(Sheffield)*

Fernão Lopes THE ENGLISH IN PORTUGAL 1383-1387
edited and translated by D. W. Lomax and R. J. Oakley
(Birmingham)

THE POEM OF MY CID *(El Poema de mío Cid)* edited and
translated by Peter Such and John Hodgkinson *(Sherborne
School)*

Fernando Rojas CELESTINA edited by Dorothy Sherman
Severin *(Liverpool)* with translation by James Mabbe

Roger Wright *(Liverpool)* SPANISH BALLADS with English
Verse Translations

GOD AND MAN IN MEDIEVAL SPAIN Studies in honour
of Roger Highfield. Edited by D. W. Lomax and D.
Mackenzie *(Birmingham)*